Fool's Bond

Book 2 of System Apocalypse: Kismet

An Apocalyptic LitRPG

By

Tao Wong & David R Packer

Copyright

Published by Starlit Publishing
PO Box 30035
High Park PO
Toronto, ON
M6P 3K0
Canada

www.starlitpublishing.com

Ebook ISBN: 9781778551666
Paperback ISBN: 9781778551765
Hardcover ISBN: 9781778551772

Books in the System Apocalypse Universe

Main Storyline

Life in the North

Redeemer of the Dead

The Cost of Survival

Cities in Chains

Coast on Fire

World Unbound

Stars Awoken

Rebel Star

Stars Asunder

Broken Council

Forbidden Zone

System Finale

System Apocalypse: Kismet

Fool's Play

Fool's Bond

Fool's Last Dance

System Apocalypse – Relentless

A Fist Full of Credits

System Apocalypse: Australia
Town Under

Anthologies & Short stories
System Apocalypse Short Story Anthology Volume 1

System Apocalypse Short Story Anthology Volume 2

Valentines in an Apocalypse

A New Script

Daily Jobs, Coffee and an Awfully Big Adventure

Adventures in Clothing

Questing for Titles

Blue Screens of Death

My Grandmother's Tea Club

The Great Black Sea

Growing Up – Apocalypse Style

Interdimensional Window SHOPping

A Game of Koopash (Newsletter exclusive)

Lana's story (Newsletter exclusive)

Debts and Dances (Newsletter exclusive)

A Tense Meeting (Newsletter exclusive)

Comic Series
The System Apocalypse Comics (7 Issues)

Table of Contents

What Happened Before - McBride 1

Chapter One 4

Chapter Two 19

Chapter Three 32

Chapter Four 44

Chapter Five 55

Chapter Six 68

Chapter Seven 81

Chapter Eight 92

Chapter Nine 108

Chapter Ten 119

Chapter Eleven 131

Chapter Twelve 142

Chapter Thirteen 151

Chapter Fourteen 170

Chapter Fifteen 184

Chapter Sixteen 195

Chapter Seventeen 205

Chapter Eighteen 219

Chapter Nineteen 231

Chapter Twenty 239

Chapter Twenty-one 252

Chapter Twenty-two 263

Chapter Twenty-three 269

Chapter Twenty-four 281

Chapter Twenty-five 293

Chapter Twenty-six 315

Chapter Twenty-seven 320

Chapter Twenty-eight 321

Epilogue 325

Author's Note 333

About the Authors 335

About the Publisher 336

Glossary 339

What Happened Before - McBride

He hadn't really gotten used to the nose. The tiny tickling of the hairs on the glass wasn't exactly startling, but it still gave him a sense of unease.

Which was a little strange because this was the form he'd had for his entire life. It was just that the memory of the other life was still strong.

He wrapped his tail around his paws and sat down on the windowsill. A waft of heat rose from the baseboard heater under the window, and he couldn't help but let out a little purr of satisfaction. Warmth was good.

Jackal and Fool were almost out of sight. In another minute, they'd turn down the next road and be at the little airport the village still maintained. It wasn't much of an airport, but aircraft built in a System world could be a little less stringent on physics requirements. The McBride airport, if they got any notice of an incoming flyer, could expect anything from a flying carpet to a giant spacecraft.

No one really seemed to notice that for a remote, tiny village, just recently grown into a town, the airport was a smidge busier that one would expect.

Part of the reason for that was that the village had always been a transit point. Trains, autos, and planes had all passed through regularly enough, depending on the season, before the System. And with McBride being one of the rare nearly untouched surviving human locations, it wouldn't seem too unusual that traffic wasn't all that different than it had been before the System. After all, surviving in this world meant making strong connections, and now, more than ever, that meant exchanging goods and services. That was one reason people wouldn't pay attention to the traffic.

DM was the other reason.

He flicked the tip of his tail in annoyance as he noted another flicker of drain on his mana, then he saw that the price for further discretion had ticked up again. He wasn't too worried about that. It wasn't even a drop in the bucket of the limited resources he could access in this form. The trend was upward though. And at a certain threshold, the Weaver's minions were likely to take note of that.

DM wasn't ready to deal with that nonsense. Not yet.

Fool and his companion weren't ready yet. The puzzle pieces hadn't fallen into place for them, but they would soon. DM needed them to be at least Advanced class before the next phase could even start. They were pretty close. They'd been working hard since their return from the Valemount mission, but they were still on the cusp of their next Level. Still, they should make it on this one.

Which, he reflected, should be just about the right time.

And he was certainly ready to move on. It had been pleasant being "just a cat" for Alex, but it was time for change.

The skin was feeling itchy. He'd leave this shell behind though. Alex wouldn't see any difference. She'd still have a quirky and cute little black cat. There wouldn't be any trace of him left in it for anyone to find though.

For a moment, he thought about tagging along with Fool and Jackal. He wouldn't even need a new form—he could replicate this one as well as any others. If he did, he'd be able to make sure that things worked the way he planned them to. That critical meeting had to take place. But he had to trust

Fool to make the connection, and if he had to trust him to do that, then he might as well trust them to do all the rest.

This was one thing he'd be best off not meddling in, even if it went against his nature. This was a nurture thing. If he wanted his little kitten to grow up, then he had to trust them to handle their own business for the most part. Even if it meant they collected a few scars along the way.

It was also getting harder and harder to disguise his influence on the Foundation's Machine. They were already wondering about how some of the results they were seeing came about, and it would be best if he was gone before they put two and two together on that front.

He would miss having access to that marvelous device. Being able to see potential and possibility dance with the growth and innate abilities of humans all over the planet? That was close to the powers some of his fellows had, and it was a pleasure to have even an echo of that ability for a time. He'd made good use of it while he'd had the chance, and that was why he knew that Fool and Jackal were not only off on a very important mission for the Foundation's goals but for his goals as well. And for the world too. They'd be fine.

And really, the best thing he could do was head south and set up shop for the next stage. Timing was getting tricky, and he wanted to stay at least ten steps ahead of the Weaver. Twenty, if he could manage it.

Chapter One

The dampness filled the air with the scent of cedar. It didn't quite cover the smell of rot, but it helped. Not enough though.

Jackal had noted the strong, pleasant, woody smell as they'd made their way closer to the entrance of the dungeon. The rain had been falling heavily all day, its constant drum adding a background rhythm to their hike. The dungeon was on the outskirts of the town of Prince George.

Before the System, the dungeon had been a pulp and sawmill. They'd gotten solid instructions on how to traverse the dungeon: Start in the former Administration Center, which would open access to the pulp mill, and clearing that out would open access to the Sawmill. It was effectively a three-level dungeon, with the hazards growing at each level. The Prince George adventurers recommended they take their time with it. Regulars suggested a day for each level.

It was a good dungeon for a city. The first level was challenging enough that no one had soloed it yet, but teams of low-Level Basic classes could complete it. Mid Levels could make it through the second level. The last level hadn't been completed by anyone yet, but the first few monsters had been tough, even for the highest-Level Basic classers in town. A couple of

Advanced classers had made it through the first part of the last level but had never been heard from again.

Jackal smelled the rot again, cutting through the otherwise pleasant cedar smell. The System had transformed the inside of the administration building, according to the locals, but the outside looked the same. A long and quite pretty boardwalk passed over some neatly trimmed wide grass fields to a building that looked sort of like a school or small-town hospital, low and a bit spread out. The rain and cool spring air had resulted in a mist all around the grounds, and instead of being spooky, it had looked almost romantic.

That had been a lie.

It jumped on him from somewhere above. Probably intended to surprise him. Whether that might have worked had been made moot by the horrible burbling scream it had let out while leaping at him.

Jackal cut a backhand cut without even really thinking about it, but the face of his attacker froze in his vision. That happened sometimes. In the middle of a fight, like a freeze-frame image. It didn't stop or slow him down, but it was like a portion of his subconscious was chewing on something it saw and was reluctant to let go.

Jackal hated that. Hated it because he knew he'd be seeing that face in his mind's eye, probably just as he was falling asleep.

Wide-set red eyes and a little pug nose almost between them. Long, bat-like ears flopping out to the side...an incongruous silver loop earring hanging from the left one. Impossibly wide mouth open in a scream, with hundreds of small, needle-like teeth filling it.

It had been wearing a tattered little jacket, ragged with patches all over. Big black boots went right up to its knees, sharp hobs poking out from the soles. And a big, meaty cleaver, that it had been swinging at Jackal's head.

The image in his mind was frozen just after his sword cut cleanly through the goblin. There wasn't even any blood yet, just the smallest hint of recognition in the goblin's eyes that something horrible and permanent and irrevocable had happened to it.

All Jackal had felt as he bisected the creature was a faint *pop* that traveled down his arm from the sword. Just a minor wobble, a tiny reverberation that caused a subtle but pleasant *ting* sound, if anyone was listening.

He didn't even really feel the impact of the two halves of the body when they hit him less than a second later.

Jackal realized he'd let himself drift and pulled himself back into the moment. He took a quick glance around the space to see if he'd missed anything.

They were in a large, open space. The admin building featured a beautifully designed atrium, all wooden beams and planks and floor-to-ceiling windows, interspersed with criss-crossing, green-painted stairs leading from floor to floor, office to office. All of that was still intact but expanded.

And filled with goblins.

Fool was ahead of Jackal, swinging his warhammer with both hands at a pair of what looked like Gremlins. Or possibly goblins covered head to toe in fur. Jackal couldn't quite tell, but Fool seemed to be handling things fine. A quick glance behind him confirmed that no one had sneaked behind Jackal.

The reception area was still spattered with the lavender blood of the Sirens they'd had to fight past, but none of those bodies were even twitching at this point.

Ahead of him, the Mousekin were moving in tight formations.

Jackal grunted in appreciation of their tactics. The Mousekin looked beyond adorable, but you couldn't argue with their skills. They were a compact military patrol unit composed of two squads made up of two four-mouse teams each. Each team had a mage, two melee fighters, and ranged weapon specialist, with an additional healer for each squad. They'd clearly been trained to a high degree and moved with precision, laying down a river of damage as they engaged the enemy.

It was even more impressive because they were smaller than the goblins. Each Mousekin was just over a foot high, and the goblins doubled that. If the Mousekin patrol didn't punch way above its weight class, they'd have been swarmed under the goblins in no time. Instead, they were cutting through the goblins about as easily as Jackal was.

That accounted for everyone. Except the Mousekin leader, Roger. Where was Roger?

Jackal looked all over the room but couldn't see him or his two companions, Eric and Olivia. Where the hell had they gotten to?

A moment later, Jackal figured it out. Another goblin came flying out from the floor above... and plummeted straight down. Jackal saw the wounds on its body. Neat holes from the Mousekin firearms, and a deep stab wound that had turned into a cut, opening the body up to show the odd green insides. Jackal knew what had caused that wound.

"Fool," he said, "they've gotten ahead of us. I'm going to catch up."

He didn't say any more than that, trusting his friend to get the context.

Fool's response was a string of curses as another goblin sneaked in behind him and bit him on the ankle. Jackal managed not to laugh. Then he activated his [Potooooooooo[1]] and [Lead Zeppelin[2]] Skills and burst up across the room and up the nearest stairs.

---

[1] "Pot" followed by "8 o's" Get it? Potatoes? The greatest racehorse of all time, some say. This Skill gives Jackal a short burst of speed.

[2] Alters relationship with gravity. The user becomes either lighter or heavier as they wish. This can allow them to run on top of things or become very hard to move.

His smile faded as soon as he got to the next landing. The sign on the floor just said "Marketing."

The Dungeon Master had a low sense of humor and had been a former employee of the mill. As a result, he'd built up the city dungeon from his vision of what the worst of the company was. This was the floor all the goblins were coming from. And there were more of them up here.

A lot more.

Individually, or even in small groups, the goblins were no threat to Jackal at all. But a lot of them were suddenly charging at him.

He saw other creatures mixed in with them as well—the ones he'd originally taken to be fur-covered goblins. They now seemed to be a creature of roughly the same size, but with a sturdier build. They looked just like Gremlins from the movie his parents had made him watch. The one that had given him so many nightmares when he was a kid.

A mixed horde of them started for Jackal, but he had a moment to take in the whole situation. He was on the landing of the second floor, which was composed of a walkway going all around the atrium. The side he was facing held a row of offices going far back into the building, judging from what he could see through the dirty glass windows that lined the walkway. There were no more stairs going up, so the entrance to the next floor up had to be somewhere in those offices.

Since he couldn't see Roger or his two friends anywhere, they were either dead and piled under a mound of goblins, or they'd pushed on to the next level.

No point in assuming the worst. If it was true, they were screwed, and the mission was shot. So, he had to assume that Roger had somehow pushed through the hordes and had moved on to the next level.

Judging from the larger mess of creatures he could see at the far end of the offices, that was what had happened.

Jackal saw a commotion there, and some of that seemed to be turning back toward him.

Perfect.

He activated his [Blade Walking[3]] Skill, and he felt the corners of his grin touching his eyes. It was a Skill tailor made for this kind of environment, letting him almost literally walk across the incoming blades of massed attackers, avoiding most damage and letting him attack at will.

It was useful when facing small groups of higher-Level monsters, letting him gain a significant edge on them when they expected to have the upper hand by dint of numbers.

Against a horde of the lowest-Level monsters?

Jackal danced through them with almost no resistance. He could feel their blades slashing and rising up to him, and his spirit flared up, the grin splitting his face. This was what he lived for. He let himself go, holding nothing back, spinning and chopping and stabbing in a timeless flow, leaving a river of blood behind him.

Even with his Skill, he was taking damage. He saw his health ticking down, along with his mana, but wasn't that what they were for? Coin to be spent in service of living his life as it was meant to be.

For a moment, he cut through all of his attackers. The combat paused, and he found himself on the floor again, surrounded by a screaming mass. He heard the faint *plip, plip* of blood dripping off his twin swords. No breathing or other sounds. It was as though the entire room had frozen in

---

[3] Evasion with attack bonus, improves the more opponents there are. Dance amongst blades, never being touched, and leaving a trail of blood behind you.

time. The gleaming teeth of the creatures were all around him, dripping with a viscous saliva, twisted grins of fear and hate.

A poem his father had read to him when he was young ran through his head. A poem of his people, his father had said, but had never explained more. He understood the words now, and their meaning.

The "Poem of Antar" came to his lips, and he recited it out loud for his enemies:

> *"You were always on my mind,*
> *even when their lances drank my blood,*
> *and their shiny blades from India were*
> *soaked with my blood.*
>
> *I wanted to kiss the blades,*
> *for they glittered like the light*
> *that sparkles from your smile."*[4]

And then it was his turn to scream and leap.

He tore through the creatures like a hurricane of steel, blades flashing like lightning. The Gremlins held for a moment. A brief moment.

Then they broke, scattering with hoots and screams, and Jackal chased them, desperate to land one more righteous slash.

Then they were gone.

And his world was dimmer for it.

He had the room to himself, although he could hear the beasts chittering and shrieking in the other rooms. For a moment, he thought about turning

---

[4] Song of Antar by Antarah ibn Shaddad

back to make sure Fool was okay. Some goblins had thrown themselves over the railing and must have added to the numbers his friend was facing.

Fool was no warrior, but Jackal had learned to trust his abilities. He did so now.

Fool and the Mousekin could handle the first floor and whatever was left of this one. They may not have the best time of it, but they'd manage it.

And Fool probably needed the experience in any case. If they were going to hit their Advanced class soon, every drop of experience was needed. Which meant leaving Fool alone to fight his battles for a while.

Besides, Jackal had to catch up with Roger.

He should have expected this. The young man had seemed affable, if arrogant, when they first met him. The arrogance had only grown during the brief trip from Roger's home on the coast to Prince George. Jackal had marked it up to youthful bravado and assumed it would fade with some real-life experience.

Instead, Roger had leapt into the first battle without even a moment's hesitation. And not even an inkling of wisdom. The Sirens in the reception area had easily overcome all of Roger's resistances, and he'd been right on his way to walking into their embrace with open arms. Only Fool's Skill had saved him.

Roger hadn't stopped to acknowledge that though. Just gone from love-struck idiot to stunned, to an angry charge with sword and shield. And his two friends were too loyal to do anything other than follow along.

All of them had rushed after Roger, not wanting him to be alone in the dungeon. For a few moments, they'd all been together, fighting the first wave of goblins shoulder to shoulder. Then the second wave had arrived, and things had gotten chaotic.

Which had been enough for Roger to charge up to the next level without even thinking about everyone else.

That was stupid, and Jackal would have been inclined to chalk it up to eagerness, but he had a sneaking suspicion something else was at work. He'd dismissed some things Roger had said during their trip here, but now he was thinking he should have paid more attention.

He wasn't going to know until he caught up with him though. He'd especially not know if the idiot got himself killed.

With a sigh, Jackal jogged toward the stairs at the far end of the room. As he got closer, he heard mutters. The stairs themselves were on the other side of a set of glass doors, marked "Human Resources: Level Three."

Someone had propped the doors open with a pile of garbage. Probably the goblins. On the other side of the door was a wide set of stairs going up one flight to a landing before turning back to head up to the next floor. Jackal couldn't see the next flight, but he saw a head poking around the edge of the wall that divided the two flights.

Olivia. The mage of the trio.

She waved to him as he came into the lower landing, then ducked back.

"Jackal's here!" she shouted.

"Send him up now!" came another voice. It sounded like Eric, the other fighter of the group. There was no urgency to the voice, but there was some anger.

Jackal started up, hoping the trio hadn't done something monumentally stupid.

He had serious doubts.

Eric was sitting halfway up the next flight and waved. He'd taken off his shield and laid it down next to him. His short gladius sword was in his hand.

He'd chosen to follow a Roman Legionary motif, fairly historically accurate. He looked pissed, but he clearly wasn't going anywhere at the moment.

Olivia nodded and moved to the side to let Jackal pass. She had a determined look in her eyes, but her hands were shaking a little. No fear, but probably suffering from a solid dump of adrenaline… either a result of the long charge up here, or from whatever was on the other side of the door.

The door that Roger was leaning against, which he'd clearly wedged closed with a length of railing broken off from the stairway wall. There was the odd thump coming from the other side, and a high-pitched, chittering warble. Whatever it was, it had finally stopped Roger's head-long charge into the unknown, and Jackal was almost grateful toward it.

He took a moment to look at the three humans. There weren't any injuries on them. It had been a few minutes at least, so any minor injuries would have healed up. Their gear showed a bit more truth, with fresh tears and scratches all over.

Nothing major.

Roger himself looked fine, if a little harried. He was a burly lad, past his teenage growth spurt but not really showing any signs of slowing down. He was easily over six feet tall and had enough muscles to show his interest in bodybuilding.

Jackal figured Roger was more likely to get into a thicker powerlifter look as he aged up a bit, judging from the genetics his parents had passed on to him.

Roger was dressed in a sort of medieval armor, with a fitted, cloth-covered breastplate and banded steel armor on his legs and arms. He'd topped it with an open-faced barbute helm, with only a nasal bar protecting his face. Round shield, and an oddly short, wide sword with a basket hilt.

That had all come from his parents. They'd been high-ranking members of the Society of Creative Anachronism and had been grooming their son to be a leader in that group since he was a kid. He'd practically been born in armor and fighting with sword and shield since he could walk. His parents had also been quite well off, so when the System Apocalypse had arrived, they'd been in a perfect position to take advantage of it.

When Jackal and Fool had arrived at their home, they'd found a complete Norman-style Mott and Bailey castle, built up from local materials and reinforced by System add-ons.

The family had been vacationing at their private retreat on the BC coast with what amounted to a small army of private security. As a result, they were already a local powerhouse, and aiming to move their way up in the new world as far as they could. Roger was their pride and joy.

And he knew it.

Roger was grinning as he looked down at Jackal, and Jackal had to bite back the irritation that flared up in him.

"Just in time, bud!" Roger said. "Like, a whole mess of these shitty flying things on the other side! Total pain, could use a hand to wrap them up."

"Imps," Olivia said with a pained voice. "I told you, Roger. Imps."

"Whatevs." he replied. "They fly and they look like little demons, and they are complete assholes. Ready to go rip 'em a new one?"

Jackal really wanted to rip that grin off Roger's face, but instead he turned to look at Olivia and raised an eyebrow in question.

"Imps," she said. "Flying demons, lesser grade. They have a tail like a scorpion, poison sting. Some of them might be able to shape change. Some might be very intelligent. They probably manage the goblins. Likely report to a higher form of demon, or some other kind of monster." She gave Roger a bit of frustrated side-eye. "Looks to be about a dozen of them on the other side of the door, at least that we saw. They swarmed us, used their wings and tails to get in our way and trip us up. We barely got away."

She directed that last bit at Roger, crossing her arms and glaring at him.

"Hey, no worries!" Roger said. "We almost got them, and with Jackal here, we can clear 'em out in no time. Let's go!"

"Jesus!" Eric shouted. "Give me a minute to catch my breath, will ya? What's the rush, dude? Those things are a pain. Shouldn't we come up with a plan?"

The three of them looked at Jackal. With an effort of will, he managed not to roll his eyes. Instead, he put his swords away and opened his hands, palm up, toward them. He flicked his fingers a few times in invitation. Time to see what the young scions could come up with.

"Plan," Roger said, "I guess. Why don't I open the door, charge in? They'll focus on me, then you guys can pick them off while they do that."

"How 'bout a plan that isn't you doing what you're going to do anyway?" Olivia said, with a little less heat in her voice than her words implied.

"And don't forget how fast they move," Eric added. "The minute you open that door, they come piling through at us. They aren't just waiting on the other side, you know. They're making plans of their own."

"Huh," Roger said. "You think they can hear us?"

Jackal nodded and pointed at the door with his chin.

The squabbling noises and banging had stopped. There was only an eerie silence from the other side.

The three youngsters looked at each other, then back at the door.

There was suddenly a long, high screech from the other side, like something metal being dragged across the floor.

Eric took a step down the stairs and Olivia took a step up, putting them both on the same level and looking up. Roger looked down at them, then back at the door.

"Right," Roger said. "Not dumb. Probably a trap. Is there another way up…" His voice trailed off as Eric and Olivia made frantic shushing motions with their hands.

Jackal raised his eyebrows and pointed at the railing jamming the door.

Roger looked at him for a moment in confusion, then realized what he meant. He turned and gave the door a few tugs, but it didn't budge at all. He nodded back to Jackal.

Trusting the strength of the temporary fix, Jackal motioned Roger to come down and join the three of them. Once he'd come down to the same level, Jackal held a finger to his lips and pointed downstairs, then made a gathering motion with his hands.

Eric nodded enthusiastically, and Olivia let out a quiet "yesss…"

Roger just looked confused. "What?" he whispered.

Olivia leaned in a little closer. "Head back down. Gather everyone else. The Mousekin probably have a drill for this. We can let them breach the door."

"Or flank," Eric said. "They can probably access more parts of this office than we can."

Roger shook his head angrily. "Don't need help. We can do this. We could probably have done it on our own if we hadn't let them swarm us."

Olivia punched Roger in the shoulder, hard enough to make the metal armor ring. Jackal raised his eyebrows. She was dressed like some kind of prehistoric shaman, with bone fetishes and strips of leather, but she had a lot more strength than Jackal would have assumed for a mage. There was a flash of anger in her eyes that hinted at even more strength.

Jackal decided she'd work out just fine.

Status Screen			
Name	Fool	Class	Acolyte
Race	Human (Male)	Level	49
Titles			
Acolyte of the (Redacted)			
Health	290	Stamina	290
Mana	600	Mana Regeneration	49/minute
Status			
Normal			
Attributes			
Strength	21	Agility	38
Constitution	29	Perception	114
Intelligence	60	Willpower	59
Charisma	65	Luck	161
Class Skills			
Closseau	1	Have Faith	1
Talent Scout	2	Pants on Fire	1
Transform Object	1	Kiss it Better	2
I know a Shortcut	2	Truth or Dare	1
Dry hair is for Squids	1	Oh god, don't hit me!	2
Mint?	1	Location Scout	1
Face Swap	1	No Fair	2
Geas	2	Feign Death	1
Aura of *	2	Regeneration	1
Spells			
Sparkles			

Status Screen			
Name	Jackal	Class	Eternal Warrior
Race	Human (Male)	Level	50
Titles			
(None)			
Health	560	Stamina	560
Mana	650	Mana Regeneration	110 / minute
Status			
Normal			
Attributes			
Strength	61	Agility	58
Constitution	56	Perception	110
Intelligence	65	Willpower	162
Charisma	10	Luck	10
Class Skills			
Pain don't Hurt	2	One Punch	2
INTIMIDATE	1	Mana Steal	1
Knock back	1	Mr. Freeze	1
Only a flesh Wound	2	Death from Above	2
Neo	1	Indomitable Will	2
Maestro	2	Blade Walking	2
Red Rover	2	The Wall	1
Eye of the Tiger	2	Boomstick	1
Spells			
(None)			

Chapter Two

By the time they'd backed out of the stairwell and made their way back to the walkway over the atrium, all the fighting appeared to have ended. Jackal looked down and waved to Fool, who waved back with a wry smile. There was quite a pile of goblins around him.

The Mousekin were rapidly looting and stacking the corpses of the goblins into an actual wall. It was a coldly brutal process, entirely at odds with their unmistakably cute appearance, but their efficiency at the task spoke to their professionalism.

Mousekin were badass soldiers.

Fool jumped up the stairs and met them as they started down. "You kids have fun?"

Jackal smiled and shook his head. Fool got the message. The other three said nothing and tromped down the stairs.

"Holland!" Fool called to the Mousekin leader, Cadet Holland.

Jackal had asked Holland about that title, thinking it was some sort of translation error for lieutenant. It was roughly an equivalent rank, but the System had chosen the word carefully.

In the Mousekin's case, it had chosen "Cadet" from the early modern European usage, meaning someone who was a representative of the overall military organization. It implied a level of not just leadership, but also panache. A sort of mascot with a bite, apparently.

For a unit the size of the Mousekin present, being led by a Cadet was a sign of very high favor amongst their military.

Holland was chatting with one of the sergeants, who was next to a couple of privates being tended by healers.

The Mousekin, despite their ferocity and Skills, had not come out of the battle unscathed. Holland took a moment to complete what he was doing, only waving at Fool to acknowledge that he'd heard.

"So, what happened?" Fool asked.

Jackal shook his head. He didn't want to explain it twice, so he'd wait for Holland to finish up his business. Roger and his friends took their cue from him and stood quietly. At least somewhat quietly. Roger lasted less than five seconds before he let out an exasperated sigh.

"Holland!" he yelled. "Let's get moving! Lots to cover today."

Holland looked up and started over. Jackal couldn't tell if he was pissed or not, but something in the Mousekin's body language spoke to a sense of resigned frustration. Maybe it was the way his tiny paws kept clenching and opening. Whatever it was, a quick glance around showed Jackal that no one else had noticed, except for Fool.

The frown on Fool's face and his look at Roger told Jackal that there was going to be a problem there.

The Mousekin leapt up on a chair next to Roger, which brought him to chest height. Jackal noticed that Holland's uniform gear, almost identical to modern military kit but with a shiny silver breastplate, looked crisp and neat. Except for the blood. There was a lot of blood. At least most of it seemed to be goblin blood.

Roger didn't wait. "Buncha imps two floors up, barricaded behind a door. You gotta somehow break 'em up so I can properly kill them without getting swarmed."

Holland tilted his head and looked up at Roger. "Sir, if you can give me more details, we can try to come up a plan of attack. We will need a bit more time to refresh the troop. The fight was hard, and we used up some resources."

Before Roger could interject again, Fool jumped in. "Your folks did good, Holland. Do you need any help getting them ready?"

Holland nodded at the compliment. "It's within our abilities. We just need about five more minutes. I gather you have some healing Skills? If you can assist our healers, we can get moving faster."

"Absolutely," Fool said, then he glanced at Roger. "Might make for a better plan if you give him some details, like how many imps there are, what kind of barricade, where the barricade is, that sort of thing?"

"Obviously," Roger said with a roll of his eyes.

Jackal flicked a glance at Fool. His friend was slowly letting a smile creep up on his lips. That was a bad sign.

"Fantastic," Fool drawled slowly. "I'll check in in a bit."

He spun off to walk toward the Mousekin troop. Jackal made a note to check in with Fool later. Not much got under his skin, but he could be vindictive when someone did. Roger was clearly pushing his buttons.

Disregard for the little people usually did it. This time, literally.

Roger seemed oblivious. He wasn't bothering to say anything more to Holland, just gruffly telling Eric and Olivia to fill in the details, then leaning back and crossing his arms.

From what Jackal had been told, the troop of Mousekin had been a gift from Roger's parents. A gift, but also a test. He'd been told he needed to learn to be a leader, and Holland would be evaluating him and reporting back to his parents on how he did.

Roger didn't seem to give two shits about that. Not in any way that Jackal had noticed. Worse, he seemed to think that giving blind orders and walking away was leadership. Not surprising, from what Jackal had gathered of his parents. Another minor puzzle for him to solve.

But not yet.

They'd only been traveling as a team for a few days. One day to meet the teens at their coastal retreat, then another day traveling *Mad Max* style in an armed and armored convoy. Jackal had rather enjoyed that part. It definitely fit his idea of a proper post-apocalyptic experience.

Definitely not enough of that in the System.

Jackal pulled his attention back as Olivia finished giving her details. She'd given a surprisingly comprehensive report, and Jackal was already seeing the best way to overcome the problem of the massed swarm of imps ready to break through. He'd see if his hunch was right, and Holland had the same idea.

Holland stroked his whiskers while he thought and, for a moment, looked just like an adorable little mouse cleaning himself. It took an effort of will for Jackal to keep a straight face and not coo. The warrior mouse was unlikely to be amused.

"We can do this." Holland said, once his thinking was over. Roger was still doing his best to look as if he didn't care, but Jackal saw him straightening up a little bit. "It's a trap for us. We open the door, they come flooding out. The small space at the landing gives them a perfect area to hurt us. Our only retreat is back down the stairs, which is straight and narrow. We could try to bait them down to the second floor, but you said they didn't seem to want to go down the stairs?" He directed that at Eric, who nodded.

"That makes sense," Holland continued. "They can keep the bulk of their force in the main room, and if we are only accessing from one door, then they have a perfect kill pocket on the other side. And the sharp turn of the stairs means the landing outside the door is an almost perfect kill pocket as well."

"So, like I said, we just charge it," Roger said. "No point in waiting around for them, letting them do what they want. We blow through. With your extra troops, we'll overwhelm them in no time, and I can push on to the next Level."

Holland chewed his jaw from side to side. "We can do that. If you order it, we will. But please consider it is likely to be costly, and this is only the third area out of thirteen in this dungeon. We risk significant attrition with a direct attack. I do have a plan though. We can reverse the trap."

Jackal leaned forward. That was enough of a sign of interest to stifle the objection that had been forming on Roger's face. Jackal took that as a good sign.

Roger was young and arrogant, but he was perceptive. Which meant there was some intelligence to him. He could be trained if Jackal approached it correctly.

"Like all System monsters," Holland continued, "the imps will default to aggression when the opportunity presents itself. They are intelligent enough to have built a trap for us, but we can still bait them into thinking they are getting what they want, without too much risk of them noticing its only bait.

"We open the door but pull slightly back. Roger, you and Jackal can form a barrier for them. They will swarm out to attack you... and then we slam the door closed on them. Basil will be behind the door with A team, and B team will be just behind you. Jerry's Second squad and I will be on the landing below. The minute the door is closed, we will charge up to it, and Basil will re-open as soon as we arrive."

"So you'll charge into the room while we keep some of them distracted?" Roger snarled. "Bullshit. I take all the damage while you get all the experience? Do better, Holland. You're here for me, remember?"

The Mousekin's eyes didn't have a visible pupil, so Jackal wasn't really sure he saw an eye-roll from Holland, but it seemed likely.

"Noted, sir," Holland replied. "However, the enemy in this case has not seen us yet, so the element of surprise will allow us to establish a quick foothold on the other side of the door. At that point, we will likely be outnumbered. We will be trusting you to dispatch the first wave of enemies quickly enough to relieve us as fast as possible. That should give you the access you need to the room to fight the remaining monsters. Is that acceptable?"

Roger "hmph'd," but he nodded his acceptance. Holland had either been around the young man long enough to know how to appease him, or more likely, had dealt with spoiled commanders before. Either way, Jackal approved of his solution. It would get them into the room with minimal risk.

At least, as minimal as anything could be, in a dungeon full of goblins and imps.

Ten minutes later, they were arranged on the stairs, ready to open the door. Fool had elected to stay back with a small reserve. A few of the gremlins from Marketing had poked their heads back into their former office space. They'd have to rely on Fool to warn them if the gremlins rallied enough for another attack.

Other than that, they were ready to go. Jackal silently walked up next to Roger, who was tightening the strap on his shield and watching Sergeant Basil and his team set up behind the door.

Basil was currently leaning against the door, his round ear pressed right up to it, his sallet helmet held in his other hand. The higher the rank of Mousekin, the more they dressed like modern military troops. The lower the rank, the more they looked like medieval soldiers, armor and all.

Basil had on combat boots and baggy pants with lots of pockets, but his upper body was covered in a tough-looking brigandine, and he had full plate arms to go with his helmet. Along with a jaunty-looking bright red scarf.

Roger nodded to Basil once he'd secure the shield strap. Jackal rolled his shoulder and thought for a bit, then drew out a sabre and a long Bowie knife from his weapon storage. He was tempted to go with his usual double swords, but the space looked a little tight. He was expecting to be smothered as well, and having the knife would let him deal with anything that got past the sabre.

"You should have a shield," Roger said. "Make 'em work to get you. You can hit 'em with it too, you know."

Jackal turned to Roger and thought about how to respond. He was familiar with shields. A big slab between you and your opponent could be a good thing. You could block shots with it, you could smash into your opponent, you could use it to hook and grab on to parts of them. The issue Jackal had with shields was they had a sort of double-edge sword built into them.

They were excellent for hiding behind, and using the way they limited your opponent's vision to surprise them. But that also meant that a cagey opponent could hide themselves, or their weapon, from you the same way.

Besides, Jackal liked the options having two blades gave him. So, he smiled at Roger and said, "Watch."

As if it that was the signal he was waiting for, Basil blew out a sharp whistle and leapt up at the door. Fortunately, it had a lever handle, so the Mousekin could grab the handle with one hand and let his body weight pull it down. The momentum of his leap, plus a little kick with his feet against the door frame, was enough to yank the door open into the stairwell.

With a startled shriek, three imps tumbled out onto the landing. A fourth stuck its head down from the top of the door frame and shrieked as it lost its grip, tumbling halfway to the floor before its wings flared up with an audible *wump* and it caught itself.

Roger yelled something fierce and slapped his sword against his shield.

All four imps turned to look at him. Skill use, Jackal knew. Some kind of taunt.

And then a half-dozen other heads popped around the door frame.

The air turned nearly red from the flurry of wings flapping at them. Roger tried to charge, leaping up the half-dozen steps between him and the upper landing, but the imps were on him before he reached the top.

Jackal just had time to see how they attacked. One of them clotheslined Roger with an outstretched wing and used its momentum to wrap itself right around his head, blinding him while stinging him over and over with its scorpion tail.

Jackal ducked, his perception helping him see the blurring red wing just before it reached him. He threw a backhand with his sabre as he crouched down and felt the satisfying wet smack of the blade slicing through an imp. On instinct, he lunged with the Bowie and caught another imp in its open mouth as it was diving in to bite him.

Two down.

One more step up the stairs.

A quick glance up showed him that Roger was now struggling with three imps, who'd wrapped him up in their wings like Saran Wrap. Jackal could sense Eric and Olivia pressing up from behind him—they'd take care of Roger.

Four more imps flared up in front of Jackal suddenly, little needle-filled mouths opening and shrieking, and their stinger-tipped tails darted in at his shoulders and hips.

Smart little bastards.

Attacking his four quarters at once made it harder to dodge. So he didn't. He felt the burn of the acid venom in their stingers as all four struck him. The words of Antar flooded into his mind as he retaliated:

"My quick hands beat him to the blow,
striking him before he could strike me;
and the blood flew from that deep cut,
red as the dye of Brazil wood."[5]

Jackal was still holding his blades in the same position they'd ended with his last attacks: Bowie in front, sabre behind.

Ignoring the pain of the stingers, he whipped the sabre over his head to deliver a backhanded diagonal cut, slicing two imps in half. His Bowie flicked out, just under the cut of the sword, and disemboweled a third. He didn't pause after the backhand cut with the sabre, but instead torqued his body clockwise. He sliced off the tail of the last imp with his Bowie, then decapitated it with the return forehand stroke of his sabre.

---

[5] Song of Antar by Antarah ibn Shaddad

He looked up as the bodies of the four creatures seemed to drop in slow motion. The last imp in front of him was being piled on by one of the Mousekin fireteams, who were ripping it to pieces with little daggers. They'd already slammed the door closed again, and the other team was bracing it as best they could.

When he turned to see how Roger and his friends were doing, each of them was finishing off an imp in their own way. Eric had somehow managed to get one to the ground and was repeatedly stomping on it. Olivia was strangling one to death with some kind of arcane green vines of force. Roger was flicking a corpse off his sword and looking up at Jackal with wide eyes.

"Ah…" Roger said. "I see what you mean about two blades."

Jackal smiled at him, then turned to look up the stairs. The Mousekin had dispatched the last imp, and Sergeant Basil was just turning to look down at them.

"Ready for the next?" he asked.

Roger slammed his shield with his sword in answer. Jackal took a quick glance at the other two. They looked fierce and ready.

Which was perfect, because right on schedule, Holland and Jerry were charging up between and around their legs, hell-bent for leather on getting as much speed as possible to charge through the door when Basil opened it. Jackal turned, and they swarmed past his legs as well, gathering speed as they went.

He waited until the last Mousekin had passed and sprinted after them. The other Mousekin had already stepped back from the door, and Basil was about to open it again when it slammed open.

Imps, it seemed, were not creatures of patience.

A group of them had barreled full tilt at the top of the door, winging into it hard enough to open it. The only thing that stopped them from swarming down was that they hadn't really been prepared for the door to open.

That became apparent when they paused as soon as the door was open. A chorus of angry shrieks behind them revealed that the imps at the top of the stairs hadn't been expecting it to work either.

Holland didn't hesitate. The door had opened only about a second before he expected it to, so he screamed a little mouse-y scream and charged under the flying imps into the door.

The timing worked out perfectly. The flying imps, caught up in the moment, reacted to the biggest motion they could see and spun around to try to catch the Mousekin invaders.

Angry screeching from the other side of the door exploded out, and it was clear that Holland and the second squad had engaged the enemy.

Jackal activated his [Potooooooo] Skill. There was no time to wait. Holland's group was effectively alone and outnumbered, and if the door somehow closed, they'd be trapped and killed.

Jackal had to get up there, get inside with them. Basil's first squad was already pouring through the door, and Jackal wouldn't be surprised if both squads together weren't enough to clear the room. But he wasn't ready to let them pay what that would cost them.

In a heartbeat, Jackal was up on the landing and into the next room. His perception was high enough that it could easily match his Skill.

It was a bit like a flood of adrenaline, with its accompanying time dilation. The chief difference was that adrenaline slowed down time and sped up mental processing by shutting off some of the senses, effectively creating a sort of tunnel vision.

Running at high speed with his System enhancements? It was more like everything else in the world slowed down. Sounds pitched down, and the high-pitched shrieks of the imps turned to lower growls. He had time to experience the rotting, damp leather and wet dog smell the imps had imprinted on the room, and to see that the sun was cutting through the clouds outside.

There were a lot of imps in the room. It was a big room, and they weren't all rushing the door. Some of them were milling about at the far end, and some of them were darting outside of the doors. Jackal frowned, hoping they weren't going for reinforcements.

Suddenly the room was lit up with bright flashes and the sound of thunder.

Each of the four Mousekin teams had one gunner, and those gunners opened up in concert now. Instead of the beam weapons Jackal had expected from an advanced, System-integrated species, the Mousekin military still used some kind of gunpowder equivalent.

Whatever it was, it was pretty effective. They fired in short bursts, but each burst was enough to take out one imp. And they didn't seem to miss very often either.

Jackal shut down his Speed Burst. He didn't want to get in front of their firing line, even at whatever small caliber of weapon they were shooting.

Too bad Roger had no such compunctions. He burst into the room with a roar and leapt over the careful defensive half-circle Holland had formed his squad into. Fortunately, they had enough discipline to cease fire as the large mammal blocked their fire.

A heartbeat later, Eric and Olivia joined Roger in charging into imps' home base.

The imps had shown another level of intelligence, as the bulk of them had adapted swarm tactics to deal with the firearm attack. They rushed about the room in a tight murmuration, like a massive airborne blood-red snake.

It was a smart thing to do, because just like everything else infested with System Mana, they could heal relatively quickly. So, spreading out damage amongst as many of them as possible gave even more strength to their numbers.

Worse, Jackal could see they had already started a second wave of attacks.

Chapter Three

Small groups of imps were clawing across the walls and ceiling, moving in bursts. It looked like chaotic motion all across the room, but Jackal could clearly see that almost all of the imps' chaos was resulting in them slowly but steadily advancing. Even outpowered, they were doing a credible job of swarming and overpowering their attackers.

They hadn't counted on Jackal though. With his near-Advanced Levels and Skills, he couldn't quite take on the entire room by himself. But almost.

Under his breath, he whispered another line from the poem:

"A challenge, Antarah, charge, and ruin the enemy."

Jackal rolled his shoulders and activated Speed Burst and Blade Walking, then stepped into the fray. The wall to the right was his first goal, and a red tentacle of flying imps was in his way. He surged into them, laying about with sword and knife. Stings and bites struck him like hail from the leaping front of a storm, but he met them all with edges of steel. His health dropped in a smooth, flowing tide, but the imps broke first, wheeling away for easier targets. At least, those of them that were left.

Almost a third of the imps from the wall lay scattered, dead and dying, at his feet. He didn't pause, leaping to the nearest creeping wave of them on the wall.

Having seen his speed and prowess, the imps on the wall changed tactics. Half of them took to the air and tossed bits and pieces of office stationery at Jackal. He was amused to see a red stapler flying at his face before he batted it away.

Of course, it was just a distraction. The other half of them dropped off of the wall and slunk across the floor, intending to trip him up and bind his legs. They were already close enough that some of them turned to whip their tails into him. The stingers dug in, but not before they encircled his ankles and bound him into place. Then more and more joined in, and again his health dropped—edging below half now. And his Mana was dipping as well.

Jackal ignored the wounds to his legs and the immobilization. The real threat was the airborne attackers, who were trying to do the same thing that they'd done to Roger—blind him. He was feeling the pressure. Quantity had a quality all its own. But Jackal didn't have to beat every imp in the room. All he had to do was take the pressure off the others. The mission was to Level up Roger, Eric, and Olivia. Roger and his allies had shown themselves to be tough, but only passably so. They really needed to do a lot of Leveling up if they were going to handle the wilds of Wells Gray Park.

Still, there were enough imps in this room to cause some genuine issues for Roger and his team. Holland's team could take them out. And Fool and Jackal together would be through the room in no time. Roger would probably survive. Maybe. But they had a lot more dungeon to get through, and Jackal figured that even with Roger's ego, having him continue with a bit of confidence was the most likely way to keep him pushing as things got tougher.

33

So, Jackal didn't really have to spend much more time keeping the flying pests busy. He couldn't risk even a quick glance to the side, but he'd have to assume that Roger, backed up by Holland and his Mousekin, was getting an upper hand on the remaining imps by now. If they weren't, Jackal would have to intervene more directly.

That decided, he stopped holding back. To anyone watching, it would have looked like the imps near Jackal just suddenly decided to explode. In reality, he was letting loose with his full speed and blade Skills, delivering multiple cuts to every imp in the area.

He was drenched in blood when he finished, and his Mana was getting dangerously low. His health was down to a quarter, but it was already ticking back up, even with the effects of the imps' poison.

When Jackal turned to see how Roger was doing, he was only slightly surprised to see they had gotten the upper hand on the swarm of imps. They'd broken it into smaller chunks, and Roger, Eric, and Olivia were each dealing with their own clump of imps.

Holland and the massed Mousekin were doing a superlative job as support, using a mix of gunfire, explosives, and magic to pick off any extra-sneaky imps and to break up any new swarms that looked to be forming. The overall number of imps in the room had been reduced drastically, so Jackal took a quick Mana potion and made his way back to the Mousekin line. He wanted to watch and see how the trio of young adults handled themselves.

Roger was moving pretty much as expected. He had a strange sort of fighting posture. It didn't seem to be related to any martial art that Jackal had heard of. Roger took a wide stance and was using strong and fast hip snaps to keep his sword flying about, balancing all that out with some truly impressive shield work. The shield was mostly tight to his body, but angled enough that he could see clearly around it, and it was in almost constant motion, moving as a unit with the sword. Weirdly enough, his sword kept returning to a resting position with the hilt near his head and the blade angled a little down. It was somewhere between the Unicorn guard of the early Italian school and the St. George guard of the English school. Jackal made a note to ask Roger about that later.

Eric's style was like Roger's, but he seemed to move himself around his shield instead of moving the shield. That made more sense, since he was using a proper Roman scutum, and there was no way that shield lent itself to agility. Instead, he was treating it like a portable tower and picking off imps as they took the obvious paths to work around the shield to get at him. Eric deftly avoided the obvious weakness of that style by not relying on defense, but by using deception, darting out from behind his own shield sometimes, delivering deft stabs with his short sword. He had the makings of a formidable fighter down the road.

Olivia was a bit of a monster. Almost literally. Her outfit of leather strips and bone fetishes jangled and moved and hid her entire body as she conjured arcane blasts and other effects, through a sort of warping dance. She pulsed and shook, stomped and swayed, and power rippled out from her. It looked less like she was casting specific spells than shaping Mana in the moment to reflect the moves of her dance and to her needs. The overall effect was frankly scary. She seemed like such a nice young lady otherwise. During the trip, she'd been quiet, polite, and friendly. Jackal had been tempted to write her off, except that her quirky outfit had raised his curiosity.

She was clearly from one of the coastal First Nations, but the outfit wasn't. It looked more like some of the older European shamanistic recreations. Whatever it was, and whatever its source was, Jackal found himself wanting to know more. Something about Olivia appealed to him.

She was clearly more than she seemed, and what he was seeing now showed that she had some immense raw potential. Plus, she kind of reminded Jackal of himself when he was that age. Not really afraid to be a little weird, but not expecting anyone to really care… or see the actual person underneath the look.

The group had clearly found their rhythm, and the remaining imps seemed to draw into them, attacking in a frenzied rush to kill them all. In a concerted movement, the imps launched a mass attack at the three.

Jackal was almost tempted to step in and help, but they clearly had things in hand. Not easily—they were all covered in blood that wasn't just imp-sourced. And they were slowing down. But the imps might as well have been throwing themselves into a blast furnace for all the good they were doing now.

Jackal guessed that all three had Leveled up in the fight.

A minute later, the sound of gunfire dwindled down to almost nothing… just the odd shot to finish off a wounded imp.

With a nod, Holland released the troop to glean the corpses, divvying them up in piles based on who had the kills for efficient looting.

"That looked like fun," Fool said.

Jackal turned and saw his friend poking his head around the door frame. Jackal shrugged and tilted his head with raised eyebrows in partial agreement. No serious injuries that he could see, nobody dead, lots of experience for the kids? That was about as good as Jackal would have expected.

Jackal flicked his eyes toward the entrance Fool was leaning past.

"No problems," Fool answered. "We watched for a bit, but the goblins and gremlins are well and truly done with us for the day. Scarpered off, the lot of them. And since we're not going back that way, I figured it would be more use to bring the rest up here." He looked back down the stairs. "We aren't going back that way, are we?"

Jackal laughed softly and grabbed Fool by the shoulder. That was about as much affection as Jackal was willing to show in public. He knew his friend hated dungeons, in general and on principle, but Jackal had to admit that the separation of the two of them, even for one room, had been more stressful than he'd expected. He liked to know where Fool was.

And not just because Fool had lately discovered a bit of a thrill in pulling tricks on people. Jackal trusted him. Mostly.

"*Yes!*" Roger roared from the middle of the floor and fist-bumped and high-fived his two friends repeatedly. "*Level up!*" he shouted with a massive grin. "We are *kings!*"

That led to another round of hooting and hollering. Jackal didn't turn around to see who let out the loud sigh—it was clearly Fool. But it might have been Holland, judging from the set of his shoulders as he walked up to Roger. Jackal followed along, and he sensed Fool joining them.

"Congratulations, sir," Holland said. "Shall we take a moment to recuperate and finish the looting while you sort out your upgrades? Do you need any healing?"

"Nah, we're all good!" Roger said. Jackal noticed Eric had been about to say something when healing was mentioned, but Roger had plowed through that. "We all leveled up! That was awesome! This kicks ass. I can't wait to hit the next room."

"Did you all Level up?" Fool asked. "All three of you?"

"You betcha," Roger said, throwing his chin forward. If he hadn't been wearing a helmet, Jackal figured the motion would have made his hair flip backward. It looked like the kind of habit that someone like Roger would have. A touchdown ritual almost.

"Lovely!" Fool said. "Let me know if you need any advice on new Skills. I'm a bit of an expert on that. You don't want to choose the wrong things and get stuck with a bad Skill down the road, do you?"

Jackal frowned, and he could feel Fool leaning into his charisma. He was up to something, and Jackal wasn't sure what it was. Nothing too harmful, he was sure, but also not something too helpful either, if Jackal was any judge of his friend.

It was looking like the Trickster had come to play. Jackal would need to keep a weather eye out on that. Fool had been showing some new power since their adventures in Valemount, and Jackal didn't think his friend was really aware of the extent of it.

Roger was looking around the room with all the energy of a puppy at walk time. "Where's the entrance to the next level? This is level three, right? Let's get on to the next one. We can manage our Level-ups at the end of the day!"

Eric and Olivia rolled their eyes at that, and Fool shrugged. Jackal was a little surprised. The next level should be tougher, and some new Skills might help the three. But showing some restraint and a desire to actually plan out his next Level growth showed more maturity than Jackal had been expecting from the headstrong young man.

Holland stepped up, edging his way into the middle of the group. "The troop is ready to go, but we are getting full on loot. Do we plan on returning this way? We can leave some of it behind to recover after, in case there is more valuable loot to be found ahead."

Roger nodded. "Yeah. Let's do that. Everyone okay with that? And what's next? The nerds?"

"Not quite," Fool said. "Past HR and the imps, the next floor up is the IT department. The information we got said it was 'Goths' at that level. Someone called them 'Richmonds,' but I don't get the reference."

Jackal smiled, but managed to keep the chuckle in. Clearly, the Dungeon Master had a similar taste in TV shows to him. This should be fun. He nodded at Fool to get his attention, then did a quick motion. He drew his forearm across his chin, as though he was covering himself with a cape.

"What?" Fool said, looking confused. Then a look of comprehension filled his eyes. "Right! Vampires. Or something like that."

Fool sat on a nearby chair, miraculously intact and clear of blood. Being Fool, he made sure to turn the chair around and lean forward against the backrest. He didn't say anything for a moment, but he'd caught everyone's attention, so they waited.

He nodded to himself. "Right. Let's take our time on this one, shall we? Roger, I know you want to Level up, but what do you say we take a peek at this one first? If it's possible, maybe you three can solo this one."

"Now we're talking." Roger was nodding and rolled his shoulders back, putting his hand on the hilt of his scabbard sword's hilt. "Who's gonna scout? I'm not good at that." He pointedly looked at Holland.

The little Mousekin shook his head. "Sorry, sir. Our troop isn't spec'd for scouting activities. We're strictly a line unit. A scout team would have cost about as much as our entire troop, I'm afraid. They weren't included in the contract as a result."

Roger frowned. "Figures. My parents spend all the money to hire a show troop but skip on the important stuff. Typical."

Holland visibly bristled. "Sir! I can assure you that we are the finest—"

Roger waved him quiet. "Doesn't matter, Holland. I'll make do somehow."

Jackal couldn't see any exposed skin on the Mousekin, but Holland certainly gave off the impression of turning white. Jackal didn't blame him. The fact that Roger was oblivious to the insult he'd just offered Holland and his troop didn't help at all. Jackal was about to say something when Fool spoke up.

"From what I've seen of Holland's troop so far," Fool said, "your parents got an amazing deal, no matter what they paid. You've all done an exceptional job, Holland, and I expect you will continue to do so."

Holland only nodded back. He seemed pacified enough at the moment, but Jackal expected the damage had been done. A talk with Roger and Holland in private, later, seemed like something he would need to arrange and moderate. Maybe this evening. Fool wasn't done though.

"However," Fool said, "I happen to have some scouting ability myself. If we can have a quick look around and see where the next set of stairs up are, then I can use one of my Skills to get a rough idea of what the layout is and what we might be facing. Once I've got that, we'll see what sort of plan we can come up with. Sound good?"

Roger nodded.

Olivia stepped forward. "I can help with that. Roger, you and Eric finish up the looting here. I'm done already, so I can help Fool. Should only be a moment."

That seemed to decide matters, and Fool and Olivia wandered off toward the other end of the large room. It seemed to turn off to the right some distance ahead, but Jackal figured it was safe enough for two people. Fool could handle any surprises.

With nothing to do for a moment, Jackal sat back and reviewed his notifications. As he'd thought, he'd Leveled up earlier as well. It was one of his "in-between" Levels, so he didn't have any skill points to distribute. And his Attributes were all auto distributed. That had been convenient for his growth... up until a point.

It kept him well-balanced. That had sucked for the first few Levels, as he'd been around other people who had min-maxed themselves to gain an edge. But as he broke out of the teen Levels and up to the forties, the constant steady growth worked out really well. There was always someone who had a stronger Attribute than him in something, but he seemed to always have most of his stronger than everyone else. Growth was logarithmic, so the outliers were coming to be less of an outclassing experience, and his overall growth had been putting him in a better and better place when it came to fights with people his own Level.

Being on the cusp of his Advanced Class was making Jackal see the downsides of the approach though. It would be nice to pour some points into other Attributes and fine-tune something, but he didn't have that option. Which meant that as he Leveled up, he would need to look for more devices to assist him or make more purchases in the Shop.

Or maybe some of his locked Advanced Class skills would help. At the rate they were going, he'd find out sooner rather that later.

Fool and Olivia came back almost immediately, and everyone gathered around them.

"Different layout," Fool said. "In the typical System fashion, the inside of this place makes no sense, but it's clear enough. Around that corner is a single wide set of stairs going up about half a flight. At the top of the stairs is a pair of glass double doors. My Skill shows two rows of what look like server racks down the middle, and a lunch room at the end. There are two monsters, about Level 20, in the server room. Four more in the lunch room. At the end of the server rows is another set of doors that leads to the upper management area. That's supposed to be the second-to-last room for this part of the dungeon."

"So, what's the plan?" Roger asked. "I mean, me, Eric, and Olivia are now almost Level 20. That means we can probably take out six of these guys by ourselves, right?"

"Maybe," Fool said. "My Skill doesn't really tell me any specifics, so they might have some Skills that counter what you've got. All I can do is tell you where they are and roughly what Level they are. The rest is up to you."

Holland cleared his throat. It was probably meant to be less cute than it sounded. "Sir, I'd recommend that you don't solo this. I realize you need the experience, but over the course of this dungeon, you'll have ample opportunity to gain that. Rather than take the risk now, we can enter as a team and ensure that we have you covered if anything unexpected happens."

"Or you could try it without babysitters," Fool said. "I mean, we'll be right behind you. How bad can it be?"

Jackal turned and looked at Fool.

"What?" Fool said. "They're adults. And they're almost Level 20. This will help get them over the hump. It's not like we had anyone other than each other at that point. They can handle it."

Jackal had to concede that point. When they were both Level 20, they'd been pretty cocky and thrown themselves into all kinds of fights that were over their heads. And they'd paid for it. But they'd Leveled up and gotten the attention of the Foundation. Jackal still had the sense that Fool was up to something, but six Level 20 monsters should be manageable by the three youngsters.

With a sigh, Jackal nodded his agreement.

"I recommend against this," Holland said.

"Chill, dude," Roger said. "We got this. Let's go!"

Holland bristled his whiskers, which was enough sign for his troop. All the Mousekin formed up in teams.

Roger smiled at that and started for the end of the room. Eric and Olivia formed up on either side of him.

Jackal leaned into Fool and said under his breath, "I thought there was supposed to be a plan?"

Fool grinned at him. "The follies of youth. But don't sweat it. They got this. And if not, we'll be right behind them."

Jackal shook his head in anger.

"Fine," Fool said. "Holland! Let's all get ready on this side of the door just in case. One squad each side? Jackal and I will listen for issues, and we'll bust in if anything seems to be going wrong. Sound good?"

Holland nodded but didn't say anything. The two squads of Mousekin were already formed in lines and heading out behind Roger and his team. Jackal and Fool fell in behind them, and they all crossed the room.

By the time they got to the far side, Roger was already up at the glass doors and peeking inside. "I can't see anything. You sure they're in here?"

"Sure thing," Fool said. "Can you see the server racks?"

Roger squinted into the glass doors. "Yeah. I mean… it's kinda dark, but there's a lot of glowing lights on either side."

"Perfect! That's them. Should be two lovely hosts for you inside, hiding on either side of those racks, probably in the darkest spots. And don't forget, as soon as you start the fight, you'll have four more coming in to help them out."

Roger nodded and turned to his companions, conferring for a moment. Then with a yell, they yanked open the doors and charged in.

Chapter Four

It was quiet for a few moments. Jackal and Fool split to either side of the doors and kept watching through them. They could clearly see Roger's team slowly and carefully making their way through the middle of the two server racks, but nothing attacked them.

And even though Fool had said there was a set of doors at the end of the room, they couldn't see the end of the room. The server racks seemed to go for quite some distance, and after a while, in the darkness and blinking lights, Roger and his team disappeared.

"Huh," Fool said. "That's weird. Jackal, can you see them?"

When Jackal shook his head, Fool turned to Holland and asked the same question, and got the same response.

"We should go in," Holland said.

"Yeah, I think you're right about that," Fool said. "Might be some kind of illusion or something. I'll stick to the left. Jackal, you take the right. Holland, split your teams as you like and stick close to us. Let's all keep together in case it's one of those 'lose yourself in the fog' kind of traps. And if you run across Roger or the others, remember to let them get the fighting in unless they look like they're losing."

Holland nodded, and Jackal had a moment of amusement at how quickly Fool had taken the leadership role. Jackal wasn't surprised at all. Fool had a natural aversion to rules and hierarchy, but given the slightest chance, he always took charge. He just didn't like other people having any kind of control.

Jackal moved in unison with Fool, the two of them in sync from long practice. The pulled open the two glass doors at the same time and stepped into the room. Jackal opted for a longsword this time and was a little surprised to see that Fool wasn't holding any weapon. He'd ask Fool about that later.

The room smelled like a server room; a smell Jackal was intimately familiar with. His first two doctorates where in astrophysics and particle physics. That translated into a lot of time sitting in rooms much like this one, tinkering on keyboards and with soldering irons. There always seemed to be something to try to get a little bit more speed or power out of whatever computer system he'd been assigned time on, and he'd learned to work closely with the computer science department, helping them kludge together new hacks. They'd been happy days, because at least most of the time, the people he interacted with had gotten to know him online first and had been less surprised when they met in person. He'd eased them into his personal quirks as best he could before meeting them, so all he ever ran into was acceptance. That had been a rarity in his old life.

Something felt odd though. The server racks looked normal. The dim lighting was odd, but not too out of character. The warmth of the room, the steady background hum of fans, the occasional waft of air from a stray current, all normal.

It hit Jackal a moment later. Cables. No cables. Immaculate server rooms where something you saw in movies. Actual server rooms tended to be a bit cluttered. Even the neatest team was always working on something, and as a result, there was always an open cabinet somewhere, a tray with tools… and cables. Always a pile of stray cables somewhere. And if a team wasn't super neat, then you'd run into a real problem with a cable nest.

Jackal turned to warn Holland and saw that the entire team of Mousekin was gone. Fool noticed at the same time and spun about to see if they'd missed something.

"I guess this is a 'fog of forgetting' room after all," Jackal said.

Fool shook out his hands and took a few hesitant steps to the side. "I hate these things. This is why I hate dungeons."

Jackal nodded and took a few steps until he was just behind Fool. He thought he'd seen something…

A thick vine of ethernet cables came tumbling over the nearest server rack, looking like a blue wave, the little plastic connectors looking like snakes' heads.

Fool shouted and jumped back, easily dodging the grasping heads. Jackal swept through them with his longsword, and though they were tough, he cut through them without too much resistance.

Something was moving on the other side of the rack, but before Jackal could follow up, he heard a muffled shout from behind him and turned to see Fool being hauled up in the air. Jackal was just able to see that the ends of the writhing ethernet cables were actually penetrating Fool's skin, and little rivulets of blood ran back up the cables.

"Admins!" Fool shouted, using a temporarily free hand to pull the cables away from his mouth. "Cables feed them."

He was abruptly yanked higher up and only his ankle hooking onto the side of a server stopped him from disappearing over the side. "I got this one, get the other!"

Fool was suddenly torn back over the server to the other side. Jackal fought the urge to go after him. This was a low-level dungeon, so Fool could probably handle himself. The cables Jackal had cut had retreated afterward and were coming after him again.

Instead of running from them or attacking them, Jackal instead leapt over the server rack, aiming for roughly the place where he thought the Admin controlling the cables would be.

He nearly botched the landing in shock when he saw what was on the other side. The room stretched off seemingly to the horizon, and the ceiling faded into a stormy, wicked red sky. The floor was nothing but alternating static-resistant flooring in black and white, as far as the eye could see.

The real horror was the Admin.

A faceless, gaunt figure. It looked at least twelve feet tall, but unnaturally twisted and warped, as if someone had taken a normal human and stretched them to fit. Somehow the process seemed to have flattened the creature, so that it looked more like ribbon than flesh. Where its legs would have been was only a mass of cables.

And they were clearly vampiric cables, judging from the struggles of Olivia and the Mousekin that were caught up in them.

The cables bound tightly around their bodies, wrapping so firmly that their flesh bulged out wherever it could escape the cables' grip. Blood ran across their bodies from where the cables had punched in.

Jackal heard the wet snap of a bone breaking and saw one of the Mousekin shuddering helplessly in the cables' grip.

Jackal turned to face the Admin, and the creature was staring at him with eyes that flickered, changing colors in a dead flat cycle like the blink of an LED. Its mouth opened and let out a whirring moan, and Jackal recoiled in horror as he realized all the teeth in the creature's mouth had been replaced with miniature tongues.

Some instinct warned him just in time, and he leapt to the side as a bundle of cables came back over from the other side of the server racks and tried to snag him.

His revulsion passed quickly. The Admin looked like a twisted, warped human, but it wasn't. It was just another System monster, a creation made to challenge him. And he was more than up to the challenge.

Jackal made a single leap, and the creature's head slipped free from its body, set loose by his longsword. By the time he landed on the other side of the Admin, the cables had slumped and loosened all of their prey.

Holland was already cursing and tearing himself free, and even as his blood was still pouring from him, he set about freeing his people.

Jackal turned to where he had seen Olivia. She was down, buried in cables. He ran to where he'd last seen her, but she was already freeing herself.

With a groan, she sat up. "I'm okay. Just need a moment."

Jackal nodded and went to check on Holland as well. All the Mousekin reported in as okay, but all were drained of health and mana down to nearly critical Levels and would need to recover before they could move on.

Once he'd determined that everyone could hold tight for the time being, he leapt back on top of the server rack. Weirdly enough, he could see over to the other side, over the top of the other rack of servers. The room looked oddly big on that side, but not nearly to the same extent. It actually seemed more like what Jackal would have expected to see: stacks and stacks of old computers and routers, spools of cable, scattered workstations and monitors, a big screen TV, and old, ratty couch. And at least four different coffee machines next to a glass-doored fridge full of energy drinks. Definitely the lair of the SysAdmins.

He couldn't see Fool or any of the others though. He leapt to the other rack and just stepped aside as a sword licked up at his foot. With a small adjustment, Jackal reset himself and took a much deeper leap into the other side of the room, spinning and turning in mid-air to face his attackers.

"Oh, pretty!" Fool said. "Do it again!"

Jackal glared, but he was relieved to see Fool leaning back against the server rack, with a jittery-looking Roger and Eric flanking him. Fool had that grin, and Jackal braced himself for a smart-ass remark.

"Taking up air-bending, are we?" Fool didn't disappoint. "Let me know if you're shaving your head. I can probably get good money for your hair."

Jackal didn't bother to reply to that. Roger and Eric looked freaked out but otherwise fine, so Jackal took a quick look around.

There was a dead SysAdmin farther down, toward the entrance to the room. That must have been the one that attacked Fool, and probably Roger and Eric before that. That was two down, which left the other four.

Fool had said they were in a lunchroom, but Jackal didn't see where that would be.

"Over there, down at the end," Fool said.

Jackal turned and looked where he was pointing at the other end of the room. There was, about a hundred feet down the way, dim light sneaking out through the crack of a barely open door. It was just the kind of creepy invitation that Jackal would have expected.

"I assume you found the others and they're okay?" Fool asked.

Jackal nodded and raised his chin to indicate the other side of the server racks.

Fool turned to the other two. "Yeah, they're okay. We're going to have to collect them though. I suggest we go back to the entrance, since the server racks didn't start right away. The alternative is knocking them over, but I suspect that will draw out the remaining SysAdmins. Probably better if we at least get Olivia back here, yeah?"

Roger rolled his eyes, and Eric gave him a swift elbow in the side.

"Yeah," Eric said. "I guess we can do that. Maybe... might be good to have some backup for four of those things."

"Sure you don't want to handle them yourself?" Fool asked. Jackal was impressed with how well Fool managed to keep the mocking tone out of his voice. If not his eyes.

"Hey, we could have handled that one just fine ourselves if it hadn't surprised us." Roger was already walking toward the lunchroom, sword in hand.

Jackal stepped in front of him and leaned forward. Jackal put his hand on the young man's chest and looked him in the eye.

"Olivia?" he said quietly.

"Oh." Roger looked almost shocked for a moment. Part of it, Jackal knew, was the same thing that happened with a lot of people. Until they got close to Jackal, they tended to forget how big he was. The other part was the recognition that he'd forgotten something important. "Right. Oliva needs the points too. We should get her back with us first."

Jackal noted the way Eric's shoulders relaxed. He'd clearly been willing to go along with Roger alone, even against his own misgivings.

Jackal nodded to Fool, who only gave a slight rolling of his eyes. "All right, you three go back and get the others. Jackal and I will stay here and make sure nothing sneaks out before you get back."

Roger gave a quick nod, and he and Eric headed back to the entrance.

"Ouch!" Fool grabbed his arm where Jackal had just punched it. "What the hell was that for?"

"Can you try not to get them killed maybe?" Jackal asked.

"I wasn't!"

Defensiveness didn't suit Fool very well, and Jackal saw him struggling to answer in any other way. He decided to shortcut the attempt.

"I can see he's gotten under your skin but try to keep it under control. We've got a simple mission. Escort him through this dungeon and retrieve one thing from a park. That's it. Do that and take him back to McBride. Get that done, and you never have to see him again. Fair?"

Fool bit back his reply and leaned back against the server rack. "Yeah. Sorry. Did you ever have bullies like him when you were a kid?"

Jackal cocked his head and thought back a bit. "Not... no, not really. I had a different kind."

Fool blinked and looked up, then took a deep breath. "Right. Sorry. I guess you did. Thing is... Roger just..."

Jackal hugged Fool. "You're not that kid anymore. No more than I am."

Fool gave a wry little smile, and Jackal could see the effort it cost. Both of them had their own demons haunting them, and even though they had aged well past that, sometimes old behaviors caught up with them from time to time.

"All right," Fool said. "I'll keep an open mind, 'kay? He's pushing some buttons, but I'll remember he's just a kid, and admit that I'm looking for the worst."

Jackal nodded. "We'll talk later, okay? Grab some time tonight?"

Fool nodded back. "Good plan. Be good to deal with some of that shit, and I don't think I ever told you that much about my childhood, did I?"

"No," Jackal said. "Not a word. I guess some stuff, but a talk will do us good."

"Deal," Fool said.

Jackal gave Fool one more quick hug and wondered a little at that. The two of them had been good and strong friends almost from the moment they met… but they hadn't really hugged before. It felt right, but also a little strange. And no small part of that, Jackal had to admit, came from his own childhood. It was an odd thing to suddenly come up in the middle of a dungeon, but what was the System if not an excuse for constant change? Hopefully, they could turn it into a change for the better.

"So," Jackal said, "four of the same in that room?"

"Yup. And no worries about them coming out. They already know we're here. Pretty sure they've got a different kind of trap ready for us."

"No more cable things?"

"I'm thinking not." Fool paced. "Ambush predators, vampire cables. That's feeding behavior, right? Different from fighting behavior. The one I fought here went down pretty fast once I freed the two kids. I distracted it, and they chopped it up. How about the other one?"

"One hit." Jackal mimed a baseball bat swing, which made Fool smile. "But it was sort of just staring at me like it expected a different response. And it had taken down Olivia and Holland's entire troop, so whatever it was doing was effective on them."

Fool nodded. "Right. The staring thing. Did that to me too. Just that creepy look. Probably a mental influence thing, but low-level enough to not even register on us. But good enough for everyone else. Think that might be what they're planning in there?" Fool pointed at the sliver of light coming out of the door.

Jackal thought about it for a moment. A mental attack was likely, but it seemed a little too simple. Fool was right—they had a lot of ambush skills, but there was no reason for them to rely on the same skill when they knew their ambush was going to fail. The most likely form of attack would be one the monsters used against each other in mating or territorial contests.

Nothing came to mind. "How would real Systems Administrators fight? Trivia contest?"

Fool snort-laughed, and his grin removed the last worry that Jackal had about him being stuck reminiscing about the past. "Probably, but I have no idea how the System might twist that. But if we charge into that room and you see a giant *Jeopardy* setup, I officially give you license to be smug."

"I'll take it," Jackal said. "But really, no plans? Did you see anything? I assume you ran your Talent Scout Skill on them?"

Fool made a noncommittal little noise. "Yeah. All I really paid attention to was the vampire cable thing, honestly. They also have a good bit of stealth and some mental misdirection related to that. I was running my buffs on everyone to shut that down, but they still surprised us. My bad, I guess. Got too cocky?"

Jackal nodded. It made sense and explained most of what happened. And truthfully, there probably wasn't anything to worry about.

He looked up and saw Roger and everyone else coming back from the other side. Time to move then.

Just vampire cables and a little misdirection. How bad could it be? If all they were going to see was what they already saw, then it shouldn't be too bad.

"Right!" Roger said, as the rest of the party joined them. "Let's go kick some nerd ass!"

Fool looked at Jackal, who shrugged. Why not? What was the worst that could happen? They'd taken out two of the six creatures pretty easily once the initial surprise wore off.

Eric was still looking a little nervous. "Shouldn't we have a plan for this?"

"I think I might have something for this," Olivia said. "They surprised us when we came in the room, but now we know exactly where they are, so that's not going to happen again. Now it's our turn to surprise them."

The smile she let loose was backed by a crackle of electricity running across her fingers. It surprised Jackal enough that he took another look in appreciation. She hadn't shown any abilities with electricity before, so she'd either been holding back a Skill, or her Skills lent themselves to more adaptability than Jackal had expected. In either case, electrical-based attacks seemed like just the thing to bring to a fight with monsters mostly made up of cabling.

That sounded like a good plan, at least.

Chapter Five

Roger, of course, decided that the best approach was for him to step up and fling the door open. On one hand, it was nice that he was showing enough confidence in everyone having his back if it got out of control. On the other hand, he was once again being a selfish git and trying to charge ahead and be the first one to score any kills.

A special kind of hell was released when the door opened. The SysAdmins had clearly been waiting for this moment. The entire open area behind the door was a solid mass of blue cables and ethernet connectors, pouring out in a writhing mass.

Roger and Eric were ready for that. They had their shields up, and the cables conveniently split themselves between the three young folk.

Roger was driven back and just barely managed to keep his feet.

Eric had clearly spent more points on defense, and he had a Skill that enabled him to hold his ground as the cable ends smashed into him with a titanic roar.

The remaining cables made a beeline for Olivia, who was just a hair to the side of the other two. The cables reached out for her with the same speed and ferocity as they had to the other two, but just before contact, there was a loud, snapping *pop* and a brilliant arc flash. It looked like an enormous snap of static electricity, and every cable reaching for her went limp at once.

The air filled with the smell of ozone and burning plastic, and Jackal felt the hairs on his arm standing up in response to the residual atmospheric charge.

A quartet of hideous screams ripped out of the room, and the cables attacking Roger and Eric faltered as well.

With no hesitation, Roger leapt forward, swinging his sword like a scythe mowing down blue vines and grasses. Eric roared again and trudged forward with the steps of a leviathan. The cables collapsed and parted before him, even without the licking stabs of his sword.

The trio reached the door all at the same time and dove into the room.

Jackal looked at Fool. Fool looked back at him, shrugged, and crossed his arms. A glance back showed that Holland and his Mousekin were all poised for action. They'd inched closer, into four columns, and were all literally balanced on their toes, their little tails stretched out behind them, ready to charge at a moment's notice.

It was cute. Deadly, but cute.

Jackal wasn't sure what to do, but he didn't think the trio needed any help really. He was tempted to keep an eye on them anyway, but he didn't want Roger to see that and think he was being babysat.

Suddenly Fool grinned and walked forward. He reached the open door and leaned against the door frame, arms crossed again, and looked in. "Nice cut, Roger! Eric, look out for those cables below you!" Then he burst out laughing. "Told you! Olivia, let him get himself up, watch your back! It's coming right up behind… Oh, very nice. Good job, Olivia! Only three more to go!"

Jackal decided to watch rather than listen to Fool's disjointed play-by-play.

The lunchroom was as twisted as the rest of the rooms, somehow tripling in size from what it should be. The SysAdmins were using their cables as tentacles. Each of them had bundled all of their cables into eight thick tentacles and were flailing at the trio with them. It was a strong showing of force, and any lesser adventurers would have been crushed. Roger and his friends were handling it quite well.

Mostly.

Jackal winced as he saw Roger dart in front of Eric, trying to land a shot on the SysAdmin Eric was fighting. The creature had temporarily retracted its cables and seemed to be in pain. Clearly, Roger was trying to score the kill on what looked to be a wounded creature. Unfortunately, Eric had been about to do the same thing and nearly stabbed Roger... and when Eric tried to pull his blow back, he lost balance. Just enough for another cable-tentacle to knock him off his feet.

Luckily, Olivia was right there. She was still channeling electricity through her hands and delivering thundering punches to every tentacle she could see. In no time, she had the cables off of Eric. She was about to help him to his feet when things got very bad.

Roger had put all his focus into finishing off the weakened SysAdmin, but the other two were still very much in the fight. Even the one Olivia had been punching the cables of looked to have recovered. Both of them were closing in on the pair.

And Olivia's electric sparks were noticeably dying down. It looked to Jackal as if she had used up all her juice.

With her back temporarily turned to pull Eric up off the floor, the two creatures saw a perfect opening and took it. Ten pairs of tentacles lashed against her back, and she screamed in agony.

Some of the tentacles had already been chopped off, so only two more were left after the attack on Olivia to latch onto Eric's ankles and snap him across the floor toward the SysAdmins.

One of them pulled its tentacles back from the attack on Olivia and wrapped them all around Eric. Instead of flaying him or sucking the blood out of him, this one seemed to want to straight-up crush the life out of Eric.

The remaining SysAdmin lashed out at Olivia again, and this time she dropped without a sound. Jackal started to jump into the room, but Fool held him back. Roger had killed the SysAdmin he was fighting and was turning to attack the one attacking Olivia.

The one crushing Eric was starting to struggle. It had almost completely covered Eric in thick wraps of tentacle, but Eric's shield was holding up under the crushing pressure. And Eric was able to use the large concave on the back of the shield to give himself just enough room to maneuver and land some stabs with his short sword.

Since the beast had tried to crush Eric against its own body, Eric lost no time stabbing through the tentacles and into the creature's actual body. It only took three thrusts to bring it down, and the creature collapsed in death.

Onto Eric.

The last two combatants in the room were Roger and the SysAdmin he was fighting. This one had a few tricks and had pulled the individual cables out of its tentacle form. Instead, it used the hundreds of cables in a sort of lashing spray, striking everywhere on Roger that it could find where there was no armor protection.

Roger screamed as the beast struck his face, and Jackal winced when he saw multiple cables stabbing into Roger's eyes. Even with all that, it was clear that the creature, like the others, wasn't built to take punishment. Roger took the pain and kept screaming as he leaned into the creature, slashing wildly with his sword and delivering punishing blows with the edges of his shield. In a span of heartbeats, the last of the SysAdmins dropped.

Jackal didn't wait anymore and dove in to pull the dead creature off of Eric. His fears that Eric might have been smothered were relieved almost immediately. As soon as he started to lift the weight of the creature, he had to let go in order to dodge the stabbing sword that came up from below.

"Hold on!" Jackal said. "It's all clear, I'm just lifting the body off of you."

Eric seemed to have heard that, because the sword stopped stabbing up through the pile of cables. A moment later, Eric was sitting up, free of the cables and gasping for air.

Jackal glanced over and saw that Olivia was still down and unmoving. Fool was tending to Roger, who was curled up on the floor and clutching at his eyes. Jackal saw that Fool was using some of his healing Abilities, so he stepped over to Olivia.

The young woman was curled on her side, the bone fetishes splayed all around. Jackal carefully pulled the ones away from her face and was relieved to hear her groaning in pain.

"What hurts?" he asked. "Anything broken? Should I help you up?"

Olivia groaned again, then winced. "Mana. Headache."

"Ah, gotcha. One sec." Jackal leaned back up and yelled at Fool, "Mana potion!"

Fool didn't look up from his work on Roger, just tossed a needle filled with glowing fluid at Jackal. Jackal grabbed it out of the air and stabbed into Olivia's triceps. She let out a shuddering sigh of relief a moment later. Jackal hadn't actually ever run out of Mana, but he'd heard it was a horrible feeling. Olivia must have been running on overdrive for the last fight, with her electrical attacks.

Other than that, though, she seemed fine. Jackal patted her shoulder and got up to see if Fool needed any help with Roger. His healing Abilities seemed to have worked well, along with the normal System healing and regeneration. Roger's cheeks were still wet with blood and aqueous humor... clearly, his eyes had been punctured.

If it wasn't for the sped-up healing, Roger would have been permanently blinded. Even with the healing, he wasn't uttering anything more than soft groans and whimpers.

Jackal turned to look over the room. Four dead monsters, three very wounded young people. A few years before, this would have been a terrible tragedy. A warning to everyone, followed by new rules, strict signs, systematic changes.

Now? In the world of the System? A good learning experience. No permanent physical injuries. As far as mental injuries? The impact of the trauma on their systems?

That was harder to judge. From what Jackal had seen so far, the System took measures to alleviate mental trauma. The long-term effect of that was something that would need to be watched over time, and he knew that some parts of the Foundation were working on that.

For these three though? What they'd just gone through would be giving them nightmares at some point in the future.

Odds were though, they'd have worse things happen and lose more. The future had a lot of potential for people these days. They lived in a violent world, but once you got control of that, it was a world were everyone had access to not only superhuman powers, but also technology beyond most people's wildest dreams. And contact with alien life. The potential of actual, real space travel to distant stars.

Wasn't some sharp and hard trauma a small price to pay for that, if somehow that trauma didn't result in a hardening of thinking and a brittleness of persona?

Jackal turned and looked at Fool again.

It was worth it.

Trauma was something people had gone through before the System. Horrible trauma, suffered by many people all over the world.

Growing up in a good suburb of Vancouver, Jackal had had the privilege of thinking that horrible things were rarities, news or events that happened only on the other side of the world or to random people you would never know.

But those were real people, people just like him. And they'd all lived through horrible things, and suffered mentally afterward, and tried to make a new life with what they had.

Was any of this world worse for those people? It certainly wasn't for Fool. What he'd gone through the latter half of his life had broken him completely. But now he'd found a kind of healing and a new potential.

Trauma would happen no matter what the world offered, but at least now its cancerous damage was muted and more than balanced by the potential of growth on the other side of it.

Instead of being a thing that broke a part of your soul, trauma was now a sort of rite of passage. A price, and in the grand scheme of things, a small price to pay for a bigger and grander life.

As long as you lived, it was now truly a life where that which did not kill you only made you stronger. Not just in spirit, but materially, physically, even financially.

That was the reality of the world.

But Jackal couldn't find it in himself to not feel a bit broken after what these three kids had just put themselves through. And what they still had to endure. It might be a better world, but in many ways, it was a crueller world. He was finding his own balance with it.

A few hours later, everyone was as good as new and well fed. They'd moved the bodies of the SysAdmins out of the lunchroom, because it turned out to be an actually pleasant lunchroom.

The monsters had been hideous, but the room itself had a nice long window with a counter and stools against it. The view looked out over the grass, to the parking lot, and to the woods beyond. It was an excellent place to recoup and plan the next foray.

They also had to kill a little time. It turned out that the organic cables from the SysAdmins had a very high loot value, so Roger decided that they would harvest all they could, then they passed them off to the Mousekin who was the logistics specialist. He had a sort of limited access to a Shop, so he headed off to sell the loot before it spoiled. It would take him at least an hour to do that, so they had time for a rest.

Fool was watching the Mousekin, and Jackal didn't blame him.

They looked like the cutest little caricatures of humanoid mice. They were all cute, even the third team heavy melee specialist, Whiskers. He was the most muscular mouse of the bunch, with completely ripped forearms, and wore only bracers on his wrists to show off the muscles. He could spin the big halberd he favored as though it was a toy, and it was large enough that even Jackal wasn't sure he could one-hand it. But Whiskers still looked like a chibi mouse in armor. He was insanely cute.

That cuteness was belayed by their eating habits.

The System monsters, unless they used a nasty poison, were almost universally edible. And the Mousekin had clearly found that the SysAdmins were not only edible, but also very much to their tastes.

Problem was that, once stripped of their tentacles, the SysAdmins looked surprisingly human. Which made Jackal very uneasy to watch the Mousekin tear into them as though they were cake at a toddler's party.

It was even worse when the cute little devils looked up at the humans and *grinned* when they saw how uncomfortable they were.

Jackal would have been worried about that, but he'd had a family friend who was military, so he had a bit of a sense of what kind of humor they liked. It seemed common across species military too.

The Mousekin clearly knew exactly what the humans thought of them and what they thought of them eating human-like corpses… so they were playing it up. Just to mess with them.

Of course, that made Jackal like them more. Fool was probably never going to turn his back on them again though. He'd probably go out of his way to make sure he was never alone with any of them either. He'd stopped eating his own lunch after a few moments.

Roger and team didn't seem to really care. That had surprised Jackal a bit, but it did appear that the younger generation was going to be a lot more open-minded than anyone who'd grown up before the System. They took it for granted that monsters were monsters and sometimes looked like humans.

Even so, something was bothering Roger. Jackal saw that he was distracted, so with a sigh, Jackal got up off his stool.

Fool looked at him for a moment with a raised eyebrow. Jackal nodded in Roger's direction, and Fool turned to look. He seemed to see the same thing as Jackal and nodded in response.

Jackal walked over and tapped Roger on the shoulder. The young man stopped himself mid-bite and turned to look up. Jackal jerked his head toward the door and walked out.

It was only a short distance from the doorway to the server rack, and Jackal stopped when he got to it, turned around, and leaned on the rack with arms crossed. A moment later, Roger joined him and looked up at him.

Roger wasn't short. He was probably just over six feet and taller than most people Jackal knew. He looked at the older man, then looked up again. He tried to be smooth about it, but Jackal could see Roger's discomfort and surprise as he again realized just how large Jackal was. He only came up to Jackal's chest.

"What's up?" he asked.

Jackal didn't say anything. He wanted to. He knew the right things to say, but he'd learned that silence had power. He'd learned it years ago, going through therapy when he was trying to learn who he really was. His therapist had been a remarkable woman, and she'd used silence like a scalpel to slice through a younger Jackal's lies. Over time, he'd learned to use that power himself.

After a moment, Roger stopped fidgeting. He scuffed his foot for a moment, then looked back at the lunchroom.

Finally, he spoke. "They took my eyes."

Jackal didn't say anything. Didn't move or react in any way, just kept a steady gaze at Roger.

Roger looked down, unable to keep the eye contact. "I mean, I knew I could get hurt. I've been hurt. I know a lot of people who died. My rugby team, they all died when the System came. All of them. I wasn't there, but I heard."

He stopped and looked back toward the lunch room again. Took a deep breath.

"I've never seen anyone die." It was just a whisper, and it was echoed with silence.

Still, Jackal held himself. And waited. He saw the small signs in Roger, the way he cracked his shoulders and patted himself. He reached up with one hand to grip and massage the triceps on his other arm. Little motions seemed to occupy each part of his body.

Self-soothing was what it was called. Jackal knew all about that. It was a way of dealing with stress and uncertainty. And the smaller motions. Some part of Roger wanted to run away, to not be a part of this oddly silent conversation.

Still Jackal said nothing, keeping his gaze steady on the young man.

"It hurt," Roger said. "When they took my eyes. It was just a moment, but it felt like everything broke and I wanted to scream. I don't know if I screamed or not. It was like my brain… like myself… just went away. Like there was no room for me anymore. And then it just kinda stopped, and I was angry. I couldn't see anything, but I knew… I *knew* I was going to die. If I didn't move, if I didn't fight back. I didn't even have time to think about how to fight or wonder what I could or plan or… I just started to fight. Swinging my sword, but it was like it was something inside me that took over."

Roger stopped for a moment, and he wasn't even trying to stop hugging himself anymore. In the uneven light of the room, Jackal saw a liquid glimmer in Roger's eyes.

"It's like… I wasn't even there anymore. One moment I'm fighting, and the next, it was like a long, grey tunnel. And at the end of that tunnel, like it was down below, I was looking down at myself, watching myself fight. I could feel all that rage and anger and every swing and blow, but it was like I was watching it from above. I was kinda still connected to myself, but kinda… kinda…" He stopped talking, and his voiced hitched. His breathing got ragged, and he took a big deep sniff. "It was… kinda like maybe I wasn't there anymore, like maybe… I was just gonna let go."

As he saw a single tear crest free from Roger's lower eyelid and slip down his cheek, it took all of Jackal's self-restraint to not reach out. He knew Roger needed to get this out. He couldn't interfere, couldn't help. Only listen. And witness.

"And then I was back in myself, and I was flailing away and I had no idea what I was doing and it was all over, and somehow I was on my back and I could hear Fool saying something, then I could see again, and then it started to hurt, and then it went away."

Roger looked up at Jackal, his eyes brimming with tears.

"It went away," he said, "but it's still there. I can still feel it inside me."

Slowly, carefully, Jackal gripped Roger's shoulder. Roger's eyes darted up to meet Jackal's, and Jackal held that look for a moment.

He knew what Roger meant. So did Fool. And probably most people these days. He'd been in that lost moment himself, that dark and lost place where you realized you had no more control over your destiny or even your sense of self. The place where you started to end.

The place where you learned what it would be *like* to end.

He held Roger's gaze until he saw the look in the younger man's eyes, the look that showed he understood that Jackal didn't have an answer, but Roger wasn't alone. He wasn't the only person to be in that place and come back and wonder how in the hell you were supposed to live the rest of your life after that.

When the look in Roger's eyes turned the corner, going from a cascade into terror and despair and back into fear, Jackal nodded at him and spoke.

"It will never leave, but it will get smaller every day. Make your life so big that it fades into nothingness."

Roger looked at him and didn't say anything. His eyes still churned, and emotions ran across them like wisps of fog over a river.

Then he hugged Jackal. Hard. After a moment, Jackal hugged him back.

Chapter Six

The pulp mill was gigantic in a way Fool hadn't expected. Intellectually, he knew that it was a major regional mill, in a major pulp-producing part of the world.

Knowing that and seeing the actual thing were different though. The closest he'd ever come to a pulp mill growing up was to smell the unmistakable stench of them when the wind shifted, in whatever town he'd been living it. That sour, reeking stink was a staple smell of his childhood, just as the *shush-clank-whirr* rhythm of the pump jacks was a sound that never left.

The tall stacks, the wide, round silos, the clouds of steam coming from all over... those he'd seen from the highway, but never up close. And that giant pile of wood chips? Again, seen, but the scale had escaped his notice completely.

Now, about to step into the second part of the Prince George dungeon, he had no choice but to come to grips with the size of the thing. It pretty much spanned as far as his eye could comfortably see in front of him. They were standing on the railway tracks, and once they crossed them, they would be in the dungeon proper.

But from what Fool could see, the parking lot was larger than some dungeons they'd run previously. There were wrecks of cars and logging trucks scattered all across the place, and the fact that they looked like toys gave some truth to size.

He'd been a bit scornful of the rest of the team yesterday. They'd wrapped up the Admin Center portion of the dungeon in the early afternoon. Fool had wanted to press on to the second part right away. Admittedly, because he really wanted to get this whole farce over with as quick as possible.

He'd never been a fan of the whole "chosen one" trope in fiction. Now that the System seemed to have made a reality where such things were more reasonable, he was even less of a fan. On top of that, having two chosen-one-recruit-and-retrieve missions in a row for the Foundation?

It was really getting under his skin. Fair enough with Yagnar. She'd turned out to be exceptionally useful. Her logistics skills were going to ramp up the Foundation's support levels to a whole new level. She was a commonsense resource.

But Roger? What a damned waste. Jackal wanted Fool to take it easy on the kid, and Fool had made the right noises. And he'd try to keep an open mind and see what value the kid had.

So far, all Fool had seen was a spoiled rich bro.

Wealthy parents had used every penny at their disposal to get the kid and his friends every advantage in the world. Sure, the monsters had come to everyone, and you couldn't throw cash at them to kill them.

But Roger's parents had pretty much done exactly that. They'd been vacationing on their retreat with a bevvy of private security. The security had protected them against the initial rush, and the parents had used their money and connections to keep things rolling in their favor ever since.

Fool hated the lot of them. Even when they were nice, it was the kind of nice that came from never really understanding what hardship was.

He'd seen it all before. Hell, he'd lived as a rich kid for a while. When his dad had briefly landed a plum job, all the rich kids were super friendly. They could afford to be. Life gave them everything, and there was no competition except for their made-up ones. And coming into that world late, Fool was already out of the running, so they could afford to treat him nicely.

Except the nice only lasted a short while. Privilege always had a way of showing its cruelty when things turned against it. And usually that cruelty was out of proportion to whatever triggered it, because they never had to balance anger against consequences.

Not like the poor kids, who learned pretty quickly that anger resulted in violence, usually from authorities with more power than any of their peers would ever have.

It was a different world and a different system.

One of the reasons Fool loved the System was that it leveled the playing field. At least, gave it a reset.

But Roger was putting the lie to that belief, and Fool hated him for it.

Even though Fool knew he was being a spiteful prick, he felt as though he had to show the Foundation why it was wrong in this choice. It wasn't like Professor X was going to know the real soul of the little shit otherwise. Professor X and everyone else in the Foundation had also come from a place of privilege, but at least they had the common sense to understand it and work around it. But they'd clearly also always had a soft spot for people of the same class.

So, it was up to Fool to reveal the truth and help stop them from making a mistake.

And looking over the parking lot, at the giant pulp mill Dungeon, he figured he'd have lots of chances.

As long as they didn't all get killed. He knew this dungeon was rated a fair bit below him and Jackal, but this place could have killed him before the System. He knew enough about pulp mills from growing up in mill towns to know the threats, even if he'd never seen one before. Toxic chemicals, extreme temperatures and pressures, nasty machines that chewed up and spat out humans… all of that *before* the System and its transition to a dungeon. God knew what horrors were in it now.

The Admin area had been the first part of the dungeon and had shown how the Dungeon Master was using art to imitate life. Sirens for receptionists. goblins and imps for marketing and HR. Creepy vampire cable things for IT.

The last two rooms had featured giant leeches for the Upper Management area, and a particularly horrid automaton that was in a room just labeled "Susan in Accounting."

He shuddered. Fool would be happy never to see that thing again.

All told though, they'd gotten through it in pretty good order. Whatever Jackal had said to Roger had seemed to calm him down for the last two fights, and Roger had been more open to working with Holland and his troop as partners, rather than backup. It had made clearing out the last part of that level quick and efficient.

If the Dungeon Master kept up his design philosophy though, Fool was hard-pressed to imagine how he'd managed to keep the levels down low enough to be survivable.

He shrugged. In any case, they were committed to the dungeon, and it was time to get started.

As big as the building was, there was only one entrance. Killing Susan in Accounting had given them the key to the pulp mill level, and the key unlocked the gate to their far right. That gate opened up into the chip pile.

Fool let the rest of the party get ahead of him as they crossed the parking lot. The wind was just right, so instead of the sour stench of the rest of the mill, it was mostly the fresh smell of chipped cedar and pine that greeted him.

And that came from the giant dunes of wood chips. Fortunately, the giant chipper chutes were turned off, so new wood wasn't being piled up. The path forward was still going to take them through those enormous mountains of chips.

Fool was betting that monsters were in the chips, and he hoped that they wouldn't be the piles themselves. He found himself wondering if Treants could be chopped up into sentient piles of wood chips. Sort of like a wood elemental, maybe? That would not be fun.

It got weirder as they got closer. Fool was holding up the tail end of the group. Roger and his friends out front, Jackal shadowing them, then Holland and his Mousekin, split into four teams and doing some kind of military formation thing as they moved. From his place at the back, Fool could see that he wasn't the only one feeling as though something was weird.

It wasn't obvious, but everyone slowed down a little as they got through the parking lot and closer to the gate.

It felt like… potential. Fool couldn't really think of a word to describe it, but the whole pulp mill, and especially the chip pile, looked ready for business.

The System had been in effect for over two years now, almost three. In that time, almost all the former businesses had either shifted to a noticeable "System" standard in appearance, or showed the crumbling decay that comes from neglect. Not that the neglect was intentional, but when most everyone had died off, there just weren't enough employees left to run most businesses. And the people left alive are too busy staying that way to try to get any kind of large manufacturing back together again. Not to mention that many of the factories had been obsoleted overnight.

But the pulp mill felt as if it had just been closed for the weekend, and in a few hours, a fresh crew would arrive, and it would be back to business as usual. It was so normal looking that it stuck out like a sore thumb.

There wasn't any single thing that stood out. It was just an overall expectation that hung in the air.

Just in case, Fool activated his [Dry Hair is For Squids[6]] Skill. There was nothing. It was just some sort of odd artifact of the Dungeon-creation process, Fool figured. At least he wasn't the only one feeling it. If nothing else, it gave them a nice little burst of adrenaline as their brains tried to wrap around the unsettled feeling. That would help them deal with whatever was on the other side of the fence.

Despite all the weirdness and the unsettling shit, Roger strolled right up to the gate, pulled out the shiny bronze key, and opened the gate. Typical.

Fool thought that Jackal would have talked Roger out of that. Yesterday, when the little shit had nearly gotten his friends killed—after nearly getting the whole team killed—Fool had had a moment of eye contact with Jackal. Jackal had taken the hint and given the young man a talking to about taking risks with other people's lives. He'd meant to ask Jackal about that during the wind-down from the first day, but they'd somehow never found the chance to talk.

And this morning, it didn't look like Roger had learned anything.

---

[6] Remove Fear or other mental influences. Because you have just temporarily become too cool for that kind of thing.

Fool sighed and picked up his pace. If the little shit hadn't learned anything, then this morning was going to go just as bad as yesterday, if not worse. What Roger should have done was hang back and let Jackal, or Holland, open the gates and scout the territory. Hell, Fool was pretty sure Jackal would have sent Holland ahead in any case. The Mousekin were trained for this sort of thing. At least, for military engagements. That was almost the same thing as dungeon crawls, Fool was sure. But no, Roger was heading right in, taking Eric and Olivia in with him, not even bothering to let anyone know what he had in mind. Typical. Rich glory hound. Fool had no problem with Roger killing himself, but the other two seemed like good folks.

It was easy to pace past the Mousekin, though it wasn't because they were smaller. It was because they were doing the smart thing. Spreading out, covering all approaches—the sides, behind, and above in equal measures. They had a scurrying speed which made them move at about Fool's fast walking pace. They moved out of his way with ease though, flowing in behind him to cover the rear area that Fool was now ignoring.

Roger was already past the gate and into the giant chip collection area. The smell of fresh pulped cedar was even stronger here, and Fool found that it wasn't so pleasant up close. There was another smell mixed in too. It had started subtle, but now up close, it was overriding the pleasant smell of the cedar. It was like a base note in a perfume, but it was rising to a top note.

It reeked of fermented cat pee. That was the only thing close to the smell Fool could think of.

With DM, Fool had learned that smell all too well. He kind of missed that little bugger, but something about the entire quest had put the cat off.

Possibly another reason he disliked the boy as much as he did.

Jackal noticed the look of disgust on Fool's face and let the tiniest bit of a smile cross his lips. "Cottonwood."

"What?" Fool replied. "That doesn't smell like any wood I've ever smelled before."

"Cottonwood," Roger said, turning back to the two of them. "That's what the pissy smell is. Must be some of it mixed in with other woods. It smells really bad. Worse when it's wet."

Fool glanced at Roger out of the corner of his eye. He didn't think Roger was wrong, but something about him stepping in to add his two cents really got under Fool's skin. He could feel a flash of anger stirring in him before he stomped it down.

No matter what he thought of the little shit, they still had a job to do. Fool would be damned before he'd be the one to fuck it up. It struck him suddenly that he did have a path to fix all of this.

Same one he'd used in one of his old jobs. Let the little fucker hang himself. If he was going to act like a smartass boss, then Fool would encourage him to keep it up. Roger would see where that got him.

"Good to know," Fool said. "Not something I've ever smelled before. You sure it's not some sort of monster scat?"

Roger shook his head, eager for a chance to show his smarts. "Absolutely not. I know this smell. My dad had the river near us dredged to build a new dock, and there was a whole bunch of old sunken cottonwood at the bottom of the river. Had to pile it at the edge of our property. Stunk like shit for a month. I'll never forget that."

Eric and Olivia were nodding along, grimacing in recollection.

Fool nodded. "All right. What's our next step then? Got a plan for how you want to deal with this?"

Roger looked around for a bit. "I think we have to walk all the way over to those buildings over there, right?" He pointed at the far side of the chip piles, where the first part of the main pulp mill assembly was.

There was an odd sort of building there, like a bunch of different sized rectangles all stacked next to each other. And behind it were a few large cylinders. The buildings were connected to the chip piles by what Fool figured were conveyer belts. Probably sucked up all the chips and dumped them in the first building for some kind of processing, then into the cylinders for storing or something. The path to the building was anything but clear.

"I think you're right," Fool said. "Are we going to skirt the edges of the chip piles, or try to work our way through them? What do you think?"

As expected, that got Roger puffing up a bit and looking proud. "Probably safer to skirt around, but we aren't here to be safe."

Fool bit his tongue and managed not to say anything, and instead tried to imagine which of the many possible movies Roger had pulled that line from. He was clearly, if subconsciously, imitating some actor's idea of a heroic stance.

"We're here to earn some ranks, so let's work our way through the chip piles," Roger finished.

"Can do," Fool said. "How do you want us to come along? Do you want Holland to scout a path through first, or me and Jackal? We can probably find some good monsters for you, make it easier to get the experience points."

Roger almost looked as though he would take that advice at first, and Fool was worried he'd phrased it wrong. He was trying to get Roger to reject the good advice by appealing to his ego. Fool still remembered being a teenager trying to prove himself, and at that age, he'd have scorned any offer to make things easier. Especially if it came from an older man.

Even presented in the best light, Fool expected that Roger would want to make the best impression he could. By outwardly offering to make things easier, he was bluntly telling Roger exactly how he could impress Fool.

And Roger took the bait perfectly.

"No," Roger said. "I think we need the most experience, so we'll take the lead. The piles are probably the home of whatever monster we're meant to fight here, so we'll start by walking between those two piles nearest us. That looks like a trap to me, so we'll trigger it. Holland, we'll need you to support us. You'll need to hang back far enough that you aren't noticed by whatever's in there, and close enough to hit them from the back when they jump us. That should stop us from being overwhelmed."

Holland nodded and turned to his Mousekin, who immediately dispersed to the sides. Fool was surprised by how much they looked like mice scurrying in a sudden bright light. Amused as well, because that sort of scurrying was typically used as an example of cowardice or weakness. Seeing a full troop of armed warriors, even mini-warriors, doing it? It sort of flipped the trope on its head.

Given maneuvering room, he was quite sure that a troop of Mousekin would be a formidable fast-strike military force.

Maybe they'd get a chance to see that at some point in this mission.

Roger continued. "You and Jackal will be our ace in the hole. In case there is a boss, or something we can't handle, or we're getting overwhelmed again, you two jump in and kick ass. Does that make sense?"

"Good plan," Fool said. "Let's get started."

He had to admit, as he looked at Jackal and shared a nod, that it was a good plan. It could have been done better, for sure. Fool would have used the Mousekin to scout in small groups and get a full lay of the land. Or asked

Fool to use his Location Scout Skill. But without those? Fool had to admit that Roger was maybe showing an inkling of good leadership.

Fool was tempted to use Location Scout anyway and see what kind of monsters were in the wood pile. But something of Lexi and her Mountaineering Guild had rubbed off on him.

The Guild climbed mountains with as little System-enhancements as they could, for the thrill of it... and also to have a more honest experience. So, while Fool was tempted to use his Skills, he also wanted to just enjoy the experience.

It was different from how he'd been before Valemount. He used to hate using his System Skills. It had taken an extraordinary fight and a good talk with his "Patron Saint"—the Trickster God—for Fool to overcome his prejudices and willingly use his Skills as much as possible.

That was the real difference. Before, he'd been avoiding. Now he was looking for chances to be surprised. Chances to let chaos reign a little, and to let himself be in the middle of it.

It felt like good practice for something big that was coming up, but he didn't have any idea what that was.

In any case, Fool gave himself license to be cocky and not use any crutches. He'd survive.

Probably.

Roger wasted no time following through with his plan. Once Holland and his troop had dispersed, the trio strode forward. They made it about halfway through the narrow gap between the nearest chip piles when the attack started.

Fool noticed it at about the same time as Jackal, and the two of them shared a quick look. They were poised to leap forward, and they smiled at each other as they relaxed back down. Time to see if Roger could handle himself properly.

Olivia gave the first warning, a shout as she saw movement in the pile to her right. Eric stepped to her side, his shield raised.

Roger turned in the opposite direction, and Fool grunted in surprise. Roger hadn't even glanced to see what Oliva was yelling about, just immediately turned on the expectation of being flanked. That showed more trust in his friends than Fool would have expected.

Fool had expected another attack of swarm beasts. The first level of the dungeon, the Admin Center, had featured swarms of goblins and Imps. And the SysAdmins had pretty much been swarms-in-one. The chip piles seemed to be going the other way.

With a roar and a shower of chips, a beast rose up from each chip pile, one on either side, flanking Roger and his team. Whatever they were, they were big. Easily the height of two normal humans.

At first glance, their bodies looked to be made of wood chips, but after the initial impression, Fool saw that it was actually a sort of armor made of wooden scales. It covered the creatures from neck to feet. Their heads were encased in wooden masks, white with red and black streaks on either side, with a short beak in the middle. They were each wearing cedar-bark capes and had two-handed axes with obsidian blades.

They both roared again, then charged the three youngsters.

Roger was already charging toward his cedar monster, shield out and sword brandished over his head. Eric was crashing his sword against his shield and settling down strong and defensive. Olivia was crouched behind him, bent over and waving her hands in a fluttering motion.

Fool turned to Jackal. "Bets?"

Jackal grinned and nodded.

"Five says Roger takes his out first," Fool said.

Jackal shook his head. "Nope. Olivia."

Fool raised an eyebrow. "Interesting. Deal!"

They fist bumped in agreement and settled back to watch the fight.

Chapter Seven

Fool watched as Roger charged up the slope to the Cedar Demon. He couldn't discount Roger on bravery. Charging a much taller opponent, uphill, on uncertain ground? That took a lot of courage.

And maybe not a lot of brains.

In some circumstances, it might have worked out well. If you had a good defense—and Roger's shield work was up to the task—you could have an advantage fighting someone on higher terrain. It was true that they could land many shots on you from an angle you didn't expect, but it was also true that to do that, they would need to lean forward and reach down. It was an awkward arrangement for both, and the best outcome would fall to the one who was most familiar with the situation.

To Fool's surprise, it was Roger. He slipped and stumbled on his way up the chip pile, which was to be expected. Wood chips in bulk weren't the most stable surface. The Cedar Demon took advantage of that and stepped forward to deliver a mighty swing with its axe.

The black obsidian axe head flashed like a bolt of dark lightning in the sunlight, and Fool found himself tensing, almost willing Roger to dodge the blow.

Roger seemed to have anticipated the attack and ducked forward, angling his shield up and over his head. It was the perfect response. He'd angle the shield in just the right fashion so that the sharp axe head would be wedged up and over Roger's head.

That would give Roger the perfect opening to slash right into the monster's lead leg. It was almost as if the creature was stepping right into Roger's cut, and Fool expected to see it crashing down in a minute as it tried to put weight on the stump of its leg.

It was a good plan.

What actually happened was very different.

Fool felt himself start to move forward and was unsure where the impulse came from. He was absolutely no fan of Roger, but he still found himself stepping forward to help him when Jackal's hand grabbed him by the shoulder.

Roger was still airborne.

What had happened was that the axe edge had indeed been turned by the shield and angled to skip over Roger completely. The missing factor in that plan had been the strength of the Cedar Demon. The flat of the axe blade hadn't skimmed over the surface of the shield but blasted into it with all the considerable strength of the beast.

The flat struck with enough force that Fool had flinched from the sharp *crack* of the blow, and Roger's shield arm had collapsed against him... and he'd cartwheeled over and off the pile.

Such was the force of the blow that Fool expected it would have snapped Roger's knee if he hadn't been standing on the loose pile of chips.

As it was, Roger landed in an awkward sprawl a few meters away from the base of the pile. The Cedar Demon was unharmed. Roger's blade had only skimmed its leg.

Things on the other side were going slightly better.

Eric's defensive posture had him waiting at the foot of the pile, and the Cedar Demon in their pile had stopped at the edge of the pile and was delivering ferocious blows against Eric's shield.

The larger shield that Eric used was paying off for him. Fool was pretty impressed with the design. The large Roman scutum shield was a solid design, and it was proving itself in this exchange. The pummeling blows were landing with just as much force, but instead of trying to block them, Eric was crouching as each blow landed and letting the force of the blows drive the shield into the ground, transferring all its force there.

Still, the impact was tremendous, and Fool winced as he saw how much damage Eric was taking even through the shield. And the shield looked as if it was on the verge of rattling apart. Even the asphalt under their feet was cracking under the force of the blows.

For some reason, the Cedar Demon attacking Roger wasn't following up on its success. Roger had gotten to his feet almost immediately. His body was System-enhanced enough to deal with the kinetic impact with no real consequences. He'd spun to face the creature and was slowly advancing, but the Cedar Demon hadn't moved since it had knocked Roger off its pile.

"King of the Hill," Fool said.

Jackal nodded. It looked as though the monsters were only interested in defending their chip piles and the passage between them. Since Roger was already through, the beast was only watching him.

Fool figured it out. He could see the next pile and a few off to each side. Each pile had a single peak, and each pile was separated at the base by about a half meter of asphalt, clear of any bits of wood chips. It was territory. The wood chip piles were the territory of each Cedar Demon, and they defended their territory. Likely from each other, as well as from intruders.

Fool looked at Eric and saw that while he wasn't stepping on the cedar pile itself, he was facing into it. He probably looked like a challenge to the Cedar Demon.

Which would mean…

"Uh oh." Jackal said, seeing the same thing that Fool had expected to happen.

The Cedar Demon had knocked Roger off of one chip piles and into the base of the next pile. Which was more than enough to trigger the next Cedar Demon, who exploded out of the wood chips behind Roger, roaring as it raised its axe to cleave him in two.

Roger spun to face the new threat and, in doing so, stepped out of the chip pile. He was still facing the Cedar Demon, which meant it didn't see any reason to stop attacking. It was taking sliding steps down the pile, roaring and closing in on Roger.

Roger took two steps back and crossed over the middle line separating the two piles. That was far enough back that the new Cedar Demon started to slow down, and the one now behind Roger roared and stepped forward as well.

Fool was almost amused. Roger was carefully maneuvering himself to be flanked by both. It would have been amusing if it wasn't likely to result in his death. Roger was stuck spinning between the two, feinting with his sword and trying to keep his shield up in motion… and hadn't quite realized that the two had stopped attacking him.

They were still roaring and making threatening motions with their axes.

It finally clicked for Fool. They weren't roaring at Roger now. He was between the two beasts, and they were caught up in a territorial dispute. Each had stopped just out of range of the other's axe swing. If they decided to cooperate, they would likely mince Roger in seconds. More likely, as Roger swung his sword more aggressively toward them while shifting from side to side, they'd wind up tearing him in half.

"I can get them to fight each other," Fool said to Jackal. And he could, he knew. He'd watched them long enough to know that he could slide between the two, draw them close enough to tangle up each other, then sit back and watch them tear each other apart. It would absolutely be his kind of fun.

Jackal let out a small laugh. "I believe it. But you don't want to mess up our bet, do you?"

Fool shook his head. Jackal had a little more confidence in the youngsters than he did. Fool didn't want Roger to die—just to screw up through his own ego. As he turned back to watch the fight, he had to admit that Roger was holding his own. It wasn't looking quite as likely that he was going to die as it did a moment ago.

The two Cedar Demons were attacking him in earnest now, anticipating his spins as they brought him into each of their ranges. He'd figured out the trick to using his shield to bounce off the axe attacks as well. He had developed a little snapping roll that seemed to spring the axe away on contact, and he used the impact to power a fast turn and cut toward the attacker that was behind him.

Their two-handed axes were being swung at the limit of their reach, with both hands toward the base of the handle, so Roger couldn't quite reach them. He kept slicing at them though. It looked as though he was trying to keep them at bay. It was working, but that was likely because the two creatures were clearly wary of stepping into the territory of the other.

Then one of the axes snapped, the head spinning away. The startled Cedar Demon looked stupidly at the shortened handle for a moment. Roger had been ready for that. Fool realized he'd been using his sword cuts in conjunction with his shield parries to whittle away at the axe handles.

Fool had to give Roger credit. He was smarter than he looked. And acted.

While Roger was sprinting toward the now disarmed Cedar Demon, Olivia had finished her spell preparations, and Fool was amazed to see flames spring from her hands, the same way lightning had sprung from them yesterday.

Jackal had talked Fool into not using Talent Scout on the trio when they'd first met them. Something about thinking that Fool needed to learn to use his Perception more. It made sense for some reason Fool couldn't remember now, and there was no reason for him not to look now.

Ah.

She wasn't a Wizard, but rather some kind of Sorcerer. She had a number of Class Skills that relied on an innate understanding of Mana, the result of which was that she had a level of flexibility in spell use that differed greatly from the usual spell-casting forms. It combined with some elemental affinities in a way that looked completely broken to Fool. She had a potential for power that astounded him. It was way overpowered for her Class and the System, frankly.

And somehow… familiar.

The flames didn't spray from her hands or shoot out in fireballs as he expected. Rather, a thin sheet of flame ripped up from her feet and slashed right up to the top of the chip pile… and through the arm of the Cedar Demon on the way. The beast let out a keening whistle and nearly dropped its axe. It didn't surprise Fool at all to see that they were vulnerable to fire-based attacks.

Eric didn't even pause. He and Olivia seemed of one mind, and his attack happened less than a heartbeat after hers. He drove into the Cedar Demon, slamming the front edge of his shield into its armpit. It completely exposed Eric to the beast, but its arm was missing on the exposed side, and the shield, pressed into the creature's armpit, effectively prevented it from bringing its axe around. The Cedar Demon leaned forward with a bird-like snap, and its wooden mask spilt in two, to reveal a mouth lined with flat, grinding teeth. It meant to snap Eric's face right off.

Too bad Eric's sword was much harder to nip off.

Eric drove the blade home, pounding the sword hilt against the roof of the monster's mouth, the tip of his sword bursting out of the top of its skull.

One down.

Fool swore and transferred five credits to Jackal.

Roger wasn't doing quite as well, but he seemed to have figured out the territoriality of the two creatures. He'd stepped forward onto the pile of the one he'd partially disarmed and was fighting it to a standstill. He'd probably have finished it off right away—he was clearly faster and more nimble that the creature—but the Cedar Demon was proving to be fairly capable with just the handle of the axe, laying blows all over Roger.

Roger could fend them off though. It looked as though the tremendous impact of the axes had been somehow tied to the obsidian axe heads, and with that gone, it was just using a very effective club.

And Roger was more than a match for that. A flurry of stick blows later, and Roger delivered a chop to its leg that nearly severed the limb. The creature screamed and faltered, but Roger hadn't stopped with that chop, slicing his sword free and snapping a forehand cut that took the top half of the creature's masked head clean off.

He spun in place, not even waiting for it to fall, and charged right back into the next creature.

The Cedar Demon swung its axe with force, driving a low blow intended to knock Roger off his feet. The axe slammed into Eric's scutum with a ringing clash, and Roger used the lead edge of his shield like a sledgehammer, smashing down on the wrists of the creature. He followed up a split second later with a wild downward cut, clearly aimed to cut off both arms, but there was no real need.

The shield bash had knocked the axe right out of the creature's hands, and it looked at Roger with a dazed expression, just in time for its forearms to be lopped off. A moment later, Eric and Roger finished it off with combined thrusts, then turned to high-five Olivia at the base of the pile.

Fool and Jackal sauntered over.

"Nice work," Fool said. "Got a plan for the rest?"

"The rest?" Roger said.

Fool nodded and pointed at the dozen other chip piles that lay between them and the entrance to the next building. The building was clearly the next step through the dungeon. The piles appeared to have been arranged so that there was no way to approach the entrance without going through the tight gaps and facing more Cedar Demon attacks.

Roger looked down the path and let out a sigh. "I guess we just go through? They were tough and had some good tricks. It was close, but we didn't take any damage at all, so I guess we can just push through?"

Fool nodded, and Jackal made a slight throat-clearing noise. Fool turned to him, but even as he did, he realized what he'd overlooked.

"Maybe grab one of those axe heads first?" Fool said. "Did you notice that when you chopped the head off that one, its attacks got way weaker? Go grab your loot and see what kind of properties they have."

Roger's eyes popped open, and Fool shook his head. Kids. In his excitement to get the job done, Roger had totally forgotten about looting. And Fool had a hunch those axe heads were worth a lot.

Eric followed Roger, leaving Olivia behind.

"Nice work with the flame," Fool said.

Olivia cocked her head to the side in a quick motion that made all of the bones framing her face jingle. "Seemed the thing to do."

Fool looked into her eyes, but she only smiled. The smile didn't quite go to her eyes. There were some secrets there, but Fool had been running with Jackal since the beginning. He didn't need as many words as most to understand what someone meant. Olivia was a little proud of herself and trying not to show it.

Fool liked her.

She was absolutely going to work out. And Fool had confirmed his theory as well. The term "chaos" had shown up a lot in her Skills list. Sure enough, back in her eyes, behind her stoic shell, Fool recognized the touch of the laughing Trickster. She wasn't aware of it yet, but that was why Fool was the Acolyte. It was his job to share the truth of the connection. Somehow. He'd known that it was another part of his deal with the Trickster, to preach and grow his flock in some strange way.

Olivia would be another debt payment for Fool. Maybe in this case, he was paying forward a bit. He'd have to figure out a way to get that started though. He'd been a rebellious youth himself, opposed to learning anything that didn't come from his own work, so he hadn't really learned how to teach someone.

He did know that any teaching first required an agreement between two people to be teacher and student, and he had no idea how to go about that.

He glanced at Jackal as Olivia walked over to help Roger find the far-flung axe head. Jackal looked at Fool and shrugged.

"Got a plan?" he asked.

"Shit no," Fool said. "I was hoping you would. Am I supposed to be some kind of teacher now?"

Jackal's face lit with a smile, and a silent chuckle rolled across his frame. "Be about time, honestly. You'll figure it out. I have faith."

"Gah." Fool grimaced and shuddered. "Watch your language, man."

That made Jackal laugh out loud, and they both turned as Roger shouted and held up the missing axe head. Eric had already grabbed his, and Oliva was nudging the body of the third Cedar Demon aside so that Roger could grab the axe from that one as well.

It only took another moment for them to come trotting back to Fool and Jackal like kids grabbing presents under a Christmas tree, eager for their parents to give them permission to open the packages and share what fun toy they'd gotten.

"These are amazing!" Roger said. "The axe heads give a huge bonus to strength. I bet they're worth a fortune, and we can even use them on our own gear once we've collected enough of them." The kid was practically bouncing up and down in excitement.

Fool held out his hands in a placating fashion. "It's the first thing in the morning, so we can probably clear out the lot of them. Do you want to spend the morning farming them and getting experience yourself, or make a speed run?"

Fool was pretty sure Roger would opt for speed run, in response to how Fool had phrased it. But Eric surprised him.

"Can't we do both?" Eric said. "Roger was right, they weren't that hard to beat once we dealt with the attacks. My gear is a bit worn, but not that bad. But these guys are pretty static and predictable. I bet Holland's teams can deal with them pretty quickly, and we won't lose much time if we all work together. Best of both worlds, I think? Maybe?"

The initial confidence Eric had spoken with was fading rapidly with each word, and he ended the tiny speech with a string of mumbles, a red face, and some investigation of his feet.

Fool found it adorable, but it was absolutely the right suggestion. He couldn't argue with that, even if it foiled his next plan of getting Roger to screw up.

Holland had somehow made his way back from whatever scouting he'd had the Mousekin doing and patted Eric on the hip. "An excellent suggestion, Eric. We've already completed our scouting and came to much the same suggestion. We can take down four chip piles at a time, one team per pile." He looked at Roger and continued. "As long as we have your permission to do so, sir. We can have most of this area cleaned up in less than ten minutes if you humans will deal with the rest."

"Hell yeah!" Roger said. "Let's get some!"

Fool managed not to roll his eyes at that. Mostly.

Chapter Eight

It took closer to half an hour, but they cleared all the chip piles. Roger, Eric, and Olivia got cocky and tried to each solo a Cedar Demon. They were able to, but it took them longer than they expected. They all wound up taking damage and needing time to heal. Fool spent some time playing with his. A nice easy monster was the perfect chance for him to work on his non-combat skills, relying on luck and random chance, along with judicious use of his Skills to frustrate and confuse his opponent.

That, and he and Jackal were so close to Advanced. They had to let Roger and the kids get all the kills, so they were passing up the XP that would push them over. A little play time took the edge off the frustration.

One of his first-Level Skills, Clouseau, had actually turned out to be useful in the fight. At its basic Level, the Skill allowed him to alter one physical feature at will. It was one of the first Skills he'd learned. He'd used it as a basic disguise kit, altering the color of his eyes, changing his hair length or color, growing a beard, that sort of thing. It had allowed him to get away with a fair bit of petty theft in the first few days of the System and kept him fed.

Once he'd hooked up with the Foundation and gotten access to good equipment, he'd relied less on it. When he got his Geas skill, he'd completely abandoned Clouseau. But facing the Cedar Demon, he suddenly had a bright idea and decided to use it.

He grew his nose to a ridiculous length—sticking out in front of his face almost a foot. Then he darted in and bopped the Cedar Demon with it.

That had been a bit of a mistake. He'd expected the nose to be almost fake, but it was as real as his usual nose, and poking it into the hardened wood mask of a Cedar Demon had really hurt. Fool's eyes had watered immediately, and it was only instinct that let him dodge the next few blows.

Once his vision cleared, he was able to test out his plan. It worked perfectly. He was able to dangle the nose out like a target, enraging the Cedar Demon into attacking it, then instantly shrank it back so that the swinging axe whiffed through the space the nose had been occupying. He had enough Perception, Agility, and Luck to play with the Cedar Demon all day, but adding in altering body parts kept the game fresh and interesting for him.

Eventually Fool had finished off the creature with a few swift blows of his warhammer to the back of its skull, then went to check on the others. He felt a little guilty about sneaking the kill in, but everyone looked like they had their hands full enough.

Jackal hadn't played around at all and had simply walked up and beheaded the first Cedar Demon he saw. He didn't even have to climb into the pile to reach it. He just stepped on the first few chips to call out the beast, then lopped its head off with a flick of his sword. One and done. Even if he had piled a bunch of Skills on to increase the damage of the first attack, it still was entirely unfair.

After that, Jackal had kept an eye on the kids.

Fool decided to catch up with Holland's team and see how the Mousekin were doing. He was constantly fighting the urge to cuddle the cute little bastards, but they sported some decidedly predatory gazes when they wanted to. And apparently, they wanted to whenever a human made cooing sounds at them. He hadn't bothered to push that, having learned that sort of lesson many, many years ago.

They were performing as expected. The first pile he got to was the perfect example.

The Mousekin team, what would have been called a fire team in other militaries, was a group of four Mousekin. Three privates and a corporal. Roles in the team were pretty stratified. Two privates were melee specialists, heavily armored, looking like squat little medieval knights, and used either sword and shield, two-handed swords, or pole weapons. The other private was a ranged weapon specialist.

The ranged specialist was wearing what looked to Fool to be almost modern military kit, complete with about a million pockets and what looked like a scaled down assault rifle loaded with accessories. The lead of the team was the corporal, who was always a mage. Each team seemed to have a mage with different specialities, so the troop as a whole had some utility against most threats. There was a healer and a sergeant split between the two squads, and at the moment, they were both with the other team.

Nicodemus was the mage of A team; the one Fool was watching. Blossom was the ranged weapons specialist. Nibbles and Pinky rounded out the team as the melee specialists. Both of them were armed with halberds, which they were using to hack away at the Cedar Demon while Blossom peppered it with carefully placed support fire. Nicodemus was tossing darts of fire, which had set most of the chip pile smoldering.

The Cedar Demon they'd been tasked to take down seemed to be quicker than some others and a bit cagier. It was also smaller than the other ones Fool had seen. He figured it was younger, or maybe the runt of the pack. It was causing a bit more trouble for Nicodemus and his team than the others.

As Fool came up to them, Pinky was batted right off the pile by a savage swipe of the obsidian-headed axe. Pinky's armored body folded up all around the axe head, and Fool's heart had frozen at the sight. He darted into action as he saw the little body flying through the air and caught Pinky just before he smashed into the ground.

Fool gave a bit of a grunt as the compact little body struck him. The Mousekin himself didn't weigh much, but stiff armor and the force of the blow from the Cedar Demon made for a compact punch. It was like being hit in the chest with a kettlebell being thrown by a little league baseball pitcher.

Fool managed to keep his feet anyway and held on to the Mousekin.

With a little groan, Pinky unfolded in Fool's arms, and his halberd dropped from his tiny paw to clatter on the ground. Quickly, Fool set him down and summoned his Kiss It Better skill. Tiny little cartoon kisses appeared all over Pinky, and Fool saw his health rise out of the danger zone. He was tempted to give him a healing potion, but Pinky's System-enhanced healing seemed to have kicked in already, so Fool let him be. He could also see Gadget, the squad healer, hustling over. Nicodemus must have let her know.

They were down a member of their team, so Fool stepped in to see if he could help.

It didn't look as though he would be needed, but it was close. The Cedar Demon had followed up after knocking Pinky loose by attacking Nibbles with a berserk fury. And Nibbles could barely keep up with the pace of attacks. She was blocking each blow, but not able to counter. With the force behind them and volume, the attack was piledriving Nibbles farther and farther into the chip pile. She was already down to mid-thigh, and a few more blows would have her hip deep.

Blossom was on top of it though. With only one Mousekin left, and mostly covered, he risked switching to the grenade launcher on his rifle.

It was very much a System-enhanced grenade.

Fool saw him slam the grenade into the launcher, and when he raised the rifle to fire, Fool had expected a hollow *thunk* noise. That had been what he'd heard and seen in movies. Instead, there was a mighty whistling *crack* and flash. Fool felt the impact from the force of the round being launched punch into his chest and blow his hair back.

The projectile came out looking like a solid bar of white light that punched right through the Cedar Demon. Its backside exploded into a mighty spray of giblets and bits that drenched the chip pile behind it, and it collapsed, motionless.

Nicodemus let out a high-pitched shriek. "Dammit, Blossom! We talked about this. Save those rounds for the higher-Level monsters. That's a month's pay you just wasted. It was down to almost no hit points!"

Blossom shrank down a little. Only a little. He fidgeted a bit with his rifle and said softly, "Boom."

The rest of the team burst out laughing, and Nicodemus clutched his tiny paws into fists and visibly marshaled back a retort.

Instead, he stomped up the pile and grabbed Nibbles's hand, helping to pull her up out of the chips. She was wedged in pretty good though. Blossom ran up to help, and a minute later, Pinky joined them.

"No one else injured?" Gadget asked from down by Fool's knee. Even for a Mousekin, the healer was on the short side.

"They all look okay," Fool said. "I've also got some healing skills, if not. How are the rest of the teams doing?"

Gadget looked down for a moment, fidgeting with her supply pouches, as if looking for something. She replied without looking up. "So far, no problems. Penny, Ralph, and Frederic got clipped pretty good, but me and Holly got them back on their feet. Jerry stepped in to help Ralph and Frederic when they got knocked down, and it was touch and go for a bit, but he's stabilizing." Gadget swore a little more, then took off her backpack.

"Missing something?" Fool asked.

"Regen poultice. I could have sworn I had it in here. I was going to head back and use it on Jerry, but I can't find it now."

"Regen? How hard did he get hit?"

"Lost an arm and a chunk of his skull when he tried to block a cut meant for Ralph."

That raised Fool's eyebrows. "That's... no problem? Huh."

He looked over the Mousekin again, looking at their gear and how quickly and efficiently Nicodemus was getting his team sorted out and ready for the next engagement. They'd impressed him with their professionalism earlier, but there seemed to be more to them than just having good drills.

Gadget made a little cooing noise as she found the poultice she was looking for and turned back to the other piles, but Fool stopped her.

"Gadget, how often does this sort of thing happen to you folks?"

Gadget gave him a mousey little grin. "Follow me while we head back to Sergeant Jerry, and I'll fill you in."

Fool nodded and sauntered along with Gadget as she hustled back.

"You probably don't think much about it," she said, "but imagine you had to face the universe the way we do. Imagine being in a universe full of giants. System-enhanced giants. How's that going to shape you?"

Fool thought about it for a moment. Humans had reacted with a lot of fear when the System dumped its monsters on earth. And there had been a lot of racist reactions when actual aliens showed up shortly after. But Gadget had a point. Some aliens were larger than humans, but most were in the same rough range of height.

If every monster had been a kaiju and every alien a giant?

"You get it, I see," Gadget said. "Sucks at first, but just because something sucks doesn't mean the universe makes it go away or gives you a way to hide. So, most of us decided we'd rather fight back. Better to build a rep as a giant-killer than hide at home and hope for the best. So yeah."

She stopped as they reached the other team. Sergeant Jerry was on his back, being tended by Holly, the other healer. His right arm was a stump, but not actively bleeding. The top of his skull was missing, a diagonal shear that started just above where one ear had connected to his skull and ending just past the midpoint. Fool had to clench back the knee-jerk wave of nausea that hit when he realized that the pasty lumps mixed in with red were the Mousekin's brain.

Fortunately, the Sergeant didn't seem to be aware of the issue. His mouth was hanging open, his tongue lolling about, and his eyes were rolling about patternlessly. They had a flat lifelessness that did not look good to Fool.

"Can I help?" Fool asked. He had resisted the urge to jump in and apply a healing spell, because Gadget and Holly didn't seem concerned, and they also seemed to be working with a goal in mind. It was best not to impede a medic at work.

Holly shook her head. "No worries. He'll be fine. Looks worse than it is."

"Looks pretty bad," Fool said. Even as he said that though, he saw the edges of the wound were slowly growing back… and then they grew together rapidly, knitting into whole flesh before Fool's eyes.

"There we go!" Holly said. "These regen poultices are great. Gotta restock next Shop visit for sure."

"You weren't kidding on those," Gadget added. "Much faster than the stock ones. Take me with you next time you Shop. I'm gonna grab a few more of those as well."

With a last check on the poultice, Gadget stepped back and turned to look up at Fool. "So, yes. Yes, this is pretty normal for us. We Level up like you folk, but every blow that hits us is more likely to kill us than it is to kill you. System balances that a little with some faster Leveling, but you can't Level when you're dead."

Fool shook his head. "Doesn't make a lot of sense to me. I mean, I can see running dungeons on your world, but stepping out in the wider galaxy, coming to a Dungeon World like this? I guess it must pay pretty well?"

Gadget grinned. "Yes. Yes, it does. But we do this for the same reason you do. The more you can Level up, the more you can do in the world. For us, our entire society has been rebuilt around Levels. You can't do much unless you Level up. You want an apartment? Kids? Maybe a farm? Doesn't matter how much money you have, you won't get permission without the Levels. So, we hire ourselves out to have a better life back home. Basic training and one mission gets you set up for life with basic income. Joining a professional group like this? If you can last more than a few years, freedom. You can do whatever you want back home. And our home is an amazing place to do whatever you want."

"Must be," Fool said.

Jerry groaned and sat up, the dead look in his eyes replaced with one of confusion, growing into a sour awareness. Holly squatted next to him and filled him in on what he'd missed, and Gadget wandered off to check on the other teams.

"Going to run with us for a bit?" a voice said.

Fool jerked and turned to his left. Holland was grinning up at him from just below his left elbow.

"Might do," Fool said. He hadn't been surprised by anyone in a while. "Roger ready to tackle the next bit yet?"

Holland nodded. "Jackal's holding him back until we get there. He's eager to enter though, so we'd best hurry if we don't want to get left behind." Holland pulled a whistle to his mouth and blew out a series of short, sharp tones.

The Mousekin came pouring out and snapped into four lines instantly. Some of them looked a bit ragged, but even Jerry was on his feet and at attention… if a little wobbly. Holland gave them only the quickest glance before turning about and heading off, and the Mousekin dropped into two lines to follow.

Fool found himself following from the rear, more intrigued by the miniscule soldiers with every step.

Roger hadn't waited. When they'd cleared the last of the chip piles, Jackal was waiting for them, leaning against the steel door leading into the first part of the building. From inside, shouts and clangs could be heard.

"Where's Roger?" Fool asked.

Jackal opened the door and waved in Holland and the Mousekin, who hustled in rather than answer. Fool walked up to Jackal, who was looking a little bored.

"Something fun inside?" he asked.

Jackal shrugged. "Golem, I think. Some kind of construct, steam powered. It's another 'larger on the inside' room, and the thing is rampaging.

I think Roger's having fun anyway. He stuck his head in the door to peek and got punched right in the face, lost a chunk of his health. Off he went."

"Think they'll need our help?"

"Not yet. He seems a little pumped up after the Cedar Demons, so this will let him blow off a little steam. It's a tough beast, but the three of them can take it down. Should only be a few more moments."

Fool nodded and leaned back on the other side of the door frame. The sun was shining. It was warm, and the air held that promise of deep summer heat.

"Still got an issue with Roger?" Jackal asked.

"Don't you?" Fool replied. The sun felt nice, and he was happy to spend a moment letting it settle into his bones. He supposed it was as good a moment as any for this talk.

"He's a good kid."

"Spoiled."

"So what? People grow and change. Can't hold their upbringing against them."

The building suddenly shook hard enough to bounce Fool and Jackal slightly off the frame. There was a titanic roar, and Fool heard the screams of the youths inside and a burst of volley fire from the Mousekin.

"Should we head in?" Fool asked.

"Nah." Jackal pulled out a piece of jerky from a pouch at his side and chewed on it. "It's just the golem doing its last power up before it dies. They got it. Stop changing the subject."

"His parents paid for his Skills. He didn't earn them."

"That's true," Jackal said. "But he didn't have a choice about that, did he? You gonna give him a chance to make his own choices and see who he's going to be?"

Fool let his "humph" speak for him and crossed his arms. To be fair though, Jackal had a good point. Roger hadn't had a choice in how he was raised. And Fool's reaction to him was likely to something that shaped Roger's character... and maybe what Fool was planning wasn't in the kid's best interest.

After all, it's not as if Fool was free of biases in this. He shook his head to clear it of a memory better repressed for the moment.

He leaned his weight forward and stepped away from the wall, turning to face Jackal. "He's not making good choices. He's being selfish."

Jackal nodded. "He's making the choices the world told him to make. Seems to me like a Trickster might be the perfect tool to show him some other choices."

"You're a rat bastard, you know that?"

"Nah. My parents were happily married."

Fool squinted with one eye as hard as he could at Jackal, but the giant warrior refused to be intimidated. Fool gave up, rolled his eyes, and opened the door.

It was bedlam inside. The screech of wrenching metal, screams, and shrieking steam blasted his eardrums.

The inside of the building was one huge open space, with all sorts of containers scattered about, conveyor belts galore, and the ceiling and walls seemed to be made entirely of different kinds of pipes. Some part of it looked as if they had been connected to something that had torn itself off of them. Fool figured it was the golem, probably warped by the System from some of the original equipment in the building.

The golem looked to be in its final death throes.

It was a rather huge golem, probably about two stories tall. It was covered in Mousekin melee fighters, who were scrambling all over it and delivering smashing blows everywhere they could.

Roger and Eric were at its feet, dodging oven-sized fists and driving blow after blow into the mechanical construct.

Olivia and the other mages were directing arcane blasts at its joints and other weak spots.

It was absolute, mad chaos. The air was filled with dust and steam and bits of torn insulation.

It all came to a shattering halt as the golem finally gave up the ghost and died.

But it didn't die the proper way. No slow tumble to the ground, no last gasp or collapse onto its back. Instead, it just crumbled apart. All the metal bits disconnected from every other bit, and the whole thing tumbled into one gigantic pile.

Fool winced as he saw the Mousekin caught up in that. They'd instantly lost any purchase, so they'd had no chance to jump free. Instead, they fell into a jumble of hard steel pieces… and worse, had some of those hard steel pieces fall on them from a height.

Before the System, that alone would have been an industrial accident, likely with multiple fatalities. Falling pieces of steel broke things when they landed because they weighed a lot. Hopefully, Holland's people were tough enough from their System enhancements to escape without too much trouble.

It didn't look like anyone had escaped this match without injury though.

Roger and Eric had broken arms. Eric's shield arm was clearly broken, and he screamed as his scutum slipped off his arm and clattered to the floor. Fool saw some bone sticking up from his upper arm. That was a nasty compound fracture. Roger's right forearm was bent at the wrong place, and his shield was nowhere to be seen. He'd switched his sword to his left hand to finish the golem.

Olivia's face and exposed skin looked bright red and was already peeling. The golem must have had some sort of steam-based attack as well.

Holly and Gadget, at least, were in good shape, and they ran around healing up everyone they could find. Gadget was running for Roger, but Fool waved her off, indicating that he would handle the healing. His healing Skill wasn't as good as the Mousekin's, but with the amount of blood and squeals coming from the jumbled pile of metal… they were more needed there.

Eric looked to be the worst. Roger had sat down and was clutching his forearm just above the break and letting out a bit of a whimper. The blood had stopped pouring out of Eric's arm, but his skin still had an unhealthy white pallor, and he was breathing shallowly. Fool went to him first.

"Okay, buddy. Let's just have a bit of a sit down, okay? It's all going to be okay, just give me a minute and we'll have this fixed right." The words came out in a smooth tumble, and Fool wasn't really thinking about them.

Even before the System, he'd always had a knack for first aid. Blood and broken bones didn't bother him much, and he'd wound up being the person people came to when someone got hurt. He'd added training to that whenever possible. Never had any interest in medicine as a career, he just liked to be helpful when possible. Just another skill to have. It had come in handy when he was homeless. In his lucid moments, he'd been able to help when people weren't willing to go elsewhere.

With Eric sitting down, Fool could already see the signs of the normal System healing kicking in. The signs of shock were fading rapidly. The downside with a compound spiral fracture was the System would take its time moving the bone back to its correct alignment, and that would be painful and slow. Fool knew what to do, so he stepped in.

Setting a bone is never easy, but setting a compound spiral fracture is a whole other world of danger. Broken bits of bone are sharp, and movement of any kind can result in important blood vessels being sliced open. Not something Fool wanted to cause.

This one didn't look too bad.

"You ready?" Fool asked Eric. "I'm going to speed the healing up for you a bit, but it's going to hurt. I'll be quick."

Eric looked at him, and for a moment, it looked as though shock was going to set back in, but then he nodded.

Fool didn't wait. The procedure was straightforward. If it had been a piece of wood, you could untwist the wood until it was back roughly in place. But with bone, it was surrounded by tissue and blood vessels, and you didn't want to get anything pinched. You also didn't want to lose any more bits of bone by scraping them against each other.

The first thing he did was slowly pull the limb back to its normal length. While he did that, he gently rotated the bone back to its normal position. He couldn't see where it was going, because the jagged ends were already slipping back under the skin.

As he felt he was getting close, he activated his healing skill. It was as if the bones became magnets, and he could feel the two ends pulling together. Working with the healing Skill, he gently guided them together instead of letting them snap together.

Eric let out a big "whooooo" of relief as Fool felt the bone slip to its original shape. The flesh was already closing, and Fool gave a small prayer of thanks that infection wasn't something they needed to worry about in the same way anymore.

"All good?" he asked.

"Hell no," Eric said. "This is stupid. And I'm stupid. But yeah, I'm okay. It feels much better, thank you."

Any concerns Fool would have had over Eric's words were alleviated by the smile on the younger man's face. Fool smiled back. Give the kid another few months of this, and he'd have developed a proper black humor.

Roger was already standing back up, and his forearm was mostly straight.

"I know you and Eric are friends, but don't you think breaking your arms at the same time was a bit too much?" Fool said.

Roger rolled his eyes. "Yes, Dad. I'm sorry, Dad."

That rocked Fool back for a moment, and he wasn't really sure why. He blinked, then pressed past it. "How's the arm?"

"Hurts. A lot. It's healing, but my health is going up slower than I expected. Can you help?"

"Sure can. It's probably twisted, or maybe crushed. It'll heal, but it's a lot of small things that need to be fixed. I should be able to speed that part for you."

Fool put his hands on either side of the broken bone. His Mana was down a little. Healing was part of his Skill set, but not a major part. That made the Mana cost a little higher than it would be for a dedicated healer, but he didn't expect to need much for this part of the dungeon. After a moment, the arm was done. And mostly healed. That surprised Fool.

"Do you have a self-healing Skill?" he asked.

"Sure," Roger replied. "One of the passives. Nothing unusual, just like everyone else's."

Fool stepped back and frowned. "Not everyone else. Most people don't actually. They have to rely on System baseline healing. Even Jackal only recently Leveled up enough to get some healing and a bit of regen."

"Whoa. Really?" Roger said. "I thought everyone just healed up fast. I kinda wondered why Holland brought healers with him."

"Nope. Most people rely on dedicated healers, or healing potions from the Shop. Otherwise, the normal System healing will heal up just about anything that doesn't kill you outright, but it's not usually fast enough to make a difference in a dungeon, between one fight and the next, without a little boost."

Roger shook his arm out a bit with a pensive expression. "That seems… dangerous, doesn't it? I mean, I can throw myself into things. I've got regen and healing. I'm usually good to go by the time a fight's over. But why would anyone come into a dungeon if they can't do that?"

"Everyone's gotta Level up, Roger," Fool said, then turned to look over the rest of the party. Holland was shouting, and people were hustling over to help pull some metal off of the last few buried Mousekin. "We Level up or we die, or we rely on other people to protect us. It's the new world. None of us have any other choices anymore."

He didn't wait to hear what Roger said, a foreboding feeling pulling on Fool as he ran toward the remnants of the dead golem. Maybe he should have been helping there, rather than talking.

Fool made it.

Just in time to see Holland pull out a limp body and clutch it to his chest.

Chapter Nine

It was Ralph, the melee specialist from Mortimer's team, part of Jerry's squad. He'd been at the bottom of the golem, trying to lever open the back of its calf assembly, hoping to hamstring the monster, when it died.

Most of the falling steel had dropped right on him. He'd likely died almost instantly, judging from the visible damage. His helmet had been knocked off earlier, but he'd kept fighting, wanting to keep up the pressure on the much larger creature. Not the worst decision in the moment, but it was the last decision he'd ever make.

His frail and tiny body looked somehow remote and delicate, even encased in its armor. Holland held the corpse for a moment, then, carefully and slowly, passed it to the next Mousekin soldier in line. All the Mousekin formed a line, and they passed Ralph all the way down the tumbled mass of steel by a living conveyor of solemn Mousekin. At one point, his arms dropped to the sides, and Fool felt himself gasp, even as his vision clouded with tears.

Jackal's low and solemn voice spoke from beside him. Somehow, the echoing rumble of it reached through all the spaces of the building, almost in song.

"Alone and palely loitering,
Though the sedge is withered from the lake,
And no birds sing."[7]

He'd seen the same thing Fool had seen in that moment. It was as if the Mousekin soldier, in death, had been transformed into Dicksee's knight, gazing up into the eyes of Keats's muse.

Fool cleared his eyes with the back of his hand, sniffing to clear his nose. Olivia was standing by herself, and Eric leaning close to her, but not touching. Roger just stood as still as a stone, unmoving.

Fool had gotten far too used to death. Everyone on Earth had since the System arrived. The subtle way the System played with PTSD was a thing everyone was starting to recognize, and he could feel it now. The difference was in how the pain hit.

Death hadn't been distant, living on the streets before. The lower mainland had a perfect mix of weather to kill folks, like much of BC. It was pretty—one of the most beautiful places in the world—but it hid a harshness in the wilderness. That was echoed in the cities. Long, wet winters, and hot, dry summers. Illness took a lot of friends, illness that would have been nothing in a better physical or social environment.

Fool remembered the last time he'd seen someone die, before the System arrived.

It had probably been a drug overdose. Fool didn't know and didn't care. He'd rolled over one morning and saw a young fellow he'd just met the other week, lying like a piece of background scrap, like a thing unnoticed and never to be noticed. He'd been vibrant, alive the previous night. Told some good jokes, shared some food.

[7] La Belle Dame sans Merci by John Keats

Mostly what Fool remembered was that the sense of slate grey that had fallen over him at the sight. Numbness and distance. He'd just moved on, found another place to hole up, and stayed put until the feeling went away. It wasn't the first time. The part of his soul that cared had sort of given up.

But now? Now the grief hit him like a hot knife, and it sliced right down the middle of him. He could barely stand, but he did. He'd hardly known Ralph. Of the twenty or so Mousekin, he was just a face. Not even that, because he liked to keep his visor down when armored. There was no personal connection to rip a hole into Fool, but there was pain anyway.

The loss of any life was precious in this new world, and he felt the loss tear into him.

And touch on something new.

A rage. An anger at the futility of it all. Lives given for the System of all systems, the ultimate unfair, snuffing out promise and potential in random rolls of some unseen dice.

It didn't have to be this way. They'd all been blessed with power, including healing. Cheating death was common… so why did death still have to happen? Why was this damned System set up with such cruelty? And why, damn it, had no one ever fixed it?

And down deep inside him, that rage was echoed back. A keening, a sorrow, and an old anger. He felt a tugging at the edge of his awareness and looked up.

Olivia was looking at Fool with a shocked look of recognition on her face.

Part of it was a mutual understanding. Fool knew the keening rage inside was being echoed by the Trickster, an aspect of his god he hadn't known before.

But Olivia did. That aspect of the Trickster was the source of her powers too.

That, Fool had been expecting.

What he hadn't been expecting was the other thing familiar between him and Olivia. He'd felt a stirring before when he'd looked at her. Something familiar. And now he knew what it was.

It was kinship.

They shared blood somewhere down the line. And somehow, their shared connection with the Trickster allowed them to recognize that other connection as well.

That floored Fool, because he'd thought he was the last, that all of his family was dead.

They held eye contact for a moment, a tiny reaffirmation of life and a gift, before nodding at each other. They'd talk later, maybe tonight. For now, it was time for the grief to flow.

The Mousekin placed Ralph on the floor, making an empty space for him. They all gathered around him, linking arms and tails until they became almost as one, then they looked up and let loose a mournful, howling keen. An ululation of sound that rose and fell and rose again, from howl to scream to hooting a soft song and back again, the pure outpouring of souls in grief.

Fool couldn't tell how long it lasted. It seemed forever and just a moment, but when it ended, they all stood in a kinship of hollowness, and silence descended.

For the merest heartbeat, then it ended. Mousekin bent down, stripping Ralph of all his gear. They kept going until Ralph's little body was only left in its undersuit, a soft-looking unitard in pale grey. Holland held open a black bag, like a body bag, and they slipped Ralph's body into it.

Then all lined up again and bent their heads.

Holland closed the bag with a seamless sort of zipper, and when it was closed, he pushed a button on the side of it. The bag puffed up for a moment, then let out a low hissing and slowly deflated. It shrank until it was nothing more than a little black puck. Holland picked that up and put it into his backpack.

The Mousekin almost shook themselves, then it was a scurry of quick words and hugs all around, and the moment of grief was gone, like an errant drop of rain on a spring day.

The humans all had moved together by unspoken accord during this entire process. Holland walked up and stood before them and looked up. His long fuzzy face was as solemn as anything Fool had ever seen.

"Sir," he said, speaking to Roger, "I regret to inform you that our number is reduced by one. We are still combat effective and will do our utmost to make up for the shortfall."

Roger blinked a few times, and his mouth opened and closed as he thought of something to say. Fool wanted to jump in and say the right thing, before the young fool said something really stupid, but he surprised Fool.

"I know you will, Holland," Roger said. "You're the finest soldiers I've ever seen, and I have no doubt you will perform beyond my expectations."

Holland only nodded in reply, but Fool got the impression it was exactly the right thing to say.

"What are our orders, sir?" Holland asked.

Roger glanced at everyone else and made quick eye contact. "Next room. This time, you guys scout ahead and let us know what's up, and then we'll make a plan, 'kay?"

Holland nodded and moved back to his troops.

If Fool didn't know better, he'd think that maybe he'd just seen Roger grow up a little.

Fool wished they'd taken more than a breather before entering the room.

It was the second-to-last part of the pulp mill, and before the System, it was the last step of the process before the pulp was pressed into paper… and the System had focused on the bleach part.

If he squinted, Fool could imagine that maybe the fat, lustrous black beetles were originally part of the machinery of the mill. It was a stretch though. It rather looked as if the Dungeon Master had run out of thematic options for monsters on this part of the dungeon and had instead found a monster with a vaguely related attack.

In this case, the beetles were much like giant-sized bombardier beetles. They attacked by hunching up and arcing their rears forward, sort of like a reverse scorpion. The tail went under the body to attack.

And they used bleach to attack.

Super-heated bleach. It gave the entire room a gut-wrenching stench, and Fool didn't think any amount of time would get them used to it.

Some of the Mousekin were actively gagging, and the humans weren't far behind. When the beetles came swarming up, it was almost a relief to have something else to focus on.

The beetles were about the same height as the Mousekin and probably double the mass. For once, Holland's troops hadn't been forced to fight a taller opponent, and they made the most of the opportunity. Roger hadn't come up with any plan for this room, but he'd also not told anyone to stay back and let him collect all the experience either. So Holland had ordered his folk to form lines on either side of the humans for a more unified approach.

It wasn't the worst approach, but it was limiting everyone's defensive motions. They found that out as soon as the beetles attacked.

Fool and Jackal had split the line between the two of them, with Fool backing up the left half and Jackal the right. Which meant they were perfectly positioned to watch it all fall apart.

The first beetle to attack had been an easy kill, because it had come in to bite. Roger and Eric, in the center of the line, had hacked it to bits as soon as it approached.

The follow-up wave had noted that.

Two beetles approached and stopped a short distance away, just out of sword reach. Roger was about to advance on them when one hunched up, drawing its rear under its body. Fool started to step toward Roger. He wanted a closer look at what was happening, so he saw it happen clearly.

The boiling bleach spurted from the beetle's rear in a short, high-pressure blast. It wasn't very directional, spraying in a messy arc in front of the beetles. Messy enough that it actually sprayed the beetles themselves, and Fool saw a caustic steam rising from the beetles' shells. It was actually eating away some of their chitin. Clearly not an attack that the beetles would prefer then.

Everyone who got hit by the spatter screamed. Fool was wondering just how bad it was when he felt a burning on the back of his hand, then he was yelping along with everyone else as it felt as if someone had dropped a ball of molten steel on the back of his hand.

The line fell apart.

More beetles charged from the far side of the room, dozens of them. Fool felt a hard jerk on the back of his neck.

It was Jackal, pulling him back. The warrior had a spear in hand and nodded toward the entrance to the room. Time for a retreat. Fool put the pain aside and stepped up to pull back Jerry, who was managing his line in front of Fool.

"Pull back!" Fool shouted. "Regroup in the other room."

The order spread quickly. The Mousekin reacted instantly, pulling back, and forming a defensive perimeter around the door. Jackal grabbed Roger and Eric and shoved them back toward the door with Olivia's help.

They all managed to retreat, thanks to Jackal's swift work with his spear. He could dodge the spray while keeping up enough sharp jabs with his spear to keep the beetles back.

Jackal slammed the door closed behind him when he finally made it through.

"We need a better plan," Roger said.

Fool was surprised to hear that. It looked as if the little twerp was actually growing up. Admitting he needed help, or even that he didn't have everything perfectly in hand, was a hell of a big step compared to the person Fool had seen him be before this.

It smacked of potential.

"What are you thinking?" Fool asked.

Roger opened his mouth, then he closed it again. His brows furrowed, and he let out a sigh. "I guess... I think... I'm not good at this. I really just want to charge back in and hit them harder and faster instead of going in slow and steady, but that's not going to work, is it?"

He was looking at Fool and Jackal for an answer, and Fool knew that was a bit of a trap. He glanced at Jackal and held his gaze for a moment. Jackal nodded.

Fool sighed and shook the last bit of pain out of his hand. The damned beetles had a nasty sting, but it really was just a sting. Pain, and lots of it, but not a lot of damage.

The trap here was that Roger was doing a better thing, but he wasn't doing the right thing. Asking for help was the right thing, but turning to the most senior people in the room? This was a bit of a fragile moment for Roger—Fool could see that. The risk here was that he would see Fool and Jackal as people he could rely on.

Normally, Fool would be okay with that, but as much as it annoyed him, he had to admit that Roger naturally fell into a leadership role. When pressed, he was always going to default to being in charge. Which meant that as much as he was looking for help now, he was going to have to learn to get it from the right source—the people he was leading.

Fool pointed at Roger. "Talk to your people. Work out a solution."

Olivia didn't even wait. "We need to deal with that bleach bomb attack of theirs, because I'm not putting up with that again. That sucked."

"No shit," Eric added. "My shield covers me, but that isn't going to help everyone else, and we need them to push through. Maybe I can draw them in on me, and the ranged Mousekin can pick them off? Will that work, Holland?"

Holland tilted his head in thought. "Maybe. But they won't stay focused on you. And there are enough of them to swarm past you, and the room isn't big enough for us to use maneuvers to stay out of their way. We need to pin them and pick them off."

Roger stepped in. "Maybe me and Eric can charge them and split them into two groups? That might split their attention enough to let you get more shots in? Maybe we can plan to retreat fast if they push past us… can your troops reach them from the door? We could, like, sally out and back again? Would that work?"

Holland smiled and nodded. "It's not bad. But you might not be enough of a threat. It would work better if our melee fighters went with you. They have enough armor to withstand some of the ranged attacks before they will need to retreat, but if we don't push too deep, you can provide them cover when they get worn down. Our mages might work some defensive shielding that can help, if Olivia can provide them with offensive cover while they do that."

Roger nodded. "Okay. That's a plan. Fool? Jackal? Any input?"

Jackal shook his head.

Fool chewed on his lip for a bit. He could think of a couple of better ways to do this, and he was sure Jackal could think of dozens. Despite the work of the last few days though, Holland's Mousekin, Roger, Eric, and Olivia weren't a team yet. They didn't have the coordination to work together as a team, and their best chance was to try something easy.

"I think it's a good plan," Fool said. "We'll be there for backup, but I think you can do this."

Roger nodded and looked at everyone. They were ready to go, so they moved back to the door.

He may have had a moment of insight, but Roger was still all about action in his heart. There was no hesitation. He slammed the door open, and they charged in.

Nothing had been planned ahead of time of course. Roger and Eric bumped into each other as they tried to go to the other sides of the room, but they sorted it out quickly, Eric charging to the right and Roger to the left. They had caught the beetles in mid-return to their previous hiding positions, so the beetles helpfully milled about and bumped into each other while they turned around.

Holland's teams hadn't been given exact orders either, but they were well drilled. Holland gave more whistled commands, and the two squads split, one following each of the two human fighters. The ranged weapons specialist formed up on Olivia as she strode through the center.

For all that, it was a bit of a shitshow. By the time the beetles and the humans got into range of each other, it all sorted itself out, mostly because of Mousekin professionalism.

Roger made contact first, driving into a ball of beetles that were turning and hissing at each other as much as the encroaching teams. But they also acted with a fierce single-mindedness as soon as they had a clear target, and Roger was met with the combined spray of nearly a half-dozen beetles.

He had his shield up, and just as the spray happened, four armored Mousekin piled against Roger's legs, providing a little more protection against the boiling spray. And the two mages tipped the balance in their favor, applying spells to the five that had the spray splattering and bouncing off, as if they had all been covered in repellent waterproofing.

The first beetle went down to the heavy cracking of rifles, combined with a lightning bolt from Olivia.

Eric's team on the other side was faring well, and the ranged fighters in the center were punching out a beetle with every volley.

In less that thirty seconds, only a few beetles were left. They'd stopped their acid sprays after the last attack, seemingly having run out, and just in time. The last spray had finally eaten through whatever protective magic the mages had used, and Fool heard the ranged fighters screaming and shrieking as they burned… only to stop bitching as the healers, mixed in with the mages, darted forward and did their work.

The melee fighters finished the last of the beetles a moment later, in a coordinated threshing attack.

After running through the last beetle, Roger ripped off his helmet and hoisted it into the air with a raucous bellow. "That was *awesome!*"

Fool had to agree. There was definitely some potential here.

He hated it when Jackal was right.

Chapter Ten

Jackal smiled as he watched Roger's team move into place.

They'd decided to speed run the rest of the dungeon, slow down on the looting and maximize the kills and resulting experience. Working everyone as teams, instead of as random backup for Roger, had gotten them through the last of the pulp mill and the first room of the third part of the dungeon in less than an hour.

It was just past lunchtime, and they were in the second-to-last level of the sawmill. Only one more level past this one, and they'd be ready to start the journey to Wells Gray Park. The saw mill part of the dungeon had a real horror show vibe. Whatever the original building had been, the System had replaced it with an ancient twentieth-century version. On the outside, it was a creaky and spooky looking wooden structure, full of ominously shuttered windows. Inside, it was even worse. The first floor had been a large warehouse space, row after row of stacked pallets, shelves, and huge rolls of paper.

Only one monster, but it had been an absolute doozy—a demonic forklift run by a headless driver, with chainsaws launching out of it to chase people around. Worse, it seemed to have a theme song. A deliriously upbeat, cheery ditty that would start slow and distant to announce the imminent arrival.

It was much faster than a normal forklift, moving with the speed and fluidity of a hunting cat. Somehow, it always managed to surprise them, despite the music, jumping out of some pile of debris or coming around a corner that no one was watching, then disappearing a heartbeat later, leaving only a dissonant ringing alarm bell in its wake.

Tough too. It was, after all, mostly a solid chunk of metal. Stabbing the headless corpse that appeared to drive it had no effect. Eventually, they'd managed to swarm the forklift and hack it to pieces. It felt as though it had taken forever, but a check of the time afterward showed less than ten minutes had passed.

But the time they'd finished it off though? The rough edges of working in teams seemed to be gone. It hadn't even really taken much discussion.

They'd taken the initial two teams and split them into three, with Roger, Eric, and Olivia each in charge of one team.

Roger and Eric's teams were pretty much the same. Each of them had three melee specialists, a healer, and two mages assigned to them. They were the heavy teams, taking and dealing the most damage. Olivia had the four ranged weapon specialists with her to complement her set of skills. Her team was the fast-moving precision team, tasked with taking out leadership, flankers, or filling any weak spots that came up.

Fool, Jackal, and Holland made up a fourth team, along with a single melee specialist, Whiskers, as a runner. Whiskers made it immediately clear that he considered himself the bodyguard of all three and took to standing around glowering at anything and everything.

Fool had even resisted making a joke about that. It wasn't hard. Whiskers had the innate cuteness of a Mousekin, but only superficially. He was clearly a vet of many scraps, somehow even retaining a scarred appearance. He was also a powerhouse of a Mousekin, thick with muscle, and was even less talkative than Jackal was. Jackal had only ever heard Whiskers grunt once, in response to a command.

Basil and Jerry, the two Mousekin sergeants, rounded things out by fitting themselves into Eric's and Olivia's groups.

And now that they were entering the next level of the dungeon, they were going to get a chance to try out their new formations.

Roger was clearly getting into the team spirit, and he asked Fool and Jackal to scout out the level before they all went down. It was common sense, and not just because they were a good team. The entrance to the second level was down a shaky, narrow set of stairs with only room for one person at a time to go down. The second level of the dungeon was in the basement.

It was as spooky as it promised to be. Dimly lit. Cobwebs and scary-looking spiders everywhere. Lights that flickered on and off, revealing and then hiding different parts of the room. The room itself was far larger than the building above, but you couldn't really tell, because the farther recesses were hidden in the dark. The only reason they knew was that Fool had used his Location Scout skill to get the general layout first.

The weakness of that particular Skill was clearly shown. The Skill was supposed to give a map of any location Fool wanted to go to, hazards included. The layout he shared with them was simple and clear, even down to the initial, rough locations of the monsters.

None of that was visible once they accessed the floor though. The whole haunted-mansion theme of the level was being taken to its extreme. Jackal had half expected to see skeletons come flying out of the walls with a canned Halloween laugh-scare sound effect.

They hadn't been immediately attacked, so Fool had signaled everyone else down.

It was still quiet, with no movement at all in the basement, even after they'd slowly moved everyone down. Roger had wasted no time wondering about that. Fool had shrugged and said something about the bad guys being content to wait.

Now Roger was forming his team around him and pressing forward. Right in front of them was a musty pile of garbage that blocked their view of the rest of the space. Roger stepped around it, to the left. His team fell in place with him, and Jackal was pleased to see how smoothly they were all moving together.

Eric had gotten his team together, and they were following Roger. There didn't seem to be any other way into the rest of the basement. Which made it a perfect place for a choke-point ambush by the enemy.

That thought kept Jackal tense as Roger stepped through the opening. It was wide enough for three people abreast, so Roger could pass through it with half of his team spread out on either side of him and the rest pressing close behind.

Jackal expected to hear an attack the second they moved out of sight, but nothing happened. He glanced around, but there were no other entrances to the space. He could relax and not worry about being flanked, but it was in his nature to worry.

For no reason, it seemed. Eric went through the opening next, then Olivia, with no attack.

It was only when Whiskers stepped through ahead of them that the bad guys showed up. Whiskers held up his hand for a halt, but then quickly motioned them forward a second later.

As soon as Jackal entered the passage, he saw the problem.

Rats.

Giant rats.

Giant undead rats.

They were about half again the size of the Mousekin and also bipedal. Not quite skeletal, but they had chunks of flesh missing, and flat, dead grey eyes. As they saw the intruders in their domain, they let out low, squeaky moans and started forward.

The rats didn't shuffle, but rather moved with a clear purpose that suited their gear. They were dressed like Viking warriors, in long mail armor that covered their torsos and extended down to their knees and covered just past their shoulders. They had no helmets, but each carried a long, bearded axe to match the round shield in their other hand.

They moved smoothly until they formed a solid line, completely blocking the other side of the room. As one, they slammed their axes into their shields in challenge and stared at the intruders.

"This should be fun," Fool said. "Almost equal numbers, and matching Levels. Tough fight, but no real surprises." Fool had clearly chosen to use his Talent Scout Skill again.

If he was right, and there was no reason to think he was wrong, this would be the toughest fight yet. That made sense because the dungeon only had one more level after this one. This would be a good test for everyone. No easy beasts to plow through, and hopefully no major surprises.

Roger glanced back, and Jackal gave a single nod. Roger could handle this. It would be easier if they sat back and planned out tactics, but Jackal figured this was the perfect fight for Roger. Since he'd been raised in an SCA household, shield wall tactics were something he, Eric, and Olivia had been around since they were kids. They may not have had a chance to participate in any of the big battles that the organization had held every once in a while, but from talking to Roger, Jackal was certain he'd been mentally preparing for this sort of fight most of his life.

Roger grinned in response to the nod and gave a curt command to his team.

They moved forward, spreading out into a matching line. Eric split his team off to the far right. That split them into two lines, marching toward the rats' single line.

Roger wasn't aiming for the far left side though. The standard tactic that Jackal knew of was to try to wrap around the edge of the opposing shield wall. The rats had anticipated that though, and formed their line so that they anchored each end to a wall. It meant they had to space their line a bit, but they still mostly had overlapping shields.

If Olivia joined them, they could have formed an equal-sized line. With that, the usual method would be to walk up to the opposing line and attack, gradually wearing down the other side until you could exploit any opening that showed up.

Instead, they approached the single line of rats as two staggered lines. Eric and Roger seemed to have split the opposing line into an imaginary half, then positioned their lines in the middle of each half. Olivia kept her team in a line as well but staggered back from the two front lines and in between them.

Jackal frowned as he watched. It seemed a recipe for disaster because they had intentionally left a hole in their line. That meant that the rats could punch through the middle and the sides at the same time, effectively cutting off Eric and Roger's lines and surrounding them.

Then Jackal saw the logic of it. If the rats pressed through the space between the lines and tried to wrap around on the inside, then they'd be vulnerable to Olivia's line. She'd be effectively outnumbering a small section of the Rat wall in that case.

And the rats were aware of that. Jackal saw them shift in the center, pressing forward but hesitating. Roger's group was still about ten steps away, and the rats' slow and hesitant press forward had resulted in the center of their line gently forming a wedge—the usual formation for a charge between lines.

Jackal watched intently. He'd long ago made a study of classical battles, and this was looking to be a line formation battle out of antiquity. All that was missing to make it really interesting was pikes.

But the edges of the Rat line were also moving forward, and the rats on those sides were seeing the openings on the end of the lines and pressing into them. As a result, it looked like Roger was going to be flanked on his left.

As Jackal thought that, Roger yelled, "Back five!"

Then he and his team took five smart steps back. Not perfectly, because it hadn't been rehearsed at all. It was pretty clear the Mousekin had no idea what he was doing, but their own professional drilling habits kept them moving in near unison with Roger and Eric.

As they stepped back, the flanking rats moved in a little quicker, looking to take advantage of the opening before it closed. The rats in the center surged forward but stopped as Olivia's line stepped forward to almost fill the gap. The remaining part of the Rat line also stepped forward, but more slowly.

Jackal saw the plan. It wasn't much, but it was something. Given an open field, Roger probably would have been able to play an excellent bout of maneuvering against the rats and wind up encircling them. There was no room, or time, for that in the basement.

But the effect he could have was likely to be enough to decide the battle in his favor even before it started.

With the center moving into a wedge and the sides curling in, Roger had effectively split the Rat line into two lines. Not from their movements, but from how the ends compressed to flank Roger and Eric's lines. That had a downside, in that now Roger and Eric each faced a line opposing theirs that was denser—a bad tactical match. But the advantage was the lines were no longer smooth. The ends arced forward like the horns of a bull.

And those horns cost the rats the battle, because they meant that some part of their line would clash with Roger's before the rest of the line caught up. Roger's team would be able to reduce the size of the opposing line before they fully clashed.

And that was before accounting for Olivia's line and its ranged weapons specialists.

At another shouted command from Roger, Olivia's line opened fire. As expected, the rats' shields had some magically-backed portion, and the first hail of bullets that arrived was mostly blunted. The pre-System supremacy of firearms had been removed, and now they were just another tactical tool. Still dangerous, but there were more answers for them now than just other firearms.

What is known is not what is felt though. Faced with a spray of lead, the rats under fire responded the way most warriors would—by pressing forward into the threat to try to neutralize it. Olivia had directed the gunfire with this in mind. She'd had her Mousekin aim at the center of the Rat line. The result was that the center horns curved in even more... until suddenly, the Rat line was two separate horns, with a wide gap between them.

As soon as he saw that, Roger gave another, louder, command.

That was their signal.

Holland, Whiskers, Fool, and Jackal sprinted forward, dashing for the gap between the lines.

Holland and Whiskers could move pretty fast, but they were no match for Fool and Jackal. Before the rats could react, the two of them were behind the Rat lines. Jackal had ditched his swords in favor of two Bowie knives. He walked down the back of the Rat line to the right, stabbing and slicing into the Rat warriors from behind.

Fool didn't bother with a weapon at all. Instead, he madly sprinted down the entire length of the left-side Rat line, slapping Rat helmets from behind, tugging tails, yanking on half-attached ears, anything to distract them.

Holland and Whiskers opted for Jackal's usual favored tactic, and they screamed and leapt into the rats on either side of the split.

Predictably, the rats tried to deal with the chaos behind them while keeping an eye on the approaching lines in front of them.

Divided attention in combat is death, and Roger brought down the scythe.

One final command, and Olivia, Eric, and Roger brought their lines smashing into the rats. Olivia's team split into a column, two by two, and rushed into the space between the two opposing forces using their weaponry to pick off targets of opportunity.

Roger and Eric just crashed into the rats at full force. Swords, halberds, and spears licked out, stabbing around Rat shields.

The rats fought back, then fought to the last. They had been completely outmaneuvered, and even with equal numbers, they were crushed completely.

No one on the attacking side had more than a scratch, in System terms.

The entire battle had ended in less than a minute. Even Roger looked stunned by that.

"Now that," Fool said, "is how it should be done."

"Anyone hurt?" Roger asked.

"All good, sir," Holland said. "Everyone has some minor wounds, but the healers are on top of all of it. We'll be good to go in a few moments."

Eric walked over to Roger, joining Jackal and Fool. "Is that it? I mean… are there more of them? And how the hell did we beat them that fast?"

"Luck," Roger said.

"Not all luck," Fool said, and Jackal was surprised to see the serious look on Fool's face. He'd expected him to land another subtle dig, but he seemed to be acting in honest good faith.

"Well…" Roger said. "I didn't think the plan would work that well. I mean, I've seen that same thing work before, but that was…" He looked off to the side and took a deep breath. And then another. "No. It was luck. I was being stupid. I'm sorry. I saw my parents pull that off in the SCA, and I thought it would work here, but that was fake. Everything they did was fake. No one died in their game. No one. I took a chance on the same thing working here, but if I was wrong, people would have died, and it would have been my fault. I should have known better. What if something went wrong? We could have all died!"

Jackal knew what was happening. Roger's internal systems had dumped a bunch of adrenaline into his bloodstream, but the fight had ended so much faster than usual that he now had an excess of energy. With no enemy to fight, his body didn't know what to do with it all. That was why his face was alternating between flushed red and pale white, and his breath was coming in deeper and deeper.

Jackal moved forward. He wanted to get to Roger before the adrenaline dump hit his emotions. He was probably too young and inexperienced to understand why he'd suddenly cry in the middle of everyone else. Jackal wanted to save him from that.

Holland was faster. Jackal had no idea how old the Mousekin soldier was, but he clearly had much experience bringing up young leaders. It made Jackal wonder if it wasn't one of the specific things that Roger's parents had looked for when they contracted a military group for their son and his friends.

Holland stepped in front of Roger and grabbed his sword hand, abruptly pulling the young man down, closer to Holland's height. "Luck always has its way. Always. But it's never the last word in a fight. Your plan was good. I would have said something otherwise. But you are also right, you should have planned for failure." The tough look on Holland's face faded away, and he let go of Roger's hand.

"But you haven't had the training to plan for that, nor the experience yet," Holland continued. "That's what I'm here for. And Jackal and Fool as well, I'd wager. You're ready to become a leader now, in deed as well as title. That means, if you're willing, that I can teach you. Do you want that?"

Roger looked down and nodded. "Of course I do."

Holland shook his head, his whiskers making a little blur. "No, I mean really teach you. That means not telling you what to do. It also means not letting you do what you want. It means we talk everything out, but you make the decisions. You take the responsibility for what you decide. Are you willing to do that?"

That was one of the harsher things Jackal had ever heard. Also, one of the most honest. But Roger was more than due for it. He'd been an arrogant ass, unthinking of what happened to everyone else, only concerned with his own Leveling. He'd gotten past that quickly. What Holland had said was just the right thing to say to him now though.

Earlier, Roger wouldn't have been able to understand the import. After seeing Ralph die, he'd have been too raw. But now, with a solid win and an understanding of the stakes? Now he was ready to undertake the profession of war.

Roger didn't reply right away. He stood up straight and looked around. Looked at Fool, who nodded. Eric raised his eyebrows and gave a thumbs-up. Roger looked at Jackal, and Jackal nodded back as well.

"Okay," Roger said. "I'm ready to learn."

He shook Holland's offered paw.

Chapter Eleven

There wasn't time to do any real training, as much as it would have benefitted Roger. And as much as Jackal and Fool were willing to do it. They were in the basement, and the entrance to the next level of the dungeon had already been found. Roger had at least asked the leads of every team if they were ready to go, and they'd all agreed.

One last level. Kill the boss, finish the dungeon, be home in time for dinner. Or a nice cold pint, Fool had added.

The rats had been living in the basement for a long time, it appeared. The party had kept their three teams and taken turns advancing while the other teams kept a watch to back them up.

The place was filthy with debris from the rats, along with evidence that they had once shared the vast space with other creatures. Mounds of bones were scattered everywhere. Most of them seemed to be rat bones of different sizes. Jackal hoped they were corpses of pre-System rats, but when they saw some with fragments of clothes still on them, it became clear that the undead rats hadn't started out that way.

At one point there had been a community of rats living here. Monstrous rats to be sure, but still living. Judging from the ages of the bones and the random garbage around them, they'd all died off about a year ago. All the bones had gnaw marks on them, which led to the conclusion that something had effectively zombified the rats, turning them on each other until only the undead guard they'd faced were left.

The basement had eventually given way to a bare room with a crumbling back wall and a hole just big enough for one person to fit through, hewn through the rock foundation of the building. A fetid odor rose from it, rank and damp. The electric lighting had stopped, but some sort of fungus lining the walls gave off a dim light.

Fool had tried to use his Location Scout skill to see what was up ahead, but only frowned and said that he was being blocked from using it. Nor could any of the other mages use any of their divination spells.

Olivia was the only one who could get some sense of what might be down in the tunnel, and all she was able to pick up was that it was something evil. And huge. Something twisted and wrong. She hadn't wanted to share anymore.

Eventually, they'd had to scout out the tunnel. Fool went first and came back a few moments later.

"It opens up after about a block of distance, but you're not going to like what's on the other side," he said before pausing.

It looked like a dramatic pause, but Jackal saw the discomfort in his friend. And though his voice was steady, Jackal also heard a quiet shake in it.

"It's an open cavern. I can't see the bottom, but there are steps leading down. Big steps made out of what looks like some kind of translucent green jade. I'm guessing someone had a Lovecraft bug to get out of their system with this, so... expect something bad."

Roger and Eric looked uncomfortable, and Jackal could see that they wanted to ask a question. Fool noticed it as well and gestured for them to go ahead.

Roger let out the expected "uh…" before getting to the point. "What's that mean? I mean, I've heard 'Lovecraft' before, but… what does that mean? I know it's something scary, but is there a particular thing we should be planning for?"

Fool dropped his head into his hands and swore steadily and deeply for about a minute, which made Olivia grin.

Demonstration done, Fool looked up again. "Right. Sorry. I keep forgetting I'm very old. Lovecraft wrote a bunch of borderline-racist horror stories, but one of his central themes was that the world used to be ruled by an ancient race of very scary cosmic creepy gods. They were supposed to be so far away from being normal that to see them meant you would go completely mad."

"So, like a Medusa, but for brains?" Eric said.

Olivia completely lost it, laughing so hard Jackal was afraid she'd forget to breathe.

"Something like that," Fool said. "Probably a big bad guy with some sort of reality-warping power or mind control. Depending on what the Dungeon Master was thinking, might be some cultists we need to overcome before that. Might even be some sort of summoning we have to stop before an overwhelming bad guy shows up. In either case, we should expect things to get confusing. This won't be a standup battle like the last one."

Eric was still looking angrily at Olivia, so Roger took the chance to follow up with another question. "More rats maybe? Or some other kind of cultists?"

"Dunno," Fool said. "We're just going to have to get in there and deal with it. You've all Leveled up enough that we should be able to give whatever the boss is a good fight. If it's really bad, we can book it out and come back tomorrow fresh. Or run the previous levels again a few times until you Level up even more."

Roger and Eric groaned. That made Jackal grin. If there was one thing he and Fool hated, it was farming dungeons for XP or loot. Being forced to do a dungeon run was bad enough, but if the trio had to repeat the dungeon, Jackal and Fool would likely find something else to occupy themselves while everyone else did it. It was good to hear that the thought was as much of a turn-off for the kids as it was for the grownups. They'd be more committed to making it through.

"Plus side of all of this," Fool continued, "is that it's probably going to be big enough for all of you to get enough XP to make your final Levels to meet the minimum for the Park. And if it isn't quite enough... maybe we can do some hunting on the way to Wells Gray."

That earned him a round of hoots in support, and with that, it was time for everyone to move forward.

The stairs were just as Fool had described them, but he hadn't quite conveyed how creepy the giant cavern was. The fungus glow was sporadic, so you couldn't really tell how large the cavern was, but it was gigantic. Somewhere above it was the city of Prince George, the Fraser River, and miles of forests. The sheer vastness of the cavern put a creepy little twist of fear into Jackal's guts. He wasn't afraid of the dark or being underground, but something about this amount of empty space under such a large part of the world creeped him right out.

There was nothing for it but to go down. The steps were jade in color, as Fool had described, but they also had the translucence of that stone. It had a net effect that was rather like walking down steps made of gelatinous slime. That was made worse by the hardness, which gave the steps a glass-like surface. Combined with the overall moist drippiness of the cavern, and the surface was unpleasantly slippery.

It got worse as they wound down. At the top, the steps were wide and wound down with some cavern wall and small flat surfaces on either side. That lasted for about thirty meters down, then the steps took a tight right, narrowed, and clung to the side of the cavern.

There was still no sound in the cavern, other than the distant dripping that could be heard coming from different locations. After about twenty minutes of descent, the stairs turned into the void, spanning across the cavern with a narrow bridge that faded off into the darkness on the other side, with no end in sight. The party halted. The bridge looked too narrow to support its own weight for the distance it traversed, but there was no other route.

"Keep going?" Roger asked.

Jackal saw the hesitation in his eyes echoed by everyone else. Some were on the edge of fear, but everyone looked determined despite that.

Roger must have seen the same thing because a moment later, he nodded. "All right. Same three groups, columns of two, stagger each group by the length of the group in front. That work?" He looked at Holland for confirmation, and Holland nodded back.

Roger's group was first to step the bridge, and in a moment, they were far enough forward that Eric's group followed, then Olivia's.

When Jackal stepped on the bridge, he felt his stomach lurch. It was almost as if the bridge was shifting under his feet. It hadn't moved though. He was sure of that. It was something else.

Something about the bridge itself. He glanced forward, then looked right down again. The narrowness of the bridge heading off into the dark brought up a sudden dizzying sense of vertigo, like looking up at something very tall from below. Jackal could almost feel himself spinning, and he forced his eyes to only look at the surface below him and the feet of the people in front. From their stumbling steps, he could tell they felt the same.

He risked a quick glance at the groups ahead and saw that their steps were starting to stumble, just the faintest bit. And some of them weren't quite walking in a straight line anymore. It was subtle, but he could see it.

Then he was struck with the most curious sensation. It was as if the surface of the bridge was no longer flat, but somehow curved, and the edges closer than he thought. And he knew that if he stepped the wrong way, he'd slide, then he'd be falling into that terrible abyss…

"Fool…" he managed to blurt before the feeling overwhelmed him.

"I'm on it," Fool said. "It's not a spell. I tried to shut down Mental Influence, but that's not the source. As far as I can tell, it's something inherent in the geometry of the bridge. The angles are somehow not right. Just a sec…"

Fool stopped walking, and Jackal brought himself to a halt as well. Holland and Whiskers stopped and looked at the two of them in confusion.

"Is something wrong?" Holland asked.

"Can't you feel that?" Jackal blurted.

Holland shook his head. "Something feels a little odd, but it's no different from walking over any other kind of narrow bridge. Sort of feels like a rope bridge honestly. Are you afraid of heights, or is it a feeling of something approaching?"

"Nothing like that," Jackal said. "Just a feeling like the bridge itself is… somehow wrong. You don't feel it at all?"

Holland shook his head, and Jackal risked looking ahead. The other groups were still walking. They weren't entirely steady, but they didn't look to have the same sense of unease Fool and Jackal had.

"Got it," Fool said. "It's not an attack per se. It's something intrinsic to the design of the bridge. Its inherent geometry doesn't match in some way— almost as if it's only partly in this dimension, and partly in another."

"Then why are we not seeing this effect?" Holland asked.

Fool sighed and turned back to face the still-walking teams. "It's just me and Jackal, I think. We've both got Perception and Intelligence Abilities above everyone else's, from our Levels. This only affects high-Level adventurers. If we were higher Level, it would be hitting us even harder."

Jackal and Holland frowned at that. This was supposed to be a low-Level dungeon, a place for townsfolk to push their Levels before heading out into the wider world. Why would there be something that only affected high-Level builds? At least it probably explained why the Advanced Classers hadn't returned from this part of the dungeon

"I wouldn't fret it too much, folks," Fool said as he walked toward the other groups. "It might just be a side-effect of the design. Part of the atmosphere that came with an unintentional side-effect. But it probably means the boss monster is something special." He turned back to look over his shoulder. "You guys coming or what?"

Holland and Jackal looked at each other, then set off to follow Fool.

The bridge ran for another half an hour before they saw any change in surroundings.

For all the buildup, there hadn't been any other issues, or attacks, on the bridge. The strange geometry affected everyone toward the end of it, serving to increase their unease and make them jumpy, but Fool was able to use his

[Show Must Go On[8]] Skill to boost everyone's morale. Jackal could swear that whenever Fool used that skill, everyone seemed to *strut* a little.

It didn't stop Jackal and Fool from feeling almost nauseated from the effects of the geometry, but they managed to hold it together. The nausea faded when they saw the end of the bridge.

At first, it was just a vague shape at the end of the bridge, but as they got closer, it resolved itself into a huge, arched entrance.

The effect of the geometry wasn't the only change. The closer they got to the arch, the more the darkness surrounding the bridge faded away, until it was completely gone. It went away in wisps, revealing itself not as an absence of light but instead some sort of light-sucking fog that faded out.

The arch was set in an enormous cliff face that disappeared above into more of the light-sucking fog. Below was hell.

Or a city of hell anyway.

Glowing in sickly hues from an untold number of glowing fungal sources, an eldritch city ran under the entire length of the bridge. They'd been walking over it for some time now.

Nothing about the city felt right. At first glance, it was all towers and low squat buildings, and it was easy to think of it as being some variant of a modern city seen from a distance above.

As they all stopped to look over the side of the bridge, unsettling details became visible. The towers were more gothic than modern, but still the height of modern skyscrapers. The effect made them look like jagged needle-teeth hungry for flesh.

The streets were lined with odd square lumps that might have been the size of city buses, but they seemed to be squirmy as if they wanted to run

---

[8] Raise morale of allies. Almost like everyone can hear a really kick-ass theme song playing in the back of their heads.

but were unable to leave the spot they were in. The low, blocky buildings were covered in some sort of symbols, but looking at them for more than a glance made everyone's eyes hurt as if they had accidentally glanced into the sun.

The worst was the towers, because once they got a proper look at them, they saw the towers were hollow spires of bone. They had no entrances below, only square holes and openings in the upper halves, as if they were the roosts of some eldritch and long forgotten winged race.

The whole city gave off a palpable aura of age, as if it had been here far longer than any other life on Earth, as if the System had only discovered it, not created it.

As they got closer to the massive arch, more details appeared. The arch was at least three stories tall, if not taller, and a city block wide at the base. The bridge connected to it via a large, semi-circular landing. On the other side of the landing were the remnants of what had once been stairs reaching up to the platform. It made Jackal a little queasy to see how the stairs had fallen. Aside from a few steps left at the top, the entire length of the stairs, all the way down to the city, looked to have been swiped off as if by a giant hand.

The arch was composed of two curves that met in a sharp point at the top and made of the thick green jade that the first stairs had been made of. The stones were deeply carved with runic symbols of a sort Jackal had never seen before, and none repeated.

The three teams stopped before the arch in uneasy bunches. They reformed smartly as Holland finally stepped off the bridge. Roger took that as a sign and nodded at Holland, who only waved a paw in response. Roger turned to Eric and Olivia and gestured them to either side. The three teams formed an arrowhead shape and entered into the long, vaulted hallway on the other side of the arch.

The end of the hallway could be seen some distance away. A faintly glowing green opening, wisps of fog leaking out into the hall.

The overall effect was as if one was walking into a nave, and Jackal found himself expecting to see some sort of twisted altar at the end of the hallway.

About halfway down, Roger stopped. On either side of the hall were two additional arched openings. Looking inside them, they saw circular rooms arched into a dome. The walls of the dome were covered in round openings that split the walls into levels. Each opening consisted of a short cylinder of some kind of metal, going back another meter or so. All the chambers were empty and held no markings of any kind. The floors and walls were bare of any decoration. The only unusual feature of the rooms, aside from their bareness, was that the cylindrical openings appeared to be unfinished.

The lower levels had evenly spaced openings running the whole circumference. The top level only had three cylinders.

The room on the left had four.

The teams spent a few minutes looking through each room but couldn't see anything. Couldn't smell anything. What they touched was smooth and slippery.

They elected to move on.

As soon as they stepped out of the rooms and started toward the far opening, the hall shook... a tremor that started slow, built to a crescendo that nearly knocked everyone off of their feet, then faded away. At its peak, there was a sort of sharp, shuddering bellow that seemed to come from the space at the end of the hall.

That seemed to steel Roger. With a glance back at everyone and a nod, he walked forward. Only now, he'd drawn his sword and slipped his shield forward to his arm.

Everyone else followed suit, and the teams readied themselves for combat.

As they got closer to the doorway, the green fog turned into a thicker mist, tendrils of it reaching down the hall. With it came a putrid stench, a cloying wet rot of earthiness and over-filled and neglected sewers, like the waste of a thousand cities.

It reached deep into the nose and never seemed to fade. Each breath was a fresh assault on the senses.

The closer they got to the doorway, the more the tendrils of mist thickened. They became like tentacles, and when they touched anyone, they left a cold streak that lingered.

Along with that came the sharp odor of ammonia and the overall air that they were entering a place of filth no sentient creature should inhabit.

Each step brought them closer to the maw of the door, and Roger never faltered.

Despite the distress everyone felt, no one wanted to be the first one to show any weakness, not with Roger advancing as if none of it had any effect on him.

Sooner than anyone wanted, they were at the door, then through it.

Into another world.

Chapter Twelve

A vast and sickly-glowing, yellow-skied swamp, complete with towering mangrove trees, their roots plunging into the wet like greedy skeletal fingers. They held shadows in their grasping digits, and Jackal wanted nothing more than to be forever ignorant of what the shadows concealed.

The sky… the impossible sky was a roil of green and purple clouds, tumbling about each other in a great conflagration, but there wasn't the slightest wind or sound that reached the ground. Once in a while, a bare patch of sky would appear, but it was a pale yellow. A faint white blur looked like a sun turned into a dead eye.

They stood on the only clear, dry patch of ground that could be seen, a plaza carved of obsidian stone, with great blocks of jade set about in unknown patterns. A low wall of the same mix surrounded the plaza, and beyond that was the swamp.

A gigantic tree, sick and dying, stuffed with fungus and mushrooms blossoming from every inch of it, sat on an island made of flat slate rocks. Slime in garish colors ran amok over them.

Between that island and the plaza was an expanse of black water, streaked with fuzzy bands of white mold.

And something rippled through that water toward them.

Jackal got to watch Roger disappear in slow motion.

It wasn't really slow, but it might as well have been. Jackal was too far back to do anything about it.

The shape rippled under the water, and before anyone had any chance to do more than glance at it, a thick red tentacle tore out of the water. It was narrow toward the tip and covered in short, rubbery spines, and it came out of the water like a whip.

Like a whip, it wrapped around Roger in one swift motion and yanked him under the water. Or at least, toward what was under the water. Because as soon as Roger approached the surface of the water, a black shape snapped up, the upper lip of an enormous mouth. The head of the creature crested a heartbeat later, but Roger had already disappeared down its gullet.

It looked like a giant frog, only it had a cluster of eyes on top of its head, more akin to a spider than a frog. As it lifted itself farther out of the water, another difference appeared. Instead of arms, it had two pair of tentacles, four in total.

The tentacles weren't as swift as the tongue, but they still packed a serious punch. The creature wasted no time in attacking the rest of Roger's group.

A tentacle smashed back the entire team, tumbling them head over heels. Except for one unfortunate Mousekin, who was snapped up by the first red tentacle—which was clearly the tongue of the creature—and it snapped the Mousekin down the same gullet Roger had gone down.

Eric was screaming something, and his team was right behind him—just in time for a pair of tentacles to punch into them. Half the Mousekin were sent flying, and Eric was driven to his knees by the blow. His shield split with an enormous and resounding crack, right down to the center boss.

Even so, he managed to score a quick slash on the tentacle that struck him, and the beast let out a warbling howl of pain, turning on Eric to redouble its attack.

Olivia lashed out at the creature with a bolt of lightning, much faster than she'd been able to generate one before. It howled again, the tentacles on the side closest to her curling up like weeds under a burner.

Then it disappeared, ducking back under the water with a loud *blup* and a spray of muck that spattered across the courtyard.

Jackal darted forward, intending to dive into the water and cut Roger out of its belly, but Fool caught him hard by the shoulder. Jackal spun to face him.

"Give them time!" Fool raised his hand, palm forward, placating Jackal. "They're all still in the fight. Look!"

Jackal turned back and saw the beast rearing back up out of the water.

Eric was screaming at it, trying to draw it forward, but it was out of everyone's reach, upright in the water, mouth pointed up to the sky and tentacles wiggling in an obscene pattern, writhing in and around themselves.

Olivia was cursing up a small storm and waving her hands, recharging her lightning spell. Holland was pulling up downed Mousekin and directing them forward, and the Mousekin healers were working over some of the downed forms that didn't seem to be moving.

The Frog Behemoth suddenly hunched over, driving its head forward, and opened its mouth in a giant snarl. It happened so fast that even Jackal flinched back.

The beast froze for a second, then seemed to pull back on itself and vomited up a thick and disgusting pile of half-digested organic matter... and the thrashing and angry forms of Roger and the Mousekin.

The beast yanked itself back under the water, and Roger and his sodden companion staggered to their feet, the Mousekin healers already on them. The tongue lashed out again from under the water and yanked in another Mousekin.

"Fight!" Roger yelled, clearing his eyes as best he could with his soggy arm. "There's room inside to stab it. Make it barf you out!"

Eric piled into Roger, smashing him to the ground with his shield, just in time as another tentacle whipped over their heads.

The beast breached the water again, this time close to the edge of the plaza, and let out a hideous *gronk* that filled the air with an unspeakable stench.

Olivia let loose another burst of lightning, and this time it was accompanied by a spatter of gunfire and arcane flames as the Mousekin recovered from the initial attack.

Without a sound, the creature disappeared back under the waves.

"What the hell?" Fool said. "This thing is going to be a pain the ass."

Jackal nodded, but Fool was right in his previous statement too. It was a very capable creature. It clearly had the power and speed to wipe out the whole party, but even as Jackal thought that, he saw what he'd hoped to see.

Roger was turning back to face the water, and his team was forming up on him again—even the Mousekin that had been swallowed. Eric and Olivia's teams were doing to the same, and all three teams spread themselves out. They'd make the creature have to chose which team to fight, and that would leave the other teams free to attack it.

Which was a great plan.

Too bad the Frog Behemoth had other plans.

With not even a lash of the tongue for warning, it burst out of the water and flew over everyone. Somehow it turned in mid air and landed on the plaza, blocking the exit, and facing Fool and Jackal.

Fool was in motion already, darting past the tongue and leaping up on the creature, smacking it on the nose with his hand to vault up.

Jackal opted to go low, diving under the creature. His Skill brought knives to his hands, and for a moment he considered gutting the creature, but this wasn't his kill or his combat. Instead, he slashed the left side, the lower part of the hind limb, with both daggers. He wasn't sure if it would have the same effect as hamstringing other creatures, but he figured it was the best way to stop the Frog Behemoth from leaping again.

As he slid out from under the beast, he spun back to his feet in a low crouch, weapons ready. Just in time to watch Fool complete his transit of its back and slap it on the ass as he dismounted.

The beast convulsed again and let out another bellowing shriek—then vomited up its most recent attempt at a Mousekin snack. Jackal slashed the back of its leg again as he noticed Fool darting forward to recover the former morsel. Jackal idly wondered, in the way that thoughts drifted in and out, what exactly Fool had done to make it cough up its snack.

Trickster had tricks.

Jackal hit it hard enough with the double attacks that it spun again to face him—just in time for another bolt of lighting to lance into its backside. This time, it didn't try to recover or flee. Instead, it went on the attack.

Facing Jackal, it jumped right at him. Awkwardly, with one leg wounded, but still with great speed. It bounced off of the wall behind Jackal and ricocheted, this time barreling right into Eric's team.

No tentacles, no biting, just crushing the whole team with the mass of its body. A few of the Mousekin went flying from the impact, but most were crushed under its weight.

Without pause, it leapt again, this time for Roger's team.

Roger was ready, and so was his team. The Mousekin dodged to either side, and Roger... did the impossible.

He leapt up to meet the Frog Behemoth in the air.

For the briefest moment, it looked as if the two had clashed so hard they had overcome gravity. The pair seemed frozen in mid-air, forcibly joined. It was just an illusion though, and a split second later, the Frog Behemoth hit its intended landing spot with Roger latched onto the side of its head like a leech, by his sword.

He'd rammed the weapon right to the hilt in the Frog's skull, forward and just under the cluster of eyes. The moment of the jump had carried him up and over the forehead of the beast, and the abrupt landing had whipsawed Roger back in front its mouth.

The back-and-forth action had the effect of ripping the sword back and forth inside the monster, and it landed with a painful wheezing shriek. Its tentacles whipped up and across, swiping Roger right off and leaving his sword stuck in its skull.

Jackal saw Eric slowly rising to his feet, but none of the Mousekin members of his team were moving at all.

Olivia shouted and drove into the Frog. Her fists crackled and glowed with lightning, and she hooked punch after punch into the side of the creature as it howled in pain. It coiled its legs for another leap, but the remaining melee fighters from Roger's team were all there, stabbing and hacking into the leg Jackal hadn't injured.

It was enough to buckle the creature and make it spin in rage and attack the pestering Mousekin.

The other mages added their attacks, balls and bolts of flame encasing its eyes.

It flailed its tentacles, knocking over most of the clustered Melee fighters.

Olivia was dodging the tentacles and still landing punches, but the fiery sparks were fading in intensity.

Then Holland came charging in. He'd always had a sword at his hip, but Jackal had never seen him draw it. He had it out now, and Jackal was surprised to see that the blade was golden and shimmering. Clearly some sort of magical blade.

He charged toward the monster, a tiny mouse against a mountainous toad. He had no hope. None at all.

And then Roger was between the Frog Behemoth and the charging Mousekin, and he knelt and lifted his shield to cover himself. Holland leapt up on the shield, then leapt again as Roger sprung him up in the perfect arc.

Holland reversed the grip on his sword as he flew through the air, and the Frog flinched away from Olivia's last punch and turned, mouth gaping, toward Holland, who passed over the open mouth…

And landed on top of the creature, in the middle of its hideous cluster of eyes, and stabbed his sword straight down. It sliced through the skin, the bones of the skull, and the mucosal brain with no resistance. Then Holland screamed and ripped the sword down in a forceful motion as a longer and wider energy blade showed beneath it. He twisted and tore the blade out through the center of the Frog Behemoth's face.

It didn't even shudder as it died, just collapsed into a wet and rubbery puddle.

Holland stood on top of the corpse, gore-covered sword in hand, looking out with defiance as if all he wanted in the world was for another beast to come and try his mettle.

After a moment, he shook himself, looked at the dead beast under his feet, and pulled out a long white scarf. With a snap of his wrist, he flicked off the gore on the blade, then wiped it clean with the scarf. The blade slid back home in the sheath with a muted click.

Holland walked forward, but there was no easy way down from the beast. He took a few more steps across what was left of its face, then leapt down.

Jackal walked forward to meet him as Holland walked up to the rising Roger. Somehow, he'd managed to recover Roger's sword, and he presented it hilt first to the young man.

"Orders, sir?" Holland said.

Roger smiled and took the sword. "You are one badass mouse, Holland."

"Mousekin, sir. And thank you. You're not bad for a naked ape either."

The two grinned at each other for a moment, then Jackal cleared his throat to get their attention.

"Gentlemen," he said, "congratulations. First to complete the dungeon."

"Indeed," Fool added as he walked up. "And nice job too. I just checked in, and we didn't lose anyone in the Boss battle."

Jackal turned, surprise on his face.

"It's true," Fool said. "Couple are in bad shape, but the brunt of the weight of that thing landed on Eric, and he wound up taking most of the crush damage. He's going to be recovering for a bit, but not too long. Gonna need a new shield though."

"We can probably afford that from the loot," Roger said. "But seriously, I was sure we'd lost a few people. I kinda went all berserker there for a bit, I think. I was pretty pissed off at that thing."

"I noticed," Fool said. "Nice job, by the way. Looked like you maybe got all your Levels there."

"Uh…" Roger's eyes glazed over and darted from side to side. "Oh. Yeah. Wow. I guess. Uhm… I need to think about this…"

Fool laughed and clapped him on the back, and Jackal stepped back. Holland and Fool would give the young man all the advice he needed.

Jackal looked over the plaza and was glad that Fool had stopped him from leaping in to help too early. The cost had almost been too high, but that was the only way to grow in this new world.

Chapter Thirteen

Most of them collapsed as soon as they got to the Wells Gray Park entrance sign.

They'd had to leave all the vehicles about ten kilometers back, so before they collapsed, they dropped off all the extra gear they'd been carrying.

The five-hundred-kilometer journey to the park had been the easy part, taking up only a half days travel to reach the town of Clearwater.

The town had looked in better shape that expected. It must have had survivors after the System arrived, but something appeared to have either killed them or driven them all off sometime in the not so recent past. Something about that bothered Jackal, but it wasn't too unusual these days. It wasn't a safe world anymore. They hadn't bothered to look too closely. The road to the park was a left turn, and the town was to the right. They'd left early but no one wanted to get to the park without lots of time to setup camp before dark.

They'd hardly started on the road before having to stop, a slide having made the road impassible for the vehicles they'd brought. The only way forward was on foot.

"Can we do one more load today?" Fool asked. From the look on his face, he was hoping the answer was no.

Jackal turned to see the answer, after dropping his load—and half of Fool's—into the big pile in the middle of the parking lot.

Roger groaned and dropped on his back.

"I'll take that as a no then," Fool replied. He looked up. The sky above was clear, and their walk had been extra fun with some direct solar heat. The long winding mountain road had provided only sporadic shade. "I can't tell with these mountains. Jackal, any idea how much daylight is left?"

Jackal tilted his head up, shading his eyes with his hands. The sun was about a handspan over the nearest mountain peak, but the next one over was lower. It was late afternoon, and on a flatter bit of land, the evening would be a good many hours away. But here, deep in the valley between the big peaks?

He held up two fingers to Fool.

"Two hours?" Fool said. "Not bad. Time to finish getting camp set up and get dinner ready, I guess."

The Mousekin had already done most of the work. They couldn't carry as much as the humans, and someone had to guard the first load of supplies they'd dropped off, so the Mousekin had set to work building a camp.

They'd followed a nearly Roman model in that. No slacking off for the ones left behind to guard. They'd been felling trees while everyone else had made the return trip for another load of supplies, back to their abandoned vehicles. A spring storm had closed off the main entrance to the park, dropping enough logs and stones that there was no way to clear that and bring the vehicles through. Which meant they had to hike the remaining ten kilometers to the park entrance, then the remaining thirty kilometers to their destination.

And fight any monsters they encountered on the way.

Which meant setting up the park entrance as a basecamp.

It had been a lovely little parking spot once upon a time. A long, winding road and a pleasant afternoon's excursion. The park entrance was strangely intact, if a bit worn. It still looked just like any other provincial camp site entrance. The big sign was there, dark brown painted wood with "Welcome to Wells Gray Park" carved into it and painted in a fading white. The sign sat upon a stone cairn.

The parking lot in front of the sign was a small roundabout, with a few outhouses and two well-set-up information signs. Jackal had been amused to see that the last notice posted before the System arrival was a warning that bears and cougars were active currently.

The Mousekin camp would easily repel those animals. They'd dropped a number of trees and hadn't bothered to skin the branches all the way off. They'd initially stacked the trees on their sides in an overlapping diamond formation three trees deep. It would be a right pain to climb over. They were currently stripping all the branches on the inside part of their makeshift wall, so they could get close to the trees and have overlapping fields of fire against anyone who tried to attack.

The extra branches, foliage intact, were tossed over to the outside. It was really a quite clever wall. The outside branches were partially intact, and with the new branches tossed over, the sharp sheared ends of the cut branches were completely hidden. It looked like a short, lumpy, ugly cedar hedge. Not a thing any attacking force would want to climb over. Not perfect, but it would do for the duration. If they had to stay longer, they'd build it up more.

Holland and the other Mousekin had dropped their loads and were helping set up the second stage of the camp, marking off locations for tents and communal facilities.

Jackal had looked at the outhouses when they'd arrived on site and had Fool check on his suspicions. Then they'd firebombed them out of existence.

It was easier than dealing with the hordes of poisonous insects that had made them a home. They'd make do with slit trenches.

Jackal grabbed his and Fool's expedition tent from the pile and went to the spot Holland pointed out for him.

"I'll help."

Jackal looked up. He wasn't surprised to see Olivia. He'd heard her coming, and since the party had left Prince George in a caravan of vehicles, she'd been casting more than the occasional glance at him.

He nodded and tossed the second tent bag to her. The main tent had a second accessory tent. It was a useful add-on.

Olivia looked over the instructions with a glance, then pulled out the parts, aligning them correctly with the main tent. After a few moments, they connected the poles and threaded them through. With some careful balancing, they got the main tent up.

"Can I ask you some questions?" Olivia said, once that was done.

Jackal nodded. The next step was mostly running the guy lines and hammering home stakes to attach them to, and Olivia had anticipated that by grabbing a handful of stakes and a hammer. They set about securing the tent.

"How long have you known Fool?" she asked.

"Since the start of all this," he answered.

"Do you know much about where he was from before this?"

"Few places. Vancouver mostly. His family was there."

"Family..." Olivia's eyes went somewhere else for a while. "You know anything about that? He ever say anything about them?"

Jackal shook his head and held out a hand for the next stake. She passed it over, and he hammered it a little bit into the ground, then hooked the guy line around it and hammered it into the ground at an angle until it was snug.

When he stood to move to the next spot, Olivia was looking across the parking lot.

Fool was animatedly talking to one of the Mousekin, his hands flying all over as he spoke. The Mousekin made little stabbing motions with his hand, and Fool shook his head and talked again. Arguing about things was a habit Fool was developing these days, and he looked to have found someone new to practice on.

There was something wistful in Olivia's look, and Jackal turned to look at Fool again. With a sigh, Jackal stepped over to Olivia and took the rest of the stakes from her.

When she looked up, he said, "Go talk to him."

She turned back to look at the woods. "I'm not ready for that yet. Let's just get this finished, 'kay?"

It only took them a few more minutes to finish, and Jackal could see that Olivia was getting a little more antsy. When they finished, she crossed her arms and looked around a bit more. She'd changed out of her combat clothing. Without the mask of jangling bone fetishes, she looked like what she was—a young woman with a lot of strength and ability, but very unsure of herself.

Jackal stood and waited for her.

After a moment, she turned toward the road and started walking. "C'mon, Let's walk."

They didn't go far down the road they'd come from. Just far enough that no one could overhear them, but still close enough to be seen. Oliva walked over to a rough set of boulders by the side of the road and sat on one, then gestured Jackal toward the other.

"My family was fucked up," she said. "My whole childhood was fucked up, but my family loved me. I loved them."

155

She didn't seem to want any reply as she stared down the road. Jackal was happy to sit and listen, and the silence between them became comfortable after a bit.

"Me, Eric, and Roger used to hang out at the dock. Family made fun of me for that, but we were friends. Didn't make much sense. Rich kid, cop's kid, and me. But it worked, you know? We made each other laugh, and all our families had shit we wanted to get away from." She snorted and shook her head.

"I mean, shit we thought we wanted to get away from. Just wanted to bitch a little bit, you know? Wasn't a big town. Not much else to do. Went hiking, went hunting. Fishing. Couldn't take 'em home for the same reason we couldn't go to their places either. Families all had reasons not to like each other."

After that, she was quiet for a while, and Jackal saw a lot of emotions running across her face. Wasn't hard to imagine what she was thinking.

The silence carried on its own conversation for a while, until a sharp, high-pitched series of whistling chirps joined in. Jackal couldn't quite figure out what it was, and he spun about trying to locate it.

"Chill, big guy. Just a hummingbird. See?" She pointed up at the remnants of the power lines running next to the road.

Sure enough, Jackal saw an incredibly tiny bird perched on the wire, chattering away. It almost sounded like some sort of insect. The closer he looked, the more details he could see. It had the bright red sparkling chest and the long, needle-like beak he'd expected, looking just like a pre-System hummingbird. Until one of the big, fat, nasty mosquitos showed up. The hummingbird ripped into the bug like an arrow, leaving two halves of the mosquito to flutter through the air and drop to the ground with delicate little plops. There was no sign of the hummingbird. It must have just kept going.

"Badass. That's what my uncles told me. Hummingbirds are badasses. Tough little bastards, don't take shit from anyone, stand up to anyone. He said they bring happiness wherever they go."

She was looking back up the road toward Fool. He'd moved to their tent and was setting up a chair outside, a can of something in his hand.

It was, Jackal figured, a sign that the hummingbird could be trusted. Fool had a knack for bringing happiness to things. Jackal wasn't sure exactly what Olivia was hoping for from the older man, but he'd noticed Fool glancing at her from time to time as well.

Jackal figured it was the connection to the Trickster. He'd noticed that the two of them seemed to draw their abilities from the same source, even though they expressed it in vastly different ways. That association with what was likely a Legendary was enough to form a bond of camaraderie between the two. That was what Jackal had thought was happening.

This seemed to be something more though.

There was some kind of common thread, some kind of attraction between the two, but for the life of him, Jackal couldn't figure out what it was. He wondered briefly if it was romantic, but something even more ludicrous than the forty-year age gap between them made that seem unlikely. It was more like they had something in common that neither of them really understood, but both knew. Something under the skin that connected them.

As he watched her looking at Fool, something in her profile finally clicked for Jackal, and he hoped he was right. As much as he loved Fool and as much as the man was a walking stereotype of carefree, he had to admit that Fool had always had an echoing loneliness inside him. He'd lost his family long before the System, and that emptiness was a hollow weight he carried everywhere.

He deserved some happiness.

Eric was busy, and Jackal didn't think much of it. Then he noticed Holland and a few other Mousekin staring at Eric, so he took another look.

He wasn't doing anything special. Eric had kicked a few rocks into a circle to make a rudimentary fire ring and had stacked up some dried wood he'd found. Clearly, he was in the process of getting a fire going for the night, but something about that process was confusing the Mousekin.

Roger figured it out first. "Haven't you guys ever made a fire before?"

Holland cocked his head sideways. "Of course. It's part of our survival kits. It's not even expensive. Probably the cheapest of all of our supplies. But what has that got to do with whatever Eric's doing?"

Now it was Eric's turn to look confused. "Wait. How do you guys start a fire?"

That was a reasonable question. Jackal hadn't thought about it much, but the entire time they'd been together, there hadn't been any need for a campfire. It was only now that their vehicles had been left behind that they were going to have to rough it.

The Mousekin leader touched one of the pouches at his side. "Fire kit. Place on the ground, pull the tab. It expands out into the standard frame size, with a flame in the middle for cooking or heat. Push the button on the side and it collapses back. Good for at least a dozen uses before it needs to be recharged. Same system most sentients use."

Eric raised his eyebrows, pursed his lips, and nodded. "That's pretty cool. Less work. I guess we can do that instead."

"Wait," Roger said. "Have you ever made a fire? Like, from scratch?"

"Never had a need, and no, it's not part of our training. I remember reading something about rubbing two sticks together that primitive Mousekin used to do, but there is no need for that in modern times."

"Man. Wow." Roger shook his head. "That's crazy. Okay, like, this is Canada. You can do that modern stuff, but you really gotta know how to make a fire. Eric, you got a flint?"

Eric shook his head.

Olivia piped up from the side. "I saw some over by the road. Give me minute."

"I've got some tinder," Eric said. "I was just gonna use a match though."

Roger smiled. "Yeah, let's do this old school. Holland, why don't you grab anyone you think should know this? You never know when you might be stuck with none of your stuff and have to make a fire from almost nothing."

Holland nodded and spoke into his com unit. Roger sat down in front of the fire ring and moved things around, waiting for Olivia to come back. Once she was back, he didn't waste any time waiting for the other Mousekin. Most of them were already drifting in.

"Okay, so you can use the rubbing sticks thing, but it's a pain in the ass. Flint and steel is a better way to go. I mean, it means you need to have a knife, but if you haven't a knife out here, you're pretty much dead anyway. That was true even before the System. See this rock?" He held up the stone that looked like a piece of quartz. "Normally you want to find some flint or something. But any kind of hard rock you can chip to make sharp will work. This one looks freshly chipped. Olivia, did you already do that?"

"Just smacked it against another rock," she said. "Don't gotta make arrowheads or nothing."

"Yeah. That. Thank you. Anyway, once you have a sharp edge on it, you just have to graze it against your metal." He gave the rock a quick little knock against the back of his knife, and a spatter of small sparks rained out. "Right. Like that. Next bit is the hard part."

Roger squatted next to the wood pile and grabbed the smallest piece of wood he could find. Eric was already stripping some lichen and dried moss off of the other chunks of wood. The Mousekin were fascinated, gathering around to watch the demonstration.

Roger used his knife to split the small pieces into a couple of thin, almost sliver-like pieces. He then cut his knife into the edges of the wood until he had a few bits of wood that were heavily feathered with little curls of wood.

"Probably only need one of these, but it's kind of a challenge we gave each other a few years ago. To start a fire using only one match. Way harder with flint and steel, but we got good at it. It's gonna take you a lot longer, so if I get this done in one, then the other two? Holland, you can have your guys try it on those. Everyone can get a chance."

Jackal grabbed one of the larger pieces of wood lying around and propped it up to sit on—with instant regret. He hadn't sat on a "camp chair" in years, and not since he'd become himself. His larger self. After a moment of painful probing, he moved the chunk of wood back into the pile and settled into a squat.

He wasn't watching the demonstration as much as he was watching the Mousekin. And Roger. The kid had a knack for teaching. And from the way all the eyes were locking in on him and nodding, he also seemed to have a real knack for leadership. It was interesting to watch.

Roger showed them how to carefully place the different kinds of tinder into a little pile to catch and hold the sparks, and to lay the feathered wood over that to keep the initial fire going a little longer. And over that, how to tent progressively larger pieces of wood.

A single strike of the rock against the knife sent sparks that caught in the tinder, and he was down on it in an instant, blowing gently to get it to catch. A moment later, a small but steady fire was going, and he showed them how to build a lattice of bigger logs around it, like a little wooden house, to dry wetter logs and let them tumble into the fire. He explained how to drop bigger logs in once the coals were going, and how to bank the fire for cooking and how to extinguish it at the end of the night.

Then he split them all into groups. Before long, there were a few little fires going on all over the place with grins all around.

"Not bad," Fool said.

Jackal turned, startled. "How the hell did you do that? Did you kill a squirrel for experience?"

Fool chuckled. Both of them were now only a handful of experience points away from their respective Advanced Classes, and it was taking a fair bit of self-control to not go off hunting. They'd given their word to Professor X that they'd put Roger and his mission first though.

"Nah," Fool said. "Just muted your perception a bit. Not much though. You're pretty focused there."

Jackal nodded. "Kid's doing all right."

"Looks like it. This thing might work out all right, I guess."

Jackal nodded and didn't say anything else because Fool was doing that thing he sometimes did. Not so much of a fidget, just a bit of stroking his sparse beard while he kept glancing off into the distance. Something was on his mind. Jackal knew that if he waited long enough, Fool would find a way to say whatever it was.

It didn't take long.

"I'm thinking we might want to hold off on our Skills. Something tells me we're gonna Level up quick enough, but I feel a cold wind blowing. We're gonna go through some shit before this is over. So, hang tight. I figure when the time comes, we'll know."

Jackal didn't even nod in reply, but a conviction settled over him. Fool wasn't wrong. This was supposed to be a bit of a cakewalk, but he felt the same cold wind blowing. More, he smelled blood on that wind.

The weather changed with the fury of a dragon.

The first clouds came skudding down the valley almost out of nowhere, shortly after the camp was set up. A solid grey, almost black wall, a rolling wave of a cloud. At first, it was a silent line on the horizon, but the first distant rumble followed. And then flashes. The bottom edge of the storm was obscured by the trees.

But it came fast. As the wall of clouds got closer, more clouds poured over the mountains and the light from the sky turned a pale yellow-green. The first gust of the storm front ripped though the camp, a buffet that swept across the whole front of the valley.

When Jackal looked up to see how the storm was developing, his heart dropped. The clouds were swirling, changing before his eyes. He'd never seen a storm like this. As the black lead wall rolled toward them, Jackal saw the underside of the rest of the clouds roiling and spilling in a tumultuous uproar.

Backlit by the eerie light, three different sections of clouds spun and turned inside the main cloud, and some of those spinning bits extended down.

It was impossible. This part of Canada was too far north for tornadoes, but this storm was showing all the classic signs.

As the black wall rolled over them, the lightning ripped loose. Bolt after bolt tore apart the sky. The thunder beat hard on their chests, and even Jackal flinched at the anger in it.

Buckets of rain could be seen, sheets pouring out of the clouds. They'd be soaked once it hit them, but there was still a bit of time to stand and watch.

He saw the trees on the mountainside churning in the downdraft. The forest swayed and rippled as if it was a tilted ocean, a wave slowly rolling toward them.

The rest of the camp stopped to look too. They were all caught in a moment of indecision. The smart thing to do, the instinctual thing, was to head for shelter. That was at war with the logic that most of their shelters were fabric tents. Tents that might be snatched up in a bad enough storm. Or crushed by a falling tree.

At that errant thought, Jackal looked back at their own tent. It looked distant enough from the trees, and Fool was wasting no time running around and checking all the guy lines, giving each stake a few extra hammers. The tent itself had a bit of a slope to its design, so it should hold up.

The Mousekin didn't use tents, but rather some System-enhanced instant shelter that sprang up on its own and drove in its own supports. Roger, Eric, and Olivia had been given an upsized version. They looked like little huts, and from the casual air of the Mousekin, they should be strong enough to survive most storms. That didn't stop them from watching this one to see if it would exceed that limit.

The wind bellowed again, and Jackal turned back to look at it. The clouds were visibly lowering, still swirling. The tendrils still reached down, but instead of coalescing into tornadoes, they seem to swirl themselves apart after a moment, only to be replaced by another.

There was a madness to it, and Jackal found himself grinning.

With one last powerful gust, the storm hit. The rain struck, first with fat drops. It gave just enough warning for everyone to dive into their shelters, then the sky opened.

Heavy rain pummeled Jackal, but he just stood. Lightning flashed all around him, and thunder ripped the air apart in a steady beat. Each drop of rain that hit him seemed to go right through him. It wasn't the coldest rain. It was almost warm, as was the wind. He didn't notice in any case, as caught up as he was. The storm blew through him, and he felt himself becoming one with the storm.

A memory. Him as a child, looking out a window, lightning crashing on some distant part of the city, the rain not reaching the glass, turned aside by the overhang.

The air inside was stifling. Hot. His parents wouldn't let him open the window, even though he knew the air would be fresh and cool outside, alive with the ionic tingle of the storm.

No, they said. They didn't want the barely working AC to fail. His parents didn't hate change; they just loved things to be just right. That was the real reason.

Young Jackal had stared out the window and dreamed. His mother made some noise behind him, part of her incessant cleaning and organizing. Some small thing had dared to move an inch maybe and upset her need for things to be an eternal just-so.

The window had a touch of moisture at the bottom, and the faintest bit of fuzzy mold had escaped his mother's attention. He held his fingers against the glass, just above, and wondered who he'd be in the future. If he'd be the kind of person that could see the lightning up close and feel the rain. And he made a promise to himself, in that moment, that he would remember this moment when he was older and check back on himself and compare who they were to who they had been.

The rain drenched Jackal, and he remembered and smiled. And his tears blended in with the rain, and he felt all that he had become, so much more than he had ever dreamed when he was that distant youth.

Then he froze, as something distant moved on the mountainside.

On the mountaintop. A figure, small in the distance, backlit by a bolt of lighting striking just next to it. A humanoid, stepping up and over the peak of the nearby mountain, then instantly covered by the clouds billowing down to cover the mountaintop.

To be seen at that distance? It had to be at least as tall as some of the trees on that mountain. And those were not small trees.

In a moment, he was at Holland's cabin, hammering on the door.

"Giant," was all Jackal said, pointing toward the mountain.

Holland swore and tumbled out of his dry warmth, hollering for the two sergeants, Jerry and Basil.

Roger, Eric, and Olivia were already coming out of their tents to see what the commotion was about. Jackal waved them to Holland, and he moved to his shared tent with Fool.

Fool was sitting in a camp chair, his feet up on a stool, reading a book. He'd set up an extra sturdy tarp for himself, with opposite corners tied to trees and staked into the ground. Jackal approved. It looked like a Bedouin tent and would probably hold through any winds they got. And keep out the rain. At least in the center.

"Some fun out there?" Fool asked.

Jackal sighed. "At least one giant, on the peak of the facing mountains. Looks like the park is living up to its reputation."

Fool carefully folded the corner of the page he was reading and closed the book. "What kind of giant?"

"No idea. It was on top of the mountain, so I suppose a mountain giant? I'm not that familiar with the varieties." Or even if there were varieties. Mana bleed helped a little bit but not much.

"Me neither. I was kinda hoping you were. Kids might know."

"We can ask them." Jackal came to the realization that Fool wasn't going to rush up any time soon, so he decided to imitate him. He grabbed his own chair and set it down. "Figure we'll get stomped to death in our sleep then?"

Fool smiled. "Nah. Way I figure it, no fires lit yet, we're down in the forest, big storm… Giant probably doesn't know we're here. Might be some sort of storm giant chasing the storm in the mountaintops."

"I should tell Holland to not set up patrols then."

"Oh hell no, are you… you're kidding. Ha ha."

Jackal grinned.

Fool was right though. The giant probably wasn't any kind of immediate threat, any more than the storm was. And they'd at least confirmed one type of monster that was roving the park. Jackal had never fought an actual Giant. Giant monsters seemed to be pretty normal, but a giant humanoid? That was new. He'd heard stories about them, and they seemed to be pretty damned tough.

Folks from other worlds spoke of them with the same kind of awe they spoke of when they mentioned Dragons—creatures of vast power and different levels of intellect. Giants might be dangerous simpletons or sentient beings. Either way, they represented a stupendous threat.

They'd have to plan some strategies for dealing with them.

Jackal sighed. Might as well get together with Holland now and figure out something.

Fool just opened his book and went back to reading.

The rain outside was as bad as it had been, but the wind had slackened off. There was no longer any view of the mountain—or anything beyond the edges of the camp. The downpour blocked the view of everything. Jackal couldn't even see the swirl of the clouds anymore, just a dark grey somewhere above the rain.

It seemed, at least, that Fool was right. They were safe from anything seeing them in the storm unless it literally stumbled across them. And there was little sense planning for that because their surprised reaction was likely to be the same as a planned reaction. Once the storm was over, things might change, but for the moment, it was probably better to relax. The more relaxed one was, the faster one could react.

Holland was already walking toward Jackal. "Jackal, we're going to run patrols tonight, but in case the giant approaches, we're going to need to some backup. We can't handle that kind of threat in this weather at night. Are you and Fool able to keep watch in shifts tonight?"

Jackal nodded. "Fool will take the first shift."

"Thank you," Holland said. "We'll send someone to get you when the patrols go out." He didn't wait for a reply, walking past Jackal to go talk to the next person.

Fool was back to reading his book, so Jackal opted to take a walk and check on everyone.

A small mess area had been set up by the band of trees that separated the parking lot from the road. It was made of a single large tarp tied to the trees overhead. As the rain and wind had picked up, some of the Mousekin had hurriedly changed it around so that two of the corners had instead been pulled down and staked to the ground. That left it as two inverted triangles, which helped stop most of the rain from reaching the table and chairs inside. It also gave the tent a stronger structure, which stopped the wind from tearing it loose.

Roger, Eric, and Olivia were sitting inside, huddled around the table where someone had set up a mana-powered heater. They all waved at Jackal when he came in, and Eric offered a mug of something steaming.

Jackal took it gratefully. The rain and wind were making him feel rather chilly. He knew the effect was entirely psychosomatic, but the hot mug was still blissful. He sat down in the chair and took a sip.

"Hot chocolate. Lovely. Thank you," he said.

"My pleasure," Eric said. "I've been hoarding a few packets, and this seemed like the right time to use them. Do you think Fool would like some?"

"He's good," Jackal said. Fool loved hot chocolate, but he seemed to be happy in his covered shelter with the book. He wouldn't miss what he didn't know about.

"Was there really a giant?" Roger said.

Jackal nodded, and the three youths looked at each.

"How... big?" Eric asked.

Jackal shrugged. "Maybe twenty meters."

That made the three of them sit back and get quiet again. Roger was looking at the other two, and he looked worried. Jackal didn't have to guess why.

Roger had started this whole thing full of confidence and pep, and without much care. Since then, they'd seen the cost of what they were doing. And now, facing something as strong as a giant, Roger had to be thinking how he'd feel if his friends died. It'd be a hell of a price to pay for the quest, and Roger had to be wondering what he'd gotten himself into.

Not that there was any way out of it now. The quest had to be fulfilled.

None of them said anything after that.

The storm abated half an hour later. During a brief pause in the wind and rain, the three youths used the excuse to head back to their tents for the night.

Jackal stayed in the mess tent. From time to time, Mousekin came in and warmed themselves. The evening patrols had started already.

The storm blew through the night in waves. It didn't end until just before dawn.

When dawn came, it brought a bright blue sky. A welcome warmth, and a steam all over the ground as the sun started to dry away the storm leavings.

When the morning roll call came, it was found one of the Mousekin soldiers was missing.

Chapter Fourteen

The door of the soldier's cabin had been forced open, and no one had noticed. Their team had been the second to last to patrol. They'd come back on schedule and had all sacked right out. Sometime between their patrol return and the wakeup call, the lock on the door had been forced open quietly enough that no one noticed.

Then someone had entered, also without waking anyone else, and somehow captured and silently removed the soldier.

It had taken a bit to find a single set of tracks leading away from the camp and into the woods.

Fool had found it. Because of his and Jackal's higher perceptions, they seemed to have the best chance of tracking, along with one Mousekin with some Levels in tracking. They were hastily sent out to try to find where the trail led. Holland and a tactical team would follow up once they got some intelligence on what had happened. Everyone else was spending the morning securing the camp and setting up alarms and traps.

The prints were roughly human-sized, but of a different shape. And they left a deeper impression than any but the heaviest human would leave. The kidnapper was either extremely high Leveled in stealth or was using some high-tech equipment. Neither option presented anything they'd expected in Wells Gray Park.

They'd expected high-Level monsters, but this spoke of sentients. Holland had warned them to be extra careful, as he had a hunch this was the work of a military outfit. He wouldn't say more than that.

Jackal's gut was telling him the same thing. Something was odd about all of this. What made the most sense was that someone had grabbed the Mousekin to gather intelligence about the whole group. If that was the case, then they likely had a small window to actually rescue him. Once the enemy had everything it wanted, they'd kill him and dump the body somewhere. Same if they figured they couldn't get any information.

As a bonus though… if the enemy hadn't kidnapped the Mousekin, their group would probably not know an enemy group was in the park, and they might have walked into an ambush later. So now they had some warning.

The question was, who or what were the opposition? If Holland was right and it was a military group, what were they doing here? Wells Gray Park had been one of the remotest places in BC before the apocalypse, being that it was in the middle of the province. The terrain was starkly inhospitable, consisting of near endless mountains with no clear way to build a road or railway through it. It was remote enough that even though it was mineral and resource rich, it had been almost completely ignored by colonization.

It had also been the site of the most recent vulcanism in the area, with eruptions as recent as a few hundred years ago. But even for the advanced tech of the System civilizations, there was nothing here that couldn't be found easier elsewhere. There were no trappings of civilization at all, so no reason for a military operation to take place.

Adventurers, for sure. The System had taken this remote area and done what it had done to all the big natural areas—turned it into a massive, high-

Level outdoor dungeon area. They'd had a relative torrent of warnings on entry, almost guaranteeing all of them death.

It was possible that someone else was doing the equivalent of what Roger had done in Prince George and using the park to do some serious Leveling up. Which also didn't make sense. Why bring a full military group along? Anyone high enough Level to use this park for those purposes was probably better off running it alone.

Unless they were planning something major.

Jackal brushed the thought out of his mind. It wasn't important at the moment. What was important was finding the kidnapper and rescuing the Mousekin victim. Odds were that the more he focused on that mission, the more likely he was to finding answers to his other questions.

The best they'd been able to determine, the kidnapper had about a two-hour head start on them. They'd been tracking them for almost an hour now. The tracks had been almost impossible to see for the first half hour, showing that the kidnapper was moving with real caution, taking care to hide. It had taken all three of them working together to keep up, following the faintest of hints—the slightest disturbance in the soil, a branch that had been moved aside and flipped back into position with just a little less moisture on it than the others.

After that though, the track had been easier to follow. The kidnapper had picked up their pace. They'd found the odd footprint as well and had come to a few conclusions. The kidnapper was still carrying the Mousekin, and the kidnapper was huge.

The breadth of the disturbance on either side of the trail marked out a being as tall as Jackal, but even broader across the shoulders. Something that large and able to move with that much stealth spoke of some serious Levels. They'd likely have a good fight ahead of them.

Fool was in the lead, and Jackal froze as the diminutive older man held up a finger. Jackal turned to pass the message on the Mousekin tracker, who was following in parallel to help make sure they didn't miss anything, but the Mousekin had seen the same signal and stilled into almost invisibility in the woods.

Fool moved his hands slowly, indicating that Jackal should make his way up next to him. Jackal hunched lower to the ground and inched forward. It took him almost five minutes to make his way to Fool, but in that time, Fool didn't move at all.

The sun had been up long enough to start to clear away the leftover wet from the storm, but only a bit. The path they'd been following looked to be a game trail, and the forest floor was covered with pine needles and cones. Only the soggy wet stopped their passage from being noisy.

The trail ahead led down a steep ravine, and the trees were the dominant life form, so undergrowth in the area was sparse. As a result, they had a pretty good view down through the trees. There was a small clearing which looked like it had once been a streambed, cut off from the main hydrology some time ago.

The result was a dry little curve surrounded by rocks, with no trees in the area. It would have made a cozy camp site. The sun had warmed the pine needle flooring and small shrubs in the clearing, enough that there was a lazy steamy fog floating about in the gust of wind, almost twinkling in the sun.

Frederic was bound tightly in ropes, and those ropes were hung on a hook tied to one of the trees. His mouth was covered with some kind of tape, but he looked to be okay for the moment.

A very large humanoid was ripping chunks of raw meat off a haunch of fox, while sitting on a log and looking at Frederic. The creature was toying with a large, wicked looking knife, and it was clear that the knife was intended to be a threat to Frederic, because the creature hadn't bothered to use it to dismember the corpse of the fox.

The little animal looked to have been torn in half, and the humanoid was happily tearing off pieces, grinning to show its sharp, hooked teeth. It had small legs in proportion to the rest of its body. Its shoulders, chest, and back were so large it looked hunchbacked, but as it ripped off another piece of fox, Jackal saw clearly that all that mass was muscle. It had tiny beady eyes, a dark liquid red visible even at this distance, and large, pointed ears that reminded Jackal of the goblins they'd fought back in Prince George.

It wasn't a monster. It was wearing forest-camouflage pants bloused into sturdy combat boots. Its belt was loaded with pouches and a sidearm, in addition to the knife sheath. It was wearing a desert-tan muscle shirt, with a mottled dark green beret on its head. Next to it on the log was a camouflage uniform jacket, with a shoulder patch of some kind.

Catnip was tugging frantically at Jackal's jacket, and when he turned to look at him, the Mousekin gestured for them to retreat. Jackal nudged into Fool, and they carefully backed up until they were around a curve where any sounds were unlikely to reach anyone below them.

Once they were a little hidden away, Catnip got them to lean in close and whispered, "Bugbear. Bad news. He's going to be a scout for Hobgoblins, and if they have a scout, there's a lot of them. We need to let Holland know right away."

Jackal nodded, but Fool interrupted. "What about Frederic? Is he safe to leave here? I'm trying to keep an open mind, and I'm assuming that military groups have some kind of prisoner protocol? Something like no torture?"

Catnip shook his head. "Doesn't work like that. Hobgoblins we can negotiate with, but only if they see any benefit. There's no telling why they're here or what their mission is. They might just want to wipe us out to keep their presence secret. But the Bugbear… they do what they want. They like torture. Frederic won't last the day."

Fool swore softly, then sat back and thought for a moment. "All right. You go back and inform Holland. Jackal and I will deal with the Bugbear and get Frederic loose. We'll—"

Jackal stopped him with a firm shake of his head. "No. Can't risk it. Holland needs to know."

Fool frowned, but he seemed to get the meaning. One of them had to go back with Catnip. The most important thing was to get information to Holland and let everyone else know about the threat. Saving Frederic was secondary.

"Fair point," Fool finally said. "Do you need any help?"

Jackal shook his head. He could take out the Bugbear unless he'd missed something obvious.

"All right," Fool said. "I ran Talent Scout on it. Nothing really outstanding. He's built for stealth. He's a little higher Level than you, but you've got him beat in combat skills. Just be very careful. If he gets away from you, you're screwed."

Jackal could only smile in response to that.

He didn't think the Bugbear would get away.

With no time to waste, Fool and Catnip started back to the camp.

Jackal slowly made his way back to the top of the ravine and looked down. The Bugbear was finishing its meal. It didn't even bother to wipe the bloody mess from its face. It stood and stretched, spreading its arms wide, then looked at Frederic.

Its voice, when it spoke, was surprisingly high-pitched and reedy, and Jackal was reminded of the villains from some of the eighties' animated movies his parents had loved to watch.

"Well, my little friend. I think we have some time to play before we meet up with the Major, so why don't we have a little fun?" As if the leer in its voice wasn't enough, it played with its knife again.

Jackal saw Frederic was frightened but trying not to show it. Which was probably wise, because from the way the Bugbear was posturing, creating fear was a big part of what it was after. And Jackal doubted it would wait long before putting that knife to use.

He thought of a few things he could do. Probably the best thing would be shout, gain the Bugbear's attention, and then attack. Or run away and make it chase him. The risk was that the uniform might not be for show. A well-trained soldier would do just what Fool and Catnip had done and book it back to report to the rest of its unit.

And while that was tempting—Jackal figured he could turn the tables and follow the Bugbear back to its headquarters—that would leave Frederic alone. And more than likely, Jackal would be setting himself up for an ambush by the Bugbear.

The better thing in this case was the more brutal thing. And the real reason he'd wanted Fool gone.

The smart move was to kill the Bugbear as swiftly as possible and make sure it didn't report anything to its commanders. Better would be to keep it somewhat alive and see if he could get information from it, but Jackal didn't think he'd be able to take it down without killing it. If Fool was right and it was higher Level than him? He couldn't risk going for a nonlethal takedown. There was just too much at stake.

He was amused to realize just how much he didn't want Fool to see this. They'd fought next to each other and killed many opponents, sentient and not. But that had always been in some kind of pitched battle. Jackal didn't intend this to be a fair fight at all.

Nothing else for it, but a direct attack.

He activated his Speed Boost skill and burst down the slope.

He was about halfway down when he saw the Bugbear react, turning in slow motion to see what the noise was. Jackal's Speed Burst increased his perception enough that everything was moving in slow motion, and he had all the time in the world.

Jackal activated his next skill: Death from Above. He leapt, an impossible powered arc, and he could practically feel the extra power coursing through him. This was his one-shot kill Skill, able to punch through armor and doubling his damage. And in preparation for the fight, he'd equipped himself with his longsword.

The Bugbear was fast. And clearly well-trained.

As Jackal neared him on his descent, the Bugbear had managed to turn to meet him and was raising the knife to block his longsword. The outline of the Bugbear was changing as well, fading and becoming blurred and indistinct—a stealth Skill at work, clearly.

It wasn't going to help.

Jackal didn't roar or shout, just threw the cut with as much force and precision as he could.

The Bugbear managed to block. Jackal's longsword hit the knife just above the hilt, and the Bugbear had angled it just right so that the blade slid all the way down into the hilt.

It should have been the perfect block and the start to a more equal fight.

If Jackal hadn't been so strong and so perfectly tuned for this blow.

His longsword struck, and he saw the Bugbear's eyes widen as the sword shoved the knife back around, the force of the cut nearly ripping the blade out of the Bugbear's grip, as the longsword finished its inexorable path down.

The block saved the Bugbear though. It moved the blade just offline enough that it cut into its shoulder instead of splitting its head in half. Even so, the blade split down a quarter the length of the Bugbear's body.

A testament to its skill and ability. The blow should have split the creature in half.

Jackal didn't waste any time, using the last pulse of his Speed Burst to draw the blade out and raise back to a guard position.

Just as the Bugbear threw a forehand cut with its blade, bloody spittle bursting from its mouth as it screamed in rage, ignoring its own pain.

Jackal had no desire to see how strong the Bugbear was. And combat was never really about face-to-face contests. As he saw his opponent shift weight to throw the cut, Jackal did the fastest thing he could—pulling his knees up to his chest and letting gravity drop him toward the ground in a low squat, easily dodging under the Bugbear's slash. As soon as he landed, he lashed out with a one-handed backhand cut, leaping forward with his left leg at the same time.

He wound up angled slightly behind the Bugbear, and it howled again as his longsword slammed into its hamstring.

But it didn't cut through. The blade stopped and only caused the Bugbear to buckle a little bit. Clearly it had activated some kind of Skill.

Jackal's back flared, and it was his turn to flinch and yell as his back turned to lava. Some kind of burning attack with instant heat. Marshalling his will, he ignored the pain and shifted all his weight to his left foot, pulling his sword back to an overhead guard while lashing out with his right foot…

Success. The Bugbear might be temporarily invulnerable, but it couldn't defy gravity and physics, not against Jackal's pinpoint attack. His right foot slammed into the ankle of the same leg the longsword had struck, and this time the pressure did the trick, buckling the ankle.

The Bugbear started to fall, but even as it fell, Jackal could see it turning into a rapid breakfall, so he did the smart thing and sprang back to give him time to deal with any surprises. Creating distance meant the opponent would need to come to him, and he'd have more time to react. And time was what a wounded opponent didn't have, because they were bleeding out.

The Bugbear leapt back to its feet, and Jackal realized his mistake. It was still wounded, the huge cut down its side rendering one arm useless. System healing aside, the wound was bad enough that blood was still pouring out of it. A few moments, one or two more cuts, and it would be dead.

But it was an experienced veteran of the System world, and it knew how to deal with lethal blows. Giving it space gave it time to use its Skills. The Bugbear shimmered in place, its outline blurring. Jackal had forgotten about its stealth Skills, and if he didn't move quickly, he would lose the chance to stop the Bugbear from reporting back to its unit.

He sprang forward with another cut, this one two-handed and aimed at the forehead of the Bugbear. It moved to block the cut, but the cut was a feint. Jackal pulled the cut a little short by crossing his wrists, the tip of the sword looping down in front of the Bugbear's knife, making its block pass harmlessly by.

Jackal's sword was now a diagonal line between him and his opponent, and he took a deep lunge forward while lifting his hands up over his head. The Bugbear was fast and was already throwing a return cut back down toward Jackal.

It was too late though. The lunge had driven the tip of the longsword into the lower torso of the Bugbear, just above its belt. The blade slipped in easily, and Jackal found he was a hair faster, and in a better position due to the angle of this strike.

With a slight lean to his right, the incoming cut from the Bugbear stopped. Not because it was blocked, but because the part of the longsword closest to Jackal's hands, the sharped strong of the blade, had been put in the path of the Bugbear's wrist.

The edge cut halfway through, and the Bugbear grunted and pulled back its hand. But not before delivering a crushing kick to Jackal's midsection.

Some kind of Skill backed that kick, because the pain was immense and Jackal flew back to crash into a tree trunk, where everything was swirling. He couldn't make sense of up or down, and his longsword was gone.

Everything shifted. The Bugbear was gone.

Jackal had been around Fool since almost the arrival of the System. He knew deception when he felt it. This was some kind of illusion, but it was acting right on his brainstem. There was no trick to look around, no faint visual clue, just a spinning world and a growing sense of nausea every time he tried to stop the spinning. The only thing he knew was that his opponent was massively wounded, but also going to kill him.

A face swam into reality in front of him, seeming to coalesce out of nothingness. The Bugbear, like some sort of evil reverse Cheshire cat, grinned at him.

"I'm going to enjoy killing you, human."

Jackal had no doubt about that at all. If he couldn't overcome this, he was going to die. He had a moment of regret for sending Fool back. Fool would have been able to blow through this illusion Skill, whatever it was, in a breath.

"It's nothing personal though," the Bugbear continued. And winced at some pain sneaking back through. "You hurt me, but that's part of the job. I'm going to enjoy cutting your body up and delivering bits of it to your friends over the next few days, while we slowly surround them and chop them up, bit by bit. The meat is sweeter when it's had a few days to marinate in fear."

The Bugbear grinned, and Jackal grinned back.

"And why is that amusing?" it asked.

"Pain don't hurt," Jackal said.

Up until now, he'd been managing the fight on only a few Skills. He'd wanted to see what the Bugbear had.

It wasn't enough.

Pain Don't Hurt was his body-toughening skill. And as he hoped, activating it cleared his mind. It didn't matter though. Because Maestro, his unarmed combat Skill, gave him the ability to fight blindfolded, and this illusion was no different.

Intimidate was strong enough to rattle the Bugbear, then it was all One Punch. No weapon needed.

Jackal's hand flashed out, fingers spread, and drove into the Bugbear's eyes. Jackal felt how tough they were as they compressed against his fingertips. That compression had the same effect on the Bugbear as it did on humans, overloading the optic nerve and causing a shrieking spasm of pain to run through its body, strong enough to shut down all of its Skills for a second.

Its legs buckled, and Jackal found himself standing face to face with the Bugbear.

Just before he rammed his knife home where his fingers had been.

The Bugbear went rigid in shock, but it was already dead. That was just its body having its last fight for survival. Jackal held the corpse on his extended arm for a moment, feeling the weight of it on his blade.

He disliked killing sentient beings. Always had. There wasn't much room for that in this System world though, and he had no problem acting when he had too. And this creature was evil. Its intended act of torture was not a first-time thing. Jackal knew he had just removed something from the world that was responsible for more pain and grief than he wanted to know.

Still. He looked up at its now lifeless face. The remaining eye was slack but hadn't yet reached that deflated look of death. A few tears still dripped down, in response to the eye-thrust he'd given it with his fingers.

Someone had loved this Bugbear once. It had grown up and had friends, and even if it had been a jerk and a bully, it had still been a living creature who had tried to do the best it could every day.

"I'm sorry," Jackal said. Then he yanked his knife back and let the body drop to the forest floor.

He walked over to where Frederic had been hung and carefully cut loose the Mousekin, then undid his bonds.

"Can you travel?" he asked.

Frederic looked up at him, then back at the Bugbear. His little body shook—with sudden revulsion or anger, Jackal couldn't really tell. Likely both.

"I can walk. Run if I have to. Thank you. I owe you," Frederic said.

"It's what we do," Jackal said. "Head back, run if you can. Catnip and Fool left a moment ago. They'll be moving slow for the next bit. You can catch up to them if you hurry. I'll follow once I've cleaned this up."

Frederic nodded, and after stretching his limbs, he started up the ravine slope at a slow jog. Jackal watched him go, then turned back to look over the clearing.

It really was a beautiful spot, and Jackal felt he'd done the forest a disservice with the violence he'd participated in. The best he could do was try to find some balance.

He thought about hiding the body. The Bugbear's companions would come and look for it eventually. The longer it took them to find it, the better it likely was for Jackal and everyone else. But he found himself reluctant to do that. He had no idea what the burial methods for Bugbears were.

In the end, he decided he couldn't just leave things the way they were. He stripped the body and carried it to the river he'd heard through the trees. He clambered down with the body until he was in water deep enough to support the weight of his dead foe, then leaned down and kissed it on the forehead.

"May you find peace," he said and let the body go, watching it float down in the gentle rapids.

He walked back to the clearing and looked around, extending his perception as best he could. No one was around. He gathered up all the gear, bundling it into the Bugbear's clothing to make it secure to carry, then spent some time walking all around the site to clear up the evidence. The blood and scuff marks were all covered up by fresh pine needles, and he used a recently fallen branch to smooth out all the evidence of any fights. Once all that was done, he hoisted up the bundle and started back.

Chapter Fifteen

"Spitetooth ain't back yet." The lieutenant looked more annoyed than worried.

Hellgaze nodded. "Give him another hour. If he's back before then, half rations for the week. If he's not back after that, take the rest of your scout group and go get him. Then it will be half rations for the scout group for a week."

"Yes, sir. Won't happen again, sir." The lieutenant knew better than to complain.

Running the scout group was usually a cherry post for a young up-and-coming Hobgoblin looking to make their mark. Part of what made it such a prestigious post was that the Bugbears tended to make up most of the scout groups, due to their natural affinity for stealth.

The downside was their affinity for cruelty and a tendency to think they were superior to their Hobgoblin cousins, which made them extremely difficult to manage. The good officers learned the tricks quite quickly. The bad ones got eaten.

Well, not really. Maybe back in the old days, when things had been a bit rougher and wilder. But this was the modern world, and the old days of

Hobgoblin bands being led by cruel Bugbear warlords were long gone. Even the older military models and harsh punishment were gone.

So, Lieutenant Sparkflint wasn't likely to be eaten, but if he couldn't manage his group, he might be moved to a more suitable post. Something in logistics, maybe. Still, he'd been doing a good job so far. And Seargent Spitetooth was a particularly troubling soldier. He'd been written up a few times in the last cycle and reduced in rank. If he wasn't such a superlative scout, he'd have been bucked back lower or spent more time in the stockade.

This, Hellgaze decided, would be Spitetooth's last chance.

It had been a simple scouting patrol, and Spitetooth had run it regularly with no issues in the last two weeks. He was due to rotate to one of the other patrols next cycle. Hellgaze had no idea why he'd decided to slack off this close to that.

There was always the possibility that something in the park had gotten to him, of course. Wasn't likely, but it was possible. Giants had been sighted moving about during the last storm. Not a surprise, given all the recent activity. Poor things probably wanted nothing to do with what was going on and were running for the nearest safe spot. Spitetooth was one tough Bugbear, but even he would have been made short work of by a giant.

But the other scouts would have noticed one of the Mountain Giants coming down south of Battle Mountain, and he hadn't any reports of that. More likely Spitetooth had just taken the chance to take a nap or found some lesser being to torture for a while. If that was the case, he'd have a chance to see how Sparkflint handled discipline.

Or worst case, something serious had happened? Well, they had enough troops to spare sending a group or two to take care of any serious issues. It wouldn't be enough to change the plan at all. They had troops to spare for this.

Hellgaze looked up. Sparkflint was still waiting at attention, and Hellgaze managed to hold back a sigh. Sparkflint would make a good officer in time, but he was fresh out of an advanced training course and still stuck in the rules loop. He was going to have to coax the initiative back out of him.

"Dismissed, Sparkflint," he said. "Wait. Before you go, where's the employer now?"

"Back in his quarters, Major. Just returned from Flourmill."

"Hm. All right. Get back to your group then."

Sparkflint gave an academy-crisp salute and turned out, closing the door neatly behind him.

Hellgaze leaned back in his chair and put his not-too-muddy boots up on the desk. He was tempted to go talk to the employer and let them know about Spitetooth, but troop discipline wasn't anything to do with the contract. He'd let him know if they ran across any opposition or if it looked as if something serious was going to throw the plans off, but aside from that? He didn't think the employer would really care at all.

He looked over his office. Field office, but still, he'd set it up as nice as he could. He knew a lot of officers liked to keep their offices sparse and barren when on mission, thinking that it gave them a more professional military appearance.

Hellgaze thought that was so much crap. The walls had all his decorations and unit citations, holos of him with various celebrities, and more than a few combat trophies he'd collected over his career. His desk though, the part that faced him? That was all photos of his wives and his brood of fourteen children.

The family photos had the same purpose as the flash on the wall though. War was a fickle business. All those officers who kept their crap in storage did so with the full expectation that they'd be setting it up in their perfectly dressed home study, and they'd wile away their retirement having fond memories and some drinks with the boys.

Hellgaze knew better than that. He figured one mission, maybe this one, and he'd be a dead Hobgoblin. He had no illusions about an afterlife, and he knew he'd blink out as if he'd never been. The flash on his walls was his to enjoy now because he couldn't count on later. Same with the family photos. Trophies of what he'd accomplished in life, and a reminder not that the best was going to come, but that he'd already had the best.

So many of his friends, better Hobgoblins than he, had died before attaining even half of what he had.

The show wasn't for others, and in a way, it wasn't really for Hellgaze either. It was for his lost friends, a little call to the memory of them that he held deep inside himself, that he hadn't wasted his life, that he was doing the best he could.

He leaned forward, sliding open one of the desk drawers. In it was a bottle of the local brew, confiscated when they'd cleaned out the closest town. Some kind of mashed plant, fermented and distilled with an insect residue. Sounded disgusting and tasted rather unpleasant. At least at first. He'd been curious enough about it to try a second sip and found some strange flavors. About half the bottle was left now, and he was finding himself hoping that they hadn't somehow destroyed the only source of this "Honey Shine". He poured himself a thin shot, just enough to enjoy the flavor, and spent a minute enjoying the aroma.

Most pleasant. Then he tipped back the small glass and let the booze roll around his mouth for a moment. It burned wonderfully on the way down, a promise of the joys of a longer life, and he raised the empty glass in the direction of the holo of his lost friends.

"Cheers, boys. Join you soon enough."

Hellgaze got a System notice about an hour later that Sparkflint had left the base with his scout group.

Something struck Hellgaze as a little off, but he couldn't put a claw on it. He got up from his desk and walked over to the display wall, calling up a holo of the operations area. The wall filled first with a flat display of the area, then grew the geological features in, then put on an overlay of current know entities in the space and overlaid the whole thing with labels.

"Wells Gray Park" was what the locals called it. Its System Levels were high enough that only Advanced class soldiers were out in less that squad size patrols.

The staging base, where they were now, was near the bottom of the park, about thirty kilometers up. They'd been dropped by their ships at what was labeled as a ranch of some sort. Whatever it was, it had been tromped flat by some kind of megafauna since the System had arrived. But it was an excellent flat spot with a good line of sight, and far enough from what was going on in the rest of the park to be relatively safe.

North of them was Clearwater Lake. West was Mahood Lake, and east was the very large Murtle Lake. The main action was taking place between Clearwater and Mahood, at what was listed on the map as the Flourmill.

Flourmill was a recently erupted volcano, as were most of the range of mountains that ran between Murtle and Clearwater Lakes. Whatever the geology of this place before the System, it was rapidly becoming something else. Which was why they were there.

"Special Resource Collection" was the euphemistic phrase they had been given, which made about as much sense as the slavery that had been visited upon the people of Clearwater.

Hellgaze had no illusions about that. Hobgoblins used to be quite known for their slaving activities, back in the old days. Since then, they'd grown and changed as a civilization and people, and now they looked at the practice with if not hatred, then serious disgust. If it hadn't been the massive debts that a certain politician had run up with their employer, Hellgaze would have walked away from this contract. But that politician had been a relative of Hellgaze's, and he had his own debts to pay. So there they were, on a vicious Dungeon World, in one of its most dangerous areas, working for the cursed Thirteen Moon Sect.

Hellgaze shook his head. He'd wrestle his demons as he tried to sleep. Daytime was for doing the job.

If something had happened to Spitetooth and it was enemy action, it was entirely possible some other faction had found out what Thirteen Moon had. They couldn't have come from the east. The volcanoes and their special companions would crush anything on this world. The north was impassible to anything that wasn't airborne, and Hellgaze had sensors in place that would have picked anything like that up. From the east, they would have had to have to gone through their target area, which made no sense.

Which left the south. An enemy would have had to come up the road from Clearwater. Any sizable force landing in that area would have triggered any number of sensors they'd set up, so the only option was a small unit. Possibly a scout group?

Or locals, but Hellgaze was confident they'd cleaned them all out and moved them to the Flourmill. Still… it was a potential avenue of attack. Something might be up. It was probably best if he gave the Thirteen Moon

Sect representative a heads-up. Likely it was just Spitetooth being the throwback he acted like, but just in case? With this employer, it was better to look prepared.

Mind made up, Hellgaze marched out of his office.

The command staff all jumped to attention, and he briefly saluted them. Likely the employer rep was still in his quarters. He rarely left. So Hellgaze didn't bother to have anyone check on his location. He just walked out, telling his attaché he would be back shortly.

The camp was still sparse, and there wasn't much going on. That was the whole point. As a staging area, they were the place the main force would come back to or occasionally request resupply from. Security was the main focus, which was why most of the scout group had stayed with them, as well as most of the artillery. Frequent patrols, with good hefty explosions to back them up when they made contact.

And the shuttles. Very important, to get the hell off of this world as soon as the mission was complete. They'd landed in the main transport ship, but it was safely back in orbit for the time being. The shuttles were for their return and occasional supply trips.

Everything looked neat and orderly, the way it should be. It was an attractive enough location, if you liked being in the mountains. Hellgaze didn't. He rather hated them. The way they blocked the horizon left him feeling trapped all the time, like a constant low-grade claustrophobia. Given his druthers, he much preferred a plains deployment. Open skies as far as the eye could see, that was the good life.

There was one remaining building left from when the location had been an active ranch, some sort of guest lodge with a strange look to it, as though it was supposed to be old and out of touch with the architecture of the nearest town, but it was, behind the facade, entirely up to the most recent technological standards. That was where the Thirteen Moon Sect's representative had set himself up.

Hellgaze knocked on the door and announced himself, then opened the door when the voice from inside invited him in.

The room looked barely lived in. The bed was slightly rumpled, as if the resident had chosen to sleep sitting up, curled into a fetal position at the top by the wall. There was a desk by the window, and it only held a single data terminal, closed. The air in the room had that musty unused smell. The representative was apparently one of those sophonts who preferred to use clean spells instead of liquids to wash themselves. Or just didn't wash themselves.

Hellgaze couldn't tell. He had found the representative to have a foul odor from the moment they met, and it hadn't changed in the entire time he'd known him.

He was sitting in a chair by the desk. As always, his face was completely covered by a reflected glass-fronted helmet, a smooth and featureless oval that only showed the room and Hellgaze. The rest of the helmet was a dark iridescent surface that seemed to organically flow back from the mirror-front. If it wasn't for the lumps, power ports, and bits of extra armor added on, Hellgaze might have assumed that it was the representative's actual face. That, and he could hear a bit of hollow echo when the representative spoke.

The rest of him was covered in what looked to be a skin-tight leather suit that covered him from head to toe, without even seams before it covered the hands and feet. The soles of the feet were covered with a fairly standard military sole, but the hands were uniform. Dark red streaks ran over the entire suit, with no real pattern or purpose to them. Again, Hellgaze was tempted to think that this was the natural skin of the creature, but there were square lumps and protrusions underneath the suit, and he'd noted how the leather slid over those covered protrusions.

There were two large boxes of ammo next to the desk, and leaning on the wall next to them was the representative's only other possession—a comically oversized sniper rifle. It had a barrel almost as long as the main gun on a scout tank, and the suppressor on the end of the barrel was almost head sized. The scope flared into a foot-wide opening, but the eyepiece at the other end was minuscule... too small for putting an eye to. Hellgaze hadn't seen the weapon in use, but he'd seen similar designs. The optics usually plugged directly into a receptacle on the shooter's body. Often an artificial eye made just for that purpose.

"What's on your mind, Major Hellgaze?" the representative said.

Hellgaze kept himself at attention. The representative was a tricky person to deal with. He had a short fuse, very little understanding of military comportment or practice, and often wanted the most minor issues dealt with in a cruel fashion. Hellgaze didn't like him at all, but he'd learned that being excessively formal made every meeting go by faster.

"Nothing too serious, but we have a potential issue. I wanted to keep you informed in case it becomes something more serious, so that you have time to plan for the contingency."

The mirrored face swiveled as if it was a mantis head on an insectile neck, and the representative looked at Hellgaze for a moment. "Do tell then."

"A scout hasn't reported back from a routine patrol to the south. This is the area that we swept during the Clearwater operation. If you recall at the time, we decided that the risk of incursions from that area wasn't as likely as one from the other approaches, so we reduced the sensor coverage to save on expenses. It's most likely a disciplinary issue with the scout, but there is also the chance we may have erred by leaving that area more open."

"I hardly think so. We scoured that town for everything useful. And I assure you, none of the communities close by have anyone free to come and investigate. We've rather thoroughly occupied all of them. They are safe possessions of the Sect. Any of our rivals coming from that direction would have set off certain other triggers we've got set up. Aren't most of your scouts Bugbears?"

"They are."

"There you go. Ignorant and self-sighted. It's in their blood. Probably found a forest nymph to torture."

Hellgaze bit back a snapping retort. He'd protested working for the Thirteen Moon Sect, but finances dictated more than conscience. They needed employment, and the Sect was hiring an organization just their size for a reasonable job. Just not a tasteful job.

"That's possible," he said. "But as long as there is a risk, it's my job to let you know of the potential. I've dispatched the scout group to find him. If they find him, he'll be punished. If he isn't, we're best off to assume something of the worse sort happened to him. What are your orders in that case?"

The mirrored face turned to look at him again. "We are close to finishing, and we have a deadline, so I'm not pulling any troops back from the Flourmill. You'll have to deal with whatever it is with what you have here. But feel free to use as many as you want. We've got almost two days before we really need this base, so your lot are just busy playing your military games until then. You can take off and hunt for a few days. I'll keep the supplies safe."

The tone of voice was as sharp as the words, and Hellgaze mentally broke down the time until the end of the contract into days and hours. It wasn't going to end soon enough.

"Very well. Shall I assume that I have free rein to respond to whatever we find?"

The representative nodded. "Whatever you want. Just send word to me if you find something interesting to kill."

"Absolutely. Will you be off hunting for the rest of the day again?"

"Soon. Might try some night hunting. I heard this was supposed to be a high-Level area, but all I've managed to collect so far are some Forest Nymphs and a Treant. The Treant was at least a challenge, but hardly a sporting one."

Hellgaze worked hard to keep a neutral face. The Nymphs were sentient, not monsters. They'd come to settle this world and set up a colony. The Treants were their livestock, of a sort. Pets, but cherished ones. Hobgoblins had a bad rep, well earned by their ancestors, but that was an evolution away from who they were these days. The Thirteen Moon Sect acted like the old Hobgoblins and had probably hired Hellgaze thinking they were still the same.

"Well," Hellgaze said after a moment, "I suppose you could always try the Flourmill, or the other areas."

That got a harsh laugh from the helmeted Representative. "Can't Level up if I'm dead, can I? No, I'll leave those areas for your people. Maybe when this is all over, I'll take some of my Sect brothers and go on safari here. Maybe bag some of those horned beauties."

"Indeed," Hellgaze said. "In that case, I'll get back to my troops then."

"I'm done with you." The representative turned back to his display.

Hellgaze had been in the habit of giving salutes, but he decided he was done with that and just turned around and walked out.

The sooner this job was done, the sooner he'd see the last of Band Eller. And that couldn't come soon enough.

Chapter Sixteen

Jackal didn't stop to look through the bundle of belongings until he got back to the camp. He'd caught up to Frederic part way back, and they were only a few moments behind Fool and Catnip in returning.

It was enough time for Holland to have everyone up and moving, with Roger, Eric, and Olivia temporarily taking over as watch. They were patrolling close enough to the camp to warn anyone if they saw anything.

Holland and Fool came up to Jackal at a run as soon as they saw him enter the camp.

"Bugbear we know. What else have you learned?" Holland asked.

"He was a scout," Frederic said. "I heard him say something about running late, but it being worth it. Nothing else."

Holland nodded. "So we can expect a follow-up patrol to come looking for him, but they probably don't know anything about us yet. Jackal, I assume you made sure that it wouldn't report back to its command?"

Jackal didn't reply, just dropped the bundle of clothes carefully in front of Holland. The blood had stopped dripping out a bit ago, but it was still damp on the clothing.

Holland hunched down and carefully unpacked everything. He sorted and put aside the weapons and rations, then made a little "hm" noise when he saw the unit patch on the shoulder of the jacket that everything had been bundled in. He rocked back on his haunches for a bit, then stood up.

"Hobgoblins for sure. He was a scout. Must have stumbled across us and nabbed Frederic for interrogation. I assume he didn't have time for that, or do you need more medical assistance?"

"He was just getting started when Jackal arrived," Frederic said. "I owe him my life."

"No debt. We bleed together," Jackal replied.

"Indeed," Holland said. "I suspect we're all going to bleed together before this is over. This unit patch belongs to a Hobgoblin Battalion. I have no idea what a force this size is doing out here, but we are seriously outnumbered. This completely changes our mission."

"We should get the hell out of here," Fool said.

"We can't," Holland replied. "Unfortunately, the quest Roger's father placed him under was done under a rather strict timeline, with severe consequences for non-compliance. I got the impression when we were hired that his father intended the quest to be dramatic and full of consequences. The timeline was supposed to be a part of that. I don't think he understood the risks, though. He wanted his son to feel like he was doing something important. I gather humans aren't entirely well-educated on consequences when it comes to the System."

Fool snorted. "Let me guess, he added a 'or die trying' phrase?"

Holland shook his head. "That would have been very difficult to set up, even if he had intended it. But the consequences will be almost as bad in the long term."

Fool shook his head "Lovely. No. There is a habit amongst some folk to think that nothing bad can ever happen to them or their kin, because having money means they're blessed." Jackal gave him a look, and Fool sighed. "Or at least, they haven't really experienced much bad fallout, so they don't always factor it into their plans. So how bad are the consequences?"

The flat look on Holland's face was all the answer Fool needed. "Well. That's lovely. I gotta ask. Jackal? We still in on this? Holland, how big are these battalions?"

"At least three hundred soldiers, including supply. Probably a light infantry focus, since we ran into a scout. Maybe some vehicles. Armor, maybe artillery. Mostly basic soldier classes, Advanced classes for officers, but only very low Advanced class. I should point out that Hobgoblins are tough. Not as disciplined or as highly trained as the Hakarta, but their units work with more cohesion. They don't break, retreat, or give up once they have a target. Very tenacious fighters."

Fool looked at Jackal, and Jackal shrugged. Neither of them was going to let these kids face this alone. Fool looked back at Holland and asked the next obvious question.

"I have to ask, does your contract cover this? Or does this break the terms? I'm pretty sure you didn't sign on to fight another military group ten times your size."

"We did not." Holland didn't look exactly upset by the question, but he stood as tall as he could. "But we signed up in the full knowledge that we would likely be facing odds very much against us. This Wells Gray is known to have at least one Dragon, plus Giants and wyverns. We are here to support Roger, and we will stay. Our dependents will receive the full pay for our unit if we are not able to return."

Fool nodded. "Had to ask. Didn't expect anything else from you, Holland." Fool stood up straight and crossed his arms behind his back as he took in a deep breath. He let it out and straightened his arms to the sides, shaking out his hands. "Okay, so we're fighting an army. This is stupid, but what the hell. They don't call me Fool for nothing. How we gonna do this?"

"Focus on our goal," Holland said. "We are not here to fight an army. We are here to help Roger retrieve a piece of the Dragon's Tongue. The army is an obstacle to be worked around. And believe it or not, we actually have trained for this sort of thing. We Mousekin are used to being outnumbered, as well as outsized, in our engagements. Can I share with you our basic training doctrine for this? It might help for us all to be on the same page."

"Absolutely," Fool said.

Holland nodded and sent a notification to both of their System displays. Jackal saw a list of ten factors for consideration when a smaller force had a mission of retrieval against a larger force.

"Here are some factors to consider when planning your mission:

Reconnaissance: Before embarking on the mission, gather as much information as possible about the terrain, enemy positions, and strength. This might include satellite imagery, local sources, or deploying scouts to gather information on enemy movements and positions.

Timing: Choose the most opportune moment for your mission, such as night time or during adverse weather conditions when visibility is low. This will help your team to move undetected and potentially catch the enemy off-guard.

Stealth and infiltration: Train your unit in stealth and infiltration techniques to minimize the risk of detection. This could involve camouflage, silent movement, and nonverbal communication.

Divide and conquer: Divide your unit into smaller teams, each with a specific task, to increase the chances of success. For example, one team could create a diversion to draw away some of the enemy forces, while another team infiltrates the area to retrieve the object.

Escape and evasion: Plan multiple escape routes in case your unit encounters resistance or needs to make a hasty retreat. This may involve pre-arranged extraction points, vehicles, or support from other units.

Contingency plans: Develop backup plans for unexpected events or obstacles that may arise during the mission. This could include alternative routes or tactics, as well as preparing for the possibility of casualties or compromised team members.

Communication: Establish secure and reliable communication methods among your team members and with higher command. This will enable you to relay important updates, request support, or coordinate movements.

Equipment and supplies: Ensure your unit is equipped with necessary gear and supplies, such as weapons, ammunition, medical kits, and rations. Consider lightweight, compact, and specialized equipment that will aid in stealth and mobility.

Coordination with other units: If possible, coordinate with other friendly units in the area to provide support or distractions that could increase the chances of mission success.

Briefing and rehearsals: Brief your unit thoroughly on the mission objectives, plans, and contingencies. Conduct rehearsals to ensure your team is familiar with their roles, the terrain, and potential challenges.

Remember that flexibility, adaptability, and teamwork are crucial for the success of such a mission. Be prepared to make adjustments as the situation evolves and always prioritize the safety of your unit."

Fool held up a finger in question, and Holland nodded. "Can I assume point three is handled? Your teams are trained for that?"

"Fully qualified. Happened just before this contract."

"Excellent. So, I guess our next thing is reconnaissance then?"

"Not quite," Holland said. "First, we need to find a safe place and make sure we aren't discovered. Jackal, how long until you think they will find the corpse?"

"They won't," Jackal said. "But if they have trained people, they will likely find the location where the fight happened. They won't know what happened, but they will know something happened."

"Nothing we can do about that. We have to assume worst case, that they will know we are here. But they won't know why we are here or how many of us there are. I suggest we break camp immediately. Let's look at the map."

Frederic excused himself to catch up with his team, and the three of them walked across the parking lot to the map of the park.

Their current camp was just to the west of the middle of the map and about a quarter of the way from the bottom, at Spahat Falls. The main road was to the east. Jackal pointed out where they'd come across the Bugbear, at a point to the north and east from the road.

Their destination, the Clearwater Lake Campground, was due north on the road.

"Given routine scouting patrol lengths, and the timing of when Frederic was taken, I'm guessing that puts the main force of Hobgoblins about here." Holland pointed at a spot higher up on the road, labeled as a "guest ranch." It was roughly halfway between them and their destination. "If they're here, then our best path is to move north at an angle. Cross the falls and head up off the road to the north. If I'm right, they'll focus their patrols south along the road and to the more open area on the east."

"West. Follow the river." Jackal pointed at the map.

The Clearwater River ran parallel to the road. At least on the map. But from where they were, they could see the truth of it a little better. The map was flat, and the park was steeply mountainous. As a result, the road had been built much higher up on the slopes, where there was a relatively long and flat, if not straight, stretch to be found. The river was far down, and for much of the road, it was out of sight.

Their goal was just outside the Clearwater Lake Campground. The lake was the source of the river, so all they had to do was move up the river until they got to the lake, cut across to their destination, retrieve the Dragon's Tongue, and take the river all the way back down. If luck was on their side, they could avoid the area the Hobgoblins seemed to be occupying.

Holland looked over the map and took a moment to quietly think. Then he nodded. "All right. That looks like a good plan. Even with scouting and avoiding engagement, that looks like it would still get us there faster. Not as fast as the road, but fast enough. I think the best plan is for the bulk of our people to head down to the river path, then we run a small scout group slightly ahead to look for trouble. In the meantime, we send a recon party, no more than four, to get some direct intel on what's going on with the Hobgoblins. We can work out a contact schedule that should be undetectable."

Holland still had a look of discomfort on his face.

Fool noticed it as well and spoke up. "Just spit it out, Holland. What's the fly in the ointment?"

"That's a disgusting metaphor." Holland looked pained but shook it off. "You and Jackal are the strongest in our group. We'll need to split you two up for us to have our best chance at success. One of you should stay with the main group, and one of you will need to head out with the recon group."

Jackal and Fool looked at each other. They'd been a team since the beginning. They'd both run their own solo parts of missions, but they were a solid team for a reason. They covered each other's weak spots. It was one thing to go off and fight a monster solo; another thing to be apart for what was looking like a few days. It made Jackal uneasy, especially since he knew where he would do the most good.

"I'll run with the recon group," Fool said to Jackal's surprise. Fool turned to look at Jackal. "What? I'm built for stealth and confusion. You're the tank. Recon needs sneaks, not smashes. You need to be with everyone else, because if we screw up or it all goes bad, you're the one who can stand up best in any kind of fight. I'm happy to run if we screw up. They won't have that chance. They need you."

"Fool's right," Holland said. "We need you with the main group."

"I'm taking Olivia too," Fool said.

"What?" Holland and Jackal said at the same time.

"She's my charge," Holland continued. "She will stay with the main group where she can be protected. She has no stealth skills at all!"

"I know," Fool said. "But she's coming with me anyway. You're going to have to trust me on this."

"I don't have to trust anything," Holland said. "It's up to her. And I'm not seeing any reason why I shouldn't advise her to stay with the main group."

"That's fine," Fool said. "But she'll agree to come with me anyway. Trust me."

Holland glared at him. "They will be back soon, and we'll talk about it. I'm going to get everyone ready for the push north."

As soon as Holland was out of earshot, Jackal asked, "You sure this is a smart decision?"

"Feels right," Fool said, "and I'm going to work with my instincts on this one. Got a specific objection, or just something general?"

"Any idea what's up between you two? Not everyone's noticed, but some of us are picking up on the vibe."

Fool looked off into the woods. When he turned back to Jackal, the look on his face was calm and resolute. "I think it's a kin thing."

"Kin?" Jackal decided to push a little and see if he'd been right in his earlier hunch. "Pardon my biases here, but I'm not seeing any family resemblance. I mean, she's…"

"I had a bit of a thing with a woman, long ago. Coworker. I was married. She was bright, fun, challenging. Things maybe went a little deeper than they should have. Had to make a choice between her and my wife, and I chose my wife. Had a lot of regrets since then, but never saw her again after I made that choice. She took a job out of town, left the next day. She was Nuxalk."

"From Bella Coola?"

"Nah, but her family was. I think. I'm not really sure. I feel kinship, but I can't tell you why. Might be because something more happened than I know about, or it might the Trickster pulling some strings. Her magic comes from him, same way my Skills do. So, a few different ways to connect."

"And you think going out on a combat patrol is the time to work that out?"

Fool grinned at Jackal. "Hell no. But I think the Trickster does. I'm getting nudges, and I think if the two of us don't get away from the rest of you for a while, it might not go so well for everyone else. Do you really want a Trickster God paying more attention to what we're doing?"

Jackal stood up straight and looked into the forest. "Good point."

Chapter Seventeen

Fool's team caught sight of a Hobgoblin patrol later in the afternoon. Blossom was in the lead, and Fool had been paying careful attention to how the rangy, almost rat-looking Mousekin moved. It wasn't that he moved without sound, because he did make noise. Fool could see his feet touching the ground, brushing aside a rock or a twig, but somehow the sound seemed to be coming from somewhere else, from something else, like a piece of bark being tapped by a branch in the wind.

He'd almost figured out how Blossom was doing it. He altered the momentum of his steps. Fool was realizing that the normal noise people made walking through the woods had to do with how suddenly the noise started, a kind of momentum of noise caused by verticality and mass.

Blossom was slowing his steps every so slightly, but just at the last minute. The resulting sound was more natural. Not jarring or artificial at all. And he didn't look especially stealthy while he did it. He was the perfect person to be on point. He walked at a nearly normal pace and kept all of his attention on his surroundings, only glancing down every few steps to plan the next place to put his feet.

Daffodil, in contrast, was hunched over, keeping as low as he could— challenging for him, because he was the biggest and burliest of the Mousekin.

He also sported the closest thing Fool had seen to a beard on the murine race. Oddly enough for his size, and against Fool's prejudice, he was one of the Mousekin Mages.

Daffodil was predominantly a fire mage, but he'd grown up in the backwoods of his home planet and had learned to hunt before he could walk, clutching onto his mother like a possum. Blossom had picked up his stealth skills the hard way—as part of the process of qualifying as a sniper in the Mousekin armed forces. The other aspect of that qualification—a rifle that was almost twice as long as Blossom—was on Blossom's back.

Olivia managed her stealth with a bit of natural talent. Her folk were mostly at home on the sea, but she'd spent more than her share of time running through the woods. Her magic helped as well. Whatever the real focus of her chaos-magic (which she still wasn't talking about), it had a damned strong natural element that Fool could feel. Her magic just made her somehow more part of the woods.

Fool didn't bother trying to be stealthy. His skills worked better when he just relaxed and sort of stumbled about. He kept up a Geas with a simple rule that would direct anything that heard his passage to believe it was a noise they'd made themselves. Simple and easy, and it would also work as an early warning system since he'd notice a deeper Mana draw if the Skill needed more juice.

It hadn't triggered at all though when Blossom froze. The rest of the team froze in reaction. When Blossom held up his hand and patted down, they all slowly lowered themselves to a squat, but didn't move anymore.

They'd been heading steadily northwest since leaving everyone else, and they had passed the area where Jackal had killed the Bugbear about four hours previously. It had been raining about then, which was perfect. The forest floor in that area was a sponge for rain, and as a result, it was obscuring what evidence had been left of the fight.

That had seemed like good news until now.

Blossom turned, just his head, and very slowly, until he was looking at Fool. He crooked a finger and beckoned him forward. Fool dropped a little lower and crept forward. No sense in straining his Mana.

The rain had stopped about half an hour ago, and the sun dappling through the cedar boughs was strong enough to make the air muggy. At least it kept their footsteps softer.

When Fool got to Blossom's side, he was able to look over the downed log.

Fool's team had been following an old park trail, poorly maintained and constantly rising. The theory had been that if the Hobgoblins were camped out on the road north, then they would come almost directly south to the point where the fight had taken place.

With that in mind, Fool had pushed them to take this path with the reasoning that they would be outside of the most likely path any follow-up patrols would take. They would be, in effect, taking the high road, keeping up and out of the most likely patrol routes. They would gradually move more north once they passed through a few mountains.

The fallen log Blossom was looking over was on the edge of the trail, up against the trunk of a thick old tree. It was also at the top of a steep series of switchback trails. He couldn't see where the trail was coming from, but it seemed to continue on to meeting their current trail about a half-kilometer farther down on their right.

About halfway down those switchbacks, he saw a Hobgoblin patrol. They were stopped at a wider, flatter section of switchback, and some of them had dropped their packs and were drinking water. One of them was listening to two others as they talked and gestured, and Fool got the opinion, from the glances, that they were deciding which way to go next.

Fool swore under his breath. This team was way off of the predicted path. If they came up the trail, it would be a fight. There were six of them, but from here, he couldn't see if other scouts were out doing overwatch or lagging behind.

He was tempted to use one of his Skills to see if he could get a sense of what sort of Skills they had, Levels, and all the rest, but he was leery of doing that.

Holland had given him a heads-up that Hobgoblin armies were peak professionals and usually took steps to give themselves operational security. The extent of that would depend on funds. If they had the funds, they might be able to detect Fool's peeking, then it would be a fight. And that wasn't a fight Fool wanted, because if they had the funds, they probably had a much bigger army. Fool wasn't relishing the thought of running through the mountains for weeks, trying to outwit an army.

Well, maybe a little.

Still, he'd rather be cautious until he knew more, and for the moment, their quartet didn't appear to be in any immediate risk. The Hobgoblins hadn't detected them, or they'd be more on alert. So, they had a little time to talk over things.

Fool tapped the subvocal communication device Holland had issued to everyone on their team, giving them the ability to have quiet conversations. "Blossom, what do you think? Take 'em out, surprise them? Or hang tight and hope they move on?"

"No fighting. Might be more. No noise," Blossom said.

Fool nodded, then slowly backed away and crept back to Olivia and Daffodil to fill them in on the situation.

"Makes sense," Olivia said. "If they're being really cautious, they might be swinging side to side off of the main track. The missing Bugbear was probably a scout, right? So, they expect he might be coming back a different route. Don't want to walk all the way following his trail only to find he swung back and beat them back to camp. Same if he got eaten or something. Don't want to walk into a trap. It's what I'd do, work a search pattern in. Not ideal, but safe. Bet they turn back in a bit."

Daffodil nodded at that. "It's not what we'd do, but everyone has their own patterns. I guess we'll find out soon."

"No sense in taking a chance," Fool said. "Daffodil, you keep an eye on the trail ahead. Oliva, you keep an eye behind. Blossom and I will watch the Hobgoblins and let you know if they come back up. Don't worry about noise if you see another party coming from either direction. If that happens, we're in a fight regardless, and we'll deal with it."

They nodded at him, then turned to cover their respective directions. Fool worked his way back to Blossom.

It was weird to be moving slowly in the now-warm afternoon. From the trail they were on, the Hobgoblins were invisible. The trail at this point had turned into a natural sort of ditch for the last bit, with the upper part of the trail undercut against the slope of the mountain. Fool had been keeping an eye on the upper part, because the lower part was mostly hidden.

And here he was, sneaking about because the Hobgoblins were below. He felt like a kid sneaking around upstairs during one of his parents' house parties—supposed to be fast asleep but wanting to know what the grownups were doing and what all those weird noises were that happened around the laughing and shouting.

Somehow, Fool didn't think that the Hobgoblins were playing board games or cards. Still, he couldn't help but stifle a bit of a giggle at the recollection. The only thing that would make this more fun would be if he was wearing his old onesie pajamas…

He bit back that thought before an actual giggle escaped, and he joined Blossom in looking carefully over the log. He noticed that Blossom had taken the time to unlimber his big sniper rifle and set it just so along the log, ready to pull it up and into action if needed.

The Hobgoblins were clearly getting ready to move. The ones lounging about were standing back up. Bottles were put away, backpacks donned, and weapons brought to patrol positions. It was easy to see which one was in charge, the one they all kept turning and glancing at, while being careful not to make eye contact. Clearly a decision was about to be made, and they were all afraid of being chosen.

The leader was a taller, thinner, meaner looking Hobgoblin. He had the same kind of ears as the goblins did, but they spread to the side instead of rising straight up. He had a sort of nasty permanent grin and a wide mouth. It showed his teeth. His military uniform was broken up a bit by the slightly gaudy looking sword on his right hip. Clearly an officer of some kind. Fool would take him out first if a fight happened.

Fool froze as the officer looked up the hill and pointed. It took a serious effort of will not to duck his head down, but Fool had learned that against the backdrop of a pacific rainforest, sudden movement was the telltale. It was hard to make out a face against the mottled greens, yellows, browns, and greys that covered the slope. He would be seen if someone knew he was there and was looking right at him… but odds were in his favor if he stayed perfectly still.

The other hobgoblins looked up the hill as well, and Fool figured that was it.

But then they all turned back to the officer, who then pointed south, and they all looked that way.

Then set off in a march.

Fool didn't risk letting out a breath or collapsing in relief. Not yet. He kept looking, unmoving along with Blossom, until the patrol marched off to the south and out of sight.

"Well, that was fun," Blossom said. "Happy to keep up this pace the whole way."

Fool looked at him. "How so?"

"Not being seen. Works for me."

Fool snorted at that, then slowly stood and walked toward the others.

"Now what?" Olivia asked.

"Now?" Fool said. "Looks like you were right. So, I think we just keep on going. If they are searching out in pendulum sweeps, then we're probably past the farthest out they'll go. We should be clear until we get to their camp. So, we keep pushing on. Blossom, Daffodil? Thoughts?"

"Stick to the plan," Daffodil said. "Something goes wrong, the planned route is where our people will come looking for us, so best to stick to it as long as we can."

Blossom nodded as well. "Be a bit easier for the next day, but by tomorrow evening, we'll need to look out for routine patrols and defenses. We don't really know where they are or in what size, so we'll need to be extra careful then. But I think we're in a good place now, so we might as well move a little quicker, cover some territory. Move fast now so we can move slow later."

"Works for me," Fool said. "Next bit is gonna be rough though. This trail doesn't look like it's going to get any less steep, but hey, the System buffed our endurance, right? Hell of a lot easier than it would have been before this."

Olivia didn't return the smile. She was actually looking a bit grim, and Fool noticed she was holding a metal sign. She must have found it on the side of the trail. From the back, it looked like a BC Parks trail marker sign.

"How do you guys feel about omens?" Then she turned the sign around.

It was a BC Parks sign. Fool guessed it had come from the next junction up the trail. Someone or something had probably torn it off some time ago and dropped it back here. It was a simple direction sign that said "Battle Mountain: 30kms."

Jackal watched Roger carefully step around the rocks. The spring melt had mostly finished, and for some reason, the river was running far lower than normal. That was in their favor, as it gave them a much easier passage.

His real worry when they opted to take the lower route along the river was that parts of it would be impassable. The terrain was unbelievably rugged. The river had cut through the forests and down into the edges of the mountains like a knife. A sharp and jagged knife. The best parts of the river had a low, flat bit of loam on the edge of the forest, leading to an undercut bank over rocks. You could walk almost in comfort along that.

Unfortunately, those were the rarest parts of the river route. There had been, some time ago, a bit of a trail running alongside the river. It had become long overgrown to the point where it was hard to follow. And the undergrowth next to the river was impassible for the most part. If the river hadn't been so low, they would have had to occasionally hike the hundreds of meters up the steep vertical stone and climb back to the road to pass some sections.

With the low river level, they could mostly just walk on the river rocks. It wasn't fast, and it was a real challenge, but it was easier than it might have been. There'd been a steady downpour at the start of the journey, and Jackal had worried about flash flooding, but it hadn't seemed to affect the river level at all. A small mercy.

As the afternoon had drawn on, the heat grew. The rocks were absorbing some of the heat from the sun, but the breeze from the briskly flowing water was keeping that to a minimum. The real source of the heat seemed to be a hot, dry breeze that was coming down with the river. And the more they walked along, a sulfurous smell became a more pronounced part of the hot breeze.

Roger was the first to notice the issue and give them the warning they needed. As Jackal watched him, he stopped and looked down at the river, then scooped something up. He stood, looking at the thing in his hand. Jackal was only a few steps behind him, so he stepped up to see what it was.

"Check this out." Roger offered his open hand to Jackal and showed him the walnut-sized black rock. "It was floating on the river."

"Pumice," Jackal said. "Not surprising. This area used to be volcanic. Must have been knocked loose in the rain. Probably lots of it in the area."

"There's another one," Roger said and pointed into the river. "And another!"

Jackal looked a little closer and saw another of the little black rocks floating down the river, followed by another. Then he looked up the river, toward the bend just ahead of them, and saw even more coming down.

Something clicked in his mind.

"Run," Jackal said, shoving Roger toward the woods. "*Run*! Uphill!" He gestured frantically as Eric turned to look at him.

The Mousekin didn't turn to look, Jackal noticed. As soon as he'd said run, they'd instantly bolted into the woods.

Jackal sprinted forward, grabbing Eric by the shoulder, and dragged him up the riverbank. Eric slipped at one point and Jackal didn't even slow, relying on his strength to pick up the younger man bodily and carry him up and over the bank and into the woods.

Jackal kept running up, and everyone followed him as an eerie susurrus rumbled from the direction of the creek. When they got to about twenty meters up, Jackal stopped and turned to look back.

The river had turned black. It was a roiling mass of tumbling black rocks, spreading from bank to bank and hunched in the center. The black was so uniform that for a moment, the river looked like freshly laid asphalt pavement, shimmering in the summer heat.

A terrible rumbling followed from upriver, with loud splitting cracks, and the ground shook. This time, Jackal didn't have to yell anything. Everyone backed farther up the slope, unsure of what was coming.

The black pumice wave split and rolled up the banks, rising higher and higher. Then suddenly it was gone, and the river was back with a vengeance.

Only it wasn't water anymore. It was a thick brown sludge, a rolling mass of loose mud. Tumbling along with it were logs and trees of all sizes, even on occasion a small boulder. The sulfur stench grew stronger, and another rolling wave of heat came down, but this time it wasn't just on the river. It came with a single, powerful gust that howled through the trees, whipping them back and forth.

The patrol had hunched together to watch what was happening, and they looked for the threat all around them. Jackal kept his gaze down and relaxed after a moment. The sludgy flow had stopped, and only a murky, grim, slowly pulsing mass still moved along the river.

"What was that?" Holland asked from down around his elbow.

Jackal looked down at him, then back up again. The heat was gone, and so was most of the sulfur stench. "Volcano. Something seismic. Small eruption, broke a dam. Be way up the river though. Maybe at the lake."

Holland looked down at the river. The flowing water was long gone, but already the center of the slick mud was moving more toward the center, as the flowing water fought the intrusion to try to return to its original ways. His whiskers twitched as he watched. "Can't change plans now. I think we need to just keep going. Is this going to happen again, do you think?"

Jackal looked back up the slope, into the sky. It was still blue, the earlier clouds long gone. "No. If it had been a major eruption, we'd all be dead by now. And small eruptions mean a big one isn't likely. But something's going on up the river. Something more than just Hobgoblins."

Holland shook his head at that, resigned. Roger and Eric looked confused.

"I didn't think we had volcanoes," Roger said. "This is Canada, right? Not Hawaii. How do we get volcanoes?"

Eric wound up answering that. "Don't you remember geography class? BC used to have chains of volcanoes. One up the coast, and one through the middle. This is the middle one. The last eruption was only a few hundred years ago though. Wasn't supposed to happen again, but it's not like anyone's been monitoring this stuff in the last few years."

"Unless something made it change," Roger said. "I mean, that's possible, right? Holland, are there Skills that can make volcanoes erupt?"

Holland nodded, but he didn't look happy about it. "Anything is possible for someone with a high enough Level. But if someone of that Level is here,

215

then we are doomed. They would be far above what we would be able to deal with."

Jackal looked at him. Holland was chewing his cheek as if he had something worrying in his mouth.

"And?" Jackal asked.

"There are… other things that can cause changes," Holland said. "Some kinds of creatures that have an affinity for such environments. Some are not terrible in small doses, others…" He looked off into the distance.

"Oh c'mon," Roger said. "Can't leave us hanging like that."

Holland sighed. "Titans. Dragons. Elementals. I've heard rumors of spells of great power. It's a wide universe, and there is still much beyond anyone's understanding. Let us just hope it is a temporary change in this area's geography and leave it at that. Anything else is more than we can deal with, in any case."

"Fair enough," Roger said. "So now what? We keep going on the river and run for the hills when we see anything else like that?"

"Yup," Jackal said, and cut off further conversation by walking back down the slope.

Once he got closer, he saw that it wasn't too bad. It looked as though a plug of debris had been blown loose and had been running down the river for a bit. The river was already reasserting its dominance over the muck, washing it away in big, sweeping chunks. That told Jackal that the source likely wasn't Clearwater Lake, the source of the river, but something between there and where they were currently. Not too close, or the disruption would have been a lot stronger.

He looked up the river as he got back down the bank. The river, rolling over the debris, had risen to the old bank almost. Going forward would be harder for them. Hopefully, the river would wear away most of the debris before long though.

They walked almost the entire rest of the day without any more incidents, which worried Jackal. They hadn't run into any wildlife. Before the system, this park had been teeming with wildlife. They should have run across deer, bear, maybe even a cougar by now.

In the System, they should have absolutely been attacked by monsters or mutated animals by now. The overall Mana Level there was more than high enough for that.

Either something was scaring off all the animals—and increased volcanic activity would absolutely do that—or something was killing them all off. Jackal couldn't imagine an army of Hobgoblins would have that effect, unless it was a much larger army than he anticipated.

Something very odd was going on in this park, and he couldn't figure it out.

Something very odd. That seemed more likely as he realized his odd feeling wasn't just a hunch. Someone had eyes on him.

They had just passed another deep-cut canyon in the river that had required them to climb up and over, and ahead of them was another steep section, with the river dropping in a series of waterfalls. This section was a little different though, because a second, smaller river was joining the main river. That river was another fast-flowing, rocking river. Its water was more of a foaming green than the clear green of the main river. That usually meant more silt. Jackal had leaned that sometime ago. Probably there was a glacier at the head of that river. It was small enough that its waters blended into the main river after only a few turns.

Still, the forest on either side of that river was broader and more open. It still rose into another set of mountains, but Jackal saw that the landscape had been subtly shaped into almost terraces. Wide flat green, spotted with large river rocks, but looking somehow more inviting. More… civilized. It was also, he realized, not natural.

It was a built-up feature, terraforming done by an alien race.

The race that the naked, green young lady staring at him from across the river probably belonged to.

Chapter Eighteen

The Hobgoblins fired first.

It was a testament to the professionalism of their training. They hadn't even paused upon seeing Fool and his team as they came around the corner of the trail. Opened fire without hesitation. He'd almost believe that they'd expected them, except that he saw the surprise in their eyes even as they fired.

Fool's team had gotten lax on their long patrol in the second day. They should have been far away, almost at a right angle to the east from the Hobgoblin base.

The trail they were on, from the map they'd found on a post, even led away from the location they figured the army would be at. If the Hobgoblins were heading south, Fool and his team should have been behind their lines already. He'd been planning on cutting west once they got to the bottom of this trail, which was winding its way down the far slope of one of the mountains.

So close. Another half-kilometer down, and they'd be back to sneaking around. They'd all naturally relaxed. They hadn't seen a single soul since the encounter the previous day, and the afternoon's path had led them through steep trails, but trails with a much better view of their surroundings.

A large swath of the park had been scoured by a recent forest fire, and they'd taken advantage of the open view that provided to scope out the terrain.

It had been nothing but a vast and open natural area. Fool had even been able to look far enough west to see some hazy remnants of smoke from what he figured had to be the Hobgoblin camp. But nothing else, aside from some oddly stubborn puffy clouds clinging to some of the mountains to the north. The confidence the view gave them had them all sauntering a bit as they resumed their patrol.

The weather had helped too. Sunny, with a light breeze. It had been an absolutely beautiful day for a walk in one of the loveliest parks.

Until they'd walked back down into the forest and taken the turn into the Hobgoblin force.

While he dodged to the side, Fool took a quick mental snapshot. There were almost a dozen of them. All Hobgoblins. It struck Fool in that moment just how much they looked like a grown-up version of the goblins. They had the same almost-oval head shape and oversized pointy ears. Big, wide mouths filled with teeth, but not quite as sharply pointed.

The differences were telling though. The Hobgoblins were all quite a bit taller. Most seemed to be normal human height and about the same build. They all wore matching uniforms, modern military in design but with blood-red accents and rank markings. Blood-red eyes as well, but instead of a goblins' madness and keen bloodthirstiness, the Hobgoblin eyes were bright and sharp. Intelligent.

Hobgoblin Private (Blooded Hob Level 27)

HP: 370/370

MP: 210/210

That was all the time Fool had for looking, as his dodge carried him right into the side of the trail, smacking into the dirt undercut and displacing some of the rocks. Fool had been in the lead, and with the Hobgoblins coming up the trail and having to turn right, the fire that missed Fool went off into the forest instead of down the trail, giving Blossom, Daffodil, and Olivia time to react.

Blossom dropped right to his belly, drawing a sidearm. Daffodil threw up a mystic wall that repelled the few shots that came down the trail. Olivia sprinted off up the slope and into the woods overhead.

Fool was a bit surprised by that, but also relieved. She could take care of herself.

For now, he had to deal with the Hobgoblins. After firing off the first volley, they had wasted no time charging forward, still firing.

Fool didn't think, just reacted. He threw himself forward, diving for the legs of the closest Hobgoblin, and tackled him to the ground.

That resulted in the next two falling like bowling pins. The one closest to the edge tumbled over with a shriek. Fool didn't even have a knife in hand to follow up with though.

And he was flat on the ground.

He turned in time to see the rest of the patrol pointing their weapons down on him.

Only their brief hesitation at firing and wounding one of their own saved Fool. And Blossom's reaction speed.

The Mousekin fired right away, putting a charged pistol round into the head of the closest Hobgoblin. Apparently, Blossom favored "special" rounds, stacked with his Skills, as the Hobgoblin's head exploded a split second later.

It was only a second delay, but it was enough for Fool to activate his Oh God Don't Hit Me Skill. It had the intended effect of making anyone aiming at him hesitate to pull the trigger. Which would have been the perfect start of a sequence of fun, but these weren't random monsters. They were trained soldiers, and they reacted on instinct.

Ignore one target that was out of bounds. Switch to the next target.

Blossom was low-firing from a near-concealed position.

Daffodil was standing, relying on his hasty shield for defense while he prepared his next spell.

It wasn't enough.

Hobgoblin doctrine on the battlefield was to burn Mana fast. Get the kills, worry about regen later. Every attack came with a full stack of Skills.

The Hobgoblins were well-equipped, so only about three-quarters of the bullets were stopped by Daffodil's shield. The other quarter were the kind designed for a System battlefield and built to pierce armor. Half of those were meant to pierce armor and resistance Skills, and those all failed against the barrier. Of the remaining handful, two were aimed poorly and, after passing through the shield, went off into the woods.

The last three ignored the shield completely and passed through Daffodil. Not directly—that would have left him only wounded. Instead, these rounds tumbled and turned and broke apart the way they'd been designed to do, causing maximum damage on the battlefield.

They entered Daffodil as three small holes in a neat line up his torso. They exited as three large holes, scattered around his back. Daffodil didn't even have time for a final breath before he died, crumpling into a heap behind Blossom.

Blossom kept firing, and the Hobgoblins shifted their fire down.

Fool swore and used Aziz to blast light into the eyes of the Hobgoblins. They blinked and their fire jerked around, but Fool heard the sudden squeal as Blossom took some hits. Fool jerked to his feet, pulling out his warhammer.

Oliva hit them with a tidal wave.

A vibrant purple wave, looking almost like flame, lashed out at the Hobgoblins, striking them all at head height. Half of them tumbled over the side of the cliff, and the other half screamed and grabbed their ears.

Fool didn't wait now that his feet were under him. He leapt forward and smashed his hammer into the temple of the closest enemy, feeling the hard crunch of bone suddenly give way to softness. He spun to hit the next target, but there was a bright flash, and his own vision went away.

He realized he couldn't hear.

Trust. He had to trust in his instincts and in his luck.

He sat down, hard and sudden.

All around him where the distant sounds of shrieks and yells, as if they were coming from a few rooms away. He felt the heavy thumps on his chest of guns being fired close by, then a much larger bang as an explosion went off.

He blacked out for a second.

Just a second, but when Fool opened his eyes, he could almost see. There were bright and black spots all around his vision, and his ears were burning and buzzing. He'd dropped his warhammer somewhere, and he fumbled around until he found it. Weapon in hand, he stumbled over until he felt the side of the path, then he scrambled over until his back was firmly up against the mountainside.

It seemed to get quieter, and he heard a mumbling near him, a muffled voice. He blinked a few times, and that seemed to help. Olivia was leaning in front of him, mouthing some words. He nodded. She was probably asking him if he was okay, and he felt all right. She didn't look as if there was any threat, so he fumbled for his pouch and found a healing potion. Slammed it back.

His hearing came back, then his vision.

Bodies on his right. Couple of Hobgoblins crashing, downslope, and heading away. To his left, Blossom was groaning in pain, curled up a tiny ball, with Olivia frantically trying to help him.

Daffodil, flat on his back and not moving.

Fool crawled to Blossom and laid hands on him, summoning his healing skill and applying it over and over until the agony on Blossom's face turned to something more sane.

Fool looked at Olivia. She seemed unhurt, but tears were streaming down her face.

Fool stood and looked down the slope. He saw bodies down the slope, and a flicker at the edge of his vision. One last Hobgoblin soldier, running off to the west, in the direction of their camp. He looked to the right and saw a few mangled and burned bodies.

Blossom must have tossed a plasma grenade, or something stronger, right into the attacking Hobgoblins. And judging from the state of the bodies, and the amount of health Fool noticed he was repairing on himself, the grenade must have set off something explosive the enemy patrol was carrying.

"Fuck," he said and turned to face the other two. "We good to travel?"

Olivia nodded shakily.

Blossom was slowly standing. "Soon. I need to take care of Daffodil, then we can move on. They'll be back with more, yeah?"

"Yeah," Fool said. "We fucked that up. They'll be after us now. We need to get some distance before we figure out what to do next. Don't want to risk anything until we get that distance."

"Back on the trail?" Olivia asked.

"No. Too obvious. Uphill." Fool pointed up the slope of the mountain. "Head for the peak, get some height, and see what's really going on. Shoulda done that in the first place, I guess."

"Bad luck," Blossom said. "It happens in war. You just have to roll with it."

He turned around and crouched by Daffodil, and Fool saw he was pulling out the disintegrating body bag device that Holland had used earlier. It didn't seem that Blossom was as much for ritual though, and Fool stood awkwardly watching, not knowing what to do.

Olivia walked over to Fool and stood. He noticed she was still trembling and put his arm around her. She didn't say anything, but she leaned into him. Just a little. It felt right to Fool, and suddenly he felt a deep sorrow open up inside him, paired with an odd lightness and sense of something happening that was meant to be. Like something wrong was being corrected, but not quite.

"I should have done more," Olivia said, her voice little more than a whisper.

"How so?" Fool had an idea what was bothering her, but he'd gotten pretty good at not making assumptions about people's thoughts anymore.

She leaned a little deeper into him. He wasn't a tall person, and she wasn't short, but for some reason, she seemed to snug just right under his arm, and his mind shied away from why that felt so familiar.

She took a few more breaths, then let out her breath in a long gust. "What's the point of all this magic if I can't save people?"

Fool didn't really have an answer. That was a pain he wasn't entirely unfamiliar with. "I dunno. I just keep trying to get stronger, hoping I can be of more use to people and protect everyone best I can. But you can't do that for everyone. This life is pretty bad, but it was the same in the old one. I held a lot of friends as they died and thought I could have done more. I watched even more fall apart and run themselves into all kinds of ruin."

He took a deep breath of his own. Then another.

Blossom had finally wrapped Daffodil up, and now he was sitting quietly by the body of his companion. They all waited silently for a moment, then Blossom activated whatever it was that seemed to destroy the body inside, and the black bag puffed up, then shrank down to a little cylinder. Blossom knelt back down and held it in his hands.

"I put my own life into ruin," Fool said quietly, "and I ruined a lot of other lives too. Wasn't all my fault, but some of it was. Maybe, if someone had been in the right place at the right time and said the right thing, maybe my life would have worked out differently. Maybe the lives of the people I loved would have worked out differently."

He stopped and looked at Olivia. Really looked at her, holding his eyes on her until she looked back at him.

"No one can tell you whether or not you've done the right thing or the wrong thing, not in matters like this. You gotta wrestle with your own demons, there's no way around that. But I can tell you, you never stop doing better. This moment is always the start of you doing better, and don't you waste any of it dragging more of the past with you than you have to. Respect and honor your memories but keep your eyes on the future. Those that are lost are behind you and they'll hold you up when things get dark, but you have to be the right kind of person to let them do that. You put your mind into thinking of everything you did wrong to them, you won't have room left to do good for the next people you meet. Understand? Every moment, you work on being better. Every time you do something wrong, you take that lesson and learn to be better, but don't beat yourself up about it. Don't live in the past. It'll kill you. Like it killed me. Like it killed…"

He closed his eyes and stopped that thought before it went too far. He was speaking from far too much experience.

"I understand," Olivia said. "Thanks. I mean, we all lost a lot of people, but it's always been me and the guys, you know? We're a team, we work together. We screw up, but it's always us. Never me, you know?"

Fool let her have her peace for a moment as he wrestled with his own thoughts.

"Daffodil died because I wasn't strong enough to stop them," she said, and her voice was going cold. "I'm never going to let that happen again."

Fool turned and grabbed her by the shoulders. He could feel the Mana coiling inside her, and that special bit of chaos in her responding. This was his time. He'd taken on the Trickster's mantle as an acolyte. Not as a warrior, not as a mage, but as a priest. When he'd made that decision, he'd known what it had meant, but he'd also let himself forget, let himself think that it was a title of whimsy. But it wasn't. His job was to fight what the Trickster fought.

To fight evil. The evil inside, the evil that made people yield in the face of greater force, which made them bow their heads under the whip of authority, the evil that made them curl up inside and rot from despair… the despair that the rest of the world would constantly encourage them to accept. The price of fitting in, the price of taking the easy path and being obedient to the will of the herd.

That was the evil rising up inside Olivia. The evil of accepting the yoke of the System, the way it had been forced on all of them. The strong rule the weak, and the only hope was to always strive to be the strongest, because only strength had any authority. That was the evil the Trickster opposed at all costs.

And Fool could not let Olivia turn to that. Her energy, her spirit, it was worth so much more, and he couldn't let despair turn her to that darker path.

"There is no strength in the universe that will bring anyone back, that will right any wrong that you make. You're going to lose a lot of other people. And sometimes it's gonna be your fault. But the moment you take all the blame, that's the moment you really lose. Because that's the moment you turn away from the real evil."

He turned her to the side and pointed down at the Hobgoblin corpses. "You think they didn't have people who loved them? That they didn't have hopes and dreams too? You think there isn't a Hobgoblin running away right now, thinking the same thing as you? And let's be honest here, we killed them. And we didn't have a choice. If you want to win, if you really want to make everything better, then you have to drop, right now, drop any thought that this is your fault.

"They had a boss who put them in this position. They had orders to follow, but each of them just really wanted to live and go home and eat dinner tonight. Just like we do."

He stopped for a moment and let his arms drop off of her. His eyes were feeling a little wet and he supposed he was crying, but he didn't really know.

"All of this sucks," Fool said. "And the whole world is full of people looking for someone to blame. That makes up all the hate we've been suffering from for our whole history. Some of those people put the blame on themselves, and that's just another kind of hate. And some of those people, a very small number of them, put the blame on systems or governments or cultures. Hell, these days, some people can easily blame it all on the System."

He laughed for a moment. The irony of that cut him deeply, as he remembered his old life and how he'd railed against everything that seemed to have stepped in front of him and tripped him up. Always the system and never his own actions. But now it really was the System. But not all.

"It's not just the System though. That's just another tool for the real unfairness. And that unfairness is universal and eternal. It's that little seed that starts in one person and tells them they have to be in charge of another person. That's the real evil. And that's what we're here to fight. You know it."

He poked her hard in the chest. "You feel it too, don't you? Right here? Right at the core of you, and right from where all your magic comes. The Trickster lives in you, and never wants to let that other fool have his way with the universe. We're all that stands between everyone and the stinking mess of order, screwing up life for everyone."

Olivia was looking up at him, and her eyes held a lot of confusion, but also something that might be hope.

"Look," he said, "it's not ever going to be straightforward or easy, but the best thing you can do is keep your hurt, keep your anger, and don't ever let it turn inside you. Live a better life. And do your damndest to make life better for everyone else. Listen to that little punk bastard inside you that just wants to fuck shit up. That's what the world really needs. And you fuel that little bastard with all your hurt and loss. And you change the world. You break it when it tries to change you, and you never give up in the face of that. Understand?"

She nodded. She shimmered a bit in Fool's vision, and he knew that meant that he was crying, and he was afraid he knew why, but he wasn't ready to deal with that yet, so he leaned in and hugged her. She sobbed, and he held her until she was back to just sniffling.

"It'll be okay," he said. "It's just hard sometimes. I know."

She snuffled in his arms, then hugged him back, more fiercely. "Thanks."

On some strange instinct, he ruffled her bone headdress as if it was hair. "We're all in this together, kid."

"Ain't your kid," she said with a smile.

"If you two are done," Blossom said, "we need to get going. They don't need to go all the way back to their base to get reinforcements, and it's gonna get hot here pretty quick."

With a nod, Fool gave Olivia one more encouraging clap on the shoulder, then he picked up what gear was lying around that might be useful. He grabbed one of the rifles from the Hobgoblins and passed another one to Olivia, but she declined. For a moment, he thought about grabbing some ammo, but Blossom was already heading up slope, so Fool went up after him.

Time to go.

Chapter Nineteen

"Mousekin?" Band Eller stood and paced across the room, not even trying to hide his agitation.

Hellgaze tried not to roll his eyes. The Thirteen Moon Sect sniper might be an Advanced class and above Hellgaze in abilities, but he didn't know, or care to know, a damned thing about running a military operation.

Not that Hellgaze minded, for the most part. The more things military bored the pompous ass, the less he bothered to stick his nose into how Hellgaze ran things. Which was perfect, because the operation the sect had hired them for was pushing the limits of their budget as it was. Overseeing their mining operation and collecting their "recruits" to do the mining was within the budget. And since the contract was on a new Dungeon World, a fair bit of security work had been part of the contract.

Hellgaze had been prepared to cope with monsters, small bands of marauders, and pissed off locals. But that was about it. The actual higher-Level monsters they'd been encountering were almost strong enough to exceed what the contract allowed for, but Hellgaze knew he was collecting a lot of points for his outfit by skillfully managing his forces to cope with it all.

But that management took up most of his time. He couldn't afford to split his attentions according to the capricious whims of the employer's representative.

Unfortunately, Band Eller had been in the room when the long-range patrol group had returned with their report.

Band Eller paced back. "Are you seriously wanting to divert resources now? We're already running behind, and you want to pull some of your troops to hunt down a mousekin?"

Hellgaze let out a careful sigh. They were on schedule, but Band Eller had a habit of exaggerating when he was angry. "Mousekin. Not 'a' Mousekin. Are you familiar with their standard operating procedures?"

"Cheap mercenaries, tiny things. Low challenge rating."

Hellgaze took a deep breath and glanced at the lieutenant who'd brought in the report. The officer was standing behind Band Eller and wasn't bothering to hide the roll of his eyes.

Lovely. The rep was an idiot, but he was still their employer, and now Hellgaze would have to discipline a good officer for his breach. Couldn't let discipline get lax when working for idiots. Professionalism was why the Hobgoblins were able to charge premium rates, after all. But that reprimand would be later, and in private.

"They don't charge a premium price, that's true. But that's because they hire out in much smaller, more specialized units. And they are indeed small creatures, but they train hard. And they always travel in teams. If we see one Mousekin, then at a minimum there will be almost two dozen more. That's about the smallest team they hire out, and that still comes at a high cost. And this does represent a serious problem, because they're an expensive, specialized team. They simply won't randomly stumble across our operations. We have to consider that someone has hired them specifically to infiltrate the area and scout out what we are doing here. I would suggest that your secrecy regarding this mission has been breached, and you may need to call it off."

"Impossible!" The representative looked as if he was about to say something but stopped himself. He turned and looked about the room. The only other people in the room were the lieutenant and Hellgaze's attaché. "You. And you. Out." Band Eller pointed at them.

They both turned to look at Hellgaze, and he nodded. They left, the attaché closing the door behind them.

Band Eller walked up to Hellgaze, his mirrored mask stopping inches away from Hellgazes's face. "You are not to share this with anyone. The Thirteen Moon Sect is overextended here. We've recently had an issue in one of the southern towns. Some unexpected resistance has been showing up. That's why we need what we are mining, and we need it now. We're close to getting what we need. But finishing this depends on your people keeping the pressure on. Because if you don't, if it's not complete in time, then we are done on this world. You were hired to assist in this process. Nothing is more important than finishing that work, do you understand?"

"I do," Hellgaze said. "That was clearly written in our contract. I'm just advising you, as I am required to do, on what I feel is the best course of action. Secrecy was part of the original operation requirements, and that has been lost. The presence of a Mousekin team clearly indicates that someone has specifically hired them to interfere with the operation. In my opinion, we should eradicate that team as fast as possible."

Band Eller leaned back, then walked over to a window and looked out. "Just ignore them. Increase your security patrols around the site, but don't pull any troops away. They can just cut their rest periods. I recall that is allowed under the contract?"

Hellgaze rankled at that. It was true that the contract had a stipulation for skipping rest periods, but this wasn't the intended use. Still, as it was written, the representative did have the right to ask that under these circumstances. Hellgaze made a mental note to have a talk with their contract department the minute this job was done.

"I will pass those orders along," he said. "In the meantime, I will have our troops here continue to patrol the area around the base. Would that work?"

"That's fine. Whatever you need to do."

"Excellent. It seems like two humans were with them, so they are probably who hired the Mousekin. It might be related to the townsfolk."

Band Eller nodded. "These humans have no sense of place. Good fodder, at least."

Hellgaze didn't respond. He knew that the Thirteen Moon Sect had hired Hobgoblins out of a deluded idea that they were still as barbaric as their ancestors.

This assignment made Hellgaze sick, and there was a limit to what he was willing to do and justify as "following orders." The Thirteen Moon Sect was pushing those limits pretty hard but hadn't entirely gone over the line yet.

Still, the sooner Hellgaze could finish this mission, the better. And the sooner he could get out of the room with Band Eller, the better.

"In that case, I'll head out and set up some new patrol patterns for defense of this base. I don't anticipate any problems. Apparently one of the humans was very old, so they aren't likely to be much of a problem."

Band Eller froze and turned to Hellgaze. "Old? Where they accompanied by a larger male human wielding swords?"

"No, the other was apparently a younger human. Smaller. Might have been a mage."

Band Eller visibly relaxed, and Hellgaze was curious enough to follow up.

"Is there something we should be concerned with?"

"I don't think so, but I did run into a pair of rather troublesome adventurers in a town northeast of here. One of them was an older man, the other a giant. Keep an eye open. If you see a giant human, let me know immediately. I have unfinished business with them if it turns out to be them."

Hellgaze nodded and turned to leave. He found himself somewhat hoping it was the people Band Eller was talking about. He'd love to meet anyone who had pissed him off that much.

The figure was gone before Jackal was even sure what he'd seen. It had looked like a naked young woman with green skin. She'd seemed absolutely real, except that she'd been gone instantly, disappearing before he could even blink. It had happened so fast that he was starting to believe it had been a trick of his eye, but it had seemed so real. He could have sworn he even saw her green hair tossing lightly in the wind.

"Uhmm… did you see that?" Roger asked.

"I did," Eric said. "I think. What did you see?"

"A naked chick. Just standing there. But she was green?"

"Where?" Holland asked. There was a line of tension down his body that made Jackal check if there was anything else to be seen. "Did you see it too?"

Jackal nodded, and Holland signalled to all the Mousekin to stop. They all stood, watching the strange landscape across the way, while Holland scanned it. Finally, he flicked an ear and turned.

"Norli. We won't see them if they don't want us to see them. They're watching us though. No doubt about that."

"Are they dangerous?" Roger asked.

"They can be. I think you humans would call them Dryads. Or Nymphs. They run a bit different to most folk, and sometimes prefer to set up colonies on Dungeon Worlds. Something about being attuned to natural mana, I've heard. If we leave them be, they'll ignore us. And we want to leave them alone. They tend to be pretty powerful."

"We are."

They all spun as a voice came from behind them. At first, it didn't look as though anyone was there, but Jackal spotted the speaker. It was another Norli, high up in a tree above them.

Jackal fought the instinct to draw a weapon, and he heard Holland yelling out a quick order to everyone else to keep their weapons sheathed. Jackal kept his eyes on the Norli and didn't bother to check what everyone else was doing.

The Norli was crouched on a branch. The trees by the river tended to be tall and broad evergreens, with most of their branches starting meters above the ground. This one was no exception, and the Norli was on the lowest branch. She passed a glance over the party, then settled its gaze on Jackal. Her soft, lilting voice carried evenly to everyone.

Moira Springblossom, Warden of the Trees, Bane of Goblins, Hakarta, Jecka,... (Wood-Herder Level 48)
HP: 680/680
MP: 2140/2140

"You aren't with the others, are you?" she asked. "The Hobgoblins?"

"No," Holland replied. "We're trying to reach our destination farther in the park, and we want to avoid them."

She glanced at Holland, then back at Jackal. Her gaze was disconcertingly bright, but Jackal didn't look away. She tilted her head a little, then jumped down.

It was an almost ten-meter drop, but she landed as light as a feather even though her falling speed wasn't slowed in the least. Her only acknowledgement of gravity was a slight flexing of her knees on landing, and Jackal had the impression that she only did that as a habit, a touch of artifice, like a small cultural tic.

She stood and looked right at Jackal. "You're like the others. Are you trying to get them back from the Hobgoblins?"

That made Jackal straighten. "Others? Which others do you mean?"

He bit back the urge to describe Fool. He felt like trusting the Norli, but he wasn't willing to share information that they didn't know just yet. Like how many people were in their party.

"The townsfolk," the Norli said. "The ones the Hobgoblins gathered up and brought up to the mines. Are you rescuing them? They are probably still alive."

"From Clearwater?" Holland asked. "The town to the south of here? We aren't from there, but we noticed it was empty when we passed though. Were the townsfolk taken?"

The Norli glanced at Holland, then returned her steady gaze to Jackal. "They were taken about two months ago. The Hobgoblins have been using them to extract something from the mines. We don't know what it is, but we think it's related to the volcanoes that recently erupted. We thought to rescue them ourselves, but we aren't strong enough."

Jackal looked at Holland, then glanced at Roger and Eric. Holland's face was stoic and revealed nothing. Which was not unexpected. He had a contract for a mission. While Holland was more than happy to take charge and offer advice, this was clearly a situation out of his control. Despite how he might feel. And Jackal mentally chided himself for that. He'd been checking with Holland to see how the Mousekin might react, but he already knew. The real question was Roger.

Roger was looking a little green, but it was rapidly changing to a red fluster as his brain caught up to the words. "Slaves? Did they make slaves out of them?"

The Norli nodded, but didn't say anything, keeping her odd focus on Jackal.

"Fuck that!" Roger said. "We've got to free them! Holland, what can we do?"

"We're not really set up for this. The Hobgoblins are likely to outnumber us and out-Level us. The smart thing would be to head back to the vehicles, then back to Prince George. Rally a larger force. Contact your father and have him secure even more, then make a concentrated sortie to rescue the townsfolk. However…"

Roger looked at Jackal, and his eyes were wild… then they steadied. He took a deep breath and turned back to Holland. "Never been smart, Holland. But I ain't never slacked. This is our job, isn't it?"

Holland just looked up at Roger and waited.

Roger hesitated for a moment, then nodded. "All right then. Let's be heroes."

Chapter Twenty

Fool elected not to chase the remaining member of the patrol. Blossom had been in favor of it. Fool had to admit that between him and Olivia, they probably could have caught up to the Hobgoblin if they hustled and overpowered them. The problem with that was Blossom. He was healing, but he'd been hurt pretty badly. If they wanted to take out the patrol, they'd have to leave him behind.

That wouldn't be too much of an issue under other circumstances, but Fool wasn't willing to leave a wounded ally behind, in the vicinity of something called "Battle Mountain," in the middle of a high-Level area. It sounded like a perfect recipe for a dead soldier. Not something Fool was inclined to have happen.

It had been a bit of a sour point though. Their whole mission had been to stealthily recon the Hobgoblin camp and see what kind of forces they were dealing with. If they let the patrol go, then they lost the element of surprise. Instead of sneaking up to an enemy camp unaware of them, they would at the very least be facing increased patrols. Worst case, there would be patrols actively hunting for them. Worst, worst case, they'd be walking into a trap.

From Blossom's point of view, the gambit was over. Mission fail. It was time to head back and find another way to catch up with Jackal, Holland, and the rest.

Fool wasn't ready to write the whole thing off just yet though. For one, they still didn't know what the enemy force was, and the need for that information was as strong now as it had been at the start of the mission. For another?

All he said out loud was, "Have faith."

It looked as though Olivia maybe knew what he was talking about. Blossom just muttered something about following orders.

Fool's inside voice was a little bit more complex, but there was no point in sharing that with the other two. He wanted to keep going, and the impossibility of it drove him harder. There had never been a point in his life when he'd been happy to accept any kind of authority, and that extended to being told he couldn't do something.

Or that something wasn't possible.

It wasn't that this whole mission had bored him. It had, and he'd been blaming everyone else for that. The truth was he was feeling cocky, confident—there was no risk for him. They weren't slaying metaphorical, or even real, dragons. They were on a milk run. He felt wasted, as though he couldn't really contribute anything because there was no need.

Hell, even in combat, he'd been little more than a bystander. This mission had run more to Jackal's strength than his.

And maybe that was part of the problem, he had to admit. He and Jackal were pretty well matched. Jackal was the brawn and Fool was the brains. Sure, Jackal was technically smarter, but what mattered was that they each had a role they enjoyed playing. And Fool hadn't been able to play.

Now he could play.

Ever since the run-in with the Orcabear, the Trickster had been whispering more and more in his ear to let loose. And Fool had been trying. Really trying. But there hadn't been any opportunities. He'd toyed with the idea of doing the "classic" trickster things like pulling practical jokes on everyone, but it hadn't taken him long to realize that wasn't in his nature.

His nature was to challenge authority. That was what he had been put on this earth for—to cut the feet out from under all the monarchs, to ensure that everyone had a chance to be equal. To never let the mighty rest, even for a moment.

His happiness only came when he was in over his head, and the Skills he'd been gifted by the Trickster were designed to have him excel under those circumstances. Blossom and Olivia might not realize it, but their best chance for survival, not just for the success of the mission, meant diving head-first into the danger.

Fool had no idea how he would get them out of that danger and win the day, but that was the whole point. What would be the challenge if he knew what to do?

Which was why he'd talked the other two into leaving the pre-planned path and cutting right back toward where they thought the Hobgoblin camp was. Blossom had blanched at that but conceded after a bit. By Blossom's reasoning, they were just as likely to arrive at the camp before patrols went out. And if they were very lucky, they might be able to skirt the outgoing patrols in any case, because the last place they'd expect to find them was right at their own camp.

And the sparse information Blossom had on Hobgoblin tactics told him that while they had competent scout forces, they weren't up to the standards of Mousekin snipers. The Bugbears were, but they were usually only a small part of any Hobgoblin army. So they had a chance. And, Blossom had to admit, if Bugbears were on their trail, then they weren't likely to outrun them in any case. So, he'd agreed that the best option was Fool's.

Olivia hadn't really had any input. She'd just smiled and nodded.

All of which led to the current moment. Fool had let Blossom take the lead as they set out, and even with Blossom's caution, they'd made good time. Blossom had a rhythm of movement that they all fell into naturally after a while.

Slow, creeping moments when the sun lit them the right way, a steady swaying walk when they were in the middle of the trees. Sprints when it looked like a clear and open run. Fool hadn't been surprised to see the notification that he'd Leveled up in stealth. Blossom was a real master when he was given lead. As Olivia and Fool had adapted to his methods, he'd really unleashed his skill, and there were moments during the journey that Fool swore Blossom had just disappeared, even when he was right in front of Fool.

Eventually Fool caught up to the trick. It was mostly a Perception-based Skill. Blossom was looking at the environment around them and ahead of them. Sunlight, wind, curves in the terrain, clumps of trees, types of trees. All of it. He matched his motions to what he saw. He wasn't trying to be still or invisible, but rather he was trying to move the same way the environment did. If the wind was making the branches of the trees ripple, then he moved at the same tempo, with a subtle shift to his body that made his gear mimic that ripple.

It didn't make them invisible, but it did make them a part of the environment. If they were seen out of the corner of someone's eye and they looked to see what the disturbance was, they would only see what they expected to see. Nothing in nature was truly still, though it looked that way when people compared it to the movements they were used to, the hard angles and sharp rudeness of machinery and people bouncing around each other.

It had gotten them all the way to the Hobgoblin camp. What they'd found had almost been Fool's worst fear. The original ranch was still there. A cluster of quaint wooden buildings, nestled in a wide valley/plateau blend. It absolutely looked like the kind of place rich people would go to "get back to nature" and feel like rugged ranching naturalists. It also looked as though before that, it might have been the kind of working ranch that used to exist long before Fool was born.

It was something else now. The entire area had been surrounded by new System-based fencing, a nasty-looking force-field array of some kind that looked like a cross between chain-link fencing and barbed wire. The worst part was what was on the other side of the fence.

Artillery. Aircraft. Storage bins for what looked like ammo and fuel. And a few vehicles that looked like actual tanks, low, squat, and exuding a dense lethality. The aura was even more intimidating than the many-barrelled weapons on the turrets. The rapid intake of breath that Blossom had on sighting them cemented the idea in Fool's head that they were better off ignoring those things and running for the hills if they started to move.

The only solace they saw in the camp was that it looked as if everyone was gone and only a skeleton force was left. The vehicles were all be powered down, and they watched what was clearly a bored tech walking down the lines, carefully running tests on everything.

The only things that looked active were the artillery, which was all pointed outward, ready to defend the camp against attacks of any kind. Even those were only partly manned. Of the six artillery placements Fool saw, only two were crewed. And one of those crews was apparently having a nap break.

Fool, Olivia, and Blossom were crouched behind a line of boulders at the edge of the woods, remnants of a long-ago glacier. The area between them and the fence had been cleared of any major vegetation and only the lowest of scrub was left. The whole area still reeked faintly of burning, and most of the vegetation was either heavily burned or wilting in death from the heat of the fire that had been applied to the area. It was an efficient way to clear space, but it still made Fool a little bit sick. He knew full well that the trees all around the area looked green and damp, but the reality of the entire province was that summer was always a drought and the forests turned to tinder. There was a good chance that the clearing fire might have set the whole mountain on fire, had the conditions not been a hair better than normal.

The clear lines of sight worked for Fool and company. In addition to looking into the camp, they could see the line carved in the blasted remnants of the vegetation, from the routes the patrols routinely took. They'd come out between the two closest patrol lanes, and in the hours they'd been there, they'd only seen one patrol, of two guards, and that was inside the fence. They'd lucked out on arrival and had seen the tail end of a group of scouts heading into the woods in the direction of the fight they'd had up by Battle Mountain.

Overall, it looked as though the Hobgoblins had set up this camp not as their main camp, but rather as a safe rear-area staging camp. The majority of the force looked to be elsewhere. Hopefully not off hunting down Jackal's team.

In any case, Fool was pretty sure this camp was about as sparsely manned as it was possible to be. You couldn't blame him if the idea that sparked in his head was too good to pass up.

"You think this is it?" he asked Blossom. "Any idea if this is a trap and there are more troops hiding somewhere?"

Blossom put down the equipment he'd been using to monitor the camp. It looked like a pair of binoculars without glass and had a number of odd lumps scattered across the front. He stroked one of his whiskers, looking over the site for a bit.

"Not a trap," he said. "Hardly any waste, and no sanitation facilities for the amount of people needed to man those vehicles. If they'd planned to host the main army here, there'd be a lot more infrastructure. Also, not a lot of wear marks or paths in the fields. It looks like everything was moved here and dropped. This is a supply depot for a larger operation yet to come. The bulk of the forces are somewhere else, doing something else. They'll either use this for a reserve if they run into heavier opposition, or they plan to stage here for a final assault somewhere else. Either way, bad news for someone."

"One big bad in there though," Olivia said.

Blossom nodded. "I was getting to that. At least one Advanced class, more likely two. Some big Mana spikes showing up. No way to tell who or what without a deeper recon. And I'm not sure if it's worth the risk."

Fool let out a long sigh, then dropped back down behind the berm, turning his back on the camp. "No need. I know exactly who it is. See that shiny face mask that just came out of the big building? Band Eller. He's trouble. Big trouble. And a member of the Thirteen Moon Sect, so this must be something they're up to."

Blossom went rigid, then a slow smile crept up on his face. "Thirteen Moon Sect? Well, well…"

"Who're they?" Olivia asked.

"Bad guys," Fool said. "Kind of like the mafia and slavers all in one."

"Prey," Blossom said, the grin on his face growing larger and toothier.

"I'm guessing you've got some background with them?" Fool said, turning to look at Blossom and keep an eye on any motion from the camp.

"They used to be a larger outfit," Blossom said. "But they got a little too big and turned a little too evil. Tried to take over one of our worlds and pushed the limits of what the System was willing to tolerate from slavery. We benefited from the backlash against them. They suffered, but not enough. Holland will be happy to see them here. They owe us a blood debt. If they come, we're happy to collect it."

"Works for me," Fool said. "Dude is trouble. So, do we want to try to take him out now, or head back to the rest of the gang and let them in on the gig?"

"We head back," Blossom said. "Pleasure aside, we have the information we need to complete our mission. Time to report in."

Olivia sat up a little straighter. "Might want to wait and see what happens with those first."

Fool and Blossom turned to see what she was pointing at.

To the north, from where the valley joined the mountain ranges together, there was a flicker of motion in the air. Fool settled his gaze on it, and after a second, it resolved.

Flapping wings. A bird of some kind.

A very large bird.

With bat wings.

"Oh shit," he said. "Is that a dragon?"

Jackal knew the ache wasn't physical. Just a remnant of what he would have once felt from pushing himself this hard. The trail had gotten harder to follow, and the heat of the day had long ago reached into the depths of the steep river valley. They were all clambering over rocks, roots, and fallen trees at a breakneck pace. If they didn't have System-enhanced constitutions, none of them would have been able to keep up this pace for minutes, never mind the hours they'd been at it.

The Mousekin seemed to have it easier. They were smaller than the humans, but as they moved through the forest undergrowth, they were able to rely more on their slight predilection for quadrupedal gait. They'd long since evolved past being true quadrupeds, but they could swarm over the forest obstacles as if they didn't exist.

The Norli though, she looked as if they were on a relaxing Sunday stroll. The Mousekin could swarm and flow over the forest tumble, but the Norli never seemed to need to move from their path. Jackal tried to follow the trail the Norli walked, because they seemed to know where the right place was to step, but he couldn't find it. He could almost see it though.

For brief moments, it was as though the little, tiny flecks of openness connected together. A flat bit of stump, the corner of a rock, the edge of a leaf, somehow they all formed a clear path. If he could follow that, keep it in mind, he'd be able to soar through the forest like the Norli did.

He didn't stumble when he tried, but even the thought of trying to step off the path of that brief vision made it disappear from his mind's eye. It was, for sure, a Skill that the Norli used. More than that, Jackal figured it was something inherent in how they were built... or made.

He could see the joints of the Norli moving in slightly different ways than he would expect from their otherwise human-like appearance. Their joints would bend, but they'd also slide and sometimes move sideways. It made no sense to him, and it made him slightly nauseated to watch. He could only see it if he really focused and used his Perception to its maximum, and after a bit, he stopped trying.

He found that he was moving a bit more easily though. The sweat was cooling on his skin now because there was more of a breeze being caused by his passage. When he turned to look and see how the other humans were doing, he saw that Roger and Eric didn't seem to have his issues.

And Jackal had to remind himself again that he wasn't really having issues. It was just his mind telling them he should, a legacy of most of his life being spent with a body that resisted athleticism. The two young men had been exposed to the System and its enhancements far earlier than he had, and he saw the signs of that adaptation in their movement. Each step was more fluid and had a little more range of motion than would be expected from a pre-System human… or a human who hadn't put points into their stats. Anyone could step as high as they did, moving over roots and rocks, but the inevitable fatigue, even in a high-Level athlete, would show in the momentum of their steps.

A pre-System human would start a movement with a minuscule, but present, need to build momentum. And each movement would end with a noticeable slowdown, a mental hesitation of the muscle and tendons preparing themselves to absorb the impact shock of even a normal step.

Eric and Roger didn't show any of that, at least not at a level that Jackal could see. Each step began and ended as if it was a perfectly understood motion. No hesitation, just a lift, a motion to the landing spot, and a confident slap down on the surface. And like a machine, the motion repeated over and over with no delay of fatigue evident.

Jackal shook his head. In time, he'd probably catch up or even exceed how those two were moving. But for now, he was still hindered by the phantom recollection of his old body. A recollection that was aided by the wet slap of hair into his eyes, and the burn of the drop of sweat that it brought with it.

The hair getting in his face he could remember being a more common thing, from his old body. His parents had always insisted that he keep it long, and he'd lacked the knowledge at first to tell them why he hated that so much. And later, when he'd known, he'd lacked the courage to find a way to tell them.

All of those issues had been solved with the coming of the System. He'd been given the chance to become who he'd always dreamed of being inside his head—the lone hero, the stoic champion, the total badass who could casually tell the gang to back off from threatening the lady, and when they tried to stab him, he could pull the knife out of their hand, pass it back to them, and tell them to try it again. Even though he knew the road would be long and painful, he'd leapt onto this System path with nothing but joy.

His parents hadn't lasted even an hour, from what he could tell. But they'd died together, and all things considered, it had been the closest to a peaceful death that the System would ever offer. A simple death.

His father had been a botanist and kept a small laboratory at home. From what Jackal had been able to tell, one of the specimens had rapidly evolved the ability to exude a toxic gas that put people to sleep… and suffocated them. His parents had been curled up, holding each other and smiling when he found them. He'd let his grief roll through him, then moved on to his new life. Shortly after, he'd found Fool.

Jackal almost stumbled when he realized that the Norli had altered their progress. The short green woman was still moving forward with the same ease, but now they were keeping pace with Jackal from just out of arm's reach. And somehow looking at him while still moving forward and holding that strange smile on their face.

Jackal glanced ahead quickly. They were still moving uphill, and the next three steps would be one up, one to the right, then a short hop over a rock. He could trust himself to do that, so he glanced back at the Norli. "Can I help you?"

"You aren't like the others," they said. "You've grown. Will they change as well?"

Third step done, he looked over the next bit, then risked another glance back. "Not sure what you mean. Because I'm larger? That's a Class Skill."

Somehow the Norli managed to not just start to walk in front of him—and enough off to the side that he could still see the path he wanted to follow—but also to do it walking backward. "No, not that. You've changed your shell. You've blossomed. You are a mature tree now. We haven't met many humans yet, but none of the ones we've seen have done this. Are you the oldest?"

Jackal managed not to stumble, and with a frustrated glance at the easy movement of the Norli, he decided he could keep up their pace while he replied. Even if he wanted to stop and sigh and put his face in his hands. "No, I'm not like them. My shell was wrong, so the System fixed it."

"Oh," the Norli replied. "That's a shame. You glow so bright. I'd hoped the others would do so too."

Jackal nearly stumbled at that, and he felt the ghost of a blush showing up on his cheeks. "Thank you. I'm sure they will find their own way to glow, given time." He couldn't really think of anything else to say.

The Norli seemed satisfied at that and turned to face the path. "We are here."

Jackal glanced up and saw that Holland had stopped and had raised a hand. He seemed to be on a ridge, so Jackal assumed they must have finally reached the top of the long climb, which meant they were only a relatively short distance from the first target.

Which hopefully meant that they were close enough to contact Fool's group.

Chapter Twenty-one

It wasn't a dragon. It was a wyvern, a smaller version of the great beast. Two legs instead of four. More like a lizard bat, in a way. It was still a high-Level creature the size of a bus, and it was clearly pissed off.

Not that any of the Hobgoblin army cared. At least, judging by the artillery pieces flying.

The thing landed like a serpentine bowling ball, right in the middle of the stashed vehicles, and proceeded to lay about with an intense rage.

It wasn't unopposed. The Hobgoblins were military professionals, so they had a steady watch and rehearsed actions. Every thinking organization in the System universe planned for attack by big bads because they happened.

Fool, Olivia, and Blossom watched as the troops responded as best they could. The air was lit up with spells and withering rounds of technical weaponry. Any lesser creature would have been obliterated. As it was, the wyvern took some heavy damage. It had holes in its bat wings and rows of bloody wounds stitching its sides. That may have slowed it down, but it didn't stop it.

Now all the reserves were out, and just in time. Through the flashes of fire and the furious darting of the wyvern, Fool caught a glimpse of more dots on the horizon.

Three more wyverns.

The troops were showing their professionalism, as four of the armored vehicles fired at the original wyvern. The creature shrieked in agony as one of its wings was blown clean off. It was no solace for the troops it landed on though. The wyvern thrashed through them, crushing and tossing them all over the compound.

A sudden cyan flash punched a hole through its head, and Fool turned to see Band Eller and his sniper rifle, crouched and firing at the beast. A second shot flared out, and that was the end of the wyvern.

The troops didn't pause, and those standing about were being shouted at by a larger Hobgoblin, who was directing them toward manning the artillery pieces and pointing at the incoming wyverns. To Fool's eye, they might be able to handle the incoming wave. It was going to be tough though, unless they had some good anti-air equipment. And they might. So it was time.

"Back in a bit," he said to Olivia and Blossom. "Stay here."

Fool didn't pause to see how they reacted, just sprinted toward the compound. A tiny section of the fence had been ripped down by the thrashing wyvern. He figured he could just squeeze through it. He didn't have any plan in mind, just the activation of his "Have Faith" Skill and the full trust in the quiet presence he felt joining him.

No freezing of time, no voice… different from his previous experiences. But he still knew he was being witnessed by the Trickster and that his path would be guided when it needed to be.

The field between the hiding spot and the hole in the fence flew by. He wasn't dodging or trying to hide. If a single soldier looked his way, he'd have been wiped out in a hail of fire. He knew that, but he didn't feel any fear. Just a sense of righteousness.

If he had any plan at all, it was to surprise Band Eller while the bastard was busy trying to pick off more of the wyvern—and there were more of them now. The three incoming had swollen to five, and the first three were being engaged already.

Fool reached the fence without being shot. All eyes were on the sky and the incoming attackers. No one had time to look around.

Band Eller was in the perfect position, although Fool still had to cross most of the open area to reach him. If Fool could keep up his speed, he'd be on the cultist's back before he knew it.

Fool held back on pulling out his hammer, opting instead to run that much faster. He'd have a moment before he reached his enemy to draw it, then cave in his skull from behind. He'd trust in his god to guide his hand in that blow and end that threat once and for all.

Band Eller started to get up and turn, and Fool bit back a curse. In the space of a few more steps, he could see what was happening. Band Eller had weighed the risks of the fight and decided it was a lost cause. He was heading toward a small flying craft, clearly intending to book it out of the danger zone.

Fool doubled down on his speed, pulling from every reserve he had. Geas. Oh God Don't Hit Me. He wasn't going to let Band Eller get away. Not this time. And he trusted in the Trickster. Have Faith.

The impact wasn't felt, not at first.

At first, it was just the world turning, his point of view pinwheeling. A vague sense that he'd hit something... someone? A blurred face, startled. Ugly. A Hobgoblin.

Fool latched on without thought, tumbling.

And in the middle of it all, the touch of the Trickster.

A small grenade tumbled loose from belt of the Hobgoblin and burst open in a cloud of gas as it hit the ground. Fool and the Hobgoblin spun through the cloud, head over heels, but somehow only the Hobgoblin got a lungful of the gas. Both of them skidded to a halt, sliding through the dry grass.

Just in time for Fool to see Band Eller's craft rising into the air.

Which was when he felt the presence of the Trickster evaporate into nothingness.

There was an immediate sense of threat, so he took a moment to do a quick self-evaluation. He was belly down on grass. Nothing hurt. He could smell the sharp ozone of power being used all around him, hear the cracks and roars of weapons, the shrieks of the wyverns, and even a blast of wind from the wings of one of them passing overhead. He picked his head up and looked around.

Fool was in the middle of a chaotic battlefield. Hobgoblins everywhere, armored vehicles rolling about, at least two small aircraft ripping through the air. And wyverns everywhere. The tiny hole in the fence seemed to be many, many miles away.

He was in the middle of the enemy camp, in the middle of a massive fight.

When he glanced down, he saw he was holding the tactical vest of the commander of the Hobgoblins, who was fast asleep and drooling on his hand.

"Hell," Fool said.

Nothing for it but to go with it.

Pre-System, even before he'd lost touch with things, he'd never been that strong. The gym always seemed too boring. He'd tried jogging once, but that was even more boring. He wasn't strong. He still thought of himself in those terms, but Jackal had been hammering on him also from the time they'd met to spend his precious points on improving his physical stats.

His stats were no match for Jackal's, but Fool had learned that he was now stronger than a pre-System Olympic athlete. He just never really used that strength other than to crush heads and limbs. And there, he convinced himself the hammer was doing all the work. Still, he should be able to pick up the Hobgoblin.

Fool stood and took a quick glance around. No one was looking his way. They all seemed to be quite busy trying to stay alive. Even so, he figured this was a good time to use his Geas to remind everyone that they really had more important things to worry about than what one scrawny human was doing with their boss, who was probably fine.

That in place, he grabbed the Hobgoblin by his vest and hoisted him up. Fool wound up flipping the fellow around as if he was putting on a jacket. Only the jacket was a few hundred pounds of humanoid. It felt awkward, but Fool didn't want to waste time trying to get things just right. From the fluctuations in his Mana, the Geas wouldn't last long.

He booked it for the hole in the fence and tried to ignore the myriad bumps and smacks he was getting from the unconscious alien on his back. It took a lot longer to get back to the fence and out than it had to get in, but he managed it without becoming wyvern food. The fight seemed to be going on all around him without either side really getting any sort of advantage… or at least, it sounded as though the screams of pain, rage, and frustration were equally split amongst both sides.

Fool saw a hand waving anxiously ahead of him, and he darted for it. Blossom and Olivia had found a little divot of a hole in the ground to hide in, and he slid into it next to them, dumping the unconscious body between them. They could take care of the follow-up. He'd done his part.

They were both staring at him. Olivia had a bit of a smile, but it was mostly in her eyes. Blossom… Fool couldn't quite read his expression, but the Mousekin wasn't relying on facial expressions for communication.

"What the fuck do you think you're doing?" Blossom said. His voice was level and he looked calm, but his tail was visibly twitching.

"Dunno," Fool said, hunkering low in the hidey-hole. It didn't feel very hidden, but he would have run right past it if Olivia hadn't waved him over. "Seemed like the right thing to do though."

The battle continued behind him, with no abatement apparent.

Blossom's jaw worked side to side for a bit, and he took a deep breath. "This is a Hobgoblin Major. That means, at a minimum, there is a Hobgoblin Battle Group out there. Combined arms, maybe a thousand troops. Mostly combat troops, minimal support. This is a very, very powerful military force to be here right now. Something is extremely wrong. And you just made us the main target for all those soldiers."

"Oh," said Fool.

The battle kept on, and there was a brief flash and roll of overpressure as one of the armored vehicles exploded, along with all its ammunition. A minute later, there was an ear-piercing death screech from a wyvern as it was overpowered.

Blossom and Olivia were still staring at him.

"Uhm," he added, "so… we should do something?"

Olivia buried her head in her hands. Fool assumed she was laughing. Hopefully. Blossom made a cute little hand gesture with his curled-up paws. Or maybe he was balling them up in rage. It was hard to tell.

Blossom snapped his clenched hands open. "We should kill him right now. And run. As far as we can, as fast as we can. And then meet up with everyone else and get the hell out of this deathtrap of a 'park' as fast as we can. You humans are crazy, and this has gone over the edge into madness."

"I think he's snoring," Olivia said.

"Can't kill him," Fool added. "He's asleep. That would be wrong. Besides, I get the feeling we're supposed to do something with him. Maybe we can get some information from him?"

"Frosted grubs," Blossom said.

The ground shook as another wyvern smashed into the ground a short distance away from them. Fortunately, dead. Fool glanced over at the battle. It looked as though the Hobgoblins might be gaining an edge, except another wyvern or two were winging in.

The snoring stopped.

They all snapped around and looked at the Hobgoblin, who was now muttering and stirring.

"The little grenades!" Fool shouted, pointing at the small cluster on the Major's belt. "They put him to sleep. Use another!"

Blossom grabbed one and pulled the pin. "Run!" Then he dropped the grenade and sprinted away.

"A battalion?" Jackal asked.

"That's the closest size you might be familiar with," Holland replied. "Battle group is a better translation, but I'd say that force beating the crap out of those wyverns has to be at least a thousand at full size." He passed the binocular-like devices to Jackal.

They'd climbed up over the ravine and found themselves at another small rest area. There was a rudimentary trail, and someone had even set up a bench to view the ravine and surrounding mountains. They'd moved up the trail for a while until the ground sloped down, then found themselves on a small hill offering a small bit of oversight of the enemy camp.

And the battle that was being fought.

They'd arrived somewhere near the tail end of it, just in time to see a few hundred reinforcements come streaming down from the road to the north, weapons blazing, to drive off the marauding wyverns.

Or at least attempt to. The creatures were fierce and tough. The Norli had disappeared with a squawk as soon as she saw them. It was almost half an hour before the last of the wyverns were driven off, even with the weight of extra firepower from the new troops. The Hobgoblins seemed to be in a bit of disarray. Holland had commented on that earlier, and now, looking through the viewers, Jackal saw what he meant.

They fought well in small groups, but the groups themselves were stepping on each other's toes. Some of the wyverns were being swarmed by Hobgoblin soldiers, and other groups were forced to barely hold on, going solo against the beasts.

Whoever was in charge should have been coordinating their actions, but they seemed to be doing a terrible job of it. Even so, Jackal found himself cheering a little every time a wyvern bit a soldier in half or tore one apart. It wasn't that he wanted to see the Hobgoblins hurt or killed, but every one of them removed now was one less they'd have to face later. And even if their leadership was terrible, Jackal's group was outnumbered enough that bad leadership wouldn't really matter.

Jackal sighed and put down the viewers as the last wyvern turned with a defiant shriek and flew back to the mountains.

"So, what's the plan now?" he asked.

Holland shook his head. "I can't see a way for us to get anywhere with this. Even with all these reinforcements they called in to deal with the wyverns, there will still be at least twice as many wherever the main force is, and I'm pretty sure that's going to be at the slave camp."

"At the volcano," Eric added.

The Norli had provided them with some extra details. The mine the humans were being kept at had been at the base of a series of dormant volcanoes. But after the mining had started, the volcanoes had turned out to be not that dormant anymore. Something the Thirteen Moon Sect was up to was affecting the magma flow in the entire area. It wasn't exactly rare for this part of the province. Despite what everyone thought of British Columbia, the volcanos here were still somewhat active, with the last known eruption happening only a few hundred years ago.

But whatever was happening was on a whole different scale. A number of volcanoes had erupted in the park. There hadn't been any really serious eruptions—none of the big, rocking bang types. So far it was all cracks, steam, and the odd bit of lava. As Jackal had feared, the freak flood in the river had been a result of an upstream eruption and its resulting destruction.

And that eruption had likely happened at the volcano mine where the Clearwater folk were being held. The volcano they had to go to, instead of fleeing from.

"Fuck." The exclamation was quiet, but it sat between everyone, and they all turned to look at Roger. He was holding his head, and his whole body was tense. "I'm sorry. I was an ass. I didn't think about this. I just wanted to show my parents I'm an adult, that I can handle shit better than them. This whole quest was my idea. I talked them into it, and now we're all gonna die."

His voice was pure misery, and Jackal could almost taste the burning tears he knew Roger was barely holding in. He took the few steps over to the young man and laid his hand on Roger's shoulder. For a moment, he was surprised to see how large his hand was on that shoulder. Roger was not a small man, but Jackal's hand almost swallowed his shoulder, armor and all. That was more than Jackal had ever intended, but it was what he was stuck with. His path forward was written in his flesh, in his genes, but more importantly, in his spirit. He'd chosen to grow into the world in a body so massive that he'd never again feel restrained by his flesh. He wanted to walk as a giant amongst men, and if that meant paying the price of growing even more and more distant physically from other humans? He'd paid that price his entire life. He'd accept it.

And now he'd help Roger accept his own path forward.

"Roger," he said, "let it go. You are the one here now. You are the one who needs to rise up and lead us. It doesn't matter what the cause was. This is a fight we've all chosen. All of us. The old you brought us here unknowing, but the you who is here now is the one who needs to be here. You are the warrior we need. And you don't have to do it alone. We are all here with you. And we'll all go forward with you."

When Roger looked up, his face was still streaked with tears and his eyes were red. But those same eyes blazed, and Jackal watched him grow and change as he took in one steadier breath after another.

Jackal was sure he'd never really know what was going through Roger's mind, but it was a transformation that he felt in his soul, as true as the one he'd gone through when he'd realized the System could unlock his most secret dreams.

Roger was growing and changing, accepting his destiny, becoming a leader in front of all of them. He could feel Roger's resolve growing as he took in a few more breaths, and after a moment, he stood solid and straight.

"All right," Roger said. "Let's do this then. We aren't backing out, we're going forward. Holland, we're outnumbered, but we've got no choice. Stealth?"

Holland nodded. "And speed. They've split their forces and won't be able to recover for a bit. They'll have to keep an eye open for more wyverns. And while they're doing that, both parts of their forces will be focused more on coordinating with each other than looking for new threats. If we're going to have any chance at all, we need to move quickly and head to the mines. Once we get there…"

"We can't know what they've got, so we'll have to deal with that when we get there, right?" Roger said.

Holland nodded, and Jackal saw what looked like pride in his eyes.

"Right," Roger continued, "that means we don't have time to find Fool. Sorry, Jackal. I'm sure he'll catch up with us. We're going to need the others for this, but we have to trust that they'll catch up with us. Everyone good with that?"

Jackal looked around and saw only grim agreement on everyone's faces.

"Good," Roger said. "And on the way back, who knows? Maybe we'll have time to grab that Dragon's Tongue."

That brought a hungry smile to everyone's face and brought all their shoulders up.

Holland nodded rapidly twice. "Let's go."

"What, I don't get a vote?"

Jackal spun and saw Fool grinning at him as he came out of the woods. Olivia was with him, and Blossom. And firmly tied up and gagged, a Hobgoblin captive.

Chapter Twenty-two

Fool glanced at the Major, who was looking around sourly. He was still bound, but now in a chair. After they'd reunited with Jackal and the main group, they'd quick-marched far enough away from the Hobgoblin base to set up a stealthy and secure camp before sunset. A tent had been prepared, and they'd carefully dropped the Hobgoblin into the only chair anyone had bothered to setup.

They were far enough away to not hear any further noise from the Hobgoblin base, aside from the occasional distant rumble of an explosion. The wyverns either hadn't fully given up, or some new threat had arrived. Or they were hearing new volcanic eruptions, but that didn't seem too likely.

Fool watched Holland more than he watched the prisoner. The Hobgoblin had been silent since they'd captured him, only showing a brief disappointment when he'd realized that between Blossom's thorough stripping him of all tech and Olivia's use of a Skill that locked out most other communications, he was completely cut off from summoning help. Fool really didn't have any plans for what to do with the prisoner, but the Trickster had clearly delivered him into Fool's hands for a reason.

Holland had been pacing about the tent as best as the available space would let him. He hadn't said anything, but he'd been agitated enough that all the Mousekin had quickly vacated the space, as had Eric and Olivia. Only Fool, Jackal, and Roger were left to watch the interrogation.

With another of the sideways glances he'd been giving the Major, Holland finally stopped his pacing and tugged on his whiskers. He let out a little sigh, then spoke a short, quick command. "Remove the gag."

Jackal carefully untied the scrap of cloth and stepped back. The Hobgoblin looked around warily, working his jaw back and forth for a bit. Then he sneezed.

"Gesundheit," Fool said.

"Is that some sort of curse?" the captive asked.

Fool bit back a laugh and was about to reply when Holland raised a hand to stop him.

The Mousekin walked over in front of the Major, and despite the size difference, Holland's upright stance and arms crossed behind his back gave him the appearance of absolute confidence. Even if he only barely came up to the seated Hobgoblin's chest, with its simple rank badge and nametag. The two officers locked gazes and held them for a moment before Holland spoke.

"I'm not going to waste your time or mine with any pretense. I have no interest in torture, and we are in no condition to keep a prisoner. Nor does holding you give us any sort of advantage. Your troops are currently under constant attack from a wave of monsters, but so far, they are holding themselves well. I'm sure they'll do better with you to assist them, and I know you want to get back to them as soon as you can."

The Major looked down warily at the Mousekin. "What are you proposing? Do you want to surrender to me with better terms? I can see that there are far less of you than we'd been led to believe. Are you a scouting force?"

Holland shook his head. "No point in answering that, but you do get my respect for a nice try at a reverse interrogation. I'm going to be blunt. We came here on a simple retrieval mission for something unrelated to whatever your mission is, and of no value. All of our actions would have been to avoid contact with your mission and exit the park as soon as we could. Unfortunately, one of your scouts raided our camp and kidnapped a soldier. His intention was to torture that soldier. In the process of freeing that soldier, your scout was killed."

Hellgaze grunted. "No loss."

"Be that as it may," Holland continued, "we are aware this would force you to root us out and likely eliminate us. We cannot give up our quest, so we've been moving around your forces to minimize contact as best we can."

Hellgaze sighed and shook his head. "Let me guess. You want us to let you be in exchange for letting me go?"

Holland held a steady gaze, staring right at the Major. "No. No bargaining. I know the reputation your military has. And your organization. Your leaders. You are the standard for professionalism. And yet here you are, on a brand-new Dungeon World, working for the Thirteen Moon Sect. Your paymasters must have drained them dry before they'd hire you out to them. And it's still got to burn right down to the heart of what you signed on for to work for them. But you'll do it, won't you? Because your contract is your honor. So let me ask you something, Major Hellgaze…" Holland leaned in closer to Hellgaze, his little nose inches away from the Hobgoblin. "Do you know the history our race has with the Thirteen Moon Sect?"

Hellgaze sat quietly with no movement at all. The two officers stared into each other's eyes, no emotion apparent.

Finally, the Hobgoblin sighed and shook his head. "Worst goddamned client ever. Complete assholes."

Holland leaned forward and crossed his arms. "I bet. I can't imagine working for them. I've become immensely grateful that we signed up with the humans here. Good people, strong potential. I think they've got what it takes to rise up above what being a Dungeon World could do to them."

Hellgaze grunted and looked around the room, weighing his gaze on each of the humans. When he looked at Fool, Fool did his best to keep his gaze open, staring back without pretext. The Hobgoblin, he noted, had exceptionally evocative eyes. Not just intelligence there, but a wary acceptance of things that gave him a certain cachet of worldliness. Fool found himself slightly captivated, and surprised he hadn't noticed that in the walk from the battlefield to the reunion.

"You might be right about that," Hellgaze said, turning his eyes back to Holland.

Holland nodded. "I am. Which makes me wonder if you want to see the Humans see all hobgoblins as part of what's happening to the Clearwater residents."

Hellgaze didn't move for a moment. He wasn't frozen in place, but a stillness settled over him, a sense that he was calculating outcomes and trajectories.

Fool fought back the urge to bop Hellgaze on top of the head, mostly because he realized the urge was coming from a place of fear. Or more correctly, respect. The Major was sitting bound in a chair, surrounded by enemies, captured by a stranger while his soldiers were being swarmed by wyverns... and he was calculating the best outcomes from the situation.

If it had been Fool in the chair, he'd be pouring on the braggadocio to distract while he planned his way out. Anything to distract his enemies from realizing how smart and devious he was. Hellgaze though... he wasn't bothering to hide it. He was sitting there in absolute confidence, as if he were an ambassador mulling an agreement with an equal.

He was not someone that Fool would want for an enemy.

Hellgaze sighed and once more looked around the tent. This time he made sure to make eye contact with everyone and hold it for a moment. When he looked at Fool, Fool only felt a calm measure being taken of him. When the Major's gaze returned to Holland, he simply nodded. And Holland nodded back.

"Well then," Hellgaze said, "I suppose I should be heading back. Thank you for rescuing me when that Wyvern knocked me out and dragged me away. I really do need to head back to my troops though. They need me to protect them when the Great Old One is finally awoken from his slumber. Shouldn't be long now really. No more than another day. Crazy thing to find on a backwater planet like this. Makes you wonder what sort of secrets this world holds. This whole 'Dungeon World' thing wasn't all that unplanned, I should think. Anyway, I really do need to get going. Thanks much. Please try to keep out of our way."

Somehow, through all the fur, Holland seemed to have blanched in fear. He froze for a moment, then turned to Jackal. "Cut him loose now."

Jackal cocked an eyebrow but stepped forward to free the Hobgoblin.

Roger yelped. "Wait! What the hell, man! We can't let him go. What are you doing?"

Holland held up a paw and glared at Roger. It was a testament to how much the young man had grown that he instantly shut up.

Freed of the ropes, Hellgaze stood. Startled, he looked up at Jackal. "I didn't realize you folk grew so big. Are you part giant?" He'd clearly missed the scale of Jackal, looking at him from a seated position.

"Frost Giant," Jackal said.

"Truly?" Hellgaze said, his eyes bewildered.

"It's a strange universe, isn't it?" Fool said, offering Hellgaze his sidearm back. It was the only weapon he'd had on him when Fool captured him, and he'd been hiding it in a pocket. Seemed like the thing to do to return it now.

Hellgaze turned to look at Fool, taking his sidearm without even looking at it and ejecting the magazine. He shook the magazine, bounced it against his thigh, then glanced at it and slapped it back in the pistol. "Thank you. Strange universe indeed. I don't sense anything about you that tells me how you could have captured me, but I will admit you bested me."

"Just luck is all," Fool said with his most disarming smile.

"Luck. I should point more points into that." Then he left, as Blossom opened the tent entrance and motioned to him, either having been signaled by Holland or having eavesdropped.

Fool bet on eavesdropping, but Holland didn't even look over. He was lost in his thoughts. Holland sat in the chair that Hellgaze had vacated, and he sat with a heaviness that startled them all.

"Holland?" Olivia asked. "What's up? Something he said really upset you. What was it?"

Holland looked at her with blank eyes. "This fucking planet is doomed."

Chapter Twenty-three

Everyone sat quietly for a few moments after Hellgaze left, waiting for Holland to continue.

The sun had set, and with it, the heat of the day was petering away. It felt as if there'd be some cool relief coming soon, and if the rising gusts were any indication, there was the possibility of an overnight thunderstorm. Fool would enjoy that, and he also found himself smirking a little at the thought of Hellgaze grumbling his way through the dark in a downpour.

The best part of a storm though would be the increasing winds. They'd keep the worst of the mosquitoes at bay. Fool assumed there was a mutated version of them elsewhere in the world, but at least in this part of the world, they were still mostly the unchanged annoyance they'd always been.

He slapped at the one on his thigh, and was, for the millionth time, annoyed that he didn't get any notification of experience gained. As small as they were, he was still pretty sure he'd killed enough of them since coming to the BC interior to have at least made Masterclass. The damned System was so unfair sometimes.

Olivia was the one to break the silence, putting a hand on Holland's shoulder. "I think this is something we need to know about. Can you tell us what you know?"

Holland lifted his head, and Fool realized how old the Mousekin was. He'd never really noticed the touches of grey in his fur, the slight hollowness in his eyes, the fine cracks in the end of his nose, and the fact that some of his whiskers were a little more bent and crooked than the other Mousekin. It was either that he was older, or the process of becoming a Cadet of a group of Mousekin mercenaries was intensely grueling. In any case, the Holland that lifted his head looked older and more worn than Fool had noticed before.

"Yes," Holland said, "you should know. Great Old Ones. It's a word in my language, and another word in Hellgaze's, I'm sure. I can tell the translation you hear is something else, and I suspect it's not ideal."

He stopped and looked around the tent. It was one usually set up for him to use, and it had a small collection of his personal possessions. He walked over to a cabinet, opened it, pulled out a small bottle of something, brought it back to the chair, and sat back down. He didn't say anything else but twisted the top off the bottle and took a deep draught. Fool smelled something smoky like a strong whisky, but with a rich blackberry undercurrent. Strong enough that he could smell it across the room.

Holland shook his head after draining the shot and re-capped the bottle. His eyes looked a little brighter, but also a little less focused. He looked at the bottle, put it in his lap, and started talking again.

"It's a legend. But like a lot of legends in this System-cursed galaxy, it's got some truth to it. Ancient monsters, things from before any time that anyone alive knows about or has any record of. Titans, creatures of immense power. Twisted power. The story is that once they ruled the galaxy, an ancient star-spanning empire. Died off long ago, eons. That is, the empire died off.

"The Great Old Ones, those primeval abominations, they didn't all die. Some of them just slumber. They're supposed to be in some sort of suspended animation, trapped between dimensions for all eternity. The rumors I've heard, the ones that get shared by those with an ear for legends, are that some of the worst of them were imprisoned. It was the only way those who fought them could destroy them."

His little paw was shaking, but he kept on. "This was so long ago, it might have even been before the System. Hell, it might even be related to what caused the System. The scale of what those creatures were was vast beyond comprehension. I don't know if your people here have heard of Titans yet... monsters who've attained Levels high enough to destroy solar systems? Titans will avoid the places where the Great Old Ones slumber. And some of the stories..." Holland shook his head, reached for his bottle, but then decided against it. "I wouldn't even know of these stories, except that a teacher of mine brought them up when I was a teenager and that was my rebellion against my parents—researching long lost lore.

"What little of it there is. But it's said the homeworlds of these beings were outside of the System, and some writers thought that a great cataclysm was in our future, when the inevitable expansion of the System ran across an actual slumbering Great Old One. The fear was that it would be enough to awaken one."

He looked at his hands, and the trembling stopped. When he looked up again at Fool, then everyone else, his eyes were steely. Steely, but not calm. "The Thirteen Moon Sect is a dying sect. Desperate. They are here, like many other groups, because it's one last chance for survival. If what Hellgaze said is true, then they've found one of the interdimensional prisons holding a Great Old One in stasis. Gods know what they are using the slaves for, but they're probably planning on waking the damn thing, freeing it from its cage.

And they've almost succeeded. We've got a day, and even if we somehow finish the quest before that, we'll never get away in time. Hell, we'd have get off this planet. We're dead. That's the truth."

He looked at the suddenly grim faces all around him and stunned them all by bursting out in laughter.

"Could be worse!" Holland said with one last chuckle. "You're a fine group to die with. And what the hell, if we're going to die anyways, we might as well go out with a bang. Take out some of those fucking cultists."

"We're not going to die."

They all turned in shock at the stern, solid voice. It spoke with a clear and strong tenor, and it commanded them to listen. No one was more surprised than Fool to see that the voice came from Roger.

He was looking at them all with a curious expression, his head tilted slightly, and a smile rising on his lips. His eyes, though, were fire. Challenging fire. "Sure, we're outnumbered, outgunned, and all that. But they don't know shit about us. And if what that dude said was right, then they're not loving what they're doing. The cult folk are close to finishing, right? That means they've got to be totally focused on making sure nothing goes wrong at the last minute. And you can't tell me that the Hobgoblins aren't spending every second double-checking whatever escape plan they have, right? I mean, we've all seen this movie, right?"

Holland looked confused by the movie statement but had been nodding in agreement before that. The humans all grinned at the movie reference, and Fool let out the laugh he'd been holding back, then took pity on Holland.

"James Bond, Holland," Fool said. "Human tradition. Big bad guy plans elaborate end of the world, and Bond is always there to ruin his plans at the last second. Sometimes even in a volcano." Fool laughed again and shook his head. "He's right too. We can Bond this, right? That's what you're proposing, Roger?"

"Who's Bond?" Roger said. "I mean like Batman. Or *Star Wars*. But yeah. We can't punch them with a big army, right? They're all keyed up for that, they planned for it, got all the right stuff in place. But we're small, we're fast, and we've been through some shit."

Olivia and Eric were nodding, and Fool saw that Jackal and Holland were warily accepting. Fool watched Roger and saw him take a deep breath. Roger could apparently see that his words weren't having the effect he needed them to have, so he stopped his excited flow of language, marshaled himself, and tried again.

"I know we're outnumbered. I recognize that this is an honest-to-god real end-of-the-world issue. I get that." Roger looked at everyone, making eye contact with all of them, and making sure he had their attention. "But we are the right people to stop this. A small group can get in. Anything that involved this much preparation, this far away from everyone else? It has to be complex. Complex things can be broken by small things going wrong. That's as universal a rule as anything there is in this world.

"Fool, you're the biggest wrench in the works there is. Olivia, you too. You've always been the one, even when we were kids, who made everything fall apart with a touch. I trust you two. I believe in you. I think if we can get you close enough to the heart of what's going on, you can put a stop to it.

"The rest of us, we need to create a distraction to let you do your thing. And I know exactly how to do it. There was an old movie I saw, long time ago when I was just a kid. Some shirtless dude invaded an island, and he had to fight a whole army of guards. He did it by releasing all the prisoners and getting them to fight the guards. Those people from Clearwater? We find them and free them. That will give Olivia and Fool the chance they need. They don't even need to fight. Just running for the exit will help."

"Are you sure this will work?" Jackal asked.

"No," Roger said, with absolute conviction in his voice. "But like Holland said, most of this is conjecture. We don't really know what's going on, do we? Might be the end of the world, might just be Hellgaze trying to tell us that the cult-people are off their rockers and they're taking them for a ride. We have no choice though. If there's even a chance that it's real, we have to do what we can. And if we fuck up, we die. But we die anyway, right? Might as well die punching these dicks in the balls."

Olivia burst out laughing, and that broke everyone else into gales of laughter as well. Roger tried to stop the blush, but it flared up anyways.

Jackal clapped him on the back. "Not bad, Roger. We're behind you."

Roger smiled at that and shook his head at the continuing laugher.

"We'll work on your speeches," Holland said with a smile.

At least Fool managed to find out what the strange lizard badge was on Catnip's uniform. The fire mage, who was the team lead for team four, had gone to "Kaiju School." As best as Fool could tell, the translation download the Mousekin used all felt that was the most appropriate word, which...

Well. It was System translation software. It always had weirdness. In any case, that took a little explaining, since the only thing Fool had that was close to a military background was limited to having a number of friends who were vets.

Apparently, part of Mousekin military training was going to specialist schools. The more common ones where things like sniper school, which Blossom was a graduate of, leadership school, and mage school. But they were also a number of more esoteric schools a soldier could put themselves through if they qualified.

Holland's unit was made up of some of those specialized veterans. Most of them had been through the equivalent of human Ranger, Jungle, Arctic, and Mountain Warfare schools. Which made sense when Holland explained it. They were taking a contract on a Dungeon World. Only the most elite of units would have considered the job.

Kaiju School was something unique. It made sense in a System universe. The focus of the school was on military engagements against colossal monsters. Catnip had run them through the basics, and it was surprisingly thorough. The Mousekin who'd created the course had researched and observed all kinds of attacks throughout the galaxy and created a set of standardized responses.

All of which depended on having access to the right Shop and a budget for buying some highly specialized equipment. And only going up against kaiju with multiple teams of soldiers with the same training and only if you couldn't delay and run away long enough to get a Heroic or a team of Master Classers to do it instead.

Really, there was a reason why Heroics were, well… Heroics.

For his graduation, Catnip had actually been part of a team that took down a mountain-sized kaiju.

Fool's brain sort of locked up at that image. "Let me get this right. The team was all Mousekin?"

"That's right," Catnip said. "Standard unit, twenty-one of us. Airdropped in on it. Lost a few from the backdraft of the explosions it was causing. Had

275

some kind of fusion laser it was slicing a city up with. Made for lots of bangs."

"Aren't you all kind of…" Fool started, but Catnip interrupted him with a raised hand.

"Small? Yup. That was our advantage though. For a kaiju of that size, they don't really have any kind of sensory awareness of us. Hell, the biggest problem we had was fighting off the parasites on that thing to get to the bomb placement sites. You humans might be big enough to register as a vague itch, if you brushed against a hair. Maybe. Jackal for sure."

Fool wasn't sure, but he assumed Catnip was grinning at that comment. "Fine, I suppose that makes sense. But what are we looking at for beating this thing if it does arrive? We don't have the weapons you guys used, and I don't think we have time for the right training either."

"Hah, yeah, no. If this thing is as big and strong as Holland thinks? Forget winning. I suggest we learn to live on its skin until we find a way to escape." Then Catnip sighed. "Assuming it doesn't have an aura or other passive Skills."

Holland cleared his throat, and that seemed to be enough warning to get Catnip back on track.

"Right. No, that information was for context," Catnip said. "Our best bet is to not fight the kaiju, but rather to stop it from arriving. Fortunately, one of the aspects of Kaiju School is to familiarize ourselves with kaiji origins. And I believe the Otherworldly Summoning class of creatures is what we can expect to deal with. You know, demons, angels, immortal jellyfish squids that eat minds, that kind of thing.

"Generally, summoning this kind of creature involves a ritual to process the Mana—and sometimes Health—needed, with a number of required items to enact. We're going to be looking for objects that seem out of place.

We also, on first gaining sight of the location we believe the ritual is going to occur in, want to observe the orientation and movement patterns of the participants. What they are paying attention to is not as important as what they are avoiding. In general, important people will be looking at the expected location of the kaiju's arrival. Those people should all be killed as swiftly as possible.

"More important than that though is to look at the helpers, the assistants. These are the ones doing some kind of work. While disrupting what they are working on is important, the most likely thing they are working on will be some kind of device to make the summoning easier, but the device itself will not be important. It's a bit of a red herring. What we want to do is observe their movement patterns to see what they avoid. What are they afraid of? What do they instinctively avoid walking near by or looking at? What do they cluster away from? This is likely to be an important part of the ritual. It's not necessarily dangerous in and of itself, but they've likely been warned away from touching or approaching it, and that will give them habits that will act as pointers for us."

Holland nodded and stepped forward. "And that's your job in a nutshell. Fool, you and Olivia will need to identify the necessary components of the summoning and find a way to make them inaccessible to the cultists. That's more important than killing the summoners. If you have to chose one over the other, go for the objects over the people."

"Fun!" Fool said. "An actual caper. Steal the gem from the bad guys. I like this. I'm into it."

Olivia rolled her eyes. "And while we do that, you folks will be on distraction. Do we have any idea how that'll work yet? And how we are supposed to coordinate our actions?"

"Pfft," Fool said. "Spoilsport. Asking the real questions. Lame."

Jackal cuffed him upside the back of his head, and Fool turned to glare at him. They stared at each for a moment, then burst out laughing.

Holland shook his head, and Eric looked scandalized. Roger though… Roger was grinning at both of them.

Roger stepped forward into the middle of all of them. "We haven't got a lot of time to plan this, but it's not like we have much choice. So, I think we just have to depend on luck this time. We all head in together and split the second we see any hints of what each of our teams are looking for. Fool, you and Olivia come in with the rest of us, but don't even wait if you see what you're looking for. Just go.

"The rest of us, we have only one mission: find the Clearwater folk and free them, arm the ones who can fight, then make as much noise as possible. If we wind up running into Fool and Olivia, we help them out. Otherwise, we make as much of a mess as possible. If it fails, we aren't going to care. If it succeeds… Holland, what do we do in that case? The movies always end at that point, but we need a plan to meet up again, right?"

Holland had a bristly grin. "Well, we do have a small advantage now." He held up a folded bit of paper. Fool recognized it immediately. "This is a map of the park. Our recent guest seems to have clumsily dropped it on his way out. It's not marked up or anything. I assume it was intended for casual tourists, but it's pretty easy to see where we are now, and the likely location of the volcano is on here as well… but most important is this."

Holland unfolded the map, turned it around, and pointed out one of the features noted on the map. They all leaned forward and looked, and there was a cascade of sighs and exclamations.

"When it's all over, we meet here. This is clearly the end of our quest. It looks like it's not too far from where the volcano is, and this little bit of writing on the back even describes it." He flipped the pamphlet over, and on the back was a clear bit of text labeled "Sticta Falls and Dragon's Tongue."

"Huh," Roger said. "That... makes sense. My dad was a geotech engineer, before. This would be his sense of humor. The Dragon's Tongue is probably a geological feature. He would want me to bring him back a sample." He abruptly squatted and looked at the ceiling. "Fuck. Shit."

Fool watched him for a moment, and the younger man seemed to be on the bursting out in tears. Roger bent his head forward and held his face in his hands. A moment later, he stood, took a deep breath, and shook his head.

"Yeah. Fuck. This should have been simple. Dammit. My dad really didn't think this would be a challenge at all. No wonder he let me make the quest so rigid. He thought he was giving me a tourist job. Waltz into the easiest part of the park, grab a hunk of rock, come back home. What a fucking idiot. I knew he didn't trust me to handle anything serious... and now we're going to save the world. What an asshole."

Olivia gave Roger a hug and held him tightly.

Eric put a hand on Roger's shoulder. "Dude, we always knew you could do it. We always knew your dad couldn't see what you were capable of. You do this, you get this done, we all move on. Fuck them all."

Fool glanced at Jackal to see what the big man's take was on all of this. He hadn't really heard any rumblings about daddy issues from Roger before, but maybe Jackal had?

And that was when Fool's world dropped out from under him.

With a numb shock, he saw Jackal doing something he'd never seen him do.

Jackal was crying.

Fool shuffled closer to him and leaned over to whisper into Jackal's ear, "You okay?"

Jackal nodded with a discreet sniffle before quickly dabbing his eyes with the back of his hand. "Yes. Just… look at them."

Fool looked back over, and all three of the young folk were now hugging.

"They just grew up, and they did it with friends to support them. Not alone," Jackal said. Then he turned and nearly crushed Fool in a hug.

For all their friendship, Jackal had never really hugged Fool before. They'd leaned on each other, fallen asleep on each other, rough-housed and headbutted and high-fived and even given each other pecks on the forehead from time to time, but never hugged. It was a level of intimacy they'd never really felt the need for.

Fool understood, and after the briefest of hesitation, he hugged back as hard as he could. Jackal was seeing what his own transition to adulthood might have been like. They'd talked about it before. Jackal's parents hadn't known who Jackal really was. He'd never had the chance to see if they'd accept him or not. Roger was getting the chance to grow into himself, not with his parents' support, but with the support of his friends.

The same support Jackal had from Fool.

After a moment, Fool mumbled something into Jackal's chest, where his head was being squished.

Jackal relaxed his hug a little and said, "What? I missed what?"

"Can't breathe," Fool choked out.

Chapter Twenty-four

The blue sky had lasted almost long enough for them to feel a sense of hope. In no more time than it took them to cram down a rapid breakfast and start their march to where they figured the Clearwater folks were being held, it was blotted away. A roiling grey wave swept across the sky, and Jackal knew what it meant even before the grey flakes drifted down amongst them.

Unlike the previous days, they weren't covered in sweat or struggling to make time. The path was easier here, and they loped through the forest like a pack of wolves. Jackal was using his Perception to its max as they jogged through the dense trees, and he knew they were getting close. Scuffs of undergrowth, branches crossed in unnatural ways, slight compressions, signs of dust pressed into hollows. They were passing through areas that had been patrolled recently.

But all that was being covered with a layer of ash. The first flakes were wide, but as they moved closer to their destination, finer flakes layered more densely and pebbly bits of debris were mixed in. There was some evidence of previous ash-fall as well. Twice Jackal spotted the print of boot-soles in the ash, but fresh ash had covered most of it. Jackal wasn't surprised by that. With the deadline for the summoning coming up, the need for patrols had probably switched to preparing for their after-summoning activities. Likely moving to a new location—a new planet probably. If Holland's suspicions were correct.

"Something weird here," Fool said from Jackal's side.

Jackal didn't bother replying. It was Fool's "thinking out loud" voice, and after a moment, his friend continued.

"I mean, this is clearly a volcano, and it's erupting. But if it's erupting, why no earthquakes? Why no earth-shattering boom?" Fool asked.

Jackal thought about that for a moment, but there was only one real explanation. The local volcanos hadn't erupted for at least a hundred years— some for thousands of years. If the eruption had been natural, there should have been a near constant series of earthquakes and probably a few big explosions. Instead, there was nothing. But nonetheless, the clear evidence pointed to an ongoing eruption.

"Drilling," Jackal said. "Some kind of pressure relief."

Fool almost tripped over his feet but kept up the steady jog. "You're kidding. Do you have any idea what kind of scale would be required for that? Especially if all this ash and crap is a side effect of that?"

Jackal tried, but he couldn't shrug effectively while jogging. "Every day is some new impossibility. That's the world the System brought to us. Skills, Shop purchases, who knows? Hell, might be that what they're doing *is* causing earthquakes and explosions, but something else is draining all that energy to fuel something else."

They jogged in silence for a moment, and Jackal took a quick glance around. Everyone was keeping up just fine. The Mousekin looked as professional and stoic as always. Roger was next to Holland, who was in the lead. Eric was two steps behind Roger, ever the faithful companion. Olivia though had drifted away from her friends and was closer to Fool and Jackal. The three of them were forming a separate trio of runners.

Jackal glanced again at Olivia and Fool. Whatever was between them was stronger than it had been before. He'd been hoping to ask Fool about that, but the opportunity hadn't come up. There was still something nagging him when he saw the two of them, something about that closeness that had sprung up between them.

He didn't really have time to think about that. Nor, likely, would he. He flicked his eyes forward again. They were running toward what was likely their doom, if he was being honest with himself. Doom. Death, in service to a vainglorious hope of saving the world. That brought a smile to his lips. However terrible the reality might be, this was the sort of adventure he'd been dreaming about his whole life.

The oldest poem he'd learned, in secret, came to his lips, unvoiced by his breath but still truly formed.

"Tell me not, sweet, I am unkind,
That from the nunnery
Of thy chaste breast and quiet mind
To war and arms I fly.

True, a new Mistress now I chase,
The first foe in the field;
And with a stronger faith embrace
A sword, a horse, a shield.

Yet this inconstancy is such,
As you too shall adore;
I could not love thee, dear, so much,

Lov'd I not Honour more."[9]

Poor Lovelace. The old poet could only dream of a death as valiant as this. Jackal had to give him credit for having a Jocasta. It wasn't that Jackal was wanting for female companionship. The last few years had given him many lovers, and he cherished all of them and the memories they'd given him. But he'd dreamed of a single love, someone to occupy all of his heart, almost as strongly as he'd dreamed of a valiant war to fight. It seemed a shame that he was going to his death without realizing that last thing. Still, he'd had love, and that would have to be enough.

He looked over again at Fool. The older man was jogging along, his face lit with that quiet grin that always grew when he wasn't forcing another expression to the fore. That was something Jackal envied in his friend. No matter the anger or grief that affected them, Fool always found a way to joy. For all Fool's professed innocence of love, the man had also racked up more lovers than Jackal.

Jackal could see how that happened. Fool was of the moment, in all things he did. That meant he rarely carried any sort of baggage when it came to affection. Men, women, human, alien… Fool had a knack for seeing them true and letting them know that. It was no surprise that many responded to that honest regard with desire… and were happy to leave him be when that desire was satisfied. There was no desire in the man at all aside from what was in the moment. And he always found something in the moment.

Jackal would have been completely envious of that except that Fool still had some touch of empty loss inside him. He hid it most of the time, but Jackal knew well enough that Fool's quiet moments and occasional absence

---

[9] To Lucasta, Going to the Wars by Richard Lovelace

in the midst of a conversation were echoes of a longing the man had never voiced.

And while Jackal was sure that there was nothing untoward going on between Olivia and Fool, something about their proximity seemed to fill that emptiness in Fool, while somehow making him seem somehow more fragile at the same time.

That made Jackal suspicious, but he'd give Fool time to explain himself. If they ran out of time to do that, it was what it was.

They might be running out of time.

Jackal could make out a red glow coming through the trees ahead. A pillar, a flickering pillar of deep red.

A moment later, they crested up a small hill, just big enough to allow for a glimpse across the top of the trees on the far side.

The sky was hellfire.

They couldn't quite make out the volcano itself, but the ash billowing into the sky reached to the horizon all around, a rolling, churning, boil-filled underlayer to the sky. The red glow was coming from ahead of them, but the source was obscured by the rolling waves of ash clouds. The glow was fierce enough that it shot through the clouds, and an oval sphere before them was harshly backlit by it.

"Well," Holland said. The entire party had stopped to take in the sight. "I think we know where we're going now. Maybe another hour, and we'll be there. Any last questions?"

No one made a sound. They all knew what was expected of them. Run until they got close enough to see what was going on, then split and take advantage of speed. No planning. Jackal figured they'd have time after initial contact to make some sort of plan, but he was also trusting the Mousekin to have enough experience working together that he would be content to follow along.

Well, not quite follow along. He glanced at Holland and made eye contact, then flicked his gaze over to Roger and Eric. Holland nodded back, and it was settled. Jackal would keep an eye on those two and free Holland up to be completely in charge.

And with that, there was nothing left but to run into hell.

Fool rolled his shoulders as they crested the final rise between them and the enemy. The last kilometer had them running almost straight uphill, and they'd had to pause twice to refresh themselves with some last-case-only Endurance potions from the Mousekin's stash. At least they'd come up over the rise into the Flourmill Volcano area fresh.

They'd made the run-in hours. For pre-System folks or those who hadn't put points into Abilities, it would have been a punishing hike, days in duration. With points in their physical attributes and a few drill Skills and Basil's Aura of the Pristine Soldier, it had been a lot easier.

Aura of the Pristine Soldier

Strength, stamina, valor, and a little spit and shine. That's what a proper Mousekin warrior will have. Can't have the troops looking anything but the best with their uniform and fur taken care of. Otherwise, what would you be? A Kclarat?

Effects: Low grade Cleanse running in area of effect for all allies. +5% Stamina regeneration. +2% movement speed. +1 Strength

All the trees for hectares around had been ripped down, and some of the battered trunks had been pulled down to make a road. The forest had been cleared, as far as Fool could tell, for only one purpose—clear line of sight for weapons. The evidence of that was the heaps of monster corpses all around, in various states of decay. Apparently, the local fauna—and flora, in some cases—had been quite focused on crushing the interlopers. The Hobgoblins had been more than up to the task though.

But all of that was coming to an end. There were no troops to be seen anywhere on the plateau ahead of them. Just unending rows of downed trees.

And the river of lava.

One hell of a sight, after a night of running through forested mountain sides and valleys.

Ahead of them, the plateau stretched out like an open field, sloping down toward another sharp drop to the river valley that ran between the mountain ranges. On the far side was a ridge that echoed the slope, and from that ridge poured an unending stream of lava. It was a hot, bright river of red-orange, with a drifting heat-haze that obscured all the details of the far side.

Directly below them, a rough road had been carved into the debris, and it wound right across the plateau to the source of the river of lava. Right to the foot of the volcano.

Fool was reminded of the time he'd visited a hydroelectric dam. He'd hiked all the way down past the spillways to look up the gigantic concrete face, and he had noticed a gigantic slice put into the rocky wall next to the spillway. A crack in the cliffs, seemingly opening into the creek. When he'd looked closer at it, from as close as he was able to get, it had bars preventing access and was more artificial than it had originally looked.

He'd wondered what lay beyond that mysterious opening and had found out years later that it was an extra spillway shaft, part of a valve-release system for the dam. If he'd pushed closer, he would have also found a strange door part way up the cliffside, part of a monitoring and access system.

The volcano rose above them. Not the classic tall pyramid, but rather a short, squat cone. What it lost in vertical majesty though, it made up in strangeness. The smoke and fire didn't bubble up and roil out as Fool had seen in videos of eruptions, but rather shot directly up in a column, some force constraining the whole thing into a massive beam that rose into the sky.

In that beam, they could see there was already some distraction taking place. A veritable tornado of wyverns were raging around, fighting with a number of flying craft. And there was at least one giant on the slope of the volcano, dueling against tanks and Hobgoblin formations. If Fool had to guess, he would say that the locals were not happy with the dimensional rift opening in their front yard. Either that or the Norli had some sort of monster-summoning skill. In any case, it looked as though most of the Hobgoblins were occupied.

Just like at the dam, there was a spillway at the bottom of the volcano that the lava poured out of, and a vertical crack that formed a cave entrance to the side of it. In that crack, Fool could just make out what looked like an abandoned vehicle of some kind.

"That's the place," he said. "Here we go."

Jackal, standing next to him, nodded. Holland made no noise, just looked over everyone, then toward Roger. The young man looked more resolute than Fool would have imagined when he'd first met him. Roger had gone through a tremendous amount of growth in the short time they'd been running together. Fool knew it was a good thing. The boy had become something new, something he was always destined to be... and more importantly, he'd become something aligned with who he was inside. In a short time, he'd somehow managed to throw off the dreck of personality he'd built around himself and become his true, core self.

Fool couldn't help but frown at how much potential damage that rapid change might have caused the young man.

He wished he could roll the clock back a bit and be less of a jerk to Roger when he'd met him. It wasn't as though any of them had a chance to grow in healthy ways these days. The System had made sure of that. It was also true that without the System, none of them would likely have made the changes they had. More good than bad, but still Fool wished there was a better way.

Maybe, in time, there would be. After all, wasn't that why he'd joined the Foundation? The Professor had sold Fool and Jackal on a vision of a new and better future for humans, a place where they could negotiate a better relationship with the System, or barring that, find a way to flee from its effects and find a new home for humans. The Machine they had all pooled their startup resources to obtain had promised them a different and better path. Somehow, its ability to predict trends and identify important nodes of different kinds was going to lead to the eventual goal of freedom for humanity.

It was a lofty goal, and Fool and Jackal had bought right in. But since they'd started working for the Foundation, Fool found himself asking more and more questions. How would all of this work? What was the actual concrete goal of the Foundation... and how did they know the Machine didn't have an agenda of its own?

It didn't matter, Fool realized, as he watched Roger make his decision and nod back at Holland.

Jackal, Roger, Eric, Holland, and all the Mousekin took off down the slope toward the road at a run. They were in combat mode now. They'd charge into that hole and do what damage they could, and likely die in the effort.

If they didn't succeed, then it wouldn't matter what the Foundation was really planning, what the Machine's part in it all was, because there wouldn't be any humanity left to free.

It was possible the threat inside the volcano was overblown. It was possible someone or something else might rise up to stop the monster. Another human. Or maybe a Galactic or two. Rumors of creatures strong enough to destroy planets with a wave of their hand kept creeping in, but that was hard to believe.

It was possible.

But how could they risk it?

He and Olivia were left watching the team charge into their doom. He turned and looked at her. Now was the time.

"The chaos magic inside you, it's not part of the System, is it?"

Olivia smiled at him. "Sort of. Kind of. It's Mana, but not really through the process the way the System wants me to use it. Sometimes I can feel it fighting me, but I use it just enough to keep it calm. Mostly."

Fool nodded. Something had seemed off about how she was doing things, and something was also bitingly familiar, in more ways than one. "If not the System, then what is it you are using?"

"Something older," she said. "And something younger. Something not really born yet, a potential that the System, or at least the Galactic Council, is trying to crush out. Magic. The magic that should have been born into this universe long ago."

"And how," Fool asked, "did you learn all of that?"

"I've got a patron. They told me you'd be coming, and that you were the same as me. Same, but different."

Fool sighed and ran his hand through his beard. "I don't suppose it was a cat, was it?"

Olivia froze and stared at him with her mouth open. She blinked a few times, then shook herself. "I'm not even going to ask how you know that. That fucking cat. I guess that's why you seemed so familiar to me. It's got its touch on you too. I can see that now."

The urge to sit down and put his head in his hands was almost too much for Fool to bear, but he fought it. There just wasn't any time for that, not right now. He ruffled his beard and tugged on it one more time. "That's it, but I think there's more. Where were your parents from?"

"Bella Coola. Family always has been. Except for Gramma. She said she was born in Vancouver but moved back to have my mom. Why?"

Fool turned and looked at the volcano.

And smiled.

"Doesn't matter," he said. "We'll have time to talk when all this is over."

"You sure about that?" Oliva said. "This doesn't look like something we can walk away from."

Fool looked at her, hearing the hint of a quaver in her voice. She was holding it together. And she was a tough little warrior. Of that, he had no doubt. It wasn't just in her blood, but in the character she'd made for herself. That little quaver in her voice? He could see only the slightest trace of it in her stance.

Fear was rightful in a time like this. It was what would carry them through the worst of what was coming. It would prepare them best, as long as it was carried in proportion to everything else. And she was carrying it just fine.

He was glad he held back the urge to give her a hug. For what was coming, she needed to believe that he was only seeing the strongest part of her. He would respect that.

"I'm sure," he said. "For the first time since all this started, I'm sure. This was meant to happen, and we are here to stop it. Might hurt, but we're walking out of this. And then we're going to have a talk about cats. And other things. But right now?"

He looked at the volcano again.

A volcano. With a cult. And a plan to end the world.

This was ridiculous. And perfect.

Because he was the Fool.

"Right now," he said with a grin, "we got some shit to stir up."

Olivia let the grin infect her and shone it back at him. They sprinted down the hill toward their fate and the end of the world.

Chapter Twenty-five

The Clearwater folks were the first thing they found after a quick dogleg inside the tunnel. There weren't even any guards. They hadn't run into any opposition. Not during their mad sprint across the plateau, not at the cave opening, and not during the brief run into the dozens of barred cells carved into the walls of the tunnel.

That worried Jackal more than anything. No guards meant they were all busy elsewhere and they just didn't care what was happening anywhere around them. That meant they were on the cusp of doing whatever their final plan was, and that meant it was getting that much closer to too late.

Roger was the first one to the cells, and he tore the lock mechanism off the wall with strength alone. The Clearwater residents were shouting and screaming and gesturing down the tunnel, but Jackal wasn't listening to them.

He was looking over the state of the prisoners.

They weren't in the worst shape, but they were almost all covered in burns and filthy with a mix of black soot and some kind of shining mineral. Clearly they had enough energy to be agitated, so they'd been fed and not worked too hard, but the evidence of burns on them that had not healed was worrisome. Whatever had caused the burns was something toxic enough it prevented the usual System healing from working or was otherwise interfering with the System.

Holland was rapidly triaging the prisoners as they came out of the cells, looking for those who had any sort of combat Skills and sending them to one side, directing the others toward the cave entrance where two Mousekin had been assigned to escort them back to safety—as much safety as there could be. It had been an unpopular assignment for the Mousekin, but once straws had been drawn, the unlucky two had jumped into their role with professionalism. Only Holland and Catnip had been exempt from that draw.

It took less than a moment to sort everyone out, and at the end of it, their ranks had swollen by almost a hundred new bodies. The Mousekin had stripped themselves of their excess arms, and everyone had some kind of weapon.

Roger was shouting some rallying speech. Jackal didn't have to hear the words to see the effect it was having on the people. He was really tapping into his natural leadership skills, and everyone was focused on him. Jackal saw the electric ripple pass through them all as he laid out a quick plan. He didn't have to explain the stakes. The townsfolk had already put together the threat themselves, and Jackal saw a couple of them gesturing down the tunnel. Roger and Holland spoke with those two, and everyone was split into two groups behind each of them, orienting toward the tunnel.

That was all Jackal needed to know. It made the next step clear, and he wiped away the notification that had popped up, the last bit of experience he needed to break through to his Advanced class and to make his choice. This was the moment he been waiting for, holding his Advanced Class selections in reserve for.

Bearshirt Warrior of the Claven North (Level 1)

More akin to the true berserkers of history than the mythologized popular entertainment version of berserkers from Dungeon Planet Earth, the Bearshirt benefits from the strength, speed and damage resistance of their Class while retaining a degree of cunning and intelligence during their moments of rage.

Class Abilities: +4 Per Level in Strength and Constitution, +3 Per Level in Willpower and Agility. +2 in Perception, Additional 3 Free Attributes per Level. +20% Damage Resistance, +30% Pain Resistance. Doubles during Berserk State.

Jackal wasn't a soldier. His Skills, his build, were not meant to work well with others. He was the hero, the lone wolf, the one meant to take on impossible odds. He had to smile at the mental image even as he ran down the tunnel.

Lone wolf. He'd mentioned that to one of his lovers, and she'd laughed at him. Told him a lone wolf wasn't a good thing, but rather a broken and lost animal, soon to die. She'd told him that if he really wanted a powerful lone role model to base himself off of, then he should think of himself as a bear instead.

He'd laughed that off at the time, and they'd joked about her just wanting something to cuddle up against.

As he ran down the long tunnel though, he felt the power swelling inside him. A rage fueled him but did not overpower him. He became the bear in his mind. His great size, his strength, the loping power with which he moved, all changed and focused into that one image.

The cloak of the bear fell all around him and unified his mind. All his Skills flared into life, uniting themselves and aligning together in a way he'd never experienced before, and it was like his conscious mind stepped back and away from what he was becoming.

The first Hobgoblin appeared before him, and he tore through the enemy as if he was paper, not even bothering to draw a weapon. Jackal didn't even think, the Aura working together to trigger One Punch, Maestro, Death from Above with the leap all combined to finish this fight easily.

Even floating above himself, distant from the maelstrom of purpose he had become, Jackal felt the deep satisfaction the spray of blood caused.

He had no goal, no purpose now aside from battle. This was how it was always meant to end for him. Strategy was being handled by others. Fool would complete his mission or not; Jackal would never know. All that mattered was that every step he took, every life he ended, every bit of chaos he could create for the enemy, every ounce of that would be in aid of his friend. There was no room to hold anything back anymore.

Finally, the old dream was coming true. It was as if an ancient being slumbering within him was finally awakening, called forth by the promise of slaughter without end.

He grinned, and he could taste blood on his teeth.

Around one more corner were more Hobgoblins. They were startled by his blood-drenched appearance, and he added to that with a roar that came from deep in his belly. Shocked or not, they were professional soldiers and reacted with speed. He was among them before they could do much, but even so, some of them managed to get weapons out.

There was probably pain, but nothing in him had time for that. There were thumps and impacts on his body, weapons fire striking him, bullets and fragments running through his body, but somehow his swords were in his hands and the blades were passing through his enemies' bodies without pause, no effort, no effect other than leaving bodies behind.

He was through them in moments, leaving torn bodies and dismembered limbs behind. A few were still crawling, reorienting, but they'd be dealt with by others. He was charging down the next tunnel.

And suddenly he was in the midst of the enemy, in an immense open cavern, a pool of lava the center.

Some gigantic device was in the pool, physically drawing up the lava like some sort of pump, sucking into the blood of the earth like a vampire. From the edge of his perception, Jackal saw that the lava level wasn't dropping, even with the enormous quantity being sucked out... but the rising amount was slowing as if something unspeakably large was rising through the thick, viscous molten heart of the earth and blocking lava from flowing up to meet the suction.

Jackal only noted that from the corner of his mind. It didn't matter. Nor did the crimson-robed priests circling the lava pit. Nor the scientist-types scurrying about on their catwalks and platforms. The myriad of machines was so much dross at the edges of his vision.

All that mattered to him were the squads of Hobgoblin soldiers arraying themselves to fight him.

And the lone figure directing them. That one. The lean, alien hatchet face concealed almost immediately by the silver-reflective full-face mask. The one with the oversized rifle on its back. The one who had nearly killed him before.

Band Eller.

The bear inside Jackal roared its defiance, its throat howling open with the raging need to taste the blood of the mortal enemy. Nothing would stop him, not this time.

The soldiers had other plans.

Jackal's mind, passenger to the beast running his body, noted with respect how professional they were, how smoothly they moved into formations.

Moving forward was like walking into a moderate surf, waves buffeting his body and gently pushing backward. He saw the muzzle flashes and beams striking out at him, but the brief boost in toughness from his Skills was blunting the effect.

Not entirely. He felt some of the weapons going right through him, but it didn't matter. He was charging forward, and soon he'd be among them.

The fire briefly stopped as the formation of soldiers snapped into place, a slow-motion dance to his enhanced perception and altered state of mind.

Good soldiers, they formed a tight line, braced their left arms against their chests, and activated force shields. Jackal saw a faint blue rectangle forming in front of each of them, with a slightly actinic flare as the edges touched each other and locked into place. A practiced drill, they moved with perfect speed and motion. Almost as soon as the shield wall formed, the soldiers on the outer edges curled in.

The bear inside him smiled. Their tactic was clear. It was a good strategy for facing a higher-tier enemy who specialized in melee. Unbreakable shields, a small selection of soldiers taking all the attacks while the rest surrounded the opponent. Then they'd bring all their weapons to bear, and that would be the end of that.

Trained responses, which was what Jackal had hoped for. Warriors like him were harder to fight because they knew how to respond to instant changes. They lived in a world where everything was deception, and they had to keep up a unique response.

Good soldiers were sometimes soldiers who'd been trained to react on instinct though. Sometimes that was a great way to fight. Sometimes it was a trap.

Jackal was almost on them, and he gathered himself to leap over the shield wall. He stretched his steps, bouncing higher on each step, and gathering his arms for the leap. No hesitation. He'd bound over them, rolling over the shields like a high jumper, spinning through the air with his blades to slice a passage through…

But they were ready for that. Just as they'd been trained, even before their conscious minds realized he was about to leap, they moved in unison, lifting the shields and bracing their arms.

Jackal would land on the shields instead of behind them, and they'd turn his momentum back over to gravity, letting him smash onto the ground amongst them, where they'd have weapons ready to end him swiftly. There was no way he'd be able to stop that from happening. Once he was airborne, he was committed to the arc, and there was no way for him to beat that kind of physics. None of his Skills would save him. Even the temporary invulnerability his Skills granted him was already wearing off. He was doomed.

Or would have been if he'd actually jumped.

Instead, at the last moment, landing on the leg that should have been stiff, that would have recoiled him up in a prodigious leap… that leg collapsed. Just as he'd planned.

His momentum, instead of being transferred up and forward, dropped him to the ground in less than an eyeblink. He was already torquing his other leg around and pulling his arms in tight to his body, his blades crossing over his chest.

He hit the ground and spun and turned, but nothing was stopping his forward momentum.

The soldiers had no chance to lower their shields. They were still in the process of lifting them, eyes still flicking up to track his leap, when he slid under the shields like a two-hundred-fifty-pound bowling ball.

With swords.

And the Red Rover Skill.

It happened too fast for even his enhanced perception and intelligence to keep up with. Flashes, brief images, vignettes of violence that would be burned into his brain forever.

Two ankles, turning, twisting away from the legs they'd been attached to a millisecond ago, the boots' fabric not even folding yet, the legs just starting to drop now that they weren't supported.

A blade shearing across a thigh, the blade seeming to disappear into leg for a second, the faintest popping sensation traveling down the blade to his hand, and the silver metal suddenly appearing on the other side of the leg, a thin trail of red painting the air behind it.

Suddenly he was on one knee, rising in the midst of panic. One Hobgoblin soldier, faster than the others, had spun in place, dropped its shield, and was turning to point a pistol at him. Jackal stared down the barrel, his senses so keyed up in that brief flash of awareness that he saw the edge of the round in the barrel—not a standard lead bullet, but some sort of System tech, a little sliver of glass with something swirling inside it. The bear laughed, partially because it knew that seeing only part of the round meant the soldier's aim was a hair off and would miss him even at this range.

Mostly it laughed because even as the soldier turned, Jackal's blade had already thrust through him. But even a dead soldier could pull a trigger, if they didn't know they were dead yet.

The barrel flared, and Jackal's left arm kicked back with a pocket flare of screaming hot iron burning into it. The sword that had been in the soldier twisted with the impact, the sharp blade spiraling inside its body, and the bear laughed while Jackal cringed and screamed in pain.

For all the agony of the shot, it saved Jackal's life.

The cyan bolt from Band Eller's rifle crossed so close to his face, Jackal felt the end of his nose singing and burning.

Now the bear screamed in rage. The enemy. The shot had come from the left, and as Jackal spun to track the one who must die, he lurched in pain as he was run through from behind.

Once.

Twice.

Again. And again.

The weapons were torn from the hands of the attackers as the bear spun, swords slashing out, batting people aside in sprays of blood. The bear spun twice more, stepping as it went, blades a spiraling tempest, and soldiers fell where he spun.

Jackal watched from the back of his own mind as the Hobgoblin soldiers scrambled to regroup and rebuild their Mana… and to deal with the sudden influx of attacks from the Mousekin and Clearwater fighters.

And then there was only Band Eller left to kill.

Fool hadn't really expected it to be so easy. A dungeon—a proper dungeon—was what they should have been diving into. That was what the System preferred, after all. Everything he'd learned about it led him to believe that.

And hell, this was the perfect excuse for an epic dungeon. Remote wilderness? Check. Volcano? Check. Megalomaniac bad guy? Probably check. Evil cult? Check. Minions galore? Check!

With that in mind, they should have been facing greater and greater waves of bad guys, disarming traps, getting lost and finding their way back again. And moving up level after level or going down deeper.

Instead, it was clearly an industrial operation. Straight-up tunnel boring. There were side tunnels and rooms, but they were pretty much what you'd expect from a month's-long tunnel boring job. Fool and Olivia found themselves following Jackal and Holland's new army with nothing much to do. It wasn't a straight line through. The main tunnel curved and twisted, as whatever they were using to bore through the volcano skipped the harder stone.

Almost as soon as they'd arrived at the tunnel opening, only a few moments after Jackal, they had run into a stream of Clearwater evacuees. Fool had been tempted to help them out, but the Mousekin soldiers escorting them had come out almost right away, leading an even larger mass of people, so Fool and Olivia had kept pushing forward.

Jackal and crew had certainly been busy. The farther Fool and Olivia went down the tunnel, the more bodies they ran across. Some of them looked as if they'd been put though a blender, and Fool found himself feeling oddly queasy when he looked at them. It was less like they'd died in battle and more like they'd been savaged by a beast. He was wondering if something else was in the tunnel with them when they finally came across the main chamber.

It was a warzone.

Mousekin and humans in little knots all over the place. The Hobgoblin mercenary's professionalism seemed to have been lost somewhere along the line, and they'd been broken into small groups instead of the formations they trained to fight in.

Still, there were far more of the Hobgoblins than there were of the attackers, and the mercenaries were getting their act back together and responding with more skill. Fool saw the scattered groups fighting to get back to each other, instead of just responding to their attacks.

Fool was at a complete loss. All his Skills were really focused on being the single sneaky guy one step ahead of the enemy. This was nothing he had any Skills for, and he was in way over his head.

He activated The Show Must Go On to give everyone a boost in morale, and after thinking about it for a bit, followed up with Geas to give all the enemy soldiers the impression they were being slowly surrounded, that the chaos of the attackers was all for a purpose they couldn't understand.

He was surprised by how low of a Mana cost that was, but it made sense when he actually looked at the Hobgoblins. His Geas was almost directly in line with what they were thinking anyway. He couldn't see Hellgaze anywhere. If ever there was a time when strong leadership was needed, this was it.

Fool was happy the Hobgoblins were being denied that opportunity. Every little bit helped.

He saw Jackal finally and swore. Band Eller and Jackal were engaged in what looked like a death match, the two of them flying and darting all over, focused only on each other. Fool held back the urge to go help his friend. Jackal clearly wanted vengeance for his earlier near-death at the cultist's hands, and to Fool's surprise, they looked far more evenly matched than during their last battle. Jackal was moving in a way Fool hadn't seen before.

His focus was interrupted by Olivia grabbing his shoulder.

"No time, uncle. We gotta go!" She was pointing across the room, to the far side of the central lava pit, and Fool's heart dropped.

The passage had opened into an immense open chamber, circular, with an extended catwalk running all around it about thirty feet off the chamber floor. There were a number of stairs and platforms leading up to the catwalk, and the purpose of the whole thing seemed to be to support a gigantic machine hovering over the center of the lava lake. The lake made up the entire center of the chamber. The floor they were standing formed a ring around it about twenty meters wide, and the lava center looked to be over a hundred meters across.

The lava was roiling and churning and lacked the usual dark crust that should have formed from sustained contact with the air. Fool saw some kind of force-field holding the lava down, stopping it from rising higher or interacting with the air in the chamber. Which also explained why they weren't all dying from heat.

The only exception to the coverage was in the dead center, where a thick tube of lava was rising up to the machine and probably through it. That would explain the signs of eruption outside the volcano. The machine had somehow pierced into the center of the volcano and was drawing out its heartsblood.

Or had been, until a moment ago. The mad, red whirling of lava shooting up the tube was slowing, from a turbulence that looked like the exhaust from hell's jet engine to a slow, steady upwelling like a garden hose.

And something was rising out of the lava. Something opaque, and the lava was showing signs of being pushed off to the side. Fool couldn't see what was rising, but the hairs rising on the back of his neck told him he really didn't want to know what it was.

At least now he had a target. Olivia was pointing not at the slow rising in the lava, nor at the machine, but rather to the right of where they were standing. Opposite of where Jackal and Holland's soldiers were causing havoc with the mercenaries was what looked to be the control center for the machine.

And the cultists responsible for all of this.

Thirteen red-robed figures, gathered in a half-circle, faced the lava pool. Behind them, a cadre of what had to be technical workers, judging from how all of them were either focused intently on banks of machines or running around adjusting levers and switches.

In the middle of the robed figures, the focus of all of that effort.

An arcane sigil throbbing with power, carved runes all around its edges. The runes were drenched with blood, but the great sigil, as wide as a house, seemed to be made of actual lava spooling across the floor into the mystic shape.

Fool felt his tension, the sneaking sense of uselessness that had been growing in him, flow away. This was what he was here for. At a glance, he could see the robed figures, the cultists, were the real enemy. His enemy.

They were, all of them, alien. All as different from one another as they all were from Fool. Even with that, he saw one thing in common amongst all of them.

Arrogance.

If they had been desperate or struggling to perform their ritual, Fool might have felt some sympathy. If they'd been just doing their job, he might have had an ounce of mercy in him.

Against a wall of arrogance? Against the tangible wave of disdain and power coming off of them? Against that, he had only fury. Not an impotent rage, but a direct fury.

The moment he'd chosen his Class—debatable whether he'd found it, or it had been found for him—had been a moment of similar fury.

It had been a small thing. Nothing unusual, just another moment of helpless rage.

The twenty-four-hour donut shop in the strip mall. During the day, it was a busy little shop filled with happy shoppers, workers grabbing a snack on their break, schoolkids playing hooky for a treat. After dinner, it had the odd person driving through, students studying and drinking coffee… the usual.

After midnight? After the world put itself to sleep? The shop became the domain of the real night owls. Cops, security guards, taxi and truck drivers, restless drug users unable to sleep and looking for a safe place for a moment's privacy. And people like Fool, who had enough change scrounged up for a coffee.

Not that he wanted one, but that was the price to use the bathroom and give himself a quick wash in the sink. Most nights, they wouldn't let someone like him in, but he'd checked out the staff while he'd been crashing in the alley, and tonight had the soft crew on. If he could keep his visions under control, he might even be able to weasel a donut out of them. If he was really lucky, maybe a sandwich. That had happened six months before, and he held out the hope for another one. He'd noticed that the friendly night person had switched to mornings, so he had already been up all night waiting for the morning shift when the System arrived. He'd stumbled, but he had enough focus to remember where he was going after putting away the confusing message.

He'd just walked in, and his heart had sunk. A table full of teenagers, faces full of mockery. The tense looks on the faces of the night crew told Fool all he needed to know. Bored rich kids, nothing better to do, no fear of consequences, looking for something to entertain themselves. Fool knew the type all too well. Cruelty wasn't guaranteed, but stupidity was. They'd be driven to show off to their friends how edgy they were, and god help anyone who caught their attention.

It wasn't even Fool. It was Mary.

Mary was a wisp of a woman, hardly anything left of who she used to be. Like Fool, she wasn't much for imbibing in substances, because she had her own disconnects from reality. In her case, it was a spark of rage that burned inside her all the time. It took only the slightest breath to set it off. Fool had learned to be mostly quiet around her. It was how he showed his friendship. Some other people in their community tried to protect her, keep people from setting her off, but that was how they seemed to take turns trying to own her for their own purposes. Fool preferred to just keep her company once in a while, to be a quiet fellow traveler. They weren't friends really, but they often shared quiet moments when they got the chance.

They'd all been in the process of recovering from the System arrival when she walked into the shop. True to her nature, instead of looking bewildered, she looked pissed off. And aimed that anger at the first target she saw.

A stream of invective, a torrent of righteous fury, came pouring out of her, backed up with wild gestures. Fool couldn't remember what she was actually saying, but he knew how it was going to go. She'd come into the first available space—the bright lights of the donut shop—and directed her confusion at the space.

But to the young bravos? She was angry at them. With their selfish focus, they couldn't imagine that a screaming homeless woman would be mad at anything other than them. With their usual arrogance, it would have been a bad scene.

They were gamers and had already grokked the System and what it meant, so instead of being bad, it was horrible.

Fool glanced at them in time to see the mocking, silent agreement pass between them. Mary's screaming had given them an excuse to feel like heroes. And now they had powers, so they had an excuse to try them out.

Mary had no defenses. A blue screen flickering in front of her face wouldn't have been something she would think about or cope with, but something she would bat away. So, she had nothing to stop the flurry of ice bolts that slammed into her.

Even first-Level Skills would be enough to kill her. She was a fragile wreck at the best of times. The only thing that saved her was the pure inexperience of her attackers.

Fool hadn't hesitated for even a second. With a shout, he'd flung himself at the would-be heroes, fists flailing away.

And bounced off the shield that appeared on the arm of one of them. He bit clean through his lip as his teeth smashed together, and he felt the teeth shattering for an extra bit of joy. He crashed into the tables behind him, and only chance stopped his head from cracking on the edge of the table.

Even so, he fought through the tumbling haze his thoughts had turned to and stumbled up, shouting at the bravos to leave her alone, she was just a crazy old lady…

It was enough. They turned their attention on him, and Fool saw the Skills and weapons they suddenly had glow and shimmer in the light, and he knew he was going to die.

And it pissed him off.

He had no fear of dying. None at all. He'd come to grips with that potential long ago.

But to die at the hands of these useless little shits? To die at the hands of base privilege? That, that he raged against.

And in desperation, he reached out for that blue screen, toward the promise of there maybe being something that could help him fight.

But instead of that screen, the whole world had slowed to a stop, and he'd heard, for the first time, that voice and its words, "Have faith."

He'd accepted the offer. The blue screen had reappeared, and a flurry of options appeared and disappeared. Somehow, the voice was making the choices through him, a voice in the back of his head somehow guiding him.

He sold his soul in that moment. Sold it to become a unique weapon of righteousness. Seconds later, Jackal had appeared for the first time, in a completely different form, and trounced the bravos. But Fool was already on his long and arduous path.

And that path had led him here, into the path of this arrogance, with its selfish greed to spend a world and all its inhabitants for its own goals.

The red-robed cultist bastards who wouldn't give even a flicker of a thought to the lives they were about to shatter. All for power. A power, Fool was sure, that would be enough to shake the stars.

He wasn't aware of Olivia turning loose her powers on the technicians. Or of Jackal's desperate fight, or Holland or Roger or Eric or any of the others.

Fool stepped in front of the arc of the cultists, between them and the lava pool, and turned to face the robed priests. Just before he turned to face them, out of the corner of his eye, he caught a glimpse of a single, massive scale rising out of the lava.

No matter. He'd deal with that later.

For now, he had some arrogant bravos to smack down.

He stopped and looked at the central figure opposite him. The head priest, he guessed, from the slightly more ornate robes. A creature with the face of a featherless owl, and somehow the rigidness of its face was mobile enough to show a flash of indignation as it saw Fool.

Fool felt the immense rise of power as the priest focused on him.

The ground shook, low and slow, as a subsonic howling moan rose from under the lake, a creature temporarily denied its easy birth.

The priest wasn't Master Class, just a low Advanced Class, but he seemed to have some skill that let him draw from the other priests to a power Level that felt like Master Class. The power coalesced as the Skill gave it shape, an enormous fist forming in the air over Fool. He saw puffs of dust shattering off of it as the fist crushed itself into a harder form to slam him down and turn him into a fine paste on the floor, if the floor was able to hold back that force.

Fool glanced up at the fist as it formed over him, then looked into the eyes of the head priest as the priest focused his will and smashed the fist down.

"Have Faith," Fool said.

The world froze, and he was again in that place out of time.

Not entirely. He could still see the fist coming down, millimeters at a time.

"You ready for this?" the voice said from behind him.

"No choice really, is there?" Fool said.

It was the voice of DM, of the cat, but somehow Fool knew that if he turned around, he wouldn't see the cat but some other form.

"Always a choice," the voice said. "Death is choice. And you are my Acolyte. You can run away. I'd help with that. Do you want to?"

Fool snorted. "The hell. Wouldn't have picked me if I could make that choice, would you? But before I do this, who the fuck are you really?"

"Can't tell you. Not yet. I'm not really allowed to be on this planet, so anyway you see me isn't the real me in any case. I take these forms to escape the sight of those who made the rules. I can tell you I've been here almost since the beginning of this bullshit. I was like you, then I became so much more. That's all I can tell you now.

"So… you ready?"

"Yeah," Fool said, and he felt a nod of agreement as the voice faded away.

The Blue Screen was in front of him, his next Level, and his only real choice for his Advanced Class floating at the top: Adept Priest of the Trickster.

Time being slow meant he had time to read it. He didn't bother, but some of the information seeped in anyway. He felt his Skills lock into place too.

Adept Priest of the Trickster (Level 1)

For some, the System itself is an insufficient greater power to control their lives. These individuals throw themselves upon the whims of gods above. Of all the gods in the System, the Trickster(s?) are known to cause the greatest anomalies in the operation of the Galactic System. As an Adept Priest, you have committed to spreading the chaotic, unstable influence of this god through the System.

Class Abilities: +6 Per Level in Luck, +3 Per Level in Charisma and Willpower, +2 in Intelligence, +1 in Agility. Additional 3 Free Attributes per Level.

+30% Mental Resistance, +20% Chaos Resistance

He felt the Trickster's presence fade away, and the fist sped up. But he had a new Skill for that. Something more than just that.

He summoned his new Hammer of Loki, and he had a moment to admire the look of the weapon as the air pressure from the descending fist made itself known.

It looked a lot like the hammer dangling from its strap on his waist. A classic European warhammer, shaped ever so slightly like a gently curved bull's horn, with the base of the horn being the blunt striking surface. It didn't look like any sort of Skill-summoned weapon. No glowing surface, no ghostly appearance, not even a shiny decoration. Just a plain, functional warhammer. The only difference from his physical warhammer was that this one had a single mark—a stylized raven just under the hammer head.

As an Acolyte, his primary job had been to help others, to be a useful person to a potential flock of worshippers. As an Adept, he was now an advocate for his god. A warrior. The hammer granted him new abilities. At this, its first and most basic Level, he gained some of the physical attributes of the mythical Loki, the strength and durability of a Frost Giant.

Hammer of Loki (Level 1)

Summons a mystical hammer from Dungeon Planet Earth and offers bearer a degree of the legendary effects of mythical owner.
Effect: +10 Strength, +8 Constitution, +18% Damage Resistance. Adds +12 Mana Damage when used.
Cost: 200 MP
Duration: 5 minutes

He probably could have let the fist crush him. He was briefly tough enough that all it would do was take a massive chunk out of his Health. There would be a Mana cost for that though, and he had a better use for that.

Speed of the Giant. Not that they were that fast, but with his strength boost, he could move faster than ever, faster than his opponent could anticipate. When everyone had superhuman reflexes, anticipation made a lot of difference.

Time came back to normal, and he felt the ground crack behind him as the fist smashed into it.

Fool was staring into the face of the head priest.

"Boo," he said and smacked him with the hammer.

He'd expected that it would slam into the side of the priest's head. Probably knock him over. Maybe send him flying. But he'd underestimated his new strength and how the speed of the blow was as accelerated as his jump was.

The hammer passed completely through the priest. Fool could only figure that the priest had built himself into a glass cannon with no defensive skills, or more likely depleted all his Mana while summoning the whatever-it-was.

Maybe Jackal was right and putting more points into physical attributes was a good idea.

In any case, the hammer went through the priest's head as though it was made out of paper. No resistance, just a loud ripping sound.

Fool had a disturbing moment of seeing the top half of the priest's face floating above the bottom half before an impressive fountain of blood shot up and sent the whole mess spinning.

Another subsonic howl rose from beneath the lava, and Fool spun about to see the lava churning, an ominous shape rising.

The priests screamed, and Fool noticed that there was some sort of linkage between them and the body of the fallen priest. It looked like a silver chain wrapped around each of their waists. As he watched, the chain pulsed and glowed, and the priests seemed to whither a bit with each pulse. The pulsing glow was reflected in a sigil the head priest had been standing in, and a single, narrow stream of lava was flowing up a channel from the main pool to the sigil.

Fool made a small leap of reasoning. The priests had been contributing power to the head priest, who was acting as a focus and using that power to somehow pull up the creature in the lava. The machine and initial drilling work must have been focused on pulling as much lava off of the top of the creature as they could, so that whatever they were using could act as a sort of "hand up" to pull the creature the rest of the way.

And now with that priest dead, the creature was trying to claw its way up and was somehow pulling on the energy of the sigil.

Which meant even with the head priest dead, it could break through.

Chapter Twenty-six

The bear faded, but Jackal didn't need it anymore.

Band Eller had ducked the last sweep of Jackal's twin blades and was rapidly backpedaling. Jackal didn't need to see his face to know the sniper was panicking.

No surprise really. Band Eller's clothing was sliced into ribbons, and the armor underneath it was leaking blood from a dozen slashes. Jackal knew he looked much the same. The pain was an ocean all around him.

He glanced around to see what was going on and found only relief. Holland was ably leading his Mousekin, who were tearing through the scattering Hobgoblins. Roger and Eric were in front of the Clearwater folk. Eric was darting about, somehow seeing every time some part of their line faltered and shoring up the fighters with a nod or touch. Roger was in front, and those close to him were forming a wedge out of their line, crushing harder and harder into the group of Hobgoblins that had chosen to fight. Jackal saw that Hellgaze was with those mercenaries, which explained why they were holding and fighting back.

Roger was doing the right thing, forming his troops into an anvil for Holland's hammer to smash into. Hellgaze still had the numbers, even with most of his troops shaken and only barely coming back to fight, but it was still going to be a close fight.

Jackal dodged under a return cut from Band Eller, then slammed both blades down in a cross-block as the attack revealed itself to be a feint. Turning his attention fully back to the sniper, he noticed that the giant rifle the other had been using was in two pieces on the ground behind him. Jackal only had the vaguest memory of that, but it seemed he'd managed to cut it in half while the bear was still running him.

Band Eller had swapped to some sort of pole weapon with a long, curved blade on each end. He was, Jackal noted as he parried another flurry of attacks, pretty good with it. They'd traded so many blows, both were low on Health. It helped that Band Eller was a sniper, not meant to be up close, his Health traded for speed and perception.

Allowed him to keep up a little in a melee fight. Allowed him to fight and be decent.

But not good enough.

This was Jackal's world. The bear had brought him here on a trail of carnage, but the final duel against an evil opponent? That was Jackal's whole reason for existing.

Mr. Freeze slowed Band Eller, reducing his movement speed. Knock Back opened him up to attacks as he tried to resist the imparted momentum, or just did more damage. Mana Steal drew away Band Eller's Mana so he couldn't use it against Jackal while feeding it back to Jackal for more Health. Pain Don't Hurt meant he wasn't slowed down, no matter what the damage he'd taken, and there was a lot.

Finally, One Punch, trusty One Punch, finished things off.

He smiled, and the poem came to his mind again. He saw the gleam of his own teeth in Band Eller's reflective mask, his swords dripping with blood.

"You were always on my mind," he said.

Band Eller froze in confusion.

And Jackal leaned in as if to kiss his own reflection, to kiss his swords as they rose up in a snapping blur in the shine, then he was grinning again as the reflection distorted and twisted, falling away to tumble on the ground.

Band Eller's torso fell next to it a moment later, and Jackal took a deep breath of satisfaction.

He snapped his swords right and left in tight arcs, spraying the collected blood off of them, and turned to the battles going on around him.

The first thing he saw was Olivia dancing like a hurricane, a whirlwind of energy and destruction, wreaking havoc on a platform of equipment and scurrying workers.

And Fool.

Fool was standing opposite of Jackal, on the far side of the lava pool, and a dozen red bodies were scattered all around him. Something about those bodies looked wrong—too small, too oddly frail. As Jackal watched, they shrank even more, as if something was draining their essence.

Draining it toward what Jackal finally noticed.

A thing was rising out of the lava. It was vaguely reptilian, judging from the thick, jagged scales on what he assumed was its head. They rose almost like a forest of spikes, and as it rose higher, Jackal's heart froze.

It was gigantic. He had assumed the thing was huge, but if the slope of the rising skull was following the kind of curve he expected, then its head was almost the span of the entire lava pool—a hundred meters at least. There was no way they could stop that, not even if it was just a physical creature with no System Skills or abilities at all.

They were doomed. He started to shout at Fool, to warn him or something, but as soon as he opened his mouth, Fool made eye contact with him.

There was a depth of infinite sadness in Fool's eyes, as if all the despair in the world had settled into him. As he looked at Jackal and recognized him, a spark appeared in those eyes, and even across this distance, Jackal saw the flare of mischief alight in the Trickster Priest.

Two things happened at roughly the same time.

Olivia turned from her ravaging of the technicians and their equipment and saw the beast rising. As she did that, she saw a cable flare and burst off of the machine hovering over the center of the pool. She traced the line of the cable and saw that it was coming from the machines she'd trashed. Most of the other cables were already severed. Except one. She sent a disc of mana whirling through the air, and it sliced that cable just above the collar that connected it to the bank of machines.

The effect was instantaneous.

The machine, already having stopped sucking lava out of the pool, shifted in the struts holding it in place. The lava it was pulling up reversed direction and fell, splattering around in arcing splashes as the machine, not built to handle reverse flow, broke loose from its mooring and pivoted.

Then it fell like the world's biggest spear, aiming right for the head of the beast.

The other final act was the smallest. A tiny thing.

Fool looked up at the great beast.

It was still rising, and Fool knew somehow, deep inside him, that it was about to rise high enough its eyes would be free. And he knew that if that creature's gaze fell on the world, the world would end. Forever. Nothing would stop it.

The understanding was deeper than fear, deeper than screaming or despair. It was just the sure and certain knowledge that it would all end in a heartbeat of time from now.

Then he looked up, just past the beast, and saw Jackal.

Jackal, who'd saved him on that night so long ago.

Jackal, who'd been someone completely different, not even his own self yet, and had still put himself in harm's way, with no hope of winning, to save someone he didn't know, someone most people thought of as less than human for the sole reason that they had no house to live in.

Jackal, the hero. Standing over the body of his enemy, blades dripping with blood, with that perfect grin on his face.

Jackal would fight until time itself surrendered before him.

And so would Fool. He'd never let his friend down.

He knew what to do. The simplest, stupidest thing in the world.

He turned back to look at the rising beast, at the hint of its ridged forehead leading to a craggy brow.

Then Fool glanced at the thin and fading flow of lava running from the dwindling corpses of the priests to the giant lava pool.

Chapter Twenty-seven

He scuffed the lava, spattering it all over the floor and breaking the mystic seal.

"Oops," Fool said, looking back at the beast.

It had stopped rising.

And from the deep pool of the earth's blood, the hissing subsonic growls of the beast stopped and were replaced with a brief, gigantic, confused, "Mrowp?"

That was when the machine speared into its head, followed by a broken dam of lava falling out of the sky.

Chapter Twenty-eight

The scientists explained it all, after.

Holland and Hellgaze had had it a bit wrong. Once they compared notes, they both agreed that they'd been raised by superstitious grandparents.

There had clearly been a giant kaiju of some kind in the volcano, but according to the scientists, that was an unexpected side-effect. The goal all along had been to extract minerals and some sort of condensed Mana from the lava. The scientists had lots of details on how that worked, but no one could figure it out.

The closest they could get was that the last-minute process of creating a Dungeon World could theoretically weaken the barriers that would normally exist between dimensions, and the scientists had convinced the Thirteen Moon Sect they could tap into a virtual gold mine of the substance if they were right... but it would only be a temporary potential, because things would stabilize with time.

The monster itself, they figured, was a terrible freak coincidence. Some Legendary had probably been stuffed into a dimensional prison long ago, and Earth was just super unlucky to have that opening stuck there randomly.

The good news was the opening was already shifting away and healing. In a few months, it would be gone forever.

Fool, Jackal, Holland, and Hellgaze, after a long, strangely sober drinking session, agreed to never speak of it again.

THE END

Fool & Jackal will return in the third book of the **System Apocalypse: Kismet** series, *Fool's Last Dance.*

www.starlitpublishing.com/products/fools-last-dance

Status Screen			
Name	Fool	Class	Priest
Race	Human (Male)	Level (Advanced Class)	1
Titles			
Adept Priest of the (Redacted)			
Health	290	Stamina	290
Mana	620	Mana Regeneration	53/minute
Status			
Normal			
Attributes			
Strength	22	Agility	40
Constitution	29	Perception	116
Intelligence	62	Willpower	63
Charisma	69	Luck	170
Class Skills			
Closseau	1	Have Faith	1
Talent Scout	2	Pants on Fire	1
Transform Object	1	Kiss it Better	2
I know a Shortcut	2	Truth or Dare	1
Dry hair is for Squids	1	Oh god, don't hit me!	2
Mint?	1	Location Scout	1
Face Swap	1	No Fair	2
Geas	2	Feign Death	1
Aura of *	2	Regeneration	1
Hammer of Loki	1		
Spells			
Sparkles			

Status Screen			
Name	Jackal	Class	Bearshirt Warrior of the Claven North
Race	Human (Male)	Level (Advanced)	1
Titles			
(None)			
Health	640	Stamina	640
Mana	670	Mana Regeneration	113 / minute
Status			
Normal			
Attributes			
Strength	69	Agility	65
Constitution	64	Perception	114
Intelligence	67	Willpower	168
Charisma	12	Luck	10
Class Skills			
Pain don't Hurt	2	One Punch	2
INTIMIDATE	1	Mana Steal	1
Knock back	1	Mr. Freeze	1
Only a flesh Wound	2	Death from Above	2
Neo	1	Indomitable Will	2
Maestro	2	Blade Walking	2
Red Rover	2	The Wall	1
Eye of the Tiger	2	Boomstick	1
Punishment of the Bear	1		
Spells			
(None)			

Epilogue

"That's it?" the Professor asked, leaning forward and staring at Fool and Jackal over tented fingers, his elbows on the desk.

They looked at each other, and when Jackal nodded, Fool took it upon himself to answer.

"Pretty much. Hellgaze turned out to be an all right guy. Surrendered to Holland the second the big bad blooped away. From what I gather, he had to resign his commission after doing that, but he and Holland worked out a deal."

Jackal snorted, which made Fool roll his eyes. The Professor didn't say anything, but Fool had no problem reading the look on his face, so he shared the last little tidbit he'd been holding back.

"Well, more than a deal. Hellgaze and a few of his soldiers signed on with Holland, then Roger extended their contract under his name, since Holland's original contract was with Roger's dad and was successfully fulfilled when they delivered the Dragon's Tongue."

"And what was the Dragon's Tongue?" the Professor said. "Nothing from an actual dragon then?"

"Nope. Turned out to be a piece of yellow rock from a seam by an old parking lot. Roger's mom and dad honeymooned there. So, either really bad luck that being chosen as his 'coming of age' quest or really good luck, I guess."

"Bit too much luck all together. You sure that cat didn't have anything to do with this?"

Fool was finding it easier and easier to control his expressions now that he had his Advanced Class. He'd have to dig into that later. But for the moment, it was easy to lie. Especially when it was only a small lie of omission. "No cat, not at all. Last I saw it, it had been adopted by Alex. Why? Been bothering you again?"

"No. Quite the opposite. Which has me feeling very suspicious. All of this seems to be wrapped up a little pat, and you fell into it a little too easily."

"Pure coincidence," Fool said. "Anyway, you were right about Roger. Hope whatever you've got planned for him is big enough. The young man seems to attract a lot of people."

"I heard about that too." The Professor didn't look happy about that at all. "You were supposed to bring back one young man. Now I hear there's an army coming up the valley, with this Roger at its head."

"You wanted a leader, didn't you? Wasn't that the plan?"

That made the Professor look as if he was trying to swallow something he found too sour. Before he could reply, Fool took some sympathy on him. The old man was endlessly fun to tease, but the safety of the Foundation and McBride wasn't something Fool took any chances with.

He raised a hand and nodded to placate the boss. "I know, I know. The Machine identified one person and set him up as the leader type you needed. And he is. But somewhere along the line, he developed a bit of knack for it, and he's really good at attracting sound people. Of the Clearwater folk we rescued, half the combat classers basically swore fealty to him when it was all over. And once the quest was over, his parents sent a flyer over to retrieve him, but he elected to stay with the new people and march here. And everywhere we stopped on the way, he seemed to pick up more people. Mostly refugees. Apparently, some guy's been coming down from the north and kicking the shit out of all kinds of people and trashing a bunch of baby empires that were in the middle of forming. Got a lot of movement going on. Tons of people rallying to him, but more just wanted to get away from any new trouble. And lots of those folk just put themselves right under Roger's wing. And it's the right thing, isn't it? Him making them an army and bringing them here? I'm assuming it's what you wanted, just a little faster than you planned on."

The Professor chewed on that for a bit, then leaned back in his chair. "You're not wrong. And thanks to Yagnar and her organizational skills, we're actually a little ahead of ourselves here. You notice the new buildings on your way in?"

"Cavalry," Jackal said, and Fool turned to look at him.

Made sense, but he hadn't said anything to Fool about that. The buildings the Professor mentioned looked like about a dozen large stables, and Jackal had noticed a few horses prancing about. Didn't make much sense, because horses in general weren't all that useful these days. Any of the ones that hadn't evolved under the System into all kinds of hideous monsters where just kind of... food for everything else. And cavalry made no sense. This wasn't the Middle Ages after all. Hell, last he'd heard, the Foundation was actually looking to buy a for-real spaceship. So, cavalry made no sense. But the professor was nodding and smiling.

"Got it in one," he said. "But not quite. Air Cav. Apparently one of the local breeds evolved, but the owner died, and no one really noticed until the rumors of a 'wild hunt' got repeated enough that we decided to look into it. The horses are faster, tougher, and far more intelligent than we would have expected. Ferocious temper too, but Yagnar recruited a few beast tamers. Did I mention they're able to fly? We've already started a training program. The plan is to slot Roger in as lead, if he can be trained and if he passes all our tests."

"Flying horses?" Fool asked. "That sounds—"

Jackal leaned forward and cut him off. "Can I have one?"

Fool looked at him, stunned to see the raw lust and joy in Jackal's eyes.

"If it was up to me, absolutely," the Professor said. "But they bond to a rider—for life, I'm told. Not up to us. But you're welcome to try the bond process."

Jackal sat back with a smile and no more comment, and the Professor continued on.

"All of this relates to your next mission. That John fellow I was talking about after your Valemount mission? The complication has gotten quite a bit worse. And part of it is your fault."

That got Fool leaning forward again. "Our fault? What did we do this time?"

"Turns out the Thirteen Moon Sect was involved in quite a few other nefarious schemes, not just in BC but down in the States as well. And your 'accidental' conflict with them seems to have taken out most of their remaining leadership as well as one of their main drivers for being here, so… their remaining presence on Earth decided to withdraw. Completely.

"And before you get too excited about that, we now have the problem of a very large power vacuum. The Machine actually had a plan in place to deal with the Sect that we were working toward. But between you and this 'John' person, everyone's plans have been completely blown apart."

The Professor leaned back, and if Fool had been pressed, he wouldn't have said that the leader of the Foundation looked angry exactly. It looked as though he was playing at being angry, but Fool had always been good at reading people's expressions. And he'd guess that the Professor's actual expression was… smug. He wasn't done talking though.

"However, this does present an opportunity for us. Vancouver still has a rather sizable population, and while it looks like this John person has somehow managed to claim the city for his own, there are a large number of factions left that are jockeying for whatever power they can get. Everyone is playing nice for the moment, but we expect that to turn ugly sooner rather than later. Especially since this John fella seems to be intent on moving along.

"The Machine is suggesting we offer ourselves up as allies to the right parties, in the guise of being a mercenary cavalry group. You two will go along as assistants to our negotiator, Yagnar. Officially, at least. Your actual job will be to recon the situation and use, I hate to say, your initiative to find allies for our cause."

That caused Fool to sit upright. The old man had been using them for important missions, but he'd never shown any real confidence in their judgment.

The Professor must have read his mind because he held up a finger before Fool could say anything. "Wasn't my choice. The Machine pinpointed you two as the key factors here and wouldn't share one damn drop of reasoning why, so we're forced to stick with its results. Hasn't steered us wrong, but there's a first time for everything. So, you two will be heading down to Vancouver once you've had sufficient time to rest and recuperate and get some training in with the Air Cavalry. Understood? Then get the hell out of my office."

With that clear dismissal, they stood and left, and by unspoken agreement, Fool and Jackal headed back to the cafeteria. They weren't staying at the Foundation anymore but had found a place in McBride. But the cafeteria still had the baked goods from the various Grammas, and they wanted to stock up for the walk home.

Plus, Fool had left his guest there.

Olivia smiled up at them from the remnants of a giant cinnamon bun and waved with a happy expression. Fool and Jackal sat down next to her, as she'd already loaded up the table with a selection of baked goods. Jackal didn't wait to dig in.

"So?" she asked. "You get chewed out, uncle?"

Fool shook his head and tore off the edge of a cinnamon bun. Still warm, he noted. And just the right amount of icing. He savored the bite for a bit, enjoying the complex interplay of bitter cinnamon, sweet buttery icing, and the delicate touch of nutmeg.

"Nope," he said. "I think... I'm not sure, but I think we got a promotion. And a new mission. You still planning to come with us, no matter what?"

Olivia nodded. "The boys will be fine without me. And something tells me it's the right thing to do."

"Destiny," Jackal said between mouthfuls.

Fool had to swat Jackal's hand away. He was already reaching for Fool's cinnamon bun. "Get your own seconds. And I suppose destiny covers it. I know what you mean. I'm not sure why, but it feels right. I guess we'll just work it out as we go?"

"The first thing you want to do, Olivia..." said a voice from her side of the table, though not from any source Fool could see. But he didn't need to see the source. He knew who it was. "Is stop calling him uncle."

Jackal managed, barely, to stop from choking on his mouthful as DM jumped up on the table. Olivia absently patted the cat on the head with far too much familiarity for Fool's comfort.

The cat looked Fool right in the eye. "Call him Gramps instead."

THE END

Author's Note

Hey reader. Thanks for coming back to read more about Fool and Jackal. These two have been joyful companions in my head for a while now, but their story is almost done. Book three is in progress as I write this. Late, running behind…and maybe a part of this is that I know that it's almost time for these two to retire back into the cozy well of imagination and daydreams that they came from.

It's a struggle to wrap this up, to tie up all the lose ends and reach towards the conclusion that I've known had to come all along. One of the fun parts of the LitRPG genre is the stories that stretch themselves out over many books, giving you a ton of reading time to travel along with the characters and their journey. I wanted something different for these two, though. A tight, compact arc. A story, in a bit more of the traditional light. A beginning, and an end.

As I write this, Fool's Play has been on sale for just a little over a month. It's been an absolute treat to read the reviews, and immensely rewarding. Writing is a lonely life. Months of effort, with no way of knowing how that effort will be received. It's tough, but I can't imagine a better way to spend my time. Reading positive reviews is a pretty damned big reward, and the cats have gotten used to my excited exclamations when a new one role in.

It's winter up here now. Icy cold, and every day I sit down to write I can see the tall peak across from me getting more stark and snow covered. The winter sun treats it well when it shines, with a majestic glow and shine of many colours. When the wind is up, you can see the tufts of snow reaching up into the sky from the peak. The contrast from the summer, with it's dense smoke and constant forest fires, is amazing. And soothing. Every time I see it, I recall my favourite poem, by Li Bai, translated by Sam Hamill:

"The birds have vanished down the sky.
Now the last cloud drains away.

We sit together, the mountain and me,
Until only the mountain remains."

The mountain was always here, and always will be here, long after me and all my troubles have faded away. I've made peace with that, but it's always the goal of the writer to build a mountain of their imagination, and hope that it lasts just a little longer than they will, and will be just tall enough for someone else to notice. I hope you have enjoyed this, most recent, addition. I'll do my best to keep adding to this small hill.

See you in Fool's Last Dance.

- David, from the mountain village

About the Authors

David R. Packer has been a full-time teacher of historical European swordplay, a high-tech wizard, and a security professional. For a few years he was a for-pay bad guy working in police training, which once had him on the run from the entire police force, across the whole city.

Aside from that, he lives a cozy life with 2 cats and a real-life she-hulk for a wife. He has many books and likes coffee far too much.

You can find out more information on David's books by visiting his website: https://boxwrestlefence.com

Tao Wong is an avid fantasy and sci-fi reader who spends his time working and writing in the North of Canada. He's spent way too many years doing martial arts of many forms, and having broken himself too often, he now spends his time writing about fantasy worlds.

For updates on the series and other books written by Tao Wong (and special one-shot stories), please visit the author's website: http://www.mylifemytao.com

Want updates on upcoming deluxe editions and exclusive merch? Follow Tao on Kickstarter to get notifications on all projects. https://www.kickstarter.com/profile/starlitpublishing/

Subscribers to Tao's mailing list to receive exclusive access to short stories in the Thousand Li and System Apocalypse universes.

For more great information about LitRPG series, check out these Facebook groups:

- GameLit Society

  www.facebook.com/groups/LitRPGsociety

- LitRPG Books

  www.facebook.com/groups/LitRPG.books

- LitRPG Legion

  www.facebook.com/groups/litrpglegion

About the Publisher

Starlit Publishing is wholly owned and operated by Tao Wong. It is a science fiction and fantasy publisher focused on the LitRPG & cultivation genres. Their focus is on promoting new, upcoming authors in the genre whose writing challenges the existing stereotypes while giving a rip-roaring good read.

For more information on Starlit Publishing, early access to books and exclusive stories visit our webshop: https://www.starlitpublishing.com/

You can also join Starlit Publishing's mailing list to learn of new, exciting authors and book releases.

Glossary

Have Faith: Fool can ask the Trickster for a favour. Any kind of favour. In exchange, the Trickster will ask something in return from Fool. The Trickster doesn't need to really be asked the question, though, since he always seems to know what Fool needs. And Fool never has any idea of how the request will be fulfilled.

Clouseau: Inspector Clouseau was of course, the master of disguise. This skill makes Fool almost as ingenious as the great man himself.

Talent Scout: Fools most used skill, but it's not that great. Probably could have bought a basic identify spell from the Shop that would replace this.

First Nations: The people living within the Canadian legal boundary called British Columbia. Despite popular misconception, most of this land is still completely owned by them. They have a serious issues with squatters. Please note that the author is not First Nations, and everything he has to say related to First Nations people, practices, and namings is not to be trusted or assumed correct. Hopefully this encourages you to go and find more reliable sources, as there are many. Here's a great place to start: https://www.bcafn.ca/

Sto:lo: Fool's pretty off-base here, as are most of the people. Sto:lo is used in the lower mainland, and the usage of this word has spread a bit, but where Fool is located it would be slightly more proper to use either the Dakelh word: Lhtakoh, or the Tsilhqot'in word: ʔelhdawox. Locals use this word currently, anglicized to "Eldako" for some areas, but never to the river for some weird reason. Fool is Metis, but he was raised without any real education of his ancestry, so while he has a keen interest in First Nations lore, what he knows is spotty and often wrong. He sure tries, through.

Hoary Marmot: Squeak! https://www.youtube.com/shorts/WC5NnBFvfdw Seriously, Marmots are very cool. They will truly ignore you, to the point of walking right over you to get to something else, unless you bother them. Then you get to see a whole different creature.

Foundation: Professor Xi chose the name because he is a giant nerd.

Sunbeam Ecological Reserve: You can see this from McBride. It's lovely. I haven't been up yet because I don't own a 4x4.

Cariboo Mountain: Next door neighbours of the Canadian Rockies, and contain the Selkirk, Monashee, and Purcell ranges. These were my stomping grounds as a kid and the reason I get confused when I go to other places and they refer to hills as "mountains."

Opilione: I am one of the few humans to have been bit by one of these. It hurt. Very pinchy. I also had the terrifying experience of crawling through a quartz tube (abandoned small gold mine) waaay up in the mountains when I was a kid, and looking up at the ceiling and realizing it was a few inches thick mat of these guys. I got over the fear eventually, which is good because these things are seriously weird and fun to look at. They are probably the most alien looking thing that you can see commonly, and probably ignore.

Aziz: Yeah, I'm a huge "Fifth Element" fan.

Fool's Warhammer: Not really a warhammer. The head is based off of a museum piece, but the whole thing is closer in weight and usage to a Hungarian Fokos, which is kind of a walking stick with an small axe head or hammer head on one side. Lightweight, fast, and real handy for troll smashing.

Tom Cody: "Streets of Fire" If you haven't seen it yet, you're in for a treat.

Dry Hair is for Squids: Jack Deth is cool. Cooler than you. "Trancers" is amazing.

Halkomelem: One of the First Nations in the BC lower mainland area.

Friston: Karl Friston. Jackal is trying to explain how Friston's Free Energy principle might apply. You can look it up. It's a deep rabbit hole of very hard to understand stuff, but will give you a better sense of how the world works.

Tete Jaune Cache: Local's sometimes pronounce this "Tee Joan Cash." Tete Jaune means Yellowhead, as in the Yellowhead highway. Or "Blondie's road" if you are feeling catty. Tete Jaune was the nickname of a Metis scout in the area when it was "discovered." It's very pretty. Don't take my word for it. You should visit it sometime.

McBride: A tiny village in the Robson Valley. Has a pretty good coffee shop, and a town's worth of facilities. Really. It's quite strange.

Valemount: You go through this on the way to Jasper. If you want to save money on Jasper hotels, you stay here instead. Cheaper hotels but still overpriced restaurants.

Dunster: They have an ice-cream social once a year!

Beau Geste: Classic 1939 Gary Cooper film about the French Foreign Legion. The actual fort in the film is Fort Zinderneuf. Fort Whisky is the fort that gets swamped by bugs in the "Starship Troopers" movie. Did you know there is also a book called Starship Troopers, and it is also good? Probably someone will make a movie out of it someday.

Jumping Spiders: Did you know they make good pets? Very playful! So cute!

False Widows: Steodata, generally Grossa. Big black shiny spiders that might live under your sink. These are great spiders. They will eat Black Widows and Brown Recluse spiders, as well as all the other pests in your house. They also stay put, so if you see one, you can safely ignore it and it will always be there doing it's job for you. Don't try to touch them, their bite stings like a hornet.

Orcabear: I used to dream about this thing. Brrr.
A monster with top half of an orca and the bottom half of a grizzly bear.

Sheriff: You rarely see or hear of Sheriff's in Canada. They have strictly limited duties, and no political connections at all. They occasionally provide extra security, but mostly they only handle prisoner transfers and courtroom duties. A Deputy Sheriff is someone who only works in the court system, so the usage of "Deputy" in Valemount is incorrect, but is the sort of thing some Canadians would think is right because they spend all their time watching American TV and have a hard time figuring out which country they live in. Sheriff Barnes is one of those people.

Blue River: Blue River is too small to be a village.

EI: Employment Insurance. In Canada, a part of every paycheck goes into a fund. If you lose your job, this fund is used to pay you a portion of your wages until you get a new job. It's usually six months worth, but it can be extended if you are taking the right kind of classes, or working part time. Super handy.

CPP: Canada Pension Plan. You get money when you decide you are just too damned old for dealing with people's shit. It't not much money, though, so it's best to suck it up as long as you can.

Taxes: We pay these in Canada in the hopes that the CBC will eventually find a new comedy group as funny as Kids in the Hall. Or even SCTV. Someday.

Geas: I've been afraid to say this word out loud since I was twelve and got my first D&D set. I still have no idea how to pronounce it. I guess I should listen to the audiobook. Narrators research this kind of stuff, right?

RCMP: Royal Canadian Mounted Police. Sometimes called "Mounties" but only if you're buddies. Militarized FBI with horses and cool dress uniforms.

Most police in Canada are RCMP, and they go through substantial training. They are expected on occasion to be the only law enforcement for a very, very large territory.

Gitxsan: Coastal First Nation that no longer lives on the coast. Sort of like the Canadian version of Normans, who were descended from viking raiders that thought "oh gosh, wouldn't this be a nice spot for a winery. Let's learn to make croissants!" Alex is not Gitxsan. Fool is really, really bad at faces but really good at assumptions.

Maker: Alex is a nerd, and likes the book with sand and giant worms.

Piobaireachd: Traditional form of bagpipe music. Also called ceol mor or "big music" as opposed to ceol beag or "party tunes." It starts with a simple melody that is repeated, and then gets more complex variations added. This was the first music I learned to play on the pipes. Sounds great echoing off of the mountains…if someone else is playing it, because I suck.

Simpcw: First Nation that also has ownership of the area this book takes place in. First Nations don't use the same border system theory that the settlers did, and this caused a lot of confusion for people try to assign ownership to things because it makes them sleep better at night.

Aura of *: Area effect mental attack Skill that's not really defined. More specifically, it has the effect of making the targets feel increasingly uncomfortable and out of touch with reality. It builds a feedback loop off of whatever the target initially interprets this as, and rapidly spikes it up into overload.

To learn more about LitRPG, talk to authors including myself, and just have an awesome time, please join the LitRPG Group!

https://www.facebook.com/groups/LitRPGGroup/

Made in the USA
Las Vegas, NV
13 November 2024

11769931R00204